SISTER ROSA'S REBELLION

BOOKS BY CAROLYN HUGHES

THE MEONBRIDGE CHRONICLES

Book 1, Fortune's Wheel

Book 2, A Woman's Lot

Book 3, De Bohun's Destiny

Book 4, Children's Fate

Book 5, Squire's Hazard

Book 6, Sister Rosa's Rebellion

The Merchant's Dilemma, A Meonbridge Chronicles Companion Novel

THE SIXTH MEONBRIDGE CHRONICLE

Sister Rosa's Rebellion

CAROLYN HUGHES

Riverdown

Published in 2025 by Riverdown Books

Riverdown Books
Southampton, SO32 3QG, United Kingdom
www.riverdownbooks.co.uk

ISBN 978-1-7395394-2-9 (eBook)
ISBN 978-1-7395394-3-6 (paperback)

British Library Cataloguing in Publication Data
A CIP catalogue record for this book is available from the British Library

Cover design by Avalon Graphics www.avalongraphics.org

CAST OF CHARACTERS

PRINCIPAL CHARACTERS ARE IN **BOLD**.
OTHER IMPORTANT VOICES IN *ITALICS*

AT NORTHWICK PRIORY

SISTER ROSA, subprioress (formerly Johanna de Bohun, daughter of Sir Richard and Lady Margaret of Meonbridge)
SISTER EVANGELINA, sacrist
FATHER EDGAR, priest, Evangelina's half-brother

SISTER AMATA, almoness and infirmaress
SISTER BEATRICE, cellaress
SISTER DULCIA, treasuress
SISTER JULIANA, chantress/precentrix
SISTER GRACIA, mistress of the novices
Sisters *FELICIA*, Maria and Letitia, favourites of Evangelina
Sister Clarice and other Northwick nuns...
ANABELLA SITWELL, a widow and novice in the priory

HILDE, Evangelina's personal maid

RAFE BYLLYNGES, Northwick's bailiff
Sir Thomas Chatterton, Northwick's steward
Sir Toby Edenborough, gentleman

Master Henry Brougham, lawyer
The bishop's commissioners
Nicholas Foxe, the bishop's man at Northwick Priory
Richard Aylesbury, Nicholas's replacement

Humphrey Sitwell, Anabella's brother-in-law

IN MEONBRIDGE

JOHN ATTE WODE, the bailiff in Meonbridge
Alice atte Wode, John's mother, a villein and widow
AGNES SAWYER, John's sister
Jack, Agnes's husband, Meonbridge's carpenter and builder
Dickon de Bohun, Agnes's son and Lord of Meonbridge

Eleanor Nash, a freewoman
Walter, Eleanor's husband

Roger Stronge, blacksmith

IN WINCHESTER

The Bishop of Winchester, first, William Edington; later William
Longe, known as William of Wykeham

You can find a **Glossary of the medieval words** used in all the
Meonbridge Chronicles on my website at
https://carolynhughesauthor.com/glossary-of-terms/

PROLOGUE

NORTHWICK PRIORY

SEPTEMBER 1365

Edgar scuttled across the courtyard towards the chapel, his dark hood pulled close about his face, to keep off the rain but also to defy detection. Not that anyone else was out of doors on this wild and wretched evening. In an hour or so, the sisters would arrive for Compline – which he was, the Lord be praised, not obliged to attend – but of course they would take the night stairs from the dorter to the transept, and not have to face this foul weather. On evenings such as this, how he wished his lodgings were *inside* the priory and not across a dark, unevenly-cobbled courtyard.

He pushed open the heavy chapel door and slipped inside. Candles had been lit at Vespers, and he could move quickly across the nave towards the tiny chamber where he kept his vestments and sometimes composed his sermons. Evangelina used it too, as the priory's sacrist, and it was here she had bid him come. Here, she said, they could find the privacy so rarely found inside the priory, as she wanted to discuss a matter of great importance.

The door of the little chamber was ajar, and a light flickered within. Eva was already here and she had lit one of *his* own precious candles. He pressed his lips together. Why could she not have chosen to meet him during the day?

He pushed the door open a little further and stepped into the room.

'Ah, brother,' said Evangelina, her eyebrow raised. 'I thought perhaps you weren't coming.'

Edgar breathed in deeply. 'And why might you think that? You specified an hour after Vespers, and that is precisely now.'

She clicked her tongue, and pointed to the rickety stool he kept in a corner. She was settled in his chair, and evidently had no intention of vacating it. He decided not to quibble and, pulling the stool forward, eased himself onto it carefully.

'Well,' he said, 'what do you wish to talk about? I trust it *is* important, to justify dragging me out here on such a noisome night.'

'Of the utmost importance,' she said, and leaned back against the cushion *he* had provided to give comfort to his own back. 'Our aunt is close to death.'

'I know,' he said. 'I attended her this afternoon. I warrant she has only a few days remaining.' He never thought of Mother Angelica as his *familial* aunt, even though she was the older sister of his and Eva's mother. Moreover, although he recognised Angelica's gentleness and wisdom, he had never held her in particular affection. But she was the head of this priory, the priory where he was employed. Not that his aunt had either enabled, or approved of, his appointment...

'And when she dies,' continued Eva, with remarkable dispassion, 'there'll be an election...'

'Of course. A new prioress. A position, I imagine, you presume is yours?'

'It *should* be. It's my birth right.' Her voice rose slightly. 'I've been waiting many years for this moment to arrive.'

'The moment when our aunt dies?'

She puckered her lips. 'Of course not, Edgar. I meant the moment when I have my chance to rule at Northwick.'

When Eva was first sent to Northwick, at the age of fifteen, it was assumed that, in due course, she would replace their aunt as prioress.

The Godeffroys had been major benefactors of the priory since the end of the last century, and had exclusively provided the prioresses in all those intervening years. Angelica was probably forty when Eva came, and Eva might have expected to wait twenty years or so before her turn came. But, despite a period of frailty some years ago, Angelica had proved much more robust than any of her predecessors – or indeed than most people of her age. Thus, she had survived to eighty and was only now on her way to meet her maker, at a point when Eva was older than she might have hoped to be when her chance for power came.

'What then is the problem?' he said.

'The *election*,' she said with emphasis, then pouted. 'Because, if there is an election, I shan't win it.'

'Whyever not? Do you have a rival?'

'Of course I do! The blessed Sister *Rosa*...' She spat out the name. 'The favourite of the older nuns...'

Ah, yes, of course. Sister Rosa. When he was made priest-in-charge here ten years ago, Rosa had been at Northwick seven years, and was by then acting as an assistant to Mother Angelica. She had effectively become Angelica's subprioress, though that was not a title she had been given or assumed. At the time, Angelica thought she herself was dying, but it turned out to be just some early symptoms of old age, an old age she then managed to prolong for another *fifteen* years. Rosa, meanwhile, blossomed into a cheerful, energetic, if deeply pious woman, whom everyone in the priory adored, apart of course from Eva. Edgar knew very well how much Eva resented Rosa's seeming advancement, yet she seemed unable to lighten her own stern demeanour and win more favour with the other nuns.

Given her position, Sister Rosa *would* almost certainly stand in an election and, in Eva's view, would win. He could not but agree with her. If *he* had a vote in such an election, he would not choose his sister. In striking contrast to Rosa – and indeed to their aunt – Eva was sour-faced, brusque and overbearing. It was most unlikely the nuns would choose *her* to replace the kindly and warm-hearted Angelica.

'Yet, as I understand it,' he said, 'elections have always gone in favour of the Godeffroy, regardless of the other candidate...'

Eva tilted her head. 'Some sort of bribery, you mean?'

'I have always presumed so. And I have also presumed it was the bishop's man – our cousin Nicholas's predecessors – who arranged it, though I don't know. But I'm sure Nicholas would help you in that way, if you asked him.'

'Even if he did, I'm not convinced it would work this time. Rosa's so *very* much admired, I'm sure most of the sisters would refuse any inducement to vote against her.'

'So, what are you going to do about her? Arrange a fatal accident?' He snorted.

Eva clicked her tongue again. 'Don't be such a fool, Edgar. But I do want to stop her standing, or make her seem less suitable than she is.'

'And you have a plan for doing that?'

'I do.'

She told him about the Rosa who first came to Northwick, evidently quite a different girl from the woman she was now. She recalled how the young Rosa – then only seventeen – spent hours of her time upon her knees in the chapel, and at her bedside, pleading constantly for forgiveness.

'You *pried* upon her private and piteous entreaties?' said Edgar, raising his eyebrows.

Eva shrugged, but ignored the question. 'Did you know she wanted to call herself "Dolorosa"? What a ridiculous, self-indulgent name! "*I want to spend my life atoning for my sins!*"'—she affected a supposedly girlish voice—'That's what she said to the prioress.'

'You *heard* her say that?'

'Well, no. One of the older nuns overheard their conversation in the cloister...'

Edgar guffawed. 'You holy women! So quick to pry and tittle-tattle...'

Eva scowled but did not respond. 'Anyway, our aunt persuaded her to choose "Rosa" instead.'

'So what had made little Rosa so very sorrowful?'

'From what I heard, she imagined she'd committed some appalling sin, one so heinous she was consumed by remorse and shame. Though what exactly the sin was, I never learned.'

He gave a small shrug. 'Very occasionally in her confession, Rosa *has* referred to some transgression she committed as a girl, but she has never elaborated—'

'Ha! I knew it. A guilty secret... Anyway, I'm thinking, if I hint to her that I *know* of her secret and will expose it if she doesn't do as I demand, she'll decide not to stand in the election...'

'I suppose she *might* withdraw, but the Sister Rosa I think I know is surely made of sterner stuff.'

He stroked his chin, the stubble of the day rough and rasping against his fingertips. Evangelina might imagine Rosa would succumb readily to her threats, but he was not so sure. Moreover, Rosa would make an excellent prioress, very much in the mould of Aunt Angelica.

Whilst his sister, well, the same could not be said of her. In fact, he suspected Eva would make a *terrible* prioress. He was certain she never had a vocation for the religious life, any more than he did, and she was loved by no one in the priory. It did not bode well for her success. However, she *was* his sister – well his *half*-sister, but family nonetheless – and it was his duty to support her, even if it was against his better judgement...

1

For several weeks, Rosa had been taking turns with Sister Amata and Sister Beatrice to keep vigil by Mother Angelica's bed. The physician who had come a week ago agreed that dear Angelica had only days to live. Now, the old prioress lay in her great bed, her face serene, her hands folded together as if in prayer. Her body seemed small, swamped by the height and broadness of the bedstead, yet her spirit appeared undiminished by her approaching death. She was sleeping now, but every so often she would wake, hold out her hands to whomever was waiting anxiously at her bedside, and offer them a beatific smile and words of comfort for their forthcoming loss.

All the sisters had come and gone to the prioress's chamber, some more frequently than others. A few of the younger ones seemed not to have the stamina for lengthy vigils, not grasping the importance of tranquillity and waiting. They came for barely an hour or so, then made some excuse to go. Rosa, Beatrice and Amata were, inevitably, the most constant vigil-keepers.

Now, Rosa felt calm and prayerful, and also, at times, joyful. Not, of course, because she wished the Reverend Mother to die. Far from it. She loved Angelica, and would greatly miss her wise counsel, her kindness and her boundless patience.

Beatrice, Rosa thought, felt much the same as her, but, for Amata, the impending loss seemed to be making her especially sad.

Neither Rosa nor Beatrice had known Angelica for as long as Amata. But it was not just the length of time. Amata had told Rosa recently how especially close she and Angelica had been right from when they both first came to Northwick.

'We came the same year,' she said, 'although Angelica was twenty whilst I was still a little girl. She took me under her wing, not so much in the role of mother – for the prioress was that – but more like a familial big sister. I grew to womanhood, knowing I always had an ally in Angelica. And now that ally is leaving me, and I cannot help but grieve terribly for what will be a devastating and painful loss.' Unusually, Amata allowed a few tears to escape her eyes.

Rosa, too, who had blossomed under Angelica's care and tutelage, would greatly grieve her passing. But she was following Angelica's own lead when she described with elation the next stage in her journey. 'Our Reverend Mother is so looking forward to it,' she said the other day to several of the sisters gathered around the great bed. 'She will soon be in Paradise, in blessed communion with God, his Son and the Holy Mother, and all the angels. It is the culmination of everything she has striven for all her life.' She was sure her eyes were shining as she said it, and the sisters seemed to draw comfort from her words.

Later, when they were alone, Amata referred to Rosa's words. 'You are right, of course, and I do know this is dear Angelica's conviction. Yet I am finding it hard to keep my tears at bay, even when I know it's for myself I shed them.'

Rosa, Amata and Beatrice had agreed that, in these last days, one of them would be always at Angelica's side. Even if Angelica was looking forward to her passage to the next life, they could not bear to let her make that last journey all alone.

A short while ago, Beatrice and Amata had left the chamber to join the other sisters for Compline. Rosa said she would not go. 'Perhaps I shall attend Matins,' she added but thought it likely she might not.

Beatrice lightly touched her hand. 'We shan't be long.'

A single chair stood in the prioress's chamber, the chair in which Angelica had sat for much of the past few years. A few days ago, Rosa and Beatrice had carried it closer to the bed, so Beatrice herself and especially Amata could rest their aging bodies for a while during the long hours of their vigil. Now Rosa sank down into it, easing her back against the cushion, one of the few comforts Angelica had allowed herself.

Rosa smiled: Angelica did not much care for comfort, neither for herself nor for the sisters. Well, *unnecessary* comfort, anyway. Adequate warmth and clothing, sufficient, nourishing and palatable food, a bed restful enough to permit sleep, these things were important if the sisters were to live a life of serenity and contentment. The body needed its basic comforts met so that the mind and heart could focus upon prayer and learning. Angelica saw no need for a harsher way of life – as espoused by some other prioresses of their order – but neither did she think *excess* of anything was called for: fur cloaks, rich food, elaborate furnishings, none of these were necessary. But an occasional cushion might be permitted to ease an aching back...

It was this sensible, frugal but not ascetic, way of life that endeared most of the sisters to Angelica's rule. Which was why the bed the Reverend Mother was now sleeping in had always been a source of some amusement and curiosity.

For the bedstead was excessively wide and high for a prioress's resting place. Many, many years ago, a former prioress – one of Angelica's familial antecedents – had chosen to provide herself with the trappings of a manor's chatelaine. At the time, the priory had been wealthy, and the prioress had thought that, in her elevated position, she deserved to live as befitted her aristocratic standing. Thus, she installed wall hangings and carpets in her private chamber, and heavy oaken furniture, including the magnificent curtained high-tester bed. Of course, she did not believe the nuns in her charge should also enjoy such luxuries: *they* continued living in the discomfort appropriate to their order, then a much harsher regime than now existed here.

With gracious good thanks to Angelica's wise and careful management, Northwick was not poor, but she was the most reluctant inheritor of her predecessor's extravagance. She sold most of the rich hangings and excess furniture in order to make better provision for the nuns. But she did keep the bed, although she did not occupy it for most of her long reign. She kept to the dorter, to sleep with the other sisters, as required of a prioress by the Benedictine rule. Yet, these days, Rosa thought, Angelica must be glad of the comfort the bed allowed her frail and failing body...

The Reverend Mother stirred and opened her eyes. 'Water,' she whispered, and Rosa hurried to cradle her head in one hand and put the cup to her lips. The prioress opened her mouth a little, so Rosa could tip the water in. 'Thank you,' Angelica murmured and closed her eyes again. Her breathing was very shallow and Rosa feared the end was near.

And her fear was not only about losing someone who was so dear to her, but about what would happen after she had gone. There would, of course, have to be an election for a new prioress. Even if the outcome was inevitable, the processes had to be followed.

Yet, how inevitable *was* the outcome?

Everyone at Northwick knew Sister Evangelina was Mother Angelica's niece. And that, by long tradition here, she would be expecting to step straight into her aunt's shoes. It had been the way of things since the end of the last century, when the Godeffroy family became the priory's principal benefactor: the position of prioress passed always, and only, to a Godeffroy, as if by some kind of divine right.

Yet Rosa also knew Angelica never felt her niece was suitable to succeed her. She had told her as much.

'I regret Eva has no vocation,' she had said, 'nor even any piety. Sadly, she is not much liked amongst the members of our little community.' She had sighed. 'It is most unfortunate. If she is elected to succeed me, I fear she will not make a satisfactory prioress.'

In some ways, no one could be *less* fitting to be prioress of Northwick than Evangelina. Rosa despised herself for thinking ill of anyone, even Evangelina, but nobody liked her – even Rosa herself struggled to find *any* sort of amity with the woman. And, although Evangelina was a reasonably efficient sacrist, Rosa did wonder whether she could – or even wanted to – administer the priory as a whole, with all its buildings and its extensive land, not to mention the physical welfare and spiritual well-being of the sisters to consider.

The day of Mother Angelica's funeral dawned bright, and quite clement for mid-September. As her dear body, shrouded in white linen, was borne on a makeshift bier the short distance from her chamber to the chapel, the sun climbed into the sky. It cast its warming rays upon the Reverend Mother's final journey on this earth, as if in welcome to the radiance of the Paradise that awaited her.

It shone too on the line of dark-clad women who followed behind the bier, treading softly and murmuring prayers of thanksgiving for the life of their beloved prioress. Despite their grief and sadness at her passing, the sun's warmth and glow upraised their spirits, as they thought of the joy that would so soon be hers.

Sister Evangelina walked immediately behind the bier, seemingly untouched by any hint of warmth or joy. Her shoulders shook visibly and she made no effort to moderate the clamour of her grieving. Rosa was a step or two in Evangelina's wake, alongside Amata, with Beatrice just behind them. Amata lightly touched Rosa's arm, and Rosa turned to see her lifting her chin towards the back of Evangelina's wimple and habit.

'Somewhat excessive in her anguish, don't you think?' she whispered.

Rosa gave her a little grin. 'And not genuinely heartfelt?' she said, then felt her cheeks flush. How heartless of her to doubt the sincerity of *anyone* else's feelings, even Evangelina's.

But Amata rolled her eyes, then returned to reciting the prayer.

Nonetheless, Rosa wished she had not said it. Today of all days was not one for abstaining from compassion.

The bier, borne by the four youngest sisters, entered the chapel, and the procession of the other nuns followed on, shuffling inside, out of the warmth of the early autumn day and into the chill and dimness of the little church. As they approached the apse, Rosa watched the young nuns carefully lift the prioress's body – it must have weighed no more than that of a child – off the bier and lower it into the coffin, standing empty on a pedestal, candles at its head and foot. It was, Rosa could see, a fine oaken casket, much grander than Angelica would have wanted. Nudging Amata gently, she pointed to it.

Amata pursed her lips in evident disapproval. 'The Godeffroys, I presume,' she whispered.

Father Edgar stood to one side of the altar, another, much older, priest standing in Edgar's usual place in the centre of the little apse. Rosa had heard that the other priest came from Angelica's home parish, somewhere close to Southampton. Apparently, some members of her secular family had come with him, and Rosa noticed a rather elegant elderly matron beckon Evangelina to stand with her. Her mother? Angelica's sister? She murmured the question in Amata's ear.

'Oh, no. Angelica's sister died some years ago, despite being much younger than the Reverend Mother. I do not know who that lady is...'

She could say no more, as the elderly priest raised his hands and began to recite the funeral mass.

Out in the sunshine again, the nuns held back a little, as the Godeffroys – there were more here than Rosa had thought – pushed ahead to follow close behind the casket as it was carried, this time by men, towards the little graveyard set on sloping ground to the lee side of the chapel. At length everyone, Godeffroys and nuns, encircled the deep trench that Rosa had hired the sexton from the nearby parish to dig. Tears hovered in her eyes at the sight of it, and she looked away, taking in instead the fine view of the countryside surrounding Northwick that this little plot afforded. Her vision was blurry but she knew Angelica loved this part of Hampshire, her home for sixty years. Was that why she had insisted she be buried here and not taken back to that village near Southampton, which was now to her a foreign land?

The old priest coughed to quell the whispering that had bubbled up amongst those waiting at the graveside. He began the words of the committal, and soon the fine casket was being lowered into the trench. As it descended, Evangelina sank to her knees, beating her breast with one hand and weeping loudly, in a display that Rosa found most curious. For Evangelina was so much *not* given to displaying her emotions, this seemed inexplicably out of character.

Or was she putting on a show for the benefit of those she hoped before too long to rule?

Rosa knit her brow. Why was she being so uncharitable? So mean-spirited? It was most unlike her.

She lowered her gaze from the weeping Evangelina to the casket, now almost at the bottom of its eternal resting place. She let her own tears fall, but silently, and murmured prayers of love and hope to send the beloved Reverend Mother on her way to Paradise.

The Godeffroys had ordered up a splendid feast, with an array of meats, rich dishes and confections such as the nuns of Northwick had not enjoyed for years, if ever. Most fell upon the food with relish, though Rosa was modest in what she ate, as were Beatrice and Amata. They exchanged glances of disapproval tinged with humour as they watched their sisters gobble down the opulent fare.

'They might repent their gluttony tomorrow,' muttered Beatrice, and Rosa grinned.

She regarded Evangelina, no longer grieving, it seemed, but chatting almost merrily with her relatives. How strange it was to see Evangelina's face suddenly so bright. In all the years she had known her, she had never seen her expression anything other than dour. Yet, there she was, her eyes alight, her invariably tight-pressed lips now parted in what could only be described as a laugh. How extraordinary!

She leaned into Amata. 'Have you noticed?' she murmured.

'I have indeed. Evangelina is capable of merriment! Who'd have thought it?' She quickly raised a hand to cover her mouth, as a titter threatened to burst forth. 'And can you divine the reason for it?'

'Ah,' said Rosa. 'Of course.'

'Yet although she might *believe* it's a foregone conclusion,' continued Amata, 'she might find her election proves not *quite* so straightforward.'

Rosa was not certain what Amata meant. She picked up her cup of wine – a delicious luxury that Angelica had permitted only rarely – and sipped it.

The election for Angelica's successor would be soon. As she understood it, there had to *be* an election – with more than one candidate – it was the way things were done. Nonetheless, Evangelina would expect to win, because she was a Godeffroy and the prioress of Northwick had been a Godeffroy for the past eighty years. She supposed elections were held to give the *impression* that the sisters had a choice of who should lead them even though, in practice, the result was preordained.

Rosa had never before been party to an election, as Angelica was already prioress when she came to Northwick, fifteen years ago. Yet how was it that, if two or more candidates stood, it was *always* the Godeffroy who won the day? Was she inevitably the more popular candidate? In *Angelica's* case, it was true, but in *every* election in all those decades? That did seem most unlikely. She wondered idly if those Godeffroy wins had been achieved by some sort of bribery, shocking as it might seem.

Might either Amata or Beatrice, who had both been at Northwick long enough to have experienced at least one previous election, know the answer?

The next morning, the Godeffroys returned home after lodging overnight at Northwick, and the life of the priory settled down again to something akin to normal, with everyone going about their usual tasks. Of course, it was not normal, for the priory had no prioress. Yet it had been this way for many months. For, although Angelica had been with them in spirit, and indeed in body, the practicalities of priory life were organised by Rosa, Beatrice and Dulcia, the treasuress, and thus they would continue for a while longer.

Sister Amata had taken it upon herself to write to the bishop to inform him of the Reverend Mother's death and request permission to hold an election for her successor. She sought out Rosa to tell her what she had done.

'It will be some time before he replies,' she said. 'Weeks perhaps. But there's no question he will give us his permission. And, then, Rosa, we shall have to plan the election.'

'I have been wanting to ask you about that,' she said. 'How it works exactly. How there can be an *election*, with two or more candidates, and yet the Godeffroy always wins...'

Amata opened her mouth to answer but Rosa wanted to say more. 'So, if Evangelina is not favoured by the majority, why would *she* be elected and not the favourite?' She let out a long sigh. 'Truly, Amata, I am confused.'

Amata frowned. 'I've been party to three elections since I came here, all different but all with the same result, the appointment of a Godeffroy.'

'And were all of them *chosen* freely by the nuns?'

'I presumed so.' Then she blushed. 'Are you thinking they might not have been?'

'Well, does it not seem unlikely, that the Godeffroy was *always* the favoured candidate?'

'Well, it is *tradition* that the prioress has always been a Godeffroy...'

'I realise that. Then why take the trouble to have an election?'

'Ah, I see what you're saying...' Amata stroked the tip of her nose. 'Let me tell you what I recall of previous elections.'

They took a turn about the cloister.

'The first election came seven years after I came to Northwick,' said Amata. 'The prioress had been in post for twelve years and, for most of that time, had run the priory with reasonable efficiency, if without much genuine piety or affection for our community. But, in the last two or three years of her tenure – I don't know what went wrong – the priory's finances began to falter, buildings were left unrepaired, food was in short supply. All the sisters lodged complaints at the next bishop's visitation, and, at length, the prioress was removed from office, charged with some kind of malpractice. The sisters were delighted, thinking Angelica might now be appointed, for she was already much loved by everyone – *despite* being a Godeffroy.' She winked. 'But the authorities – you know, the bishop's man – deemed her too young. Well, she *was* only twenty-seven... He found some Godeffroy cousin languishing in a nunnery the other side of the country, who was longing to return to Hampshire. That time, she was the only candidate, but an election was held nonetheless. I was only seventeen at the time, and didn't think it was especially strange.' She rolled her eyes. 'And no one *talked* about it, though I do seem to recall one or two of the older sisters were disquieted by it.'

'Did you not discuss it with Angelica?'

'Not really. She acknowledged she *was* a little young to be prioress, and accepted that the cousin was more suitable. Or so she said, and, in truth, Rosa, I thought no more about it. And the woman in fact proved an efficient enough manager and lived another thirteen years.'

They sat down on the low wall of the arcade that ran around the cloister.

'And was it *then* Angelica's chance to become prioress?' asked Rosa.

'Unfortunately, not.' Amata rolled her eyes again. 'The bishop's man wielded his authority once more. As it happened, there was yet another Godeffroy at Northwick, an irascible, elderly woman, who came from a very distant branch of the family, but who evidently thought she deserved *her* turn in office. Yet again, Angelica accepted with good grace that the older woman had more right to the office than she, even though she was herself now forty – well, you know how selfless she was. However, she did suggest to the bishop's man that the election this time *must* have two candidates, and he agreed.'

'So did she stand herself?'

'She should have, but she wouldn't stand against her cousin. She persuaded another senior, non-Godeffroy, sister to stand. She never discussed it with me, but I believe she thought it was time a non-Godeffroy had a chance to become prioress, despite what had always been. Anyway, the man agreed to the election, but nonetheless the ancient cousin won.'

'But *why* did she win?' said Rosa. 'Surely, the sisters did not *choose* her, if she was so ancient and ill-tempered, when there was another, perhaps more amiable, candidate available?'

Amata knitted her brow. 'Actually, I don't know. I suppose, at the time, I assumed the majority *did* vote for her. I know *I* didn't, but there was *never* any discussion amongst the sisters about whom each of us voted for, as it was always considered a confidential matter.'

Yet it was surely most *unlikely* that the ancient cousin was selected by the majority. But she would not press Amata further on the matter. 'So did the old lady prove a good prioress?'

Amata threw back her head and laughed. 'She did not! She was hopeless, but she only lived another eighteen months, and then it *was* Angelica's turn. The sister who stood the previous time did so again, and it was a good election, for she too was well-liked and capable. But Angelica was bound to win, for she was so much *loved*.'

'And continued to be so for the next forty years,' said Rosa, smiling. 'So, who will stand against Evangelina? You, perhaps?'

Amata laughed again. 'Oh, dear Rosa, surely you know who?'

Rosa's eyes widened, as she understood at once what Amata was about to say. 'Do I?'

'*You*, of course! It's what Angelica wanted. She never thought Evangelina would make a suitable prioress, for all sorts of reasons. But she knew you would. And she told me long ago she hoped, somehow, you would succeed her.'

Rosa cast her mind back a few months. Angelica had not said that she, Rosa, was her choice of successor. Nonetheless, Amata's assertion did not especially surprise her, for she did realise the Reverend Mother had held her in high regard, a notion she found both gratifying and humbling.

'Yet I do not see,' she said, 'how my succession would be possible if the elections *always* deliver a Godeffroy prioress.'

Amata shrugged. 'I never questioned the process in the past. Why would I? I was very young when those previous elections took place.'

Rosa nodded. If she suspected some sort of corruption, it was clear Amata would know nothing of it, so she decided not to mention it. 'Anyway,' she said instead, 'that is all in the past. There is no reason to think whatever happened then will happen now.'

Although, even as she said it, she was quite unconfident in her own words.

2

Northwick Priory
September 1365

Evangelina sank back against the cushions of her chair. How much she relished being able to hide herself away here in the sacristy, away from the press and hubbub of her sisters. Not that they were especially noisy or demanding. Theirs was not a completely silent order, and moderate talk was permitted in many areas of the priory. But chatter was an irritation when she was excluded, which, invariably, she was... It was good to be able to retreat to the quiet of this little room.

Edgar used it too, to robe himself before a service, and to compose his sermons. But the rest of the time, it was hers: her own private office...

Sometimes she came here just to sit and think. But those were rare enough occasions, when there was always so much to do: taking care of the vestments and the altar cloths, ensuring the chapel's candles were trimmed and lit for every service, that the chapel itself was always in good order. As well as ringing the bell for the offices, and for meal times, though she'd persuaded one or two of the other sisters to share the task with her, for it was tedious and burdensome.

And then there were the wider responsibilities Aunt Angelica had imposed upon her years ago when she appointed her the sacrist: maintaining not only the chapel building but all the others in the priory, requiring her to engage with artisans from the nearby village, carpenters and masons, a task which had become more onerous in recent years, as old stone walls began to crumble and ancient timbers were attacked by beetles.

However, it was here she cleaned the church plate, the silver chalice and the paten, the containers for the communion wafers, the candlesticks and alms plate. And it was cleaning she had come to do, a task she rather enjoyed, handling these precious objects and polishing them until they shone... And imagining how their gleaming splendour would brighten and enhance the austerity of her monastic cell...

Space in the sacristy was limited, dominated as it was by the great oak chests in which the altar cloths and priest's vestments were kept. One wall held two cupboards with locks, to which she was the only key-holder. The larger one held her stock of candles made by the local candle-maker four times a year, and the aumbry was where the silver could be stored away but rarely was, since the chapel was in use eight times every day.

Alongside the cupboards was a narrow table where Edgar sometimes sat to write. It was also the only place Evangelina had to do her cleaning. She pushed his writing implements aside, but lit the candle he brought especially to light his work and had forgotten to take away. She knew he would be annoyed, but why use the chapel's precious candlewax when his was sitting here, available?

Evangelina went into the chapel and, returning with the alms plate and the paten, and the little wafer box, the pyx, she placed them on the table. She opened her pot of ashes saved from the frater hearth and poured a little verjuice from a bottle into a bowl. Dipping a rag first into the verjuice and then the ashes, she rubbed it onto the pyx, cleaning away the small amount of tarnish that had built up, before giving it a final polish with a clean dry cloth. Because she never permitted the precious silver to become too dirty, cleaning it was quick and easy, and it was always a pleasure to return the gleaming pieces to the chapel.

As she worked, she recalled Aunt Angelica's funeral. How relieved she was so many Godeffroys had come. Although ostensibly they had come for Angelica, she believed they had also come for *her*, to support her as chief mourner within the priory and as her aunt's successor. The splendid casket her uncles had provided, and the feast, made all too evident the commitment the family had to Northwick, a commitment they would surely confirm by ensuring her election...

Yet she feared the election might *not* go her way unless she took steps to guarantee it. For Angelica had already left instructions that a "proper" election, as she had called it, must be held, with at least two candidates, so the nuns had a genuine choice of who should lead them. But, if the nun who stood against her was Sister Rosa, she was sure Rosa would win.

For decades, the election of a Godeffroy as prioress had always been assured. She didn't know exactly how it worked, but presumed that Nicholas's predecessors – tasked with managing the elections – somehow ensured sufficient votes were cast in favour of the Godeffroy.

She mused a moment upon Nicholas's position in the priory. Like his predecessors, he'd been put forward for his post as bishop's man by one or other of the Godeffroys, to ensure *their* wishes were upheld in the day-to-day dealings of the priory, and in particular in the matter of elections, and visitations. Not that she thought he or any of his forebears bothered overmuch with the day-to-day. Rather, they did whatever was necessary, and no more. As far as Cousin Nicholas himself was concerned, he was amiable but maybe he was also sly. Sly enough, perhaps, to be of use to her...

Edgar had said the previous bishop's men must have *bribed* some of the nuns to vote the Godeffroy way, and that Nicholas might do the same for her.

Yet she wasn't entirely confident that, this time, bribery would work, when Rosa was so much admired, and she herself was so much *not*...

Which was why she needed to discredit Rosa in their eyes.

She took the items she had cleaned back to the altar and, picking up the chalice, carried it back into the sacristy. As she turned it on its side to begin the cleaning, she gasped. Spilled wine had left an unsightly blemish running down the vessel, from lip to base. She tutted. Had it been standing on the altar in that state ever since last Mass? Why hadn't she noticed it before? She rubbed fiercely at the stain with her ashy rag, ensuring every trace of wine had gone, then took up her polishing cloth and buffed and burnished until the silver shone.

She'd told Edgar of her plan to discredit Rosa, and he seemed willing enough to help her. He evidently knew *something* of Rosa's past, from what she had disclosed over the past ten years. How fortunate he was loyal enough to her to be willing to break the sacred seal of the confessional...

She'd always known Rosa came to Northwick under some sort of cloud of her own making. The girl had had a secret for which, in her early days here, she spent hours upon her knees begging for forgiveness. But Evangelina had never gleaned the exact nature of the secret, other than that it involved some dreadful sin.

Edgar had learned a little more: some transgression as a girl, he'd said, though he had no details. She asked him again yesterday if he knew anything further.

'I've already told you, Eva,' he said, rolling his eyes. 'Rosa's confessions these days hold fast to the adult sins of pride, disobedience and being selfish.' He grinned. 'She's not going to let slip some scandalous new morsel now. The time for that has long passed...'

Evangelina had tapped her fingers on the table. 'How disappointing. But perhaps it doesn't matter. I can still tell her I know her secret, without going into details and, surely, she'll be alarmed enough to refrain from standing against me...'

'As I said before, she *might* back down, but equally she might not.'

'Then, if she refuses to stand aside, I'll simply spread the rumour around the priory. Discreetly, of course.'

Edgar's black eyebrows shot up. 'Discreetly? How?'

'I've already decided to pick a few of the younger nuns to be my, what shall we call them, disciples...' Edgar laughed, but Evangelina flapped her hand at him. 'I'll offer them favours for when I'm prioress. But, in order to obtain those favours, they must agree to support my election, including spreading rumours about Rosa.' She tilted her head. 'What do you think?'

He laughed again. 'Well, sister, you are clearly made in the Nicholas mould of Godeffroy rather than the Angelica one. You are proposing to *bribe* innocent young nuns to lie for you?'

She applied her most indignant frown. 'Not *lie*, Edgar, no, but expose one who's not as virtuous as she makes herself out to be.'

He'd shaken his head, a gleam still in his eyes. But then he shrugged. 'Well, I suppose it might work one way or the other. Either Rosa will stand aside for fear of her perfection being sullied, or she will find herself sullied anyway.'

Evangelina nodded, but the question was, was she brazen enough to do it? Yet the answer had to be yes, for being prioress *was* her birth right. She'd already waited twice as many years as she expected for her chance to come and she wasn't going to let it slip through her fingers for a want of mettle.

Evangelina had already identified the young nuns she intended to invite to be members of her coterie. There were three of them, Maria, Felicia and Letitia, all seventeen or eighteen or so, all from aristocratic, as opposed to merely gentle, families. Maria and Felicia took their vows three months ago, and Letitia's, five weeks ago, was the last profession of Angelica's rule.

She wondered if she should also try and encourage one or two of the maturer nuns to join her little clique. Though, of course, the older women had known her for much longer, whereas the girls hadn't really had enough time to form any contrary opinions of her.

Holding fast to her original intention, Evangelina decided to approach the three individually. It wasn't easy to find a moment to speak to them alone. A nun's day wasn't exactly full with activity, but it was mostly spent in the company of others. Several hours were − for most − occupied in prayer, with the eight offices to be read and sung in the chapel. A light breakfast, dinner and a small supper took up a further couple of hours.

In between, the sisters carried out some work, according to what aspect of the priory's life they had been assigned: the gardens, the infirmary, the kitchens, working alongside the nuns in charge and supervising the few servants Angelica had allowed. Time was also set aside for private study, but, with a few exceptions, Northwick's nuns were uninterested in learning. Aunt Angelica tried to encourage a love of reading and the scriptures, but didn't seem to understand that, because most of her nuns – like Evangelina herself – had come to Northwick as children, or under some manner of duress, they had no calling to the religious life. One or two did find a vocation in the course of their lives here, but not her, and she suspected most of the others were the same.

The nuns' lives were prayer, eating, sleep, a little routine work... and nothing else. Angelica – and Rosa too, she imagined – were both utterly contented with this life. They embraced every aspect of it, with what for them was joy.

A joy she'd *never* felt in all her forty years of incarceration here.

But perhaps – perhaps soon – if things went her way, she could inject a little everyday *pleasure* into this priory of Northwick. Not the *so-called* joy of piety and reading and ascetism, but the delight to be found in beautiful objects, soft fabrics, fine food, outings, and even games? Who knew what might be possible?

Yet first she had to win the election. Only then would she have the power to change the life of Northwick. And now was a good time to approach the three young nuns, when they'd be alone in their cells, not "studying" but more likely lying on their unforgiving mattresses and dreaming of what might have been. Now was her chance to invite them to join her for the prospect of a much more congenial life.

3

Northwick Priory
September 1365

Rosa was unsettled by her conversation with Amata. Dear Amata seemed quite unworldly – and indeed why should she not be? She had been confined to Northwick ever since she was a child. Amata had never questioned how it was that a Godeffroy was always elected, even when she was clearly not likely to make a successful prioress. But why would she? Amata might be seventy, but she seemed innocent of the corruption in the world. After all, she had lived forty of those years under the benign and utterly untainted rule of Mother Angelica.

In truth, Rosa herself, at thirty-six, was scarcely much more worldly-wise. But she had known corruption in her past, with the terrible events that partly drove her to come to Northwick – Philip's murder and the reasons for it.

Of course, in the last election, no underhand tactics had been needed, for Angelica won easily in her own right because – despite being a Godeffroy, as Amata had put it – she was already loved by all the sisters in the priory.

But this time, the situation was different – more like it was before Angelica – with the Godeffroy candidate *not* being loved at all. For Evangelina to win, against Amata or Beatrice or even Rosa herself, would she not have to *persuade* more than half of Northwick's sisters to vote for her? Rosa counted up the community of Northwick... There would be eleven nuns to persuade... Yet were that many likely to succumb to such persuasion? Knowing Northwick's sisters as she thought she did, it seemed improbable.

She thought again about what Amata had said, that she, Rosa, was Mother Angelica's choice of successor. Had Angelica not considered that Evangelina would, somehow or other, fight for her birth right, making Rosa's path to succession arduous, at the very least? Had the Reverend Mother *really* thought that times had changed, and that the sisters who had grown to love her would also, without question, support the person she wanted to succeed her? Or, wise as she was, was Angelica also a little naïve?

Rosa knelt upon the floor beside her bed, clasped her hands together and looked up at the crucifix pinned to the wall in front of her. She would ask for guidance. Was entering the race to become the next prioress right for her? Was it what she wanted? Was she the most suitable person for the job? Evangelina might not be, but might there be another who could stand against her?

When her long-drawn-out, but totally silent, pleas for divine direction had run their course, the first shafts of daylight were seeping through the high, tiny window of her narrow cubicle and she could hear the bell calling her to Lauds. She eased herself to her feet, rubbing at her knees and kneading her thighs to tease out the strain of kneeling for so long. She quickly donned her habit and fitted her wimple over her coif then pinned on the dark veil. Smoothing her hands along and down her skirts, she slipped her feet into her soft shoes and hurried from the room, joining the other sisters as they made their way in silence towards the chapel.

It was hours later, after Prime, breakfast and Terce, that Rosa once more had time to herself to think. She was not idling; she had work to do in the small room alongside the prioress's chamber she was still using – until the election doubtless deprived her of her role. But, whilst she was working, she allowed her mind to wander, first reflecting upon what divine guidance she had received, and deciding she *had* received God's blessing to consider herself a candidate for prioress. So, she then mulled over the advantages and disadvantages that taking on the role might bring, both to herself and to the priory. She did not rush her contemplation, wanting to be sure she had examined the proposition from every point of view.

Her musings were interrupted when Northwick's bailiff, Rafe Byllynges, came asking to speak with her. She was able to answer his questions quickly and, soon, she was alone again. Yet Rafe's coming had discomfited her slightly, for she had mixed views about the man. He was charming and handsome, with a thicket of fair hair, but she was not convinced of his honesty, albeit she had appointed him herself only two years or so ago. The previous bailiff, taken on by Angelica some years before, after the death of a long-serving and much-trusted incumbent, had at length been found to be running the estate ineptly, as well as stealing from the priory's coffers for the best part of his tenure. Rosa had herself discovered the man's transgressions. After his dismissal, she recommended to the Reverend Mother they try to manage without a bailiff, for a while at least, and instead take advice from her father's man in Meonbridge, John atte Wode.

Angelica had agreed to try it, and so it was that John came once every month or so for consultations about managing the priory's domains. Rosa got on very well with John. Their familial connection, through their shared nephew, Dickon, the son of her brother Philip and John's sister Agnes, had engendered a cousinly relationship between them.

John always gave sage advice about what needed to be done at each season of the year, and about the detail of best farming practices. Rosa learned a great deal from him. It surprised her how interested she found herself in everything he had to say, but she learned it well and, at length, felt almost knowledgeable about the running of the priory's farm.

Nonetheless, despite her unexpectedly good grasp of John's advice, eventually it became clear that, after all, she could not manage the farm and all the tenants by herself, and Mother Angelica persuaded her to seek another bailiff for Northwick.

John agreed. 'In truth, Rosa, I don't know how you've coped this long. It must be too much for you to do, with all your other commitments. Let's hope you soon find a decent man.'

She thought she had. An amiable fellow, Rafe Byllynges certainly *seemed* both capable and honest. Nonetheless, she was loath to give up entirely her dialogues with John, and Mother Angelica was content for them to continue, and so they did, if rather less often than before.

The last time she had seen John was in July. The time before that – in April – was an occasion she recalled quite often, despite the distress the memory brought her.

Along with his advice, John always passed on news of her family and his own in Meonbridge, news that had invariably given her pleasure and even joy. Until, that was, five months ago, when what he came to tell her had brought immeasurable grief.

It was such a beautiful spring morning, the sky blue, the air warm if a little breezy. Birds were singing in all the hedgerows. Rosa had not yet recovered from the fever that had kept her in bed for days, but the warm weather had encouraged her to go outside for a short while. She was in the priory garden, speaking with Sister Beatrice, who, as cellarer, had responsibility for managing the potagers and orchards. The garden afforded a view of the little road that snaked through fields and woodlands to reach the priory's gate. She and Beatrice both turned at the distant sound of galloping hooves and, far away, but coming rapidly closer, was a horse, almost obscured by the clouds of dust rising from the road.

The horse slowed only feet from the gate, snorting and panting. Its rider leapt from the saddle before he had even brought his mount to a full halt and, running to the gate, hammered upon it and shouted for attention.

But Rosa and Beatrice were already hastening towards him, the folds of their skirts clutched in their hands to stop them tripping up. Rosa could see that it was John.

She called out to him. 'What is it, John? Is something amiss?'

She ran the last few yards and, when he turned towards her, John's face was grey and stricken beneath the glaze of sweat, and his eyes were wide. He stepped forward, one hand clasped to his chest, the other held out to her.

'What is it?' she said again, this time in a whisper. 'Has something happened in Meonbridge?'

She could see his eyes were filling with tears. 'Oh, Rosa...' he began, his voice hoarse, and terror overwhelmed her.

'What has *happened*?' she cried, her voice rising in panic.

'I can scarcely bear to tell you,' he said, 'but I've been sent to do so, so I must. Dickon, the lord of Meonbridge, commanded it—'

'*Dickon* commanded it?' Only moments later the implication of his words had sunk in. 'You mean our nephew is now Meonbridge's lord?'

'He is.' He brought both hands up to his face. 'Oh, Rosa, how much I wish I wasn't the bearer of this news...' He swallowed. 'Her ladyship is dead—'

She cried out then and Beatrice at once was at her side, her arm about her shoulders. Repeating his words, not quite grasping the truth of them, she sank to her knees on the dusty road, and Beatrice dropped down with her, cradling her against her ample bosom.

Her chest was tight and, for several moments, she found it hard to breathe and felt a little dizzy. At length she looked up at John, demanding to know how Mama had died and why she had not been called to her bedside if she was ill.

He shook his head. 'But Lady Margaret wasn't ill, Sister.' He lowered his gaze to the ground. 'She was murdered—'

Rosa thought she might swoon. Her gentle, noble, God-fearing mother *murdered*? How was something so shocking possible? For long moments she was unable to believe John's words. She leaned back against Beatrice, trying once more to catch her breath. At length, knowing John would not tell her anything that was not true, she looked up at him again and let out a shuddering sigh. She then braced herself and, taking Beatrice's supportive arm, eased herself once more to her feet.

'But who might have wished my mother dead?' she asked.

At that moment, the porter opened the gate and Beatrice suggested they all went indoors, giving instructions to the man to find the stable lad and tell him to take charge of John's wild-eyed, sweating horse.

Rosa was grateful for the opportunity to sit and sip a cup of wine. It calmed her. John accepted a large cup of ale, and sat in front of her, perhaps waiting for her to continue the conversation. Rosa found herself shivering, and wondered if the fever was returning. Beatrice must have noticed, for she came with a woollen blanket and wrapped it around her shoulders.

'Shall I leave you?' Beatrice whispered in her ear, but Rosa shook her head.

'No, please stay, dear Beatrice. I so welcome your support.' She turned to John. 'So, who did wish my dearest Mama dead?'

Tears were coursing down Rosa's cheeks as she recalled once more John's terrible reply. But then she realised with a start that someone was in her chamber and was hurrying towards her.

'Sister Rosa?' a small voice said at her side. 'Are you not well?'

Rosa looked up, to see Sister Juliana, looking most concerned. Wiping the heel of her hand across her face, she offered her a feeble smile.

'Is something amiss, Sister Rosa?' said Juliana, frowning. 'You seem a little... distracted?'

She shook her head. 'Oh dear, Juliana, yes, I was much more than a little distracted. Something set me remembering the day I learned of my mother's death...'

'Oh, yes, last April. The circumstances were dreadfully upsetting, I recall, though I have never known the details.'

'They were...' Rosa hesitated, wondering if she wished to share them.

Juliana bit her lip. 'Would you... would you like to tell me, Sister Rosa? Or are the memories too painful? I have no wish to pry, but... might it help?'

Rosa smiled and nodded. 'You will remember, perhaps, that, in April, I was ill with an ague...' Juliana nodded. '...and Sister Amata, bless her, insisted I could not travel to attend the betrothal of my nephew Dickon.'

Juliana sighed. 'How disappointed you were to have to miss such a joyful family occasion.'

'Yet that was the day my dearest Mama died, and I was not with her when she passed from this world, as I should have been.'

Juliana bit her lip again. 'Sister Rosa, you have never said how it was your mother died...'

Rosa spread her fingers out upon her lap. 'John told me how full of joy Mama was that day, and how gracious when, following the betrothal ceremony, she invited the folk of Meonbridge to come forward with any blessings or congratulations for the happy couple. Many did step forward, some bringing small gifts, often something they had made for the occasion...' She hesitated. 'Then, someone gave her sweetmeats that were poisoned—'

'Poisoned? But why would anyone—'

Rosa held up her hand. 'The reason is complicated, Juliana. I cannot explain it all. But the person who did it – it was a woman – believed very strongly, but quite erroneously, that her family had been wronged, and that *my* family – the de Bohuns – was responsible.'

'Wronged enough to warrant killing your mama?' said Juliana, her tone full of horror and disbelief.

It was indeed hard to believe that Margery Tyler would *kill* Mama in revenge for what had happened to her family, when it surely was her father Robert who had brought such disaster down upon their heads, when he lost his senses, and murdered Philip out of resentment and rage? But John had said that Margery too must have lost her wits to carry out such a wicked act.

'Well, of course,' Rosa went on, 'it is difficult for us to understand her reasons...' She paused. 'Yet we can perhaps comprehend that her anger and resentment so consumed her that she let the Devil in and it was he who drove her to such wickedness?'

'Yes, yes, it must have been the Devil's work...'

'Of course, I could scarcely forgive her for what she did. Only God can provide such mercy. Nonetheless, I prayed for her, as well as for my poor Mama.'

'You could do no other.'

Rosa nodded. She still prayed for both, albeit more fervently for

Mama than for her killer. Then, remembering why Juliana was there, she stood up. 'You were looking for me, Juliana.'

She flushed a little. 'So I was. Sister Beatrice bade me find you, and ask you to attend her in her office in the frater.'

'Very well, please tell her I shall be with her shortly.'

Juliana bobbed a curtsey and hurried off.

Rosa sat down again. Although she had not told Juliana all the details, she was glad to have told her something about Mama's death.

For it was curious in a way that she should mourn her mother's passing so very deeply. When she first came to Northwick, she was not on good terms with Mama, and even less so with her father. She felt estranged from the family, and was desperate to leave Meonbridge for the piety and isolation of the priory. But, as the years passed, and she settled contentedly into her life at Northwick, her feelings towards her parents gradually became more amiable.

After Papa was killed, the bond between her and Mama grew stronger. Some priories required their nuns to cut themselves off almost entirely from their secular families, but that was never Mother Angelica's way. She *encouraged* Northwick's sisters to maintain ties with their relatives, to visit them and have them visit here. Mama occasionally came to spend a few days in one of the guest chambers, and Rosa would return to Meonbridge from time to time, to help her mother with some of the decisions to be made, especially those to do with her young nephew, Dickon.

Once more, Rosa felt able to be a familial daughter in a way she had not been when she fled Meonbridge. Which was why John's news of Mama's death, and the manner of it, had been so devastating.

Rosa had never been much given to crying as a child, nor as a young woman, except when Philip died and she could scarcely contain her desolation. But, since she had come to Northwick, she had never felt the need for tears. Even when she learned of Papa's death, she could not remember weeping.

But that day last April, when John's terrible news had rent her heart in two, she most certainly felt the need for weeping... No, much more than weeping. Overwhelming *grief*.

After John left, she ran back out into the priory garden and followed the long grassy path that led through the gardens and the orchards, and on into the meadows. Soon, the grasses would be ablaze with colour, with blue cornflowers, red poppies and white catchfly but, then, only the bright flowery heads of pink campions were nestling between the whispering blades. Nonetheless, they were a sign of advancing spring, a fact that had cheered her, despite her crushing sorrow.

She sat upon a little hillock at the top edge of the meadow, from where the grassy sward rolled gently away downhill towards the little stream that ran along the valley. For a while, she gazed down towards the rippling water, glinting in the sunlight, and allowed her eyes to brim with tears.

How long had it been since she had seen Mama? Months! How much she regretted the fever and Amata's insistence that she could not travel to Meonbridge for the betrothal. Perhaps she could have *prevented* that wretched woman passing Mama the poisoned sweetmeats? But, even if she could not, at least she would have seen her mother in all the joy and happiness John had described, and been with her at the end...

She leaned back onto the grass − it was cool if prickly upon her back − and stared up into the sky, dotted with scudding clouds, like so many frolicking woolly lambs. She smiled at the sight of them, then had to sit up suddenly as choking sobs engulfed her and for a few moments she could not breathe. Taking in large gulps of air, at length she calmed her sobbing, and lay back once again.

She watched the lambs frolicking across the sky-blue sward a while longer, but time was passing and she had work to do. There would be other times to be alone, to think about Mama... and weep, if that was what she needed...

Now, Rosa shook herself to throw off her reverie. She really *must* go and see Sister Beatrice. She would surely be wondering where she was? Quickly, she tidied her table, putting together in a pile the documents she had been perusing before her musings, and Rafe Byllynges, interrupted her.

Ah, yes, Byllynges. Perhaps she should discuss her concerns about him with Beatrice? He *had* seemed capable enough, and honest, for perhaps as much as a year, but, recently, she was not so sure. Unlike the rogue she had dismissed, there was no *evidence* of Byllynges stealing, nor even of mismanagement. Yet, polite and charming as he was, she did not entirely trust him, albeit she could not put her finger on exactly *why*. The matter needed investigation but, with the election imminent, and the result uncertain, now was hardly the time to embark upon such an enquiry...

Yet, what *had* she decided about the election? There were many good reasons *for* standing... and maybe one or two against— But then she clicked her tongue. *No more musings, Rosa! Sister Beatrice is waiting for you...*

Glancing once more around the little chamber that soon might not be hers to occupy, she closed the door and hurried downstairs to the frater.

But she did not reach Beatrice nor even the frater before her passage was intercepted. As she hurried along one wing of the cloister, Evangelina stepped out from the door of the chapter house, giving her a start.

'Goodness, Sister Evangelina, you made me jump,' said Rosa.

Evangelina inclined her head in a gesture of apology, although her expression bore no sign of it. She pointed back into the chapter house. 'I was readying the chamber for our meeting this afternoon.'

'We are having a meeting?' said Rosa, astonished.

'The business of the priory must continue. We have matters to discuss.'

Rosa was momentarily perplexed. Who had decided a chapter meeting should be held? It was not the usual day and time. 'Yes, yes, of course. But when was it announced?'

'It will be shortly,' said Evangelina. 'At dinner.'

'That gives the sisters very little notice,' Rosa said. 'But I shall attend.' She made to hurry on to catch up with Sister Beatrice, who must now be thinking she was not coming.

But Evangelina placed a heavy hand upon her arm. 'Before you run off, Sister Rosa,' she said, her head tilted slightly, 'a word...'

A frisson of alarm ran down Rosa's spine. Evangelina's "word" sounded menacing. 'A word about what?' she said.

Evangelina drew her back into the chapter house and closed the door. 'One of the subjects for discussion will be the election,' she said.

'Indeed,' said Rosa, her heart thudding slightly at the ominous edge to Evangelina's voice. 'I understand Sister Amata has written to the bishop, asking for his permission to proceed. Has she received a reply?'

'I'm not aware of it. But that's not what I wish to raise with you...' She hesitated and tilted her head again. Then she swept over to the fine oak chair that was the prioress's station during meetings. She sat in it, leaned back and gestured Rosa to take a nearby stool.

Rosa's mouth was dry as she lowered herself onto the stool. Did Evangelina want to know if she was going to stand against her in the election? Rosa looked at her hands, resting uneasily in her lap: what would her answer be? She had not yet quite decided but, if Evangelina asked her, she should surely not prevaricate? 'So, what is it you wish to say?'

'As I'm sure you know, I'm the natural successor to Mother Angelica as prioress of Northwick, as I'm a Godeffroy...' Rosa nodded. 'I suspect you also know that, in the interests of fair play, or at least the semblance of it'—she smirked—'Angelica insisted an election must be held...'

'I understood that an election *always* has been held...'

'And one will be this time too. However, Sister Rosa, you must understand that I intend to win...'

'*Intend* to?' Despite her uneasiness, Rosa raised an eyebrow. 'Does not who wins depend upon the electors?'

'It follows then that no one must stand against me who might triumph in my stead...' She paused. 'Like you, for example.'

'Me?'

'Oh, don't play the coy damsel with me, *Dolo*rosa,' she snarled, and Rosa started at her hostile use of her old religious name. 'Everyone knows you hope to step into my aunt's shoes. Haven't you been working up to it all these years, acting as *subprioress*?'

'I was not the subprioress,' said Rosa, her anxiety rising, 'but merely Mother Angelica's assistant...'

'Whatever you say... Nonetheless it's *my* birth right to succeed my aunt. And, surely, with your sense of what is right and fair, you'd not deny me that?'

'What are you saying, Sister Evangelina?'

'I'm asking you, politely, to stand aside.'

Rosa swallowed. 'But why should I when I understand the Reverend Mother hoped *I* might follow in her footsteps?'

'Ha! You believe that? My aunt was *humouring* you, Dolorosa, into thinking you'd be the next prioress. She *knew* it was my birth right to succeed.'

Rosa found herself shaking. Was Evangelina right? Had Mother Angelica only *pretended* to favour her? She had never felt that was the case. Moreover, Amata was certain Angelica did prefer her.

'I am afraid I do not believe you,' she said, sounding much more confident than she felt.

'So, you won't stand aside?' said Evangelina and Rosa gave her shoulders a little shrug.

Evangelina placed her hands upon the table top before her and splayed her fingers. 'In that case, I shall have to *persuade* you.'

'Persuade me? How?'

'By threatening to expose your darkest secrets, *Dolo*rosa.' She smirked once more.

Rosa shivered. What could Evangelina possibly know of her past? 'But I have no secrets,' she said, willing her voice to steadiness.

'Oh, I think you do. I *know* you do!'

Rosa's heart was thudding. Was Evangelina referring to the reason she had come to Northwick fifteen years ago? If she was, how could she have learned of it? Of course, the priests knew something of it, but confessions were sacrosanct. Of the nuns, only Angelica ever knew why she had come, and she would *never* have betrayed her secret, especially to Evangelina.

'I do not know what you think you have discovered,' said Rosa, 'but tell me how you know.'

Evangelina grinned. 'I remember when you first came to Northwick, what a wretched and insufferably pious girl you were. I know about the ridiculous name you chose, "Dolorosa", and how my aunt persuaded you to choose something less unashamedly *guilt-ridden*.' She scoffed. 'It was obvious to anyone you were hiding a dreadful secret, some terrible *wrong* you had committed... How astonishing you now have the status of a saint—'

'I do not!' She could not stop her voice shaking.

'Well, if not a saint, then most virtuous and saint-*ly*... But of course, it isn't true. You're not virtuous nor saintly but the perpetrator of the direst wickedness!' Evangelina banged her hand down on the table with an air of triumph.

Rosa was queasy with dread at what Evangelina was saying, even though she was still baffled by how she could possibly know what happened before she came here. Perhaps she did not *really* know at all, but was merely pretending to, as a ruse to force her hand? Yet Rosa could not bear the thought that Evangelina *might* know enough to stain her reputation, and that she might divulge it to everyone in Northwick and turn them all against her.

She stood up, clasping her hands together at her waist to keep them still, and took a deep breath to calm herself. 'I do not believe that you know anything,' she said, 'and I will not be bullied. I have not yet decided whether or not I shall stand in the election. You will learn of my decision in due course.'

She swiftly left the chamber. Remembering as she closed the door behind her that she was supposed to be meeting Beatrice, she hurried to the frater, but was shaking so much she could scarcely speak.

'My goodness, Rosa dear,' said Beatrice, 'whatever's the matter?'

'Oh, just some news that has upset me—'

Beatrice's eyes were full of concern. 'More bad news? Can I help?'

But she was quite unable to say any more. 'Please excuse me, Beatrice, if I leave you now. Can we speak again another time?'

She ran all the way back to the dorter and her flimsy cell, and threw herself down upon her bed and wept.

4

NORTHWICK PRIORY
SEPTEMBER 1365

As John made his way once more to Northwick Priory, the balmy September morning matched his mood. The warmth of the early sun, and the blueness of the sky, enhanced the joy in his heart, heightening his gladness to be visiting Northwick again so soon, with the possibility of once more seeing Anabella, the young widow who'd taken refuge within the priory's walls.

He recalled the day he first saw her, back in May, only a few weeks after he'd come to tell Rosa the terrible news about her mother's death. He spoke to Rosa and Mother Angelica in the prioress's chamber, then he and Rosa went to the frater for some refreshments.

Anabella came into the frater to bring the ale and sweetmeats, and stayed as chaperone. As she told him later, Rosa noticed how he flushed as Anabella entered, and how Anabella herself faltered as she tried to set the tray of jug and cups upon the table, whilst she held John's admiring gaze. He'd never understood how such instant attraction could be possible, but it had struck him like a thunderclap, and he was certain Anabella had felt it too.

Since then, he'd come twice more to Northwick, in June, and then in August, more often than he'd been accustomed to since Byllynges had been appointed the priory's bailiff.

After the first meeting, when Anabella had left the frater for some reason he wasn't privy to, he'd taken the opportunity to ask Rosa about her and learned she was a widow. She was young, no more than twenty-five or so, and had come to Northwick to escape the persecution of her dead husband's family. She'd brought her fortune with her, to give as a dowry to the priory.

'The family are trying to force her to marry her brother-in-law,' said Rosa. 'A man she says is even more cruel and unpleasant than her husband was.' She paused. 'I could see at once you were beguiled by her. She is very comely.'

He flushed. 'She's lovely.' He scraped his hand through his hair. 'How terrible her husband's family have been treating her so ill.'

'Indeed, but she will be safe here at Northwick, especially once she has taken her vows and put herself beyond their clutches—'

At which he started, realising he might have found the woman he wanted to make his wife and lost her in the same moment. 'How long will it be?'

'What?'

'Before she makes her vows.'

'Oh, I see. A while yet...'

He gulped down his cup of ale and she poured him another. 'Is there any chance she might change her mind?'

'About her vows?' said Rosa. 'Only, I suppose, if she was offered marriage by a man she wished to wed. But you have only seen her once, John, and that for only a short time...'

He nodded, feeling foolish. 'Yet, I did feel an immediate affinity between us, even if it does seem unlikely.' He sipped at his ale. 'Do you think she might reconsider...?' He trailed off.

Rosa raised an eyebrow. 'Northwick would lose a substantial fortune if she did not stay with us. It is very much to the priory's advantage that I heartily *discourage* your new interest in Anabella.'

He then felt both foolish and downhearted. But Rosa, it seemed, wasn't as unfeeling as she was pretending to be. 'Yet, in truth, John,' she continued, 'I also wish to see you happy, as I am certain your mother does. So perhaps you should come to Northwick again before too long and see if that affinity is still there or is just a fancy.'

He'd stared at her, astonished. Was *Rosa* of all people acting the matchmaker?

When he'd returned to Northwick a few weeks later, Rosa arranged for Anabella once more to serve their refreshments in the frater and he knew for certain the affinity was real.

Before Anabella arrived, Rosa spoke quietly to John. 'I talked to Anabella after you came last time. She admitted she was much taken with the light in your eyes and the warmth of your smile. She asked me about you, and I told her what I know.' She smiled. 'I do believe she was enraptured by the thought of you.'

John's heart thudded a little at the thought of *her*, and when he looked up at Rosa, he knew he had a broad grin on his face. Until he saw her smile had faded.

'But then she looked a little scared,' Rosa went on. 'She said it was too late because she would soon have to make her final vows and be beyond the embrace of any man. I shook my head and suggested she could delay making her vows, protesting her unreadiness.'

Anabella came with the refreshments and Rosa invited her to sit with them, to listen to their continuing discussion of farming matters. If any of the other sisters had enquired, she'd explain that Anabella had expressed an interest in helping her with the management of the priory's estate. 'Which is quite true,' said Rosa, and John couldn't have been more pleased to hear it.

On his third visit, in August, Anabella had joined in their conversation, asking questions. And John's heart had swelled with joy at her apparent interest in his life.

As John approached the priory gate, his heart was thudding with anticipation. He had no reason to be here, for he and Rosa had discussed all there was to discuss in August. Rosa knew that well enough, yet seemed content to broker as many meetings with Anabella as they desired.

He rang the bell and was admitted, giving his horse over to the stable boy, then waited impatiently for Sister Juliana to come to fetch him and take him to the frater where he and Rosa – and maybe Anabella – would meet.

But, when he entered the high-vaulted chamber, his heart did a flip, for Rosa's face was long, her lips pressed together in an expression of concern.

'Is summat amiss?' he said, fighting down panic. 'With Anabella?'

'No, John, Anabella is fine. You will see her shortly, but I fear she cannot stay. Neither indeed can you, or not for long.'

'Not stay? Why not?'

'Because circumstances here at Northwick have changed.'

Anabella then came, bearing a flagon of ale and just two cups. She put them down, and raised her eyes to his, but the smile she gave him was wan. She withdrew and Rosa gestured John to sit. 'I have unhappy news,' she said, 'but more than merely unhappy. Everything here is about to change.'

The death of Mother Angelica was sad but hardly unexpected. Indeed, the nuns had been expecting it for years, but the old lady seemed to be strong and resilient, and had lived to a great age. But it hadn't occurred to him that the *consequence* of her death might adversely affect him.

'There will be an election sometime soon,' said Rosa.

'And *you'll* be elected, won't you?' He'd realised long ago how highly Mother Angelica regarded Rosa.

But she shook her head. 'No, I will not. For what I presume you do not know, John, is that, for the past eighty years, the prioress at Northwick has always been a Godeffroy—'

'A Godeffroy?' He hooted, wondering what she meant.

'The Godeffroy family has been the priory's principal benefactor for all that time.'

'Nonetheless, I thought prioresses had to be elected,' he said, though he knew almost nothing about the management of priories.

'In principle they do, but, in all those years, a Godeffroy always has been chosen.'

He scratched at his beard. 'So was Angelica a Godeffroy?'

'She was.'

'And will a Godeffroy be standing this time?'

She told him about Sister Evangelina, who apparently was Angelica's niece and expecting to be the next prioress. A woman more different from her aunt, John couldn't imagine. He'd spoken to her no more than once or twice, but he'd found her sour-natured and stern. He suspected she wasn't much liked by the other nuns in Northwick.

'But why would the sisters vote for her, when they can have you?'

Rosa flushed a little. 'I might not stand—' John opened his mouth to protest but she held up her hand. 'Even if someone else does stand – Amata, say, or Beatrice – I believe Evangelina will still win. In the past, as I have said, the election always swung in favour of the Godeffroy, regardless of her popularity, so I imagine the same thing will happen this time.'

John didn't understand quite *how* a Godeffroy always won, even when she wasn't the most popular or admired. Had some sort of corruption been brought to bear? Yet that seemed so outrageous, he couldn't bring himself to mention it to Rosa. Instead, he asked her why she might not stand.

'If it is inevitable that Evangelina will win, there seems little purpose in me opposing her,' she said, her shoulders slumped. 'However, I have not yet *quite* made up my mind.' She lowered her eyes to her hands, folded together in her lap.

A few moments later, she got up and poured them both a little ale. 'Anyway, I should warn you that, if Evangelina is elected, she is most unlikely to wish to continue our consultations...'

'Why?'

'I heard her say to Mother Angelica more than once your visits were unnecessary, when we have a bailiff here at Northwick upon whose experience and advice we should rely.'

'So, I'd no longer be able to come here...' John said, his heart suddenly thumping with alarm. 'But if I can no longer come to Northwick, what will become of Anabella and me...?'

Rosa shook her head, her face sad. 'I truly do not know.' She wrung her hands together briefly, then turned. 'I shall fetch her back here, John, so at least you can say your farewells...'

She hurried away and, returning with Anabella, took a stool at one end of the frater, whilst he and Anabella sat together on a bench at the other. They didn't have long to talk, as it would soon be time for dinner and the other sisters would be arriving.

Feeling bold, he took Anabella's hand, and she didn't resist. 'You must know how I feel about you,' he whispered. 'What of you?'

She sighed. 'My position is difficult, John. I have already committed my fortune to the priory. Mother Angelica was so kind to take me in, and accepted my offering in the spirit of a gift, as the rule allows. I owe it to her memory not to renege on my part of the arrangement.'

His heart sank. 'But not if you're not certain a nun's life is for you.'

She gave a little shrug. 'It is true I am not certain. I came here to escape my husband's vile family. All the Sitwell men are beastly, John...' She blushed, then bit her lip. 'Taking the veil seemed an agreeable enough alternative, even if it was not exactly my vocation...'

He squeezed her hand. 'But if it's *not* your vocation, Anabella, surely you could − should! − give it up?'

She frowned, and he realised he was pressing her too hard. 'As I have already explained,' she went on, 'I made a promise to the priory. Surely it would be most dishonourable to default on that—?'

Rosa was suddenly at their side. 'I am so sorry, John, but you must leave.'

His heart wrenched painfully, and he clutched at Anabella's hand, unwilling to let it go. He looked up into her lovely face, and saw her eyes were moist.

'I can't bear...' he started, but she shook her head.

Anabella gently withdrew her hand from his. 'You had best go,' she said, then, spinning away, ran out of the frater.

John rode home from Northwick in a considerable despond. The journey home to Meonbridge usually took two hours or so. But the day was still fine, and he was in no hurry to return, to Ma's inevitable questions. Underfoot, the track was dry and reasonably even, so he reined his horse in from a brisk trot to a walk. He wanted to take some time to think about the implications of what Rosa had said.

He'd been so looking forward to his visit. Yet what Rosa told him had thrown him into turmoil.

He'd miss his conversations with Rosa, but he was *appalled* he might never again see Anabella. However unlikely it seemed that he and Anabella could have formed a bond on such short acquaintance, he knew it to be true, both from his own standpoint and from hers. Of course, he realised their path to happiness was already strewn with complications, with the sisters almost certainly reluctant to give up the fortune she'd brought them, and Anabella being pressed to make her final vows. At least if he could continue seeing her, she might be persuaded to delay, even to reconsider whether taking the veil *was* what she wanted. Yet, even though Rosa seemed prepared to help, if she wasn't elected prioress, she'd have no power to prevent Anabella committing herself to God, if others, such as Sister Evangelina, were determined that she should—

He pulled hard and sharply upon the reins, bringing the mare to a sudden halt. She whinnied and turned a circle in alarm. He patted her neck to soothe her, then slumped forward, sighing deeply, and, finding tears were trickling down his cheeks, he swiped them angrily against his sleeve. Was Anabella truly already lost to him?

He understood her sense of obligation to the priory, but it was clear too she *wasn't* certain the cloistered life was what she wanted. When the alternative was further misery with one of those "beastly" men, a life of seclusion in the priory might well have seemed like Paradise. But now, when she had another option—?

He would not – could not – simply let her go.

MEONBRIDGE

It was late afternoon by the time John arrived back in Meonbridge. A few hours of daylight remained and most of the tenants were still hard at work harvesting beans and peas, in their own fields and the manor's. The grain harvest had been finished last month, and all the sheaves brought indoors, to be threshed and winnowed, and a few men would have been assigned to that.

Tired and despondent as he was from his journey, but mostly from the news, John decided to make a tour of the manor fields and the threshing barns, to ensure everything was going smoothly.

He stayed out until supper time. He knew Ma would be fretting he'd not yet returned, but he was reluctant to face her questioning about his visit to the priory. Her questions were only curiosity on her part, but with the news about Northwick so worrying and his affection for Anabella – which Ma knew nothing of – so much at risk, he was concerned his misery would show through. Ma was more anxious than ever these days that he'd still not found a wife. So, he'd not told her about Anabella on the realistic grounds that nothing would likely come of their relationship, no matter how much he might want it to. He didn't want to raise Ma's hopes.

John walked home from the threshing barns. He'd left his mare earlier at the blacksmith's, having noticed a slight lameness in a hind leg. She'd stay overnight in Roger Stronge's stables, and he'd collect her tomorrow. As he approached the atte Wode croft, he groaned, as he often did. The house and outbuildings weren't exactly dilapidated, but they were certainly a little shabby. He kept meaning to ask his brother-in-law, Jack, the authority on all building matters, to come and make repairs, but it kept slipping his mind. He supposed he could do the repairs himself, but he never seemed to have the time.

In truth, too, he didn't *want* to repair this house. He was frustrated that, at his age, he was still living with his mother in his childhood home. Disappointed too, given his status in Meonbridge as the de Bohuns' bailiff, he didn't live in a much larger, grander house...

Like the one once occupied by the previous bailiff, Robert Tyler, and his family, just a short walk away from here. But that house had lain empty ever since Robert, accused of Philip de Bohun's murder, had died, falling from the tower of Saint Peter's. Until, earlier this year, Margery, his elder daughter – left without home, property or income because of her father's crimes, and forced to become a lowly servant – returned to Meonbridge, lived secretly in her old family home, and there plotted to kill Lady de Bohun. Now, the house was derelict. Grand as it once had been, the Tylers' house was one no one wished to live in.

John supposed other substantial properties were available, but Ma didn't want to leave the house she'd lived in all her married life. The house she'd shared with her beloved Stephen, until he lost his life to the pestilence all those years ago. And it wasn't only the *house* Ma loved but the garden too, and the little orchard at the bottom bordering the river that rushed past and on towards the mill.

So, even if *he* might have liked a better house, one more suited to his status, he'd never try to persuade his ma to move. It was always expected that, one day, he *would* leave the cottage and set up his own home with a wife. But it hadn't happened. It was annoying that Matthew – younger than him by ten years – had done it, just last year, finding himself a girl to wed and moving into a tiny cot only a few steps away from here, so he was still on hand to manage the atte Wode holding.

As John pushed open the gate to their extensive croft, it creaked and was heavy on its hinges. He tutted: he really should get someone to come and deal with all these things. If he *did* get a wife and move, he could scarcely leave Ma in a house that needed so much work...

He stopped in front of the cottage door, and braced himself. He'd not decided how much of what Rosa told him he was going to share with Ma. But it was too late now. He'd just have to improvise depending upon what she asked.

He pushed open the door and stepped inside. Ma was, as she always seemed to be, bent over the fire, stirring a pot of what he was certain was a pottage. It usually was. The smell of the simmering broth and vegetables drifted to his nostrils. And he realised at that moment he was hungry, and remembered he hadn't been offered dinner at the priory. Rosa had seemed distracted, and almost eager for him to leave. So, he'd collected his mare from the stable boy and begun his journey home before the bell for dinner had even been rung.

He flung off his cloak and hung it on one of the pegs just inside the door, then sat down on the bench beneath to remove his boots.

Ma looked up, put down her stirring spoon, and hobbled over. 'At last!' she cried. 'I thought you were never coming back. You've spent a good long while today with Sister Rosa...'

'Not really. In fact, a shorter time than usual. I'll tell you why later. But when I got back to Meonbridge, I decided to inspect what's being done in the fields and threshing barns. That's where I've been all afternoon...' Not strictly true, but it would do.

'And is everything proceeding as it should?'

'It is. The new reeve seems efficient...' He stood up. 'Anyway, Ma, I'm starving. Can we eat?'

'Soon. You've time to wash.' She shuffled back towards the fire.

He watched her go. It was clear her right leg – or was it her hip? – was paining her. It had been for months, but it seemed to be getting worse. Maybe he couldn't leave her alone here anyway? Even if he did find a wife, this might still have to be his home. Yet, if that wife was Anabella, how could he expect a woman like her to live in a humble villein's cot?

He went over to the water bucket standing near the fire and, scooping a small jugful into a basin, carried it to the table, together with a rag, a towel and a little tallow soap. Taking off his tunic and his shirt, he soaped his arms, neck and face, scrubbed at the accumulated dust and grime, then rinsed it off. As he did it, he imagined Anabella's reaction to him washing in the hall, at the table on which they were shortly to take their meal. She'd expect washing to be done in private. He dried himself on the towel, pulled his shirt back over his head and took the basin outside, to throw the dirty water into the trough.

He snorted to himself as he came back in and closed the door. Anabella wouldn't deign to live like this! Even if her husband and his family were cruel, she'd not have lived in such confinement as this? She'd have had servants to fetch and carry water, *and* to make her meals... What had he been thinking, that a woman such as Anabella might even *consider* marrying a man like him? No, she'd been humouring him, pretending to show an interest in his work, fluttering her eyelashes at him like a giddy girl...

Ma put the spoons and platter of bread upon the table. 'It's ready,' she said and, ladling the pottage into a bowl, she brought it to the table.

John sat on a stool and pulled the brimming bowl towards him. 'Thank you, Ma. I'm in sore need of this.' He took some bread and at once began to spoon the warming broth into his hungry mouth.

Ma sat down with her own, much less full, bowl of pottage. He'd noticed how much less she ate these days but maybe that was to be expected, as she worked much less vigorously in the garden than she used to, and scarcely ever helped out in their fields. Matthew did all that, with the help of the cottars whose labour he deemed worth hiring.

He finished his bowlful quickly, and Ma took the bowl and refilled it from the pot. She cleaned her own out with a small piece of bread, then rested her elbows upon the table, her chin atop her hands.

'Well,' she said, 'what news?'

Still chewing, John raised a finger and pointed to his mouth.

'I'll fetch you some ale.' She pottered about a while, clearing up her cooking utensils, until John had finished eating. Returning to the table with the ale, she resumed her position with her elbows and her chin.

'Well?'

Ma greeted the news of Mother Angelica's death with sadness, but her eyes lit up when he told her of the imminent election for a new prioress.

'Will it be Rosa?' she said. 'You've said she's been acting as subprioress for years.'

'Not necessarily, Ma. She mightn't win the election.'

'But, from what you've said, she's much loved at Northwick...'

'That might be true, Ma, but other factors have to be taken into account...'

She wrinkled her nose. 'What other factors?'

'Oh, I dunno. Other candidates might have a stronger claim.'

'What other candidates?'

He took up his cup of ale and drained it. 'Ma, do stop asking questions! I don't know the answers. All I can tell you is Sister Rosa said she mightn't be elected. Even if she'd like to be the prioress, it's not inevitable she'd be chosen.'

'Well, that does seem silly, when she *must* be the best candidate.'

John thumped his cup down onto the table. He was exasperated, largely because he was dissembling, which he always hated doing, especially with his ma. 'You don't know that, Ma, because you know nothing of the other candidates.'

'And do you?'

He shook his head. He wasn't going to tell her about Sister Evangelina, or Rosa's conviction that she would win. Yet he wondered about Rosa's resolution not to stand. He imagined she'd be *eager* to be prioress. He was certain Angelica had held her in high regard, and Rosa greatly admired Angelica in return. If Rosa became prioress, she'd run the priory just as Angelica had done, with her efficiency and compassion, as well as piety, wouldn't she? Surely Rosa would *want* that? So why might she be willing to stand aside, to allow the unpleasant, unloved Evangelina to take her place?

It was a mystery, but one whose explanation he presumed he'd never learn, if he was no longer permitted to visit Northwick.

5

NORTHWICK PRIORY
OCTOBER 1365

Last night, Rosa had alternated between lying open-eyed upon her bed, staring into the dark, and dropping to her knees beside it to offer up urgent, silent, prayers. She had not had a moment's sleep. She attended both Matins and Lauds, but could scarcely recite the words of the psalms and could not afterwards recall any of the readings. She was just as agitated *after* the offices as before.

Her thoughts had drifted constantly to her conversation with Evangelina in the chapter house. Her mind churned and churned again at both what Evangelina had said to her and what she should do about it. She said she had not yet decided whether to stand in the election, but only to show Evangelina she was not cowed by her threats. Yet, in truth, she *was* cowed, and she could not imagine now how she could risk the dreadful reason for her coming here to Northwick being exposed.

Yet she was also baffled about where Evangelina might have heard of it. She did not believe Angelica would have told her. But what of the priests? The old priest, Father Anselm, would never have betrayed the trust placed in him, to anyone, let alone Evangelina. But, of Father Edgar, Rosa was not so confident. He was rather charming for a priest but, for some reason she could not identify, she did not like him. Did not quite *trust* him. Even so, why should *he* divulge her secret to Evangelina?

Rosa wracked her brains to recall exactly what she might have confessed to him, for it could scarcely have been much. Her fuller confessions had been made years before to Father Anselm, when she first came here. Edgar had been here ten years and, as far as she could recall, in all that time her confessions had contained little if anything to do with her past.

She could never resolve the "how": she would never know. But she could at least determine the "what". What *was* she going to do in response to Evangelina's threats?

In all honesty, she wanted to be prioress. Not for her own advancement, but to carry on the legacy of piety, industry and love that Angelica had left to Northwick. Whereas she feared Evangelina might somehow overturn all the good her aunt had done. Yet why did she think that? Perhaps Evangelina might want life in Northwick to continue just as Angelica had left it?

But, no, she was as certain as she could be that Evangelina would *not* want that. For, in the fifteen years she had known her, Evangelina had always displayed a marked lack of piety – absenting herself from many of the offices, even when she had no excuse to do so. It was true she was a competent sacrist but, as far as Rosa could recall, Evangelina never offered to help her sisters when extra hands were needed, in the infirmary, for example, or in the garden. Moreover, she seemed to have almost no affection for her sisters, nor even any concern for their welfare and, sadly but not surprisingly, she received little of either in return.

Indeed, Evangelina could not be more *unlike* her aunt, in both character and attitude, and Rosa was very troubled that the Northwick she had come so much to love might, under Evangelina's rule, change into a place in which she no longer felt at peace.

The bell for Prime was ringing. Rosa pulled her habit over her head and smoothed it down. Then, putting on her wimple and veil, she prepared to leave her cell. She still did not know the answer to her dilemma, but she must soon decide. She took a few deep breaths. What she must do shortly was concentrate on the office, and let it infuse her with the serenity she sorely needed.

After she had eaten her breakfast of dry bread and small ale, Rosa left her place at the table and hurried over to where Sister Beatrice was already discussing the rest of the day's meals with the cook. Earlier she had asked Rosa to meet her. Rosa touched Beatrice lightly on the shoulder then stepped back. Beatrice smiled when she saw her.

'I'll be with you shortly, Sister Rosa,' she said. 'In my office?'

Rosa walked to the tiny room off the frater that Beatrice called her "office". With a desk and stool, and a small chest to store her records, it was adequate but scarcely generous. Rosa brought a stool from the frater and, placing it next to Beatrice's, sat on it to wait.

At length, Beatrice appeared, bustling as she always did, her cheeks florid as they invariably were. She plumped herself down upon her stool and grinned. 'How glad I am, dear Rosa, to see you have returned this morning. I was concerned about you yesterday. You seemed so upset...'

'I was. Yet I am sorry, Beatrice, but I cannot tell you why. Or not yet...' In truth, she had not thought when, or even whether, she might share the reason for her distress with either Beatrice or Amata. Certainly, she could not tell them the whole story, much as she might like to unburden herself. Both sisters were kindly and forgiving souls, yet she feared they would be profoundly shocked if they knew what had driven her here to Northwick when she was still a girl, still "Johanna"...

It had been her grief – Johanna's grief – at Philip's murder that stopped her agreeing to marry Sir Giles, the man her father had chosen for her. But it was much more that made her renounce her family and come to Northwick.

For Philip's death did not only mean she had lost a brother, but that she had lost the man she *loved*. Her distress was almost insupportable. Yet loving Philip the way she had was sinful. It was not the familial affection of a younger sister but the deep-felt, burning passion of a woman. She had felt so tainted by her sinful feelings towards her brother, she convinced herself that she could never marry. Instead, she would spend the rest of her life praying for forgiveness for her sins, and hoping that, at length, God would absolve her.

But she could not say any of that to Beatrice. 'You wished to speak to me?' she said to her instead.

'Shall we go out into the garden?' said Beatrice. 'I want to show you something.'

They spent the next half hour or so discussing an idea Beatrice had for reorganising the layout of the potagers. Rosa listened, interested, but at length reminded her she was no longer "subprioress".

'I would not be in a position to agree or otherwise to your plan,' she said.

Beatrice frowned. 'But surely you'll be the next prioress?'

'I do not think so. It is much more likely Evangelina will be elected. Anyway, I have not yet made up my mind whether I shall even stand.'

Beatrice tried to protest but Rosa shook her head. 'I am sorry,' she said simply, and Beatrice pursed her lips.

As they strolled back towards the chapel, as it was time for the office of Terce, a man hailed them from the gate that led out from the gardens to the orchard. Rosa turned, to see Rafe Byllynges hurrying towards them.

'A word, Sister Rosa, if ye please,' he called out, as he came closer.

She remembered then she had intended to talk to John about Master Byllynges, but it had completely slipped her mind when he was here the other day. John had been almost as upset as she was with the news. Anyway, perhaps discussing Byllynges and his possible shortcomings was also no longer her concern. If Evangelina was elected prioress, she would almost certainly appoint someone else to the task of managing the estate, or even choose to manage it herself.

Nonetheless, Evangelina was not yet prioress, so Rosa nodded at the bailiff. 'What can I do for you, Master Byllynges?'

. . .

During dinner, Rosa chanced to glance across at Anabella. She was picking at her food, and not engaging at all with either of the sisters sitting with her. Her gaze seemed unfocused, either staring across the frater or down into her bowl. Perhaps she was listening intently to the reading, but Rosa doubted it. She just looked despondent.

Alongside her other worries about the present situation, Rosa was sad that she would likely no longer be able to talk to John. For she *was* certain Evangelina would dispense entirely with his services.

She was sorry too that his budding relationship with Anabella was now at risk. Perhaps she should have censured John's attempt to steal Anabella from Northwick, but she could not bring herself to do so, because she so much wanted to see her "cousin" settled and happy. She could see Anabella was much taken with him, despite the difference in their stations, and did she not also deserve contentment, after suffering so cruelly at the hands of her husband and his family? It was already clear she did not have a vocation for the religious life: she had come to Northwick to escape, not because she wished to become a nun.

After dinner, Rosa hurried over to Anabella and bid her join her in the garden. Anabella looked surprised but Rosa smiled. 'Just for a little chat. We can speak more privately amongst the cabbages and kale.'

They wound their way in silence through the priory's maze of passages towards the door that led outside to the gardens. Rosa waited until they reached the gate into the potagers before she spoke.

'Dear Anabella, I am so sorry that everything at Northwick is about to change, for I am certain it will not change for the better.'

Anabella's eyes widened. 'Whyever not? Mother Angelica's death is a dreadful loss, but I had presumed that you, Sister Rosa, would take her place?'

'Sadly, that is most unlikely. Evangelina is determined to become prioress. She believes it is her birth right, being Angelica's niece.'

'Yes, I understand that Northwick prioresses have been chosen from the patron family for years,' said Anabella. 'But I don't want Evangelina to be prioress. I can't imagine she will be a satisfactory replacement for dear Angelica.' The corners of her mouth turned down.

'I suspect many of the sisters might agree with you. But I am certain it will happen, one way or another.'

'But you would make such a perfect prioress!' Anabella's eyes lit up again.

Rosa acknowledged the compliment but shook her head. 'I am afraid I cannot stand against her.'

'But what of me and John?' Anabella wrung her hands together. 'He did explain to me that Sister Evangelina might become prioress – though he said too he hoped it wouldn't happen. But then he said that, if she did, it was likely he'd no longer come to Northwick.' She looked up, her eyes wide, and filling with tears. 'So, now I have the prospect of never seeing him again. I know it's silly, Sister Rosa, but something wonderful has grown between us in these past few months. I know John feels it, for he has said so, and I do too.'

'I know it also,' said Rosa. 'I could see it in both your eyes. Yet I do not know how to help you.'

'By becoming prioress!' Anabella said decisively, but her cheeks flushed pink. 'I apologise, Sister, for you clearly have your reasons for not standing.'

'I do, but I will promise to *try* to help you, even if I do have no idea quite *how*.'

Days later, Amata and Beatrice came to see Rosa in the small chamber in the prioress's quarters she was still using for her office. Amata waved a letter in her hand.

'It has come,' she said. 'The reply from Bishop Edyngton. So now we can make plans for the election.' She was smiling.

'What has to be done?' said Rosa.

'The bishop's man will come to see us, to instruct us in our duties.'

'Is that Nicholas Foxe? He organised the bishop's visitation three years ago?'

'Indeed. It was his first. The man he succeeded was a wily, disagreeable fellow, but Master Foxe seems pleasant enough, though I know nothing of his character.'

'Mother Angelica never spoke much about him,' said Rosa. 'Indeed, now I think of it, she was always unforthcoming when she referred to him and was even quite offhand when talking *to* him.' She wrinkled her brow as she recalled the Reverend Mother's rather odd behaviour towards Master Foxe.

'I agree,' said Beatrice. 'It was almost as if she wanted nothing to do with him...'

'Anyway,' continued Amata, 'Nicholas will help us set up the election. It will be his first election too, but I presume he knows what is required. But he will take no part in it. The bishop will appoint others to manage matters on the day.'

Rosa stood up and took a turn about the chamber. She was nervous, knowing that, any moment, Beatrice or Amata would be enquiring if she was going to stand in the election. Part of her had thought she should stand anyway, simply to challenge Evangelina's threat. But she could not face the possibility of Evangelina accepting her challenge and then spreading information about her that might turn all the sisters against her.

She was not surprised when Beatrice and Amata were both baffled and distraught when she told them of her decision.

'But why?' cried Amata.

'Is it related to that news you received the other day?' asked Beatrice.

'What news?' said Amata, but Rosa held up a hand and sat down again.

'Yes, Beatrice, you are right, but I apologise to both of you that I cannot tell you the nature of the news, nor give you any further explanation. Just suffice to say I *cannot* pit myself against Sister Evangelina.' Rosa hesitated, rubbing her thumbs together in her lap, then looked up. 'Anyway, is it not true that a Godeffroy always wins, so Evangelina will be elected anyway?'

'That's always been the way of it.'

'But why and how?' Rosa still had to ask, even though she was sure she already knew the answer.

'I came to Northwick when I was nineteen,' said Beatrice, 'but the only election I've known here was the last one, when Angelica was chosen. There was a good contest between Angelica and her rival, because both of them were liked and respected. But Angelica was always going to win, because she was so much *loved*.'

'The previous election wasn't at all like that,' said Amata. 'I don't know how it happened, because the Godeffroy candidate was neither suitable nor liked, and proved a hopeless prioress.'

Rosa nodded. Amata had told her about this before.

'But *why* don't you know what happened?' said Beatrice. 'Something must have been amiss for her to be elected if she was unfitting for the job.' She tutted. 'Why didn't you question it?'

Amata looked downcast. 'Because everyone knew the prioress was always a Godeffroy—'

'But not *regardless* of their suitability?' cried Beatrice. 'Some sort of corruption must have been involved, Amata. Bribery! To persuade the weakest of the sisters to elect the Godeffroy against their better judgement...'

'I suppose you must be right, Bea, but there was never any *discussion* of the election amongst the sisters – it wasn't done – so, if any were bribed, I knew nothing of it...' Her face crumpled.

Rosa stood up again and paced. She knew she looked just as she felt – agitated. 'So, it *would* make no difference whether I stood or not? Evangelina *will* win regardless?'

Amata's forehead wrinkled. 'Oh, but, surely, Rosa, you are the Reverend Mother's choice...'

'But that is immaterial, Amata dear. Beatrice must be right that bribery was used in the past to ensure the Godeffroy won, and perhaps Evangelina will use it too.' She would not tell them Evangelina had in fact *already* "bribed" her, if not with money but with threats. And she had succumbed, leaving Evangelina's path open to victory...

'Yet, there's always been a contest,' Beatrice said, 'even if only in name. I believe the Rule requires it... Should I encourage one of the younger nuns to stand?'

Rosa took a deep breath, then let it out. 'It seems pointless, even dishonest. But, yes, you should. Also, warn them Evangelina is likely to make certain that *she* wins, one way or another...'

6

NORTHWICK PRIORY
OCTOBER 1365

The mood was mixed as the sisters filed into the chapter house and took their places. Beatrice herself felt glum, and it was evident that Amata and Rosa did too. A few of the sisters looked anxious, even scared, but others – two of the youngest, Maria and Felicia – were full of excitement, as if they were attending some sort of celebration, rather than the solemn election of their prioress. But Sister Dulcia's face was tense and drawn, and Beatrice thought now it had perhaps been unkind of her to persuade the treasuress to stand against Evangelina.

'Oh, no, Beatrice!' Dulcia had said, shaking her head vigorously and wringing her hands. 'I could never take dear Angelica's place. I am not capable—'

Beatrice had grasped her hands to still them. 'You *are* capable, Dulcia, more than capable. As well as being much liked and respected.'

Yet Dulcia's eyes were wide with panic. 'But I don't *want* to oppose

Evangelina! She will find some way to vilify me and turn our sisters against me…'

Beatrice thought that possible but didn't say so. In truth, she felt rather guilty to be so set upon urging Dulcia to stand, when she clearly didn't want to.

'And if Evangelina wins,' continued Dulcia, 'as she surely will, she'll likely punish me by stripping me of my role as treasuress.' Her panic changed to misery.

Beatrice frowned. If Dulcia was right, it would be both unjust and a great misfortune. She was a gentle soul but an excellent treasuress. She possessed a sharp mind and a good head for figures, and had held the role under Angelica for many years. Northwick would be much the poorer if Sister Dulcia was no longer in charge of managing its finances.

So, should she, after all, have chosen someone else to stand against Evangelina? But there *wasn't* anyone else − except for Rosa − with sufficient gravitas and popularity to make a credible opponent. Though *anyone* would probably make a better prioress than Evangelina.

Beatrice had continued to cajole and coax, and at length Dulcia agreed. 'It's by no means inevitable that Evangelina will win,' Beatrice had said, vowing to atone for her duplicity as soon as possible, 'but, if she does, hopefully she'll realise that keeping you on as treasuress will be in her own interests as well as Northwick's.'

Now, when Dulcia looked so strained, Beatrice wondered whether it was the prospect of winning, or *not* winning, that was worrying her most. Evangelina had in fact said nothing during the past two weeks or so to disparage her opponent. Dulcia's fears that the sacrist might try to turn the sisters against her had proved unfounded. That being so, Beatrice speculated exactly what tactics Evangelina had been employing, to ensure − or try to ensure − the majority voted in her favour. Some sort of bribe, she supposed, yet what might Evangelina have to offer? As far as Beatrice knew, she had no personal funds or treasures to distribute.

She'd also speculated on who might vote for whom. Only fourteen votes were available: Anabella was a novice and not permitted to take part, and the candidates themselves wouldn't cast a vote. She was certain Amata, Rosa and Juliana would put their hands up for Dulcia, as she would herself. And she was fairly sure that timid little Sister Helen, the fratress, would do the same.

But what of the others?

It was more than likely that Evangelina would be able to convince those three silly girls, *and* Sister Gracia, the mistress of the novices. Felicia, Maria, and Letitia had taken their vows only quite recently, but all *four* young women had become as thick as thieves, with Gracia acting more like a big sister than a tutor to the girls. If any one of the four was persuaded by Evangelina, the others were sure to follow, like so many sheep.

Yet who might *resist* Evangelina's cajoleries?

Five nuns remained to be accounted for. The chambress, Sister Clarice, might go either way. Similarly, Sisters Anne and Mariota. The real worry lay with Sisters Katerina and Mildryth, both aged and deaf, Mildryth beginning to lose her wits. Beatrice had spoken to them all herself, asking them as warmly and encouragingly as she could if they would vote for Dulcia. The younger nuns had proved largely non-committal, and she had got little sense out of either of the ancients.

Briefly, she had pondered the idea of copying what she supposed might be Evangelina's tactics, of offering them all some sort of inducement. But the thought of it made her run hot and cold. She knew there were some words – in Deuteronomy, perhaps? – about the taking of bribes. What did they say? Something about perverting justice and blinding the wise? Beatrice crossed herself and vowed to pray for guidance later, appalled she'd even contemplated committing such a sin.

The result, then, was likely very close. Four definite and five maybes for Dulcia. Four almost certain and the same five maybes for Evangelina. With the two ancients who could swing it either way, depending on whether they had any understanding of what exactly they were doing.

As the sisters settled down in their allotted places in the chapter house, four men entered the chamber: a lawyer, Master Henry Brougham, and his clerk, a cathedral canon, and a representative of the archdeacon, all come from Winchester at the bishop's behest to conduct and witness this election.

Master Brougham took the prioress's chair, signalling that he was in charge of the proceedings. He held up his hand and the low murmurings that had accompanied the sisters' arrival in the chamber promptly ceased. He inclined his head.

'Ladies,' he muttered, then explained the procedure shortly to be followed. Beatrice couldn't help but mark his delivery, for he spoke slowly and carefully, as if he considered the "ladies" simple. Yet, she supposed, this *was* the first election for nearly everyone here. Only she, Amata and the two ancients had experienced an election before, so perhaps it was wise for him to spell it out.

'Please confirm,' he said as he concluded, 'that each one of you is clear about what is about to happen?' All seemed to murmur 'Aye!'.

'Very well,' the lawyer said. 'Let the names of the candidates be formally declared.' He looked up, an eyebrow raised in enquiry.

Beatrice had been expecting this. It had been agreed that she would nominate Sister Dulcia, so she stood up and announced her name. Master Brougham bowed his head. 'Another candidate?' he asked.

Not knowing who would be declaring for Sister Evangelina, Beatrice was disappointed when Clarice, the chambress, stood and gave her nomination. So, Clarice was not a "maybe" for Dulcia after all. Beatrice's heart squeezed a little. That meant Evangelina was closer than she'd hoped to winning the day.

The lawyer nodded, then looked about the chamber. 'Any more?' When no one else stood up, he nodded again. 'Very well. Sister Rosa, the voting pot, if you please?' Rosa came forward with a large wide-necked urn and placed it on a small table to one side of the chamber. 'Please come forward, ladies, in orderly fashion, and place your chosen ball into the pot. Remember it is black for Sister Dulcia, and white for Sister Evangelina.'

The sisters rose, maintaining silence for once, and shuffled forward, clutching their chosen ball tightly in their fist, so no one else could see it.

It wasn't always done this way, so Beatrice understood. In some priories, voting was done by a show of hands, a public display of allegiance, which might or might not, she thought, make for post-election harmony. But in Northwick the vote had always been taken in secret – or, perhaps, ever since the Godeffroy family became the priory's patron?

Rosa had had to search Mother Angelica's chamber to find the small wooden balls that were used to vote. When she found them, stored in a bag, hidden at the bottom of a chest, she brought them to Beatrice, her face a blend of amusement and dismay. 'Just look at them,' she said, 'how old and battered they are.'

Beatrice had picked one out of the bag – ostensibly a black one – and turned it over in her hand. The paint had mostly flaked away, and it scarcely looked black at all. 'Goodness,' she said. 'Well, it *is* forty years ago they were last used.'

'Should we have them refurbished?' said Rosa. 'I could ask the carpenter to give them a new coat of paint. What do you think?'

Beatrice had agreed, and the voting balls handed out today were crisply black or white.

Each sister filed past the pot, and covertly dropped her ball inside, careful not to let her neighbour see which ball she had chosen. Beatrice was awaiting her turn, when she noticed the bobbing heads of Sisters Katerina and Mildryth, both of whom seemed uncertain what to do. Mildryth touched Katerina on the arm and whispered something, then Katerina looked up, apparently seeking guidance.

Master Brougham sprang to his feet and, coming over to them, explained patiently that it was the black ball for Sister Dulcia – he showed them a black ball – and the white ball for Sister Evangelina – he held out a white one. He gestured to Beatrice and Clarice to cast their votes, then hefted the pot himself and, taking it over to the two aged nuns, held it out before them. He repeated his explanation yet again, and Katerina nodded. Under cover of the folds of her skirts, she grasped one of the balls and, raising her fist, held it inside the wide mouth of the pot. She let go and the ball dropped with a dull thud. Then she gestured to Mildryth to do the same.

Poor Mildryth! Did she know what she was supposed to do? She stared with rheumy eyes at the two balls in her lap. Grappling with them for a while, she leaned in to Katerina and whispered, 'Which one?'

The lawyer coughed and shook his head as Katerina opened her mouth to reply. 'Sister Mildryth,' he said firmly, 'it is black for Sister Dulcia and *white* for Sister Evangelina.'

The old woman clutched at a ball. Her wizened, shaking hand folded claw-like around it, as Master Brougham held the pot a little closer so she could let it drop more easily. Beatrice – and maybe everyone else – could see that Mildryth's chosen ball was white.

Beatrice's heart was in her mouth as Clarice tipped the balls onto a cloth. And it sank to her stomach as she could see the result immediately: there were two more white balls than black. Evangelina had won.

A cry of 'Hurrah!' went up, coming from the mouth of Sister Maria. Beatrice glared at her, and the girl flushed a moment but then tossed her head. The little strumpet!

Beatrice looked about the chamber. Evangelina, of course, was beaming. It definitely *was* a beam, but how extraordinary to see such an expression on that woman's face! Beatrice didn't think she'd ever before seen Evangelina look quite so *joyful*. A small group of nuns quickly gathered about her – Maria, Felicia, Letitia and Sister Gracia. Clarice sidled over and took Evangelina's hands in hers. How disappointing of Clarice. What had Evangelina offered her to take her side? And how had she persuaded the two ancients? Would they be influenced by the promise of money or trinkets? But *something* had swayed them.

It occurred to her that, despite the voting being secret, Evangelina's supporters were revealing themselves now in their behaviour. Or some were. Beatrice realised neither Anne nor Mariota was fawning on Evangelina. Each was keeping herself distanced from the clamour. She tried to detect if either of their faces betrayed their choice, but both looked simply melancholy. She'd never know which of them had cast their vote for Evangelina.

Suddenly Dulcia was at her elbow. 'Sister Beatrice,' she murmured.

'Ah, Dulcia, I'm so sorry the vote didn't go your way.'

'*I'm* not,' said Dulcia, grimacing. 'Well,' – raising a hand to shield her mouth, she whispered behind it – 'I *am* rather sorry Evangelina is to be our prioress, for I don't think she will make a good one. But I'm glad on my own account that I shan't have to grapple with the myriad tasks ahead of her.' She grimaced again, and Beatrice touched her arm.

'I understand. But I'm most anxious about how very different a prioress she's going to make from our beloved Mother Angelica.'

Dulcia frowned. 'But *why* wouldn't Sister Rosa stand? She's the one amongst us who'd make the best prioress.'

'I agree, but she had her reasons, to which I'm not privy.' She looked across the room to where Rosa was talking with Amata. Both their faces were long. She let out a deep sigh. 'A dreadful shame, Dulcia, for I fear we may be in for tough times under Evangelina's rule.'

The official proclamation of Evangelina's ascension, in the chapel, could have been made at once, as she was clearly more than satisfied with her victory. Yet, it was convention that the newly elected prioress *resisted* the appointment a little, to affect reluctance, even *if* she had connived at her success, as Beatrice was certain was the case with Evangelina.

She remembered Angelica going through this pretence of coyness, even though she, and everyone else, was highly delighted by her election. Angelica had rolled her eyes at Beatrice when she mentioned it to her a while later.

'Oh, yes, how silly it all was. But it has been the way of things, I gather, for many years. I suppose it is meant to reflect the modesty a nun should feel at the approbation of her peers.'

'I'm sure you are right, Reverend Mother,' Beatrice had said, 'but it does seem something of a fraud.' Prioress Angelica had smiled wryly.

So, would Evangelina too adopt this air of coy resistance for an hour or two before being "dragged" to the chapel to be proclaimed? It would be so out of character...

Yet it seemed Evangelina *had* decided to act the part expected of her.

The chapter house was cleared and all the sisters returned to their various labours, except for Evangelina, who retired to her cell in the dorter, ostensibly to pray. An hour later, Beatrice and Clarice went to ask her for her formal consent to her appointment. Clarice knocked upon the flimsy partition and, after a moment or two, when shuffling could be heard behind it, Evangelina bid them enter.

'Do you consent?' asked Beatrice, hoping against hope God might have revealed to her that she shouldn't.

Evangelina tilted her head. 'I'm still seeking guidance.' She smirked a little.

'How much longer?' Beatrice said, keeping her tone even.

'Oh, not too long,' she said and, standing by her bed, began to bend her knees. 'Three turns around the cloister, perhaps?'

When they returned, Evangelina declared she had now been vouchsafed God's will and was ready to be taken to the chapel. Clarice took her arm, a broad smile on her face. Beatrice should have taken Evangelina's other arm but held back, contenting herself with walking by her side, as they descended the stairs from the dorter to the entrance to the transept.

The chapel's little nave was full, not only with the sisters but the priory's servants too had come, as well as the four men who'd overseen the election. Amidst cries of joy from some of the assembly, Clarice and Beatrice led Evangelina forward towards the altar, where she knelt and the canon from Winchester proclaimed her the appointed prioress of Northwick.

Edgar hurried along two sides of the cloister, heading for the sacristy. Evangelina had sent him a message, asking him to meet her there. Why could he not have had an audience with her in her chamber, now she was in charge? But perhaps such an audience would not be sufficiently private, and she wished to have another of their clandestine brother-sister talks? He had imagined their secret meetings might now come to an end, but maybe he was wrong.

Eva was in the sacristy as usual, sitting in his chair, and toying with some quills he had accidently left behind on the little writing table. He slipped into the tight space and took the stool.

'Sister,' he said, 'congratulations. I imagine you are very pleased.'

She smiled and it struck him she actually did look *happy*, something he had scarcely seen before.

'Couldn't be more so,' she said.

'Why did you ask me to meet you here?' he said. 'To tell me we can no longer do so?'

'Not at all. Indeed, I rather think I might like to meet you *more* often. You can be my eyes and ears to what's going on here amongst the sisters, especially those who *aren't* pleased with my election.' She tilted her head. 'You're my ally, brother, aren't you?'

He tugged on his ear. 'Indeed, I am, but I'm not sure my ears and eyes will be all that useful. I have little personal contact with the sisters...'

'But I'm sure you can glean much from what they tell you *in private*...'

His neck warmed a little. "In private" meant the confession. Despite being less than devoted to his vocation, he had already regretted giving Eva any insight into Sister Rosa's testimonies. It had not been much, yet Eva had pounced upon it as evidence, enough for her to bully Rosa into not standing against her. He pulled at the collar of his cassock, feeling the dampness against his fingers. God surely knew of his earlier perfidy, and he was not keen to risk his wrath again.

'No, Eva. I'm not going to disclose any more such secrets to you.' Her mouth fell open, but he continued. 'I'm sorry, but I'm not willing to betray the sisters' confidences.'

'I scarcely thought you cared,' she said.

'I might not be the most dutiful of priests but...' But what? He thought a moment. 'But there are limits to my indiscretion...' He smirked. 'I'm sure you will gain information from your young disciples...'

'Disciples?' huffed Evangelina.

'That was *your* word for them, sister. Anyway, isn't that what they are, your followers?'

'They're my *assistants*. And, as they're all recently professed, with much to learn, I shall take them under my wing.'

Edgar nodded, though the idea of Evangelina, of all people, wishing to guide and counsel young and giddy girls was almost absurd.

Eva had been sent here to Northwick when he was two. Despite the disparity in their ages, the two children had already formed some sort of bond, and their separation greatly grieved them both. For there were no other brothers or sisters in the house: all had left, either to placements in other households or to marry. For the next three years, whilst Eva was still a novice, she came home every few months or so, and they always spent a little time together. Clinging together as the siblings left behind... It was only later Edgar came to realise he was an unwanted baby. And that Eva was an unloved daughter, who had failed to attract a suitor, dispatched at length to Northwick, regardless of her wishes. Just as he, many years later, begrudged being offered no alternative but the religious life, so Eva deeply resented being forced into a life she would most certainly not have chosen.

But Northwick was, in effect, the Godeffroys' own priory, the one the family had been beneficing for eighty years, so Eva did, at least, have the expectation that, one day, she would be Northwick's prioress. Some small compensation for being shut away for life with a crowd of women, none of whom she warmed to and none of whom liked her.

Quite why she was so estranged from her religious sisters, Edgar had never fathomed. When he thought back on her, at home, as his big sister, the memory was warm and happy. Their mother spent no time at all with them. So Eva was the mother he did not know, and he the child she would never bear.

But, once Eva had made her avowal, she came home rarely, and when he was seven, he too was sent away. They scarcely saw each other again until, at twenty-five, he came himself to Northwick, appointed priest-in-charge. And he found Eva had changed. She no longer seemed to laugh, nor even smile. Her face was forever dour, her tongue sharp, her mood perpetually melancholy, and she seemed to care nothing for anyone but herself.

Yet she *had* seemed pleased to see him.

Unlike Aunt Angelica, who was clearly most displeased that he had been given the post after the old priest, Father Anselm, died. Their aunt, it seemed, did not approve of patronage. She knew well enough that his appointment had been pushed through by the bishop's man, the predecessor to Cousin Nicholas, a man who ruthlessly promoted the Godeffroy advantage at every opportunity.

Angelica had summoned Edgar to her chamber, and he was surprised to find she was alone.

She glared at him, her expression belying her usual warmth and gentleness. 'I refuse, Edgar,' she said, her voice stern yet shaky, 'to let it be known here that you are my nephew, or that you are Evangelina's brother. I insist that both of you accept that, and make no attempt to thwart my wishes.'

He had acquiesced, with some sadness, for he had been hoping to renew his relationship with his sister. But maybe that would not be possible after all.

Yet, despite their aunt's command, and Eva's continuing melancholy, his sister had *wanted* them to meet, even if they had to meet in secret.

Now, he gazed at her for a few moments, seeing she had changed once again. The dourness and melancholy had gone, replaced by – what exactly? Her eyes were alight. He sensed excitement. Eager anticipation of what was ahead of her? The chance to run the priory as she wished. Yet her need for "eyes and ears" suggested she was also nervous about her new position. And the presence of her disciples, or even "assistants", implied she needed to surround herself with those who would willingly do her bidding.

'I'm sure you have much wise counsel to impart to them.'

She clicked her tongue. 'I hear mockery in your voice, brother.'

He held up his hands. 'Not at all. You've been at Northwick a long time, and have held many of the most important posts. You know a great deal about life here...' He drifted off, wanting to change the subject. 'But, tell me, how did you manage to persuade sufficient sisters to vote for you? Did you get help from Cousin Nicholas, as we discussed?'

She shook her head. 'I was perfectly capable of doing it myself.' She picked up one of the quills and twirled it in her fingers. 'In truth, it was easy. I approached each sister, catching her in private, and offered preferment of one sort or another if she supported me. I thought I might have to resort to bribery – a little money, or some trinket – but it proved unnecessary. All those who agreed, either emphatically or tentatively, did so because they believed it would benefit them to do so.'

'I assume you did not approach Rosa?' said Edgar.

'Ha! No. Nor Beatrice or Amata. Nor Dulcia, when I learned that Beatrice had convinced her to stand against me.' She puckered her lips. 'I'd hoped to be able to sway Juliana, but I might have known she'd refuse, fawning as she does on Rosa. And the fratress, Helen, said she couldn't go against Beatrice's wishes, even though young Maria, the kitcheness, who also reports to Beatrice, didn't object.'

'And the other two young nuns were happy to be chosen?'

'Very happy. They'll all undoubtedly be useful to me...'

'But what of the others?' He tried to recall all the names. 'Clarice... Gracia... Who else? And of course, the two aged ladies...?'

'Gracia came over readily enough, but Clarice took a little more persuading. I was never sure of Anne and Mariota, and in the event, one of them voted against me, but I don't know which. As for the ancients, well, I made them an offer.'

'What sort of offer?'

'They're both pretty feeble – Mildryth more so than Katerina – and make no contribution to the life of Northwick. All they want to do these days is sleep and eat the occasional small morsel. So, I offered them a life of privacy, the opportunity to live apart from the other sisters, in one of those cottages in the courtyard set aside for corrodians, to have their meals brought to them, and to forget about struggling to attend the daily offices.'

'And they accepted eagerly?'

'Well, Mildryth scarcely understood what I had said, but Katerina accepted on her behalf as well as her own. I'm certain they'll be much happier.'

Edgar rubbed at his chin. He was not at all sure that was true. Aunt Angelica would certainly not have thought so. She believed it benefitted ageing nuns to continue to live their lives *amongst* their sisters, even if they did not much engage with them. He suspected that Mildryth in particular would wither soon enough, and Katerina would quickly follow. Was that the new prioress's intention? He would not say so.

7

Meonbridge
November 1365

John had spent this morning, as he had other mornings recently, riding round the manor, checking what was being done. It was the middle of November, and it had been cold but dry for the past few days, so Meonbridge folk were out in numbers gathering in what they could for their winter stores.

Lord Dickon had followed his grandmother's example by being more generous than many lords in the matter of what of the manor's assets and supplies he would, and wouldn't, allow his tenants to share. The relationship between the Lord of Meonbridge and his tenants was no longer feudal – there was more give and take. Nonetheless, John was obliged to check no *undue* advantage was being taken. He wasn't always comfortable with this aspect of his job, knowing well enough that, even these days, most tenants, and especially those who had the least, could struggle to survive a cold, harsh winter, and needed all the fuel and food they could get.

Many families – men, women and children – had been in the woods for days collecting whatever dead wood and fallen branches they could find to swell their stores for burning in their hearths at home. As always, John had licensed a few tenants, under the supervision of the woodman, to prune some trees and fell others, to provide firewood for the manor house, and also timber for mending barns and byres. Other men were down by the river, cutting reeds and grasses, mostly for their own use, to repair the thinning thatches on their cots.

But the working year was winding down. All the animals that were going to be slaughtered had been, their meat smoked or salted, their hides tanned into leather. Over the coming weeks, men would still go out in teams to dig ditches and mend fences, but today, as the afternoon grew gloomy, everyone was ready to pick up their tools and go home to their wives and children.

John might have no wife or little ones, but at least he had a fire and the promise of a satisfying supper to look forward to.

It was still the middle of the afternoon when John arrived back at the cottage. Agnes was still there with Ma. She came most afternoons, to sit with her a while. John agreed with his sister that Ma seemed to be winding down too. She wasn't *ill*, though her hip did clearly give her pain. But, more seriously, she was much more melancholy than she ever used to be.

And the reason for *that* was, of course, the death of Lady Margaret.

Ma had been friends with her ladyship since before Agnes was born. At first, Ma had gone up to the manor house to make clothes and furnishings for Lady Margaret. She was Meonbridge's best seamstress. But it wasn't long before she visited her ladyship more often, to talk. John remembered how his pa had worried about their relationship, thinking it might not be seemly for a villein woman – one of the de Bohuns' tenants – to develop such a close friendship with her lord's wife. But, if Pa thought that, her ladyship evidently didn't, and the friendship blossomed, especially after the births of Agnes and Johanna, within days of each other. As they grew, the girls too became close friends, a bond that only faltered when they were sixteen, and Philip de Bohun's roving eye fell upon Agnes. It drove the two girls apart. Exactly what had happened, John didn't know at the time, and still didn't for the most part. But he did know his sister ran away from Meonbridge, wanting, she said later, to keep the child but not shame her family by having it born here. Ma and Pa were devastated, and the pestilence stopped anyone going to look for her, much as Pa had wanted to.

Agnes's disappearance, and the reason for it, had driven Ma and Lady Margaret apart as well. John knew he was at least partly to blame for the rift between them, for it rankled with him that Agnes had run away *because of* Philip, and maybe also because of Johanna. But Johanna refused to talk about it and, although John tried to encourage Philip to tell him what had happened, he'd prevaricated. Yet, shortly before he was killed, Philip seemed to be on the point of talking. John had been both furious and frustrated that he'd never learn the truth.

John had encouraged Ma to keep her distance from the de Bohuns, but it wasn't all that long before she'd mended the rift between herself and her ladyship, for neither of them could bear to be estranged.

Six months later, Agnes returned to Meonbridge, with her child – Dickon, Sir Philip's bastard son – and a husband, Jack. They stayed. Jack became Meonbridge's carpenter, Agnes bore more children, and her firstborn was embraced by the de Bohuns as their grandchild, and by Sir Richard as his heir. Philip was long dead by then, murdered in a vile vengeful plot. And Johanna had already decided she'd not marry but enter the priory at Northwick.

The two families were united by their shared grandson, and the grandmothers' friendship grew all the stronger for it.

So, when Margaret was killed last April, Ma felt the loss as much as any de Bohun.

And, in John's view, she'd never overcome her grief. It seemed to have aged her. She'd always been so full of energy and enthusiasm for life. Even after Pa's death in the pestilence, she recovered sufficiently from her grief to carry on supporting others in the village as well as her own family.

But, since April, she'd definitely declined in spirit. Her face was more often glum than bright. She pottered about in the cottage, always ensuring he had a good meal to come home to. She worked in the garden too, if rather less than she used to, paying a couple of cottar women to do some of the work.

Yet, if she was working less, and if her spirit was duller than before, her mind was still alert, her tongue often ready with an opinion.

'You're home early, son,' she called, as he pulled off his boots and went to sit at the table.

He wasn't thinking when he answered. 'It was getting dark, and the men were keen to get back to their wives...'

Ma came over with a cup of ale and put it down in front of him. 'What a pity *you* don't have a wife to come home to...'

He groaned inwardly, and Agnes laughed. 'You asked for that, brother!'

He grinned and took a few gulps of his ale. 'I've got *you*, Ma,' he said.

'Not necessarily for much longer,' she said, and Agnes rolled her eyes at him.

'What nonsense is this, Ma?' he said, getting up and putting his arm around her shoulder, as she bent over the hearth.

'It's not nonsense. I'm not getting any younger, and what'll you do when I'm gone?'

'You mean you think I'm incapable of looking after myself?'

'You don't have *time* to look after yourself! You need a wife to do that. Anyway, you shouldn't be living with your ma at your age. You should have your own house, with a woman in it, and some little ones.'

Of course, he did feel that too, but was loath to admit it to his mother, nor even his sister, though Agnes knew well enough it was what he wanted. In truth, he didn't understand why he hadn't found himself a wife.

He was still envious of Walter Nash, who had married the love of John's young life, Eleanor Titherige, despite Walter being a mere cottar to her freewoman. But he was an excellent shepherd, and Eleanor owned an enormous flock of sheep... Yet, it wasn't only their fondness for sheep. Eleanor and Walter had grown close years ago. Whereas *he* had thrown away his chance of making her his wife by treating her ungallantly.

He came back to the table, and Agnes locked eyes with him. It was as if she knew what he was thinking.

She straightened her back. 'I must go soon,' she said, 'but I wanted to ask you, brother, about Johanna... Sister Rosa... Ma thinks she'll be elected prioress, now the old lady's died.'

But he shook his head. He had in fact, two days ago, received a letter from Rosa, sent with a carter, telling him Evangelina had won and had already declared his services were no longer required. 'I won't be going to Northwick anymore,' he said, and told them about the letter.

Ma's mouth fell open. 'You'll not be seeing Rosa anymore?'

'I'm afraid not.' He turned away, tears filling his eyes as he thought of who else he would no longer see.

'Oh, poor Johanna,' Agnes said. 'She seemed so happy, from what you've been telling us these past few years. I do hope this new prioress won't spoil it for her.'

He looked up into his sister's face. He saw real concern there, in her eyes and in the uneasy set of her mouth. Despite Johanna's betrayal when they were young, Agnes had long ago forgiven her for what she did. Johanna had, in a sense, *paid* her penance by entering the priory and Agnes herself had, after years of despondency and unease, at last become a contented wife and mother. But now she was clearly anxious about the woman who'd once been her closest friend.

'I fear she might,' he said. 'She's very different from Mother Angelica, much less kindly and less pious. I think she might run the priory in a way Rosa will loathe.'

'Why on earth do you think that?'

'I met the woman a couple of times, and found her vinegary and cold.'

'Then why did she get elected?' said Ma.

'Because, for years, it's always been a member of one family – the Godeffroys, the priory's patrons – who gets elected.' He held up his hands. 'I don't know how it works. Maybe corruption was involved?'

'In a *priory*?' Agnes said, her eyes wide.

'I agree it sounds improbable, and I don't *know* if that's what happened. All I do know is Rosa, who was so much loved, was *not* elected, whilst a woman who apparently wasn't even liked, is now the prioress. It's hard to understand, but there it is.'

'I wonder how Rosa feels about it all?' said Ma.

'She accepts it as God's will.' He'd not say he actually thought she'd be dismayed.

Agnes stood up and put her cloak around her shoulders. 'Dickon will likely be unhappy to learn you're no longer able to bring him news about his aunt.'

'I daresay Rosa will continue to send me letters.'

Agnes raised an eyebrow. 'And you can read them?'

He grinned. Reading had never been his strength. 'I managed the letter I just received but it was brief. I might struggle with longer ones.'

He rose to bid farewell to his sister, taking her hand. 'Will Dickon be in Meonbridge for Christmas?'

She shrugged. 'He hasn't yet sent word, but I imagine so.'

For the next two weeks or so, John continued to ride round the manor, checking the tenants were taking only what was due, and keeping vigilant that the rights of the de Bohun demesne weren't being usurped. As he rode, he couldn't stop his worries about Northwick, Rosa and Anabella roiling around his head.

Despite seeming phlegmatic in front of Ma and Agnes about the new prioress's dismissal of his advice, he was actually distraught by his banishment from Northwick. Disappointed not to be talking to Rosa anymore, but *devastated* not to be meeting Anabella. He was terrified she'd take the veil before he'd had a chance to ask her to be his wife.

He imagined the prioress urging her to commit, though Rosa might try to dissuade her, or at least encourage her to delay. But if he couldn't go to Northwick, he'd not know what was happening. Rosa might write again with news but, even though the distance between Northwick and Meonbridge was quite short, it could take days before a carter, or a courier of some kind might be found to bear a letter...

Days in which Anabella might be persuaded to make her vows.

But then another worry came to him: might the new prioress not even *permit* letters to be sent out from the priory? Or if Rosa did manage to send one, even if he was capable of penning a reply, would she be able to receive it, or might the prioress intercept it? Were his means of communication with Rosa – and Anabella – now cut off?

His heart raced a while, until, at length, he told himself he might be panicking for no reason. Just because he'd found Sister Evangelina austere, and even if she wasn't much liked by the other sisters, that didn't mean she was malevolent or unkind. In truth, he'd no *reason* to think badly of her...

Yet he was still afraid that, now he'd finally found the woman he wanted to wed, their chance of happiness together might have already been snatched away.

His route around the manor's broad estates brought him to the junction with the road that headed off in Northwick's direction. He slowed, leaned back in the saddle and clicked his tongue, and the mare came to a halt. He turned to face the little track, scarcely a road at all.

'Shall we go that way?' he murmured to her, as if she understood, and, leaning forward, patted her on the neck. She whickered softly.

Should he ride to Northwick and demand to see Anabella? Yet what might come of such an action? Likely quite the opposite from what he wanted, if the prioress refused him entry. After all, she'd already said he was no longer welcome. What's more, as far as he knew, the prioress was quite unaware he and Anabella had ever met. If she learned, by his unbidden appearance at the priory, that Rosa had been arranging their trysts in secret, encouraging Anabella to consider leaving Northwick and, presumably, taking her fortune with her, the prioress might be − *would* be − deeply vexed.

No, that wasn't at all a level-headed plan. Nonetheless, he stayed there at the junction a while longer, letting the horse crop the few spikes of browned grass. He fixed his eyes upon the track, so much *wanting* to set off along it, yet knowing he couldn't. His eyes filled, with grief and with frustration, and angrily he swiped his sleeve across his face.

How powerless he felt. Yet what could he do? He couldn't − wouldn't − give up on Anabella. He had to keep in contact with Rosa and with her, and, in time, he could work out how to rescue Anabella from the priory and bring her back to Meonbridge as his wife.

8

Rosa was seeking refuge in the garden. It was cold and the air was damp and misty, but she wanted to be on her own a while, and to be out here, where in future she would no longer have much cause to come.

For Evangelina had already stripped her of her role as prioress's assistant. Liaising with the bailiff and the tenants as she used to was no longer her responsibility, nor even meeting Beatrice to discuss planting plans for the priory's food. Beatrice had kept her job as cellaress – Rosa supposed even Evangelina realised how unwise it would be to try to wrest that particular responsibility from the person who managed it so well.

Amata had kept her job as infirmaress and almoness, and Juliana was still precentrix. Dulcia had retained her position as treasuress, despite her fears of losing it. Yet she had told Rosa, she was not much looking forward to working as closely as she would have to with Evangelina.

The new prioress had chosen Sister Clarice as her principal assistant – the new, *appointed*, subprioress. Had Evangelina offered her the position in advance, in order to win her support in the election? But Clarice was as good a choice as any. She had been an efficient chambress, and was no fool. She would pick up what was needed soon enough, which was just as well. For Evangelina herself was scarcely in a position to advise her, when she probably had little understanding of the breadth of responsibility her new position demanded. Of course, Clarice could ask *Rosa* for advice, but Rosa suspected Evangelina would discourage it.

The prioress had given her the job of sacrist, which meant she would spend a lot of time alone. To some degree, Rosa was glad. For the role required her to spend more time in the chapel, and to handle and care for the priory's precious sacred objects.

But she would miss the freedom to spend as much time out of doors as she had done the past few years.

In front of the other sisters, Rosa made an effort to appear serene. Yet, in truth, she was uneasy, because of the unhappy memories that had resurfaced as a result of Evangelina's threats, and because she would no longer be able to see John. But most of all because she *feared* Evangelina's rule.

Of course, Evangelina would be a very different prioress from Angelica, but it was not just the *difference* that she feared. She was afraid the new prioress's lack of piety might mean the spirituality that Angelica had engendered at Northwick was now at risk, and her apparent craving for power might alter the tenor of Northwick's life.

Rosa tried to accept Evangelina's election as the will of God, even if she scarcely believed it was. To counter her own scepticism, she told herself that, however stern Evangelina *had* been, she might prove after all a caring and proficient prioress.

Yet it was hard to convince herself of what in her heart she felt was so unlikely.

Northwick's sisters were divided about the new prioress. Some seemed to accept her happily, others clearly wished Rosa had been elected.

One or two who must have *voted* for Evangelina seemed to be regretting they had done so.

Or so Beatrice said.

Beatrice and Amata still very much took Rosa's part, although neither knew exactly what had happened to cause her to refuse to stand for prioress. She would not talk about it, albeit part of her longed to share her worries about Evangelina.

The three women met less often than they used to. Rosa no longer had a reason to speak to either the cellaress or the infirmaress about their work.

She also sensed that she was being watched. She upbraided herself for being mistrustful, but she often found one of Evangelina's favourites – and especially Letitia – close by when she was anywhere but where she was supposed to be. She had thought of challenging the girl, but never did.

Rosa mentioned it one day to Beatrice.

Beatrice went out of her way to walk with Rosa in the cloister at least every other day. In the cloister, the sisters were allowed to talk, as long as they kept their voices low. They made several circuits, strolling sedately, their backs straight but their heads a little bowed, their arms crossed before them and their hands tucked inside their sleeves.

Beatrice stayed close to Rosa, so she could keep her voice barely above a whisper.

'Watching you?' she said, her eyes wide. 'Surely, you're imagining it?'

'I do not think so. Letitia is always there, whenever I am anywhere other than the dorter, the chapel or here. Or I suppose the sacristy. If I come to the frater other than at mealtimes, or if I go to see Amata in the infirmary, I am as likely as not to find Letitia there too. It is most unsettling.'

'But why would she be watching you?'

'I presume because Evangelina wishes to ensure I am not straying beyond the limits of my prescribed role.'

'I see. Making sure you're not plotting against her?'

Rosa frowned. 'I daresay you think me overly suspicious, but I do think that, yes.'

Beatrice leaned in close to Rosa's ear. 'Do you believe Evangelina *plotted* against you in the matter of the election?'

Rosa looked up, startled. 'Do *you?*'

'Amata and I both suspect Evangelina somehow *tricked* you into not standing against her. I remember how upset you were before the election. Something had disturbed you, yet you wouldn't say what it was...'

Rosa took a deep breath to steady her unease. Had the time come to tell the truth? She said nothing as they continued along one side of the cloister, and then another... But, on the third side, she decided. 'I still cannot tell you, Beatrice. I should like to, but I am not ready. But, yes, Evangelina *did* persuade me not to stand, to give herself a surer chance of winning...'

'But you'll not say *how* she persuaded you?'

'I cannot. Or not yet.'

'That's what you said before, "not yet".'

'I know, and I am sorry still not to be able to confide in you. Yet I believe the day will come when I can, and a great burden will be lifted from my shoulders when I do...'

Beatrice slipped one hand from her sleeve and surreptitiously laid it upon Rosa's arm. 'You do know, don't you, that, when you do, my lips will stay firm shut?'

'Of course I do, dear Beatrice. Thank you.'

'In the meantime,' Beatrice said, 'I must say I'm apprehensive about how Evangelina intends to rule. I'm certain she'll not continue Angelica's legacy of benevolence and piety, but what *will* she do?'

'I agree, albeit I have tried to tell myself she might surprise us. In a good way.' She gave Beatrice an encouraging smile.

'I admire your faith,' said Beatrice, 'but I fear I do not share it.'

'Oh, it is not faith, but simply a determination to be optimistic.'

MARCH 1366

It was not long before Rosa's fears, and Beatrice's, were realised: the purpose and tenor of the priory were beginning to change.

Under Angelica's rule, Northwick had been a place of piety and work, but also companionship and love. It was true that she had believed strongly in Saint Benedict's rule: every day was divided into periods of prayer, both private and in the chapel, interspersed with time for reading and study, for work and for sleep. Her rule was strict but kind. Most of Northwick's sisters seemed happy to accept their vows of poverty, humility and obedience, and to embrace Angelica's strictures with joyfulness, because she implemented them with love.

For Rosa, come to Northwick as an unhappy girl, wracked with guilt at what she perceived to be her own grave sin, found exactly what she had hoped for. She sought an atmosphere of godliness and devotion, relieved only by opportunities to task her body with physical labour and test her mind with study of the scriptures. That was precisely what Mother Angelica's Northwick gave her.

So much so that, in only months, the distraught Johanna had become an almost blissful Rosa. She could remember the moment she first understood how right her decision to come to Northwick had been. She had never found cause to regret it.

Even now she held no regrets, despite the changes apparently afoot.

Angelica encouraged the sisters to attend all the holy offices, unless they had a good reason not to. Rosa always found both peace and joy in singing psalms and saying prayers. The hours spent in the chapel were invariably the happiest part of her day.

But she knew this was not so for Evangelina.

Over all the years Rosa had known her, Evangelina had habitually skipped the offices, especially those at night. Angelica had, for the most part, turned a blind eye to her transgressions, which Rosa had found strangely out of character. Yet she concluded that the prioress probably knew that her niece was unlikely to reform no matter what punishment she imposed.

Now Evangelina herself was prioress, she had clearly decided that, if she did not wish to attend the offices, she would stay away. Neither would she bother to chastise other sisters who followed her example. And a few were doing so – sisters who, under Angelica's rule, *had* conformed. So had their earlier obedience been insincere, or was it more that they thought ingratiating themselves to their new prioress might bring them some advantage?

. . .

Like Beatrice, Amata also sought out Rosa's company from time to time, although, mostly, their only chance for conversation was, again, the daily exercise in the cloister.

Only days ago, the prioress had discharged Amata from her role as infirmaress, citing her increasing frailty. She had appointed Sister Mariota in her stead.

'Beatrice thinks Mariota must have voted for Evangelina,' whispered Amata.

Rosa pursed her lips, sad that Amata had been taken from the job she had done so well and for so long. 'Yet the prioress did have few choices for such a role. She could scarcely pick one of her young favourites, for those silly girls would have no idea at all of what the job demands.'

Amata nodded. 'In some ways, I'm relieved no longer to have the responsibility, for it was exhausting.'

'But you so loved the job, Amata.'

'I did, but I'm old, and weary. And Evangelina is impatient...'

'Impatient?'

'For power. She wants to sweep away the old guard and bring in new young faces.'

Rosa grinned. 'She's scarcely young herself!' Yet she had learned – from Angelica herself – that Evangelina was not quite as old as Rosa had once thought. She looked now much as she did ten years ago, when she was old before her time. Although, now, it might be true that Evangelina's almost youthful appearance was at least partly due to her new-found pleasure in life.

A pleasure she was embracing to the detriment of the priory...

Amata tittered softly. 'Indeed. Which is *why* she is so eager to impose her own regime...'

Amata was right. It *was* power Evangelina craved, the power to run Northwick as she wanted. Having lived an ascetic life for more than thirty years, ever since she was a girl, even Rosa could understand the new prioress now relishing the chance of doing things her own way.

'But it is worrying,' she said, 'that Evangelina's idea of exercising power means she is also wasting our limited funds, buying herself fine clothes and employing her own servants.'

'I agree. As do many of our sisters. They are aghast at what is happening, or at least those who are not part of our Reverend Mother's little circle.' Amata rolled her rheumy eyes.

Rosa wondered about the three young nuns who made up Evangelina's closest circle: why had such girls been sent to Northwick? They were from aristocratic families, all pretty enough to have attracted husbands, and none seemed to have a vocation for the cloistered life. So why were they here? Were they all younger daughters, whose fathers ran out of money to provide them with an adequate dowry? Northwick was almost certainly not *their* choice, yet all now seemed thrilled to be amongst Evangelina's chosen, for her form of benevolence would clearly extend to them.

'I do hope,' she said to Amata, 'Evangelina does not think to give those young nuns tasks for which they are not capable...'

'She hasn't done so yet. I was worried she might pick one of them for subprioress...'

'I too, but Sister Clarice was a sensible choice.'

A large part of Rosa's job as subprioress had been overseeing Northwick's farm estate. When she was first appointed prioress, Mother Angelica had managed it herself, together with the bailiff. But, when Rosa became her assistant, she soon proved to know enough about the running of a great estate for Angelica to encourage her to take over many of the tasks. Quite *how* she knew so much had baffled Rosa, for, as Johanna, she had never taken much interest in the management of Meonbridge's demesne. Yet perhaps her mother's close attention to manor affairs had, over the years, rubbed off on her? Anyway, when Northwick's bailiff turned out to be a rogue, and John atte Wode started coming to advise her and Angelica, her knowledge grew rapidly.

Given Evangelina's yearning for power, might she choose to resume the task her aunt had once undertaken, so she could learn how the priory earned its income? Rosa doubted it. For Evangelina appeared quite uninterested in the *functioning* of the priory. Indeed, she was almost certainly not interested in *running* Northwick, so much as gaining what she could from it.

. . .

Later, Rosa thought once more of John and her sadness that she would no longer be able to see and talk to him. Yet, how much worse must it be for John himself, and she already knew how distressed Anabella was that Evangelina's decision had torn their budding relationship asunder.

In some ways, Rosa felt she had let Anabella down. Although, she had promised to try to help ensure that Anabella's separation from John was not permanent, she had no idea at all of what she could do to help.

Immediately after Evangelina's election, she had written a brief note to John telling him the result. She hoped he could read her letter. Not much later, she found he could, for he sent a reply. It was difficult to decipher what he had written but at length she construed that he was asking her to send him news, not about herself or Northwick, but about Anabella. He had not mentioned Anabella's name, perhaps anxious that someone other than Rosa might intercept his letter. It was only then she realised that Evangelina had *not* put restrictions on the nuns sending or receiving letters. Some priories, she understood, did so, but it had never been Angelica's way, and Evangelina had, seemingly, not thought of it. So, for now at least, Rosa could write back to John, and receive his replies.

And perhaps, at length, they might devise a plan to enable John and Anabella to be together.

APRIL 1366

After a long night of fierce winds and torrential rain, the nuns awoke for Prime to find great puddles on the dorter floor. When Rosa and her sisters had arisen and left their beds to attend Matins a few hours earlier, they heard the dreadful roaring of the wind around the roof and the rain battering against the tiles. As they skittered down the night stairs that led directly to the transept, they murmured to each other how glad they were not to have to face the elements in order to reach the chapel. But Rosa had worried that the downpour might find its way between the tiles, and now she saw her fears were justified.

The leaks were only at one end of the dorter. That was fortunate but Rosa was concerned about how much damage the storm had inflicted upon the roof. For it was now her responsibility to deal with it.

Rosa thought Evangelina had appointed her to the role of sacrist as a way of keeping her out of the way. It was an important job, of course, but a lonely one. She was not required to associate much with the other nuns. She might meet Father Edgar from time to time, as they shared the little sacristy, and she would make occasional contact with the candle-maker to fulfil the priory's need for candles, and with other artisans if repairs were needed to the fabric of the building.

But, for the most part, she worked alone.

The sacrist's job *could* be peaceful and secluded, when all that was required was to keep the chapel, the precious objects and the vestments clean and in good order. But if repairs or building work were needed, in the chapel or any other part of the priory, it became a lot more onerous. Evangelina had found that herself. For, in Northwick, the role of sacrist had, for years, also included management of the priory's buildings as a whole.

Now this task fell to Rosa, and what a potentially daunting task it was. She could call upon the guidance of Sir Thomas Chatterton, Northwick's steward, whom Angelica had engaged many years ago, to advise on which local workmen to employ, to ensure the priory's funds were wisely used and that the work would be well done. Sir Thomas would help her devise the budget for repairs, then Rosa would talk to Sister Dulcia, who would allocate the funds and help to engage the artisans and labourers. Although, once engaged, it would be Rosa who dealt with the men on a day-to-day basis, as well as ensuring costs were kept under control.

She had been looking forward to the task. Yet, when she went to speak to Dulcia about the matter of the dorter roof, with the figures Sir Thomas had suggested noted down, the treasuress perused the numbers, then sighed.

'Oh dear, Rosa,' she said, keeping her voice low. 'I don't think Mother Evangelina will sanction such a great expense.'

'Not sanction it?' said Rosa, bemused. 'But why? Surely, the dorter roof must be repaired? We cannot sleep with the threat of rain cascading onto our beds, or worse, timber and tiles!'

'I agree. And Angelica would never have refused such an expense.

But, in my brief experience of our new prioress, I'm finding her most unwilling to spend money on...' She hesitated. 'On certain kinds of items...'

'What sort of items?'

She blushed. 'Cloth for new habits for the sisters, divers repairs about the farm and for the tenants.' She pressed her lips together. 'Alms for the poor...'

'Alms...?' Rosa repeated, aghast. 'Amata must be alarmed.'

'She is. But in Mother Evangelina's view we've been too generous for too long towards the manor's poor.' Her voice had dropped to the merest whisper. 'She referred to them as indigents.'

Rosa felt her hackles rise. So, *this* was how Evangelina was going to manage her priory? By flouting Saint Benedict's rule of charity. By making the tenants' lives even more difficult than they already were by letting their farms and buildings fall into disrepair? By not permitting the sisters to have new clothes?

'What gall to refuse cloth for the sisters' habits, when she has just bought new – and costly – garments for herself, and those silly girls.' Conscious suddenly she had allowed her voice to rise, Rosa clapped a hand over her mouth with an embarrassed blush.

Dulcia's lips widened in a sympathetic smile. 'I tried to refuse the silk for herself, but she insisted. What could I do, when I'm bound by my vow of obedience?'

That was of course the problem, and Evangelina knew it. Whatever the prioress demanded, the prioress was given. It was not a humble sister's role to argue, not even when that sister was the priory's treasuress. Or sacrist. Or almoness. And what of the cellaress?

'Has Beatrice also had her budgets trimmed? Are the sisters to find their trenchers empty, their ale watered down? When the prioress herself is eating God knows what delicacies in her private chamber?'

'Not so far,' said Dulcia, 'but I fear that might yet come. Mother Evangelina has mentioned hiring her own cook, even building her own separate kitchen...' She looked up, her eyes wide with despair. 'To fund it, cuts would need be made elsewhere... Less fish, perhaps? No wine?' She shook her head. 'And I'd not have the authority to counter it.'

. . .

When Rosa left Dulcia to her accounts and to her gloom, she hurried to the sacristy, hoping Father Edgar would not be there. The room was empty, and she sank onto the stool. What she had feared about Evangelina's rule as prioress was happening already. Moreover, from what Sister Dulcia had said, it was quite likely to get worse. The new prioress seemed to care little for the priory, or the manor, but only for what might vantage *her*.

Rosa could imagine Evangelina might be impatient to overturn the strictures Angelica had enacted. Strictures Rosa herself enjoyed but which, for Evangelina, were perhaps a form of torment. Yet the more easeful way of life she seemed set upon was only for herself and a favoured few, not the community as a whole.

As for the repairs to the dorter roof, Dulcia did at length agree to a sum of money somewhat less than Sir Thomas's recommendation. Rosa would have to consult with him to find a way of cutting costs. Yet cutting costs meant a poorer outcome, and she would not preside over the use of inferior materials and shoddy workmanship. Neither, she was certain, would Sister Dulcia.

Sir Thomas offered to go to the prioress to plead their case and Rosa nodded gratefully, hoping he would have more influence than either she or Dulcia. But, although Evangelina, he said later, cooed at him and promised to discuss with Rosa the details of the budget, she did not. She simply instructed Rosa to cut corners. Which Rosa was not prepared to do.

How troubling it all was. Evangelina was content to restrict funding even when the expenditure was necessary to the existence of the priory, but casual in her willingness to waste money on non-essentials. Rosa's fears were being realised.

Northwick was changing. No longer the modest, contemplative haven she had loved but a place of indulgence, fashion and amusement, if only for the few. Evangelina might claim *she* was saving money by keeping down the cost of building projects and making the sisters wear the same habits for another year, but the money "saved" was not going into Northwick's coffers for the future, but to fund the prioress's own desires.

If Evangelina continued in this vein, eventually, she would surely bring Northwick to the brink of ruin.

9

Northwick Priory
April 1366

Evangelina was enjoying herself. The day after the election, she'd moved into the prioress's chamber, with its fine bed and wall hangings, and each night since she'd slept so deeply and so well there was no question of her rising in the early hours to make the short journey to the chapel.

According to the Benedictine rule, a prioress was supposed to sleep in the dorter, alongside her sisters. But, at Northwick, ever since the first Godeffroy prioress was appointed, she'd had a separate chamber. Though Aunt Angelica baulked at flouting the order's rule, and mostly did sleep in one of the narrow flimsily-partitioned cells she'd had installed in the dorter many years ago to provide a little privacy for everyone. But Evangelina had no intention of following her aunt's example, when this large and comfortable private room was available to give her ease and relaxation.

Another of the order's rules demanded that the prioress always take her meals in the frater, in the company of the community she oversaw. A rule with which, again, Angelica was happy to comply, for all the years of her governance, at least until recently, when she'd become too frail to take the stairs.

But Evangelina saw no reason to comply. Why submit to sitting on hard, uncomfortable benches, being forced to listen to a sister often as not *stumbling* over her reading of the day's allotted scripture? When instead she could stay here in her chamber, reclining restfully in her chair, engaging or not in conversation as she wished, depending on whether or not she chose to share the meal with one or other of her favourites.

Today she'd invited Letitia to join her for the midday meal. She slightly favoured Letitia over the other two. Perhaps because the girl was evidently devoted to her: quite why she didn't know. She was less frivolous than either Felicia or Maria, more serious in outlook. Evangelina suspected Letitia's home life had been much like hers, where she'd felt unwanted and unloved. The girl came from a noble family, but was she too a youngest daughter, whose destiny was always the religious life, whether she wanted it or not? Had Letitia, like herself, come to Northwick under coercion, not from choice? She supposed she could ask her, but she found asking such familiar questions difficult.

So, for now, their conversations concerned their life here, and the changes she was making.

Evangelina speared a morsel of fish upon her knife, and raised it to her lips. She nibbled at it. 'Delicious, don't you think?

'Oh, yes, Reverend Mother,' the girl said, with enthusiasm. 'Delicious. And there is so much!'

'Indeed.' Evangelina smirked. Her instructions to her new maid were that the portions of food she brought to her were generous, twice the quantity of fish served to the sisters in the frater. The maid, Hilde, was proving diligent in doing as she was bid. Evangelina was pleased with her choice from amongst the young women from the village who presented themselves as candidates for the job. She thought Hilde might also prove useful in the matter of keeping her eyes and ears open for gossip or information. The more spies she had, looking and listening out for discord or dissent, the better.

'I'm considering acquiring my own cook,' she said. 'What do you think, Letitia?'

'To cook food just for us?' Letitia said then blushed bright red. Her spoon clattered into her bowl.

'For *me*,' said Evangelina firmly, an eyebrow raised. 'Though naturally you'd share it with me from time to time.'

Northwick's cook wasn't inept, but the food was often bland, and dull, the same fare nearly every day. She'd sent instructions for this fish to be more interestingly prepared. Yet, in her new position, didn't she deserve to dine on fine food *every* day, conceived and cooked especially for her? And to invite local personages to come from time to time, to share it with her?

Some days later, Evangelina accompanied Sister Clarice to the narrow gate that pierced one long wall of the potagers, and led out from the gardens to the closest of the manor's fields. The subprioress had arranged her first meeting with Rafe Byllynges, the bailiff, there.

'As I understand it,' she said, as they walked towards the gate, 'the farming year starts now, in April. I thought I should at least attempt to apprise myself of what that means.' She'd rolled her eyes a little. 'What tasks are undertaken, and by whom. Of course, Sister Rosa is well-acquainted with it all, so I could ask her, but I thought it best if I learned it for myself. And became acquainted with Master Byllynges...'

Evangelina bristled at the mention of Rosa's name, but managed to keep her hostility to herself. 'Sister Dulcia too is quite abreast of it,' she said, 'in particular the incomings and outgoings of the estate.' Though she'd not so far troubled herself to discuss with the treasuress the finances of the farm.

Felicia had come with them. When the girl asked her if she could, Evangelina had agreed, on the grounds that, given she was otherwise mostly idle, she'd benefit from an outing. But she dawdled as they made their way down through the flower gardens, peering at the plants, and fondling the nodding flowers, yellow, white and pink, none of which Evangelina knew. More than once, she was obliged to turn and chivvy the girl to hurry up, as they entered the potagers and headed for the wall on the other side.

In all the long years she'd been here, Evangelina had never walked much in the priory's gardens, which was why she knew so little about what grew here. She was especially unfamiliar with the potagers, where now row upon row upon row of tiny shoots were pushing up from the dark, moist soil – all vegetables of one kind or another, she supposed. Beyond the potagers she could see the vast orchard, where the trees were covered in a froth of white and pink blossoms. She pointed to them, and leaned towards Clarice.

'What are those trees, do you think?'

'I cannot tell from here, Reverend Mother, but I believe Northwick's orchard is renowned for the excellence of its plums and cherries, so maybe that's what they are?'

'Pears and apples too,' said Felicia, coming up beside them, 'judging by the pies and puddings the cook makes in the autumn.'

Evangelina turned to her in astonishment. 'What do you know of fruit trees?'

Felicia giggled. 'Oh, nothing, Reverend Mother. I know only about the fruit, for it is so delicious and we seem to eat so little of it.' She gave a little pout.

Clarice tutted. 'Do stop your prattling, Felicia. We are almost at the gate.' She gestured with her hand. 'Look, there is the bailiff, waiting for us.'

As they passed through the little gate, and came closer to Master Byllynges, Felicia squealed. 'Oh, do look at that *delightful* little dog!'

To Evangelina's eyes, the dog sitting by its master's side was coarse-looking and rough-coated and, as she came closer, she could see one ear was torn. Its demeanour seemed quiet and respectful but even so… 'A dog, indeed, Felicia,' she murmured, 'but scarcely "delightful", nor even very little…'

Clarice introduced herself and Evangelina to the bailiff, who removed his hood and grinned. 'Me'dames,' he said.

He bowed his head to each of them in turn, first, Clarice and then Evangelina. But, when he turned to Felicia, his gaze lingered, which was scarcely surprising, for the girl was undoubtedly a beauty. The loveliness of her face was plain for all to see, despite being enveloped in a wimple.

Yet again, Evangelina wondered why Felicia's family had sent her to

Northwick, when she could surely have won herself a suitable husband. But who knew what led some families to dispose thus so callously of their daughters?

As she watched, Felicia quivered perceptibly before she lowered her eyes, and the bailiff too withdrew his impudent gaze and turned back to Sister Clarice, to discuss what she had come for.

Evangelina had come merely to see what manner of man the bailiff was and to listen to the conversation. She'd no intention of asking any questions or, indeed, attempting to absorb anything of what he might endeavour to explain. Clarice could do that.

Much like his dog, Master Byllynges was respectful and polite. Unlike the animal, his face was handsome. Doffing his hood had exposed a mane of bright fair hair, and his disposition seemed as sunny. He appeared a very different sort of man from the previous bailiff, who'd not only proved to be a knave, but looked one too.

Moreover, as Master Byllynges talked, he seemed knowledgeable – as far as she could tell – and Clarice was nodding or tilting her head by turns in understanding or enquiry. Indeed, the subprioress seemed almost *captivated* by what the man was telling her.

At length the bailiff suggested a walk around some fields that were currently under the plough, and a tour of the most important of the estate's farm buildings. Clarice nodded again, and leaning forward, lifted the hem of her habit a fraction to reveal her feet were shod in heavy boots.

'I came prepared,' she said.

'Ah,' said Evangelina. 'Very wise. I, however, did not, so I shan't join you. Felicia and I shall return to the priory, and you can apprise me later of all that you have learned.'

Clarice's eyes widened. 'Oh, v-very well, Reverend M-mother. I am sure Master Byllynges is a gentleman...'

Evangelina frowned, wondering what she meant. But she took Felicia's elbow and, turning, set off back towards the priory. As they walked, Felicia giggled. 'I do hope the bailiff *is* a gentleman, and doesn't take advantage of poor Sister Clarice...'

'Advantage?' Evangelina cried. 'Whatever do you mean, girl?'

Felicia blushed a little. 'Well, you know, a woman on her own, with a strange man.' She giggled again. 'And such a *handsome* man...'

'But Clarice is a *nun*!' said Evangelina, her voice still raised. 'I can't imagine a man like Master Byllynges having any interest in a woman in a habit...'

'Yet Sister Clarice is quite comely...'

'Comely?' Evangelina said, then upbraided herself for echoing Felicia's words a second time. Though the girl was right. Clarice's face was fair and her habit and veil didn't disguise it. Evangelina realised then it was with *alarm* that Clarice's eyes had widened, at the prospect of having to continue on alone with Master Byllynges. She'd not realised Clarice expected her and Felicia to stay with her *throughout* her discussion with the bailiff...

But she'd not go back. 'Comely or not,' she said briskly, 'I'm sure Sister Clarice will be quite safe. After all, Sister Beatrice meets the bailiff often on her own...' In truth, she wasn't confident of her assertion, but it seemed likely enough. Though of course Beatrice *was* much older than Clarice...

'He was very charming and polite, don't you think?' Felicia prattled on. 'And he does have a lovely little dog.'

'And what difference might *that* make?'

Felicia giggled yet again. 'Oh, I think pets make people nicer,' she said, and Evangelina couldn't suppress one of her ungainly snorts.

'I'm quite sure Master Byllynges doesn't consider that animal of his a "pet". Mangy and flea-ridden as it undoubtedly is, it'll be a working dog of some sort.'

'You are right, of course, Reverend Mother. But I do think it must be delightful to have a sweet little creature to keep you company. It was quite the thing amongst the aristocratic ladies of my mama's acquaintance. Nearly every one of them carried a small white dog in her arms or trailed one on a leash.'

Evangelina didn't respond, but "aristocratic ladies" piqued her interest. The Godeffroys were most definitely of genteel blood, if not *quite* aristocratic. But the family was wealthy enough to endow Northwick and provide its prioresses with the trappings of a noble lady. Aunt Angelica might have eschewed those trappings for the most part, but Evangelina was eager to embrace them. And, if Felicia was right, and every noble lady these days had a little lap dog, perhaps she should have one too?

Days later, she mentioned it again, when all three girls were together in her chamber.

Felicia squealed with excitement. 'Oh, yes, yes, Reverend Mother!' she cried. 'And please *do* get more than one. It would be such fun to play with them.'

Maria eagerly agreed, though Letitia seemed a little cooler about the proposal.

'Dogs can be an awful nuisance,' she said. 'Leaving fur, and other things I'd rather not give a name to, in places you least expect to find them.'

'You have experience of small dogs, Letitia?' said Evangelina.

'Mama always had three at once. All small and white and yappy.' She rolled her eyes. 'She was quite *devoted* to them. Much more so than to her chil—' She stopped abruptly, perhaps conscious she'd let slip an intimacy she'd rather not.

'Oh, nonsense, Letty,' said Maria. 'Those little white dogs are adorable, so cuddly and warm...'

'And wriggly, and smelly...' countered Letitia, but Evangelina held up her hand.

'Enough. I haven't yet decided. But even if I do go ahead, it won't be yet.'

For, now she'd at least made herself more comfortable, she did recognise it would be a mistake to impose too much change too quickly. The sisters would resent it, or some would anyway.

A few were already begrudging some of the changes she had made...

Angelica, for all her supposed benevolence, had insisted – or tried to – the sisters attend *all* the offices, unless they had an extremely plausible excuse. Evangelina had always hated trailing to the chapel, especially at night and, ever since she came to Northwick as a girl, she'd shirked the night-time offices as often as she could. But now *she* was in charge, if she didn't want to leave her bed in the cold, dark, early morning hours to traipse down to the chapel to drone and shiver through Matins, Lauds and even Prime, she wouldn't. And if other sisters didn't want to either, she'd not complain, nor demand they pay a penance. Surely, *that* was more benevolent?

Yet some of the sisters – and especially Rosa – wouldn't agree.

Nonetheless, *any* further improvements – the personal cook and

private kitchen, the distinguished guests and the little dog or dogs –
could wait a while, so as not to test too far and too fast any of her
gainsayers' patience.

For months, Sister Rosa had done precisely what Evangelina expected
her to do in the face of the changes she was making: nothing.
Evangelina was prioress, and Rosa undoubtedly regarded her
appointment as God's will. She might not have *liked* it, but she'd
accept it.

For Rosa was the epitome of the obedient nun. Thus, it followed,
Evangelina supposed, Rosa would also feel obliged to comply with any
rules she, as prioress, imposed, regardless of whether she resented or
disagreed with them.

And so it had proved. Or at least until quite recently.

How irritating it was that the dorter roof had sprung a leak. And
how tedious that the steward had priced the work at such an
outrageous sum. When Sister Dulcia told her of Sir Thomas's estimate,
Evangelina resisted.

'It is indeed a large sum, Reverend Mother. I said as much to Sister
Rosa. Yet, if that's what Sir Thomas considers is required—'

Evangelina shook her head. 'Surely, a tolerable enough job can be
had without such *vast* expenditure?'

Sister Dulcia bit her lip. 'What, then, shall I tell Sister Rosa?'

'Make her a lower offer. A more *reasonable* offer...'

The treasurer inclined her head, and withdrew from Evangelina's
chamber.

But, the next day, Sir Thomas himself came to plead his case. A
charming man, Sir Thomas Chatterton – persuasive. Yet it wasn't *he*
who was in charge at Northwick.

Evangelina listened to what he had to say, her head tilted to one
side, and made a few conciliatory remarks. 'I'll discuss the details of
the budget with Sister Rosa,' she said at length, and he bowed and
went away, apparently satisfied. However, she'd no intention of giving
way, and simply instructed Rosa to cut corners on the work. But, to her
surprise, Rosa didn't agree to do so, saying merely she'd see if anything
could be done.

And, as it turned out, Rosa proved, in this matter, as duplicitous as she herself had been.

The work on the roof was carried out, and when Sister Dulcia was presented with the final bill, the amount was scarcely any different from what Sir Thomas originally proposed.

When Dulcia brought the bill to show her, her face was ashen. 'Reverend Mother, I have Sir Thomas's account for the dorter roof,' she said, then caught her bottom lip between her teeth.

'Sir *Thomas's* account?' said Evangelina. 'Didn't you purchase the materials and hire the men directly, as you usually do?'

The treasuress shook her head. 'Sir Thomas suggested that, in this case, he would take on the immediate expenses, and subcontract the labour to the builders rather than have them deal with me individually and directly. He said it would save us money and, given your concerns, Reverend Mother, I thought it a good plan. And Sister Rosa endorsed it strongly.'

'Yet it appears there has been *no* saving, for the bill's fundamentally the same as the steward's initial estimation.' Evangelina gesticulated with her hands, pacing up and down her chamber in a fury.

'You've mismanaged this, Sister Dulcia,' she said, returning to stand before her. 'And with Rosa's deliberate collusion, I daresay. You – and your predecessors – have always handled the outgoings for any building project directly, so you can keep a close eye on spending. That's true, isn't it?'

Dulcia nodded, her face dejected. She opened her mouth to answer, but Evangelina held up her hand.

'So why do it differently this time?'

'Because, Reverend Mother, I believed I could trust Sir Thomas to keep the costs down, as he said he would.' She bit her lip again. 'And Sister Rosa agr—'

'Oh, never mind Sister Rosa!' She couldn't contain her temper. 'She was doubtless *conniving* with the man. And it seems *he* can't be trusted after all...'

Dulcia's cheeks were aflame. 'I am so sorry, Reverend Mother.' She wrung her hands together.

'As indeed you should be! I think I might have to relieve you of your post. Find a sister less eager to rely upon the word of a man whose interests are evidently his own, rather than ours.'

Sister Dulcia gasped. 'Oh, no, Mother Evangelina, please! I did believe the plan a good one. Sir Thomas has been our steward for nearly ten years, and has always shown himself to be exemplary in putting Northwick's interests ahead of any others. Mother Angelica regarded him most highly—'

'Yet maybe, after all, misguidedly?' The prioress raised an eyebrow. 'What other self-seeking deals might our *trusty* steward have duped us into accepting?'

'None!' cried the treasuress, her face aghast.

'Yet your confidence, Sister Dulcia, might be misplaced.'

She dismissed her, and paced the floor a little more. She'd not of course replace Dulcia as treasuress. The woman knew too much about the work. Despite her criticism, it wasn't Dulcia she blamed for this debacle but Rosa. She and the steward had evidently conspired to obtain the result they wanted.

Well, Sir Thomas Chatterton had pulled his last trick on Northwick. He'd have to go. She could find another local landowner to be their steward.

Sister Rosa, on the other hand, she *couldn't* banish. She could give her job to someone else but who else was there? What she *would* do, though, was summon Rosa here and warn her off attempting to act again so recklessly with Northwick's narrow funds.

Yet, when Rosa was standing before Evangelina in her chamber, her back was straight. Her gaze was fierce and steady: no lowered, submissive eyes.

Evangelina glared at her. 'What were you *thinking*?'

'That I was responsible for ensuring the dorter roof was repaired. And that, as our steward, Sir Thomas Chatterton, had advised, the builders had to be given what they needed to do the job.' She pursed her lips. 'I understand you reprimanded Sister Dulcia for agreeing to the expenditure. That was most unfair. Dulcia expressed much concern about Sir Thomas's estimate for the work, but *I* persuaded her to agree to it—'

'Which was reckless.'

'I disagree. It was prudent. Our priory buildings are venerable and ancient, and it is our duty to ensure they are maintained in such a way that they survive for centuries into the future. It would be unforgiveable to botch such an important job.'

Evangelina groaned inwardly. How typical of Sister Rosa to deliver a sermon over such a matter. 'You're overstating the importance of the task. A few tiles had come loose and needed to be replaced.'

'Not so. A large hole had opened up beneath the tiles, and had to be properly repaired. Surely, our sisters should have a reasonable expectation that the roof above them is in no danger of rain, or worse, falling down upon them whilst they sleep?'

Evangelina spun around and glared at her. Rosa was *arguing*. Where was the exemplary obedient nun?

Later, Evangelina pondered upon the change in Sister Rosa. When she threatened to expose her past to stop her standing in the election, Rosa had seemed cowed. She'd decided to keep her that way by isolating her as much as possible, to limit her chances of gathering support against her. She'd given her the job of sacrist because she knew the work involved little daily contact with the other nuns. And she'd also dismissed John atte Wode, the bailiff from Rosa's home manor. Ostensibly this was because, with Rafe Byllynges apparently proving competent enough, they no longer needed the other man's advice. But mostly it was because it cut Rosa off from any support outside the priory.

Yet, despite these measures, Rosa seemed to be cowed no longer.

It was irritating, but was it also dangerous? Was Rosa deliberately resisting the changes she was making? Worse, might she try to turn the other nuns against her?

10

John had managed to pen a reply to Rosa's note soon after his receipt of hers. His handwriting was poor, and he was uncertain how to spell most words, so he was concerned his letter mightn't be intelligible, even assuming Sister Rosa was able to receive it.

He did think of asking Ma to help him, as he'd said he would. But what he wanted to say to Rosa involved Anabella, and he wasn't ready to tell his mother about her, knowing she'd at once leap to expectations that might never come to pass.

He hadn't mentioned Anabella to his sister either. He couldn't decide whether or not to tell her. Likely she'd just say he was being ridiculous to even imagine a woman like Anabella would want to marry him, and he wasn't prepared to face her scorn.

Mostly because he feared she might be right...

Thus, his brief relationship with Anabella remained a secret to everyone apart from Rosa, one that gnawed away at him, day in day out, as he tried to work out what to do to bring them back together.

His letter to Rosa, brief and ill-penned as it was, said how much he still wished to see her, and also the "other sister". He asked her to send him news. He hoped she'd understand his meaning. What else could he write without risking trouble for Rosa if, as he feared, her letters were intercepted? If that didn't happen, he could at length write more, but Rosa had to let him know if it was possible or not.

First, though, he'd had to find a way of getting his letters delivered. In winter, there were generally fewer carting journeys and, anyway, John wanted his letters delivered quickly. At length, he decided to ride to Northwick and deliver it himself. Well, not directly. The porter knew him, and he didn't want to risk the prioress discovering he'd been there...

Close to the priory's outer walls were a few meagre cottages, and there he found a lad who, for a coin, was happy to deliver a letter to the priory. John watched from a distance as the boy banged the great door knocker. Shortly, the old porter opened the door and, nodding, took the letter. John let out a sigh. He'd done his best. It was now in the porter's hands − and maybe those of the prioress − whether Sister Rosa ever actually read his words.

It was March before the usual carter had cause once more to make a journey between Northwick and Meonbridge. John happened to have come home for dinner when the man knocked on the door. He answered, as Ma was dishing out the food.

He'd known the carter for several years. He was quite old and grizzled now, but still plying his trade as best he could. John's heart flipped when he saw the man standing outside his door, for there was only one reason he might be there.

'Jakys,' he said, 'what brings you here?'

The man pulled a letter from the purse hanging from his belt, and grinned as he held it out. 'For you, Master Bailiff. One o' the North'ick sisters give it me.'

John took the letter. 'I've been expecting this. Will you step in for a bite to eat? You'd be welcome.' Ma'd never got out of the habit of making enough to feed a family.

But Jakys held up his hand. 'Nay, Master, thank ye kindly. I've a pie waiting for me at the ale-house, and a couple o' mugs of ale.' He grinned again.

'Have you made all your deliveries, then?'

'Oh, yes, I done that first. I left the mare with Roger Stronge for a rub down and a bale o' hay whilst I eat me dinner. Then I got a load to pick up to cart back to the nuns. You got aught for me to take?'

'Not today, Jakys, no, but maybe next time?' He scrabbled inside his own purse for a couple of coins and pressed them into the carter's hand.

The man tipped his hood and walked back down to the ale-house. 'Good day to you, Master Bailiff,' he called. 'Till next time…'

John shut the door and went to sit down at the table, where Ma was waiting for him.

'A letter from Sister Rosa?' she said, her eyes bright in enquiry.

He nodded. 'I'll read it later – or try to. But we mustn't let this good food go cold.' And he picked up his spoon and, plunging it into the bowl of pottage, took several mouthfuls before helping himself to bread. 'It's good, Ma, as always.'

She smiled through mouthfuls of her own. 'We're running low on vegetables, it being March, but I've still got cabbages and kale, and plenty of dried beans.'

'You're still using the last of the flitch of bacon too, I see.' These days, with more money and fewer mouths to feed, Ma could afford to add more meat to her pottages than she used to when he was a child. It made for a tasty meal.

When they'd finished eating, John stood up to go back to work.

'Aren't you going to read your letter?' said Ma, her tone full of anticipation.

'I'll do it later, Ma. You know it'll take me quite a while…'

'I can help,' she said, and he put his arm around her.

'I know you can, Ma, but I'll give it a go myself first.' He gave her shoulder a squeeze, then went to the bench by the door to pull on his boots. It was awkward, this business with Ma. He'd tell her Rosa's news, but not if it concerned Anabella. He had to read the letter first, so he could decide what he would and wouldn't pass on.

But he had no time this afternoon. Lady Day was fast approaching, and soon enough the plough teams would be going out to turn the fallow fields and prepare other fields for sowing. His job now, together with the reeve, was to ensure there were sufficient teams available, both for the demesne's fields and the tenants', the ploughs themselves were in good order, and the beasts and men all fit and ready for the work ahead.

It was much later when he was able to leave the reeve to finish the day's tasks, and retreat to the ale-house. When Ellota Rolfe took over the ale-house from her mother, Ellen, years ago, it was already a thriving establishment, with stabling and rooms for travellers. But it was still a drinking place for Meonbridge folk, and was always busy at the end of the working day. John could have done without the noise and raucous laughter, so he could concentrate on Sister Rosa's letter. But it was better than going home and having Ma hovering at his elbow, wanting to know what it said.

Ellota poured him a cup of her best ale, and he found a table in a reasonably quiet corner. He sat down and withdrew the letter from his purse. He blenched: it was very long.

John had drunk two cups of ale by the time he'd read through all of Rosa's letter. It was hot in the ale-house, for the fire in the hearth was burning fiercely. Yet it wasn't the fire that made John's neck and forehead sweat; it was the effort of trying to read. Sister Rosa's handwriting was neat and clear – much better than his own – but even so, he struggled to make out the words. But he took it slowly and gradually the meaning of what Rosa had to say emerged.

The most important words of course concerned Anabella.

He learned that Rosa talked to Anabella often, and it seemed Anabella was as upset as he was about their separation. How relieved he was to know that. What a relief too that Rosa wrote he wasn't to be concerned about Anabella having to take her final vows soon. "*It occurred to me,*" wrote Rosa, "*you might not know this, but she has to remain a novice for at least two years. As she has been at Northwick for almost exactly a year, it is far too soon for her or you to have to worry about vows.*" Moreover, she said, the prioress seemed to have little interest in Anabella or, indeed, any of the sisters. "*She is more interested in making her own life as comfortable as possible.*"

John grunted. It seemed Rosa didn't like whatever changes the new prioress was making. Did she regret after all not standing in the election? And why had she refused to do so? She'd said it was because Evangelina was bound to win. But was that really the reason? He'd thought before some sort of corruption might have been involved to ensure Evangelina's election, so was it that? Rosa would despise any such dishonesty.

She confirmed what John suspected, that he was no longer welcome at Northwick. If he tried to visit, Rosa wrote, *"Evangelina will refuse you entry, and might even call the constable to arrest you."* John gulped. He was, then, *barred* from Northwick. Would he ever be able to see Anabella again?

But Rosa ended on an encouraging note. Although she didn't know how to help Anabella leave the priory, she promised to continue encouraging her to look forward to a future life *with him*, rather than at Northwick.

How glad he was she'd said that. Yet why would she do such a thing? Why would she want to persuade Anabella to leave Northwick? It seemed curious, but what did he know of nuns? He grinned, drained the last few drops of his ale and set off home.

In a few days it would be Eastertide, and Dickon had sent word he was coming home to Meonbridge for a week or so. Agnes was excited, as she always was, to see her son again. Ma too was looking forward to her grandson's affectionate embrace. Though he'd not spend much time with his Sawyer and atte Wode families. When Lord Dickon came home to Meonbridge, it was to reassure himself his estates were running efficiently and smoothly, and to deal with any problems needing his attention or decisions that were only his to make.

But Dickon would, John was certain, invite the families – *his* families – to the manor house for a feast. As he'd done when he was here for the Christmas festivities a few months ago. John and Ma, Agnes and Jack, and the children, Geoffrey, Alice and Elizabeth, and Matt and his new wife, had all enjoyed several days up at the manor house, joining in the feasting, the dancing and the games. And Dickon had arranged for entertainers to come, just as Lady Margaret had done for Christmases past.

Last Christmas, for the first time, Dickon had invited him and Jack to join the small party of his squires and retainers on a hunting expedition. Neither he nor Jack knew what they were doing with bows and arrows, and didn't try, but they'd enjoyed the horseback chase, and being in at the kill had been exhilarating.

'Want to come another time?' Dickon had asked, as the hunting party all stood around their fallen prey – a fine hart, with a splendid set of antlers – drinking cups of ale.

John responded eagerly but Jack, the man who'd brought Dickon up as if he was his own flesh and blood, ruefully shook his head. 'I enjoyed the day,' he said, 'and thank you for inviting me. But I warrant I'll be suffering for it tomorrow. My old body's not accustomed to such spirited riding.'

'You're hardly old, Pa,' said Dickon, laughing, and John saw the joy that warmed Jack's eyes, hearing his lordship still considered him his father, if not the man who gave him life. 'But I suppose you don't ride so much these days...' He put his arm around Jack's shoulders. 'No matter. You can still enjoy the fruits of our outing: the huntsman will give you and John a good share of the meat, so Ma and Grandma Alice can cook you up a few fine dinners.'

It was on Saint Stephen's Day that Dickon had asked about his aunt. He'd put his enquiry to John, knowing he visited Northwick from time to time to give Rosa and the prioress advice.

John had dissembled for a while. He'd known by then the old prioress, Angelica, had died and Rosa hadn't been elected to replace her. This he did tell Dickon.

Yet he knew too something was awry at Northwick. Something had prevented Rosa from standing for election and Evangelina had won *despite* the nuns of Northwick apparently not liking her. But he did not pass that on to Dickon. Nor even that the new prioress had dismissed him. He'd supposed he'd have to tell him the full story some time, but, then, he wasn't ready.

Now, though, he surely *should* tell Dickon what he knew. Yet he was reluctant to say more whilst his ma was listening in. But, after a late meal, she was looking tired, and Agnes suggested she took her home. Ma agreed but told John he could stay. So, Agnes left, with Ma and the girls, leaving Jack and young Geoffrey to carouse once more with their lord and kinsman. And now too was John's opportunity to say to

Dickon that he thought his aunt was not as happy at Northwick as she once was, though he didn't want to overstate the case or alarm the lad unduly.

As soon as Agnes and Ma had left, he leaned in to his young lord. 'I do have more to tell you about your aunt,' he said.

'More?' said Dickon. 'Has more happened at Northwick, then?'

'Not exactly. It's rather I didn't tell you everything I knew when we spoke on Saint Stephen's Day.'

'You kept something from me?' said Dickon.

John held up his hands. 'I just didn't tell you everything, and now I want to.'

Dickon gestured to the servant to pour more wine into everybody's mazers. 'Go on.'

John took a deep breath. 'What I didn't tell you was Rosa didn't put herself forward for election as prioress—

'Why not?' said Dickon. 'Wasn't she the obvious candidate?'

'She told me there was no point, because the prioress was *always* a Godeffroy – the family that's patronised the priory for eighty years. But I don't think that was the only reason. There's something else, though I don't know what it was...'

'But you have your suspicions?'

'The nun who was elected *was* a Godeffroy... But she wasn't liked at all by the Northwick sisters... So, I've wondered if she won by some sort of corruption? Though I've no way of knowing...'

'What does my aunt think about it all?'

'I'm certain she's not happy. The last time I saw her, she suggested this new prioress might make changes she'd not approve of.'

'What sort of changes?'

'I've no idea, but I think the priory might now be quite different from before.'

Dickon frowned. 'And is my aunt in some sort of jeopardy?'

'Not to her person, I'm sure. But to her serenity and contentment...'

'Can we do anything to help her?'

'I'm not sure what.' He hesitated. 'What I still haven't told you is I no longer visit Northwick. I haven't been since November. The new prioress said my advice wasn't needed any more. But, in a recent letter,

Rosa said I'd be *refused entry* if I tried to visit. I'm no longer welcome there.' He grunted. 'It's one thing to be told your advice isn't needed, but to be *barred...*' He then had an idea. 'But you might be admitted, my lord.'

'Yet what could I say or do?' said Dickon. 'The prioress – liked or not – has total authority over her priory. It is not for me, or anyone outside Northwick, to interfere.'

'You're right, of course.' John drained his mazer. There was nothing they could do.

Yet there was still one thing he'd *not* told Dickon: about his relationship with Anabella. Neither would he. Albeit he did wish he could share it with *someone...* Agnes, perhaps? Would she be sympathetic, or just tell him he was a fool? Either way, he might risk it.

For, before too long, he had to find a way of rescuing Anabella, and he'd welcome help in working out just how.

11

Northwick Priory
May 1366

Rosa was afraid of the changes Evangelina was making at Northwick. She was grief-stricken too, for the whole tenor of the priory was shifting to one where she no longer felt at home or even comfortable. Much of what Mother Angelica had accomplished was unravelling.

She was not alone in her distress. Beatrice and Amata felt as she did, as did Juliana, and Dulcia, and Helen. All were aggrieved by the prioress's actions but, for now, were mostly lying low and getting on with their work – and with their prayers – despite them.

Rosa thought it likely that either Sister Anne or Sister Mariota might also share her views. Or perhaps both did, even though one of them must have voted for Evangelina. For, in whispered conversations, both seemed to rue Evangelina's election, so whichever of them voted for her might now regret her choice. Yet Mariota had been appointed infirmaress in Amata's stead, so perhaps her allegiance might, after all, remain with Evangelina?

Despite her "lying low", Beatrice was privately enraged by what was happening – in particular, Evangelina's overturning of the equality and even-handedness of Mother Angelica's rule. No one in Northwick, including Mother Angelica herself, had enjoyed greater comfort, or nourishment, or privilege, than any of her sisters.

But now the prioress had set herself apart, sleeping always in the great bed with its soft pillows and rich hangings instead of in the dorter. She had gathered around her a coterie of young nuns who fawned upon her and carried out her bidding as if they were her maidservants. Evangelina had also employed a girl to scurry to and fro the kitchens to bring her, and her favourites, food prepared especially for them by her new personal cook.

This last was Beatrice's particular bane, for it impinged upon her role as cellaress. 'It's unforgivable,' she muttered to Rosa, during one of their snatched close encounters in the cloister. 'The prioress is demanding the provision of particular ingredients, and her new cook's required to make special dishes from them. Whilst the rest of us are having to make do with less – less in quantity and in variety.'

Rosa nodded. She had thought the portions of fish the sisters had eaten most Fridays recently were a little reduced in size, and, one Friday, the fish was missing altogether, and replaced by extra pottage. 'Is the prioress requisitioning most of the fish?' she said.

'Indeed. And the wheaten loaves we used to enjoy once in a while – Evangelina has decided only she and her favourites are permitted to eat those now....'

'But why, Beatrice?' said Rosa. 'Is she *punishing* us for some reason?'

'If she is, then I'm baffled as to why. But, no, I think Evangelina simply wants to break free from the frugality and thrift that was always Angelica's way. I believe, Rosa, that you, and certainly I, found Angelica's gentle austerity most fitting to our calling. Our food was plain, but nourishing and not without variety. We were never hungry, and were allowed occasional treats – sweetmeats, the wheaten loves, a little meat. I never found my diet overly restricted. Yet I suspect Evangelina did. You must remember how often she complained – albeit under her breath – of the plainness of the food?'

'I had forgotten, but you are right. She often voiced her dissatisfaction, whilst the other sisters never did.'

They walked slowly and in silence along two sides of the cloister square, as a pair of other strolling sisters caught them up, then passed them. Rosa could see where Beatrice's thoughts were leading. Evangelina had always been disgruntled by her life at Northwick. She had never wanted to come here – Rosa presumed she was sent here more or less against her will – and had hated every moment.

'The other thing that always frustrated Evangelina was attending the offices,' she said, when they were sufficiently distant from other sisters so as not to be overheard. 'You know how often she would shun them—'

'And Mother Angelica didn't often reprimand her. Maybe she thought her niece a lost cause in the matter of piety?'

'Indeed. But now Evangelina is in charge, she can have it her own way, and even *encourage* other sisters to do the same.'

'So do we just accept it,' Beatrice said, 'or do something about it?'

'What can we do?'

Beatrice leaned her head close to Rosa's. '*Rebel!*' she murmured then, leaning back again, laughed lightly.

Rosa gasped. 'Yet how can we? We would be breaking our vows of obedience.'

Beatrice gave another small laugh. 'If we wish Northwick to survive, dear Rosa, that might be *exactly* what we have to do.'

Rosa had surprised herself when she stood up to the prioress so steadfastly over the matter of the dorter roof. It *was* disobedience, and Evangelina evidently thought it so. Yet Rosa simply believed that it was wrong – both practically and fiscally – not to make the best job possible of the roof's repair. If a poor, underfunded job had been done now, it would only have to be done again at some time in the future.

But Evangelina did not appear to understand, or did not want to...

The treasuress, however, agreed with Rosa, but was too frightened to challenge her, given Evangelina's unwillingness to discuss matters with which she did not immediately agree.

'I think,' said Sister Dulcia, 'Mother Evangelina wants to demonstrate how decisive she is.'

But, in Rosa's view, it was sheer pig-headedness. 'Being decisive is all very well, but not if you make the wrong decisions.'

'You're right. But I'm finding it difficult to change the Reverend

Mother's mind about an expense if, in her view, it is unnecessary, even when it most certainly is not.'

'It must be very wearisome.'

'Indeed. Mother Angelica didn't always agree to proposed budgets, but she *was* always willing to discuss them, and offer a compromise if possible.'

'Whereas,' said Rosa, 'her niece will only agree to expenses incurred upon her own behalf?'

Dulcia blushed a little. 'I could scarcely say *that* to her face. Yet I've tried to suggest some such costs might be unwise – the silk for her wimples, for example, or the hiring of her maid – but I'm not as brave as you, and my arguments have been feebly put and thus fallen on deaf ears.' She lowered her eyes.

In truth, Rosa did *not* feel brave at all, but the matter of the roof had irked her, and she was glad to have won the day. But she regretted that her victory was won only at considerable cost. For Evangelina carried out her threat and dismissed Sir Thomas, claiming – most unjustly – he did not have the priory's best interests at heart.

Rosa managed to speak to him before he rode away from Northwick for the last time. He was offended by Evangelina's action, as well he might be, but cheerful enough, nonetheless.

'The new prioress could not be more different from her predecessor,' he said. 'Yet I understand she is Mother Angelica's niece?' Rosa nodded. 'Extraordinary! I did not know. It was always such a pleasure offering advice to dear Angelica, but I am afraid to say, Sister Rosa, it has been anything *but* a pleasure associating with Prioress Evangelina. Indeed, I am relieved she has dismissed me.' He gave her a wry grin.

'Yet you must be aggrieved, Sir Thomas, at the slight upon your character.'

'Oh, indeed I am. To accuse *me*, after all my years of service to Northwick Priory, of acting purely in my own selfish interests – what an insult!'

Especially, Rosa thought but would not mention to Sir Thomas, when Evangelina herself was clearly acting in *her* own interests rather than in Northwick's.

The erstwhile steward held out his hand. 'I regret, however, Sister

Rosa, that you and I have not had the opportunity to become better acquainted.'

Rosa took his proffered hand lightly and held it a moment. 'I too, Sir Thomas. I wonder if the prioress will seek another steward?'

He shook his head. 'She might well try, but I shall be putting it about that she is a lady whose word cannot be trusted. She might have to catch her steward from *much* further afield.'

Rosa pursed her lips. Or Northwick might have to manage without the shrewd and knowledgeable advice that had been such a boon to them over the years...

As she bid him farewell, Rosa sighed. What a fool Evangelina was! First dismissing John, and now Sir Thomas, she was leaving Northwick with none of the expert guidance so essential for ensuring they managed their estates as efficiently as possible. Evangelina herself knew nothing of what was needed on the demesne farm or the wider estate. Although Rosa herself, and Dulcia, and to some extent, also Beatrice, had learned much over the years, none of them was *expert* in all aspects of farming practice.

Yet there was, of course, Rafe Byllynges.

She had not thought about the bailiff for a while. Other matters had been occupying her mind. She reminded herself that it was months ago – before the election – that she had been uneasy about his honesty. It was nothing she could put her finger on: she had no evidence of him stealing or misappropriating goods or funds. She simply felt that Master Byllynges was behaving suspiciously, not always looking her in the eye, and she had begun to wonder whether her initial confidence in him had been misplaced. Back in October, she had intended to talk to John about him, and ask his advice about how to approach the problem. She needed to investigate her suspicions, yet she had no idea at all how she might go about it.

But everything that had happened since October had driven Rafe Byllynges' possible wrongdoings from her mind, and, recently, she had had no occasion to talk to, or even see, him. Anyway, whether he was swindling the priory or not was no longer her concern: that belonged to Sister Clarice.

Rosa debated the matter with herself, whilst she worked in the chapel to get it ready for the next office, replacing a couple of candles that had burned down too low with new ones from the sacristy store.

She recalled when Rafe was first appointed. It had been the bishop's man, Nicholas Foxe, who recommended him to Mother Angelica. There seemed nothing untoward about the proposal. Rosa had been with the prioress when Master Foxe suggested Rafe as a replacement for the old bailiff, who had just been peremptorily dismissed.

Rafe was the son of one of the wealthier villeins who lived and farmed on Northwick's closest manor. 'The boy has received a little education,' said Master Foxe, 'so he can read and write, and understands basic accounting.' Then he had tapped his nose. 'Rafe *is*, shall we say, a little "adventurous" at times, but he is young withal, and, otherwise, most diligent and trustworthy.'

Rosa had no reason to doubt the truth of his words, even though, despite her best Christian efforts, she did not care for Master Foxe. She did not know why. But she thought Mother Angelica did not like him either, for she always acted most strangely in his presence. It was as if she could scarcely bear to speak to him, which was quite out of character for Angelica, who was affable and gracious to everyone. She kept her conversations with him short to the point of curtness, and Rosa had noticed that she rarely met his gaze. Moreover, Angelica had acted much the same with his predecessor...

Rosa would like to have asked the Reverend Mother why she appeared to dislike these bishop's men so much, but it never seemed appropriate to do so. After all, Angelica might have a reason she was unwilling to disclose.

Rosa had met neither man more than two or three times. It was they who organised the bishop's visitations every few years. The last one was three years ago. Master Foxe had also come here last October to explain the arrangements for the election. But, otherwise, he seemed to find little reason to visit Northwick, despite being the bishop's representative, with oversight of the priory and also, she understood, a monastery a few miles to the west.

Had Mother Angelica – tacitly or overtly – discouraged Master Foxe's visits?

Nonetheless, when he heard about the old bailiff's dismissal, he turned up, quite unexpectedly, to recommend his protégé for the post. Rosa's suspicions tingled but, when he introduced Rafe Byllynges to the Reverend Mother and her, she found she rather liked the young man. He was handsome, in a roguish sort of way, but also amiable, polite and even winning, with a ready smile and bright, warm eyes. Indeed, Rafe was not unlike John atte Wode in both appearance and disposition, and she suspected it was that that drew her to him.

How deeply disappointing it would be if Rafe *had* resorted to some sort of wrongdoing against the priory. Why might he have felt the need to do it? As bailiff, he was paid – not a princely sum, but not a pittance either – and the priory provided him with a house, which, for a single man, was more than adequate to his needs. Or was it not sufficient after all?

However, she was thinking ahead of herself. Rafe might *not* be cheating Northwick at all, and she had just imagined the shiftiness in his handsome eyes.

On the other hand, if he *was* being dishonest, the priory needed to know of it. The treasuress most certainly had to be warned.

The next time Rosa was able to speak to Sister Dulcia alone, she mentioned Rafe Byllynges and explained her worries about him.

As she listened, Dulcia's cheeks flushed a little – which Rosa had noticed they did much more often these days – and briefly wrung her hands together. Then she stood up and went to the coffer in which she kept her daily accounts and the priory's great ledgers. She unfastened the lock and raised the lid, then, bending down, she groaned a little as she heaved out one of the hefty volumes in which she recorded all the priory's incomes and outgoings. Carrying it over to her desk, she set it down.

'Come, Rosa, sit by me,' she said. 'I think I might have an answer to your concerns.'

Dulcia turned the pages, leafing back until she reached the entries for last summer. 'The incongruities have been so small,' she said, 'that, each time, I have put them down to an oversight or minor error in accounting.'

'How many times?' said Rosa. 'And what sort of "incongruities"?'

Dulcia blushed again. 'A few times, during Mother Angelica's rule... There were one or two missing accounts for purchases – one for a few items of farming equipment, I recall, and another for nails – so the expenditure recorded was a guess. On the receipts side, on more than one occasion, the income was less than usual for sales of livestock.'

'These were all the bailiff's accounts?' said Rosa, and Dulcia nodded. 'So did you raise them with him?'

'Oh, yes. He seemed embarrassed by the missing paperwork, and, now I think of it, he prevaricated somewhat over the livestock prices. But I simply accepted his explanations. Well, you know how charming he is.'

'You have never mentioned this before to me. Did you tell Mother Angelica?'

'No, and in some ways, I do regret not telling either of you. But Master Byllynges had always seemed reliable, so there was no reason for me to put these apparent incongruities down to anything but mischance. I simply thought them not significant enough to be of great concern.'

'Have there been further instances more recently?'

She bit her bottom lip. 'Several, and one or two *more* significant.' The treasuress's cheeks bloomed red. 'I had not wanted to think badly of Rafe Byllynges but, now, I do wonder if you might be right about him, although I think it would be difficult to *prove* wrongdoing on his part.'

'Yet why might he have felt the need to deceive us? With his salary and his house, is he not tolerably rewarded for his work? Or, if he thought he was not, why not say so?'

'Under Angelica's rule, he was unlikely to have been refused a small increase. Yet he might have assumed the opposite and therefore did not ask...'

'He would certainly be refused it now,' said Rosa.

Dulcia gave a strangled laugh. 'Indeed. I cannot imagine Mother Evangelina would consider the bailiff's salary one of her "necessities".'

'Given she has already dismissed John atte Wode and Sir Thomas,' said Rosa, 'she might think we can manage without a bailiff as well?'

'Oh, surely not! Who'd collect the rents and manage all the sales of our produce and livestock—'

Rosa held up her hands. 'Oh, I am sorry, Dulcia, that was a jest. I did not mean to alarm you. Of course, a bailiff is a necessity. Even if he does not do the job well, we could not manage the estate without him...' She paused. 'So, what do *you* think we should do about the incongruities? It is you and Clarice who must make any such decision.'

'Dear Rosa, could you spare the time to go through the apparent errors with me?' Dulcia said. 'It would be so mortifying to take this to Sister Clarice and then find I had misread the entries.'

'Of course I can. Especially as I imagine Clarice might take it as a personal affront, seeing as it is she who now oversees Master Byllynges' work.'

The treasuress nodded. 'And you can be sure Clarice would pass the information on to the prioress... I'd prefer to have my facts straight before I have to face a quizzing from the Reverend Mother.'

It did not take them long to confirm the errors Dulcia thought she had found, all of which were in Master Byllynges' favour. None of the discrepancies was large but Rosa was disappointed, nonetheless. Rafe was such an amiable young man, it seemed a great pity that he should lose his job. Yet, if he was stealing from the priory, albeit the amounts were small, that could scarcely go unheeded. 'I suppose the prioress will dismiss him.'

'I should think so. Oh dear, yet another man who will be obliged to get used to our ways.'

When, later that afternoon, Dulcia told Sister Clarice and showed her the evidence, the subprioress acted as Rosa had suspected she might, with outrage that the man she had come to like as well as trust had evidently betrayed her.

As she related the conversation to Rosa, Dulcia almost laughed. 'Oh dear, Rosa, you should have witnessed the *resentment* with which Clarice stormed off to find the prioress and apprise her of her bailiff's misdemeanours. It was quite a sight.'

'Was she keen for Master Byllynges to be dismissed?'

'Not really, no. Like us, she was disappointed in him. But I believe she *was* going to counsel dismissal to the prioress.'

'And did the prioress agree to it?'

Dulcia then did allow herself to laugh. 'She didn't. She told Clarice that, as Rafe had been recommended by Nicholas Foxe, she couldn't believe the bailiff's "little oversights", as she put it, were deliberate or malicious. She discounted the oversights as of no consequence.'

'How extraordinary. Evangelina must value Master Foxe's opinions highly.'

'I suppose she must. I don't care for the man myself.'

'Nor I. How surprising if Evangelina does.' Rosa grinned. 'So, Rafe Byllynges keeps his job, *and* his opportunities to carry on deceiving us?' Despite her grin, she could hear her tone was rather sour. 'The benefits of a handsome face and winning smile?'

'But you and I have always liked him, Rosa, and so does Clarice, and the Reverend Mother. However, she did tell Clarice to warn Rafe that discrepancies had been noticed, and he should take care in future to ensure the records he gives me are accurate.'

'I wonder if he will?'

'If he *was* cheating Northwick, he's been given a reprieve. He would be wise to welcome it.'

The following morning the prioress summoned Rosa to her chamber. She sent Sister Letitia to fetch her. Why she had been summoned, Rosa did not know. Was it to do with the concern over Rafe Byllynges? She did not bother to ask Letitia.

The young nun opened the door to the prioress's chamber and, having ushered Rosa inside, withdrew. Evangelina was sitting at her desk and did not look up as Rosa approached. Rosa stood before the desk and waited. The prioress appeared to be reading something, yet neither her head nor her eyes seemed to be moving. At length Rosa cleared her throat and Evangelina sat back in her chair.

'Ah, Sister Rosa,' she said, as if she had not realised she was in the room. She did not invite her to sit. 'I understand you've been interfering in matters that don't concern you.' She lifted an eyebrow.

'I do not think so,' Rosa said. 'To what are you referring?' She could hear the mutiny in her voice, and it shocked her, but she was unwilling to be submissive. Evangelina might be the prioress, yet Rosa found herself unable to owe her any deference or veneration. In truth, it frightened her, this abandonment of one of her most sacred vows. But

Beatrice was right: they had a *duty* to stand up to Evangelina before she brought their beloved priory to ruin.

'The matter of the bailiff, of course,' said Evangelina.

'In what way do you consider I have interfered?' Rosa took care to keep her voice composed.

'The bailiff and his dealings with the priory are no longer your responsibility, but Sister Clarice's.'

'Indeed, that is true, but it was not the case when I first suspected Master Byllynges might be cheating the priory out of some of its goods and income. My suspicions then were not backed up by evidence, so I did not wish to raise them until I had had an opportunity to investigate. But that opportunity never came, with Mother Angelica's death and the election...'

'And exactly how did you propose to *investigate?*' said Evangelina, her voice a sneer.

Rosa thought for a moment. What *had* she planned to do? 'Well, I always was going to speak to Sister Dulcia, to see if she had found any discrepancies in the accounts. But I had also intended to ask John atte Wode for his opinion – he had met Rafe Byllynges more than once, and I thought he might advise me how best to approach the bailiff with my concerns.' She stiffened her back against the sorrow that was welling at the loss of her dialogues with John. 'But, by then, Master atte Wode's wise advice was no longer available—'

At once she realised that mentioning John was a mistake, for Evangelina bristled.

'Wise advice?' she said, the sneer in her voice again. 'Is that what it was? Or did you receive rather *more* from Master atte Wode than merely his advice?'

Rosa's neck grew hot beneath her wimple and she suspected her cheeks had flushed. Whatever was Evangelina implying? But she did not ask, and the prioress said no more about John.

Instead, she returned to her original complaint. 'However, by the time you did raise the matter, it *was* no longer your concern. Yet, for reasons best known to yourself, you chose to meddle. To achieve Master Byllynges' dismissal? Was that your plan?' Her lips were pressed together in a thin line. 'However, Sister Clarice did *investigate*'—her tone was mocking—'and found nothing to perturb her in Master Byllynges' behaviour.'

'But what of the discrepancies in the treasuress's accounts?' burst out Rosa, unable to stop herself.

Evangelina waved her hand in a gesture of dismissal. 'Pah!' she cried. 'Of no significance. Or so little to make it quite absurd to consider dismissing such an excellent bailiff, who performs his duties towards Northwick with such diligence and care.'

In fact, Rosa was glad Rafe Byllynges had kept his job. She just hoped, in future, Clarice and Dulcia, and Beatrice too, could keep any "discrepancies" he might produce under control. These matters *were* no longer her concern, but she doubted she could simply dismiss them from her mind, if Northwick's survival remained at risk.

12

How thankful Agnes was that, whenever Dickon came home to Meonbridge – which was no more than three times a year, at Christmas, Easter and Midsummer – he invited the atte Wodes and the Sawyers to the manor house for a meal and the chance for conversation and the sharing of news. Just like any normal family...

How proud she was of Dickon. Even now, she could scarcely believe such a fine and noble young man was *her* son. Each time he came home, he seemed to have grown; in stature, but also in wisdom, in his awareness of his position as lord of Meonbridge, and in the prowess he was evidently gaining in his life at Steyning. He'd just passed seventeen, and it was four years yet before he'd be ready to be made a knight. Yet to her he seemed already the model of chivalry and nobility. Not that she was biased...

After the feast two weeks ago, to celebrate Midsummer, Jack and Geoffrey had stayed behind – John too – to drink and talk a little more with Dickon, whilst, as usual, Agnes brought Ma and the girls back

118

home. Ma had enjoyed a perfect meal and much laughter with her grandson, but was once more looking tired and needing rest. Agnes was glad, as always, to leave Jack to spend time with the young man he still thought of as his son – and who evidently considered *him* his father. And she was pleased to let Geoffrey get closer to his half-brother, when, as boys, they'd spent so little time together after Dickon was sent away.

When Geoffrey and Jack came home much later that evening, Jack was in no fit state to tell her anything of the conversation that had accompanied their drinking, and anyway it was bed time, and Agnes herself was already half asleep.

But he did tell her about it all next morning.

As usual, there'd been a good deal of revelry and banter, as Dickon told them more about his exploits as a squire at Steyning. Agnes suspected some of the talk was scurrilous, on topics she'd prefer not to know about. But that was fine.

But before the drinking and the revelry had got under way, said Jack, Dickon had asked John if he had any more news of his aunt and what was happening at Northwick Priory.

Last Easter, John had told Dickon that Sister Rosa hadn't been elected prioress, though he didn't know why, and that he was no longer visiting the priory. He'd said too that Rosa thought the new prioress might make unwelcome changes to the priory and, last evening, Jack said, John confirmed that many such changes had taken place.

'But how does he know?' said Agnes.

'Rosa sent him another letter spelling out what's been happening. Apparently, the new prioress is turning Northwick upside down, and Rosa's very unhappy about it all.' Jack frowned. 'John seems gloomy about it too. I do wonder why he cares so much about the priory.'

She agreed that John was quite often glum these days. 'Perhaps he misses his conversations with Rosa?' she said, though surely it couldn't just be that?

Jack had no better explanation. But their conversation prompted her to think more about her brother as she went about her daily chores.

For a while, about this time last year, John had been a *happy* man. She'd noticed how bright his eyes had been and how his face habitually wore a smile. Apparently, he even *sang* occasionally as he rode around the manor on his errands. He never offered to explain his uncommon joyfulness, and of course she didn't ask. But *something* had made him so particularly cheerful, and she'd wondered what it might be.

Yet, only a few months later, he'd changed, falling into despondency, and it hadn't really left him. When had it happened? She thought around the time the new prioress said he was no longer needed at Northwick. So, was it *not going* to the priory that was making him so sullen? Yet she was certain it could have nothing to do with not seeing Rosa. Then, what?

How much she wanted to ask. But John wasn't given to discussing how he felt, though he *had* confided in her in the past – when he was so upset at losing Eleanor. So, he might be glad to do so again, if he was as unsettled as he seemed to be. She'd tread carefully, but thought she might ask him later.

Yet Agnes was also anxious about how the changes at the priory might be affecting Rosa – Johanna, as she still thought of her – if they were as serious as John had suggested.

Out in her potager, she bent to the task of harvesting some early vegetables for the pot: onions and turnips, early cabbages and kale, even a few peas. She filled her basket with what she needed for the midday meal. Then, taking up a smaller basket, she hurried down to the orchard, where more cherries should be ready to be picked.

Being amongst the fruit trees often reminded her of Johanna, for, as girls, they spent long summer days playing in the great orchard belonging to the manor house, picking fruit – not only cherries, but plums and pears and apples – and sometimes making themselves sick.

She and Johanna had once been such friends. They grew up together from babies, playing together at the manor house as their mothers talked and laughed. As they got older, they spent hours talking, sharing confidences and whispering secrets. They were very close, despite the difference in their stations, just as their mothers were.

Having picked enough cherries for today, Agnes sat down on the grass, in the shade of one of the great trees. She sighed, as she often did when she remembered how that closeness came to an abrupt end. When Philip began to look at *her* with a gaze that was no longer brotherly, and asked his sister to persuade her to meet him in secret. Philip was so handsome and charming that, when Johanna suggested it, despite her qualms, Agnes had readily agreed.

Johanna had hinted that Philip's intentions were completely honourable, yet Agnes suspected – *knew* – they would not be, and she was right. The outcome drove a wedge between the girls, and, for a while, between their families.

But what she remembered with most concern was how Johanna *reacted* to the relationship she'd arranged between her best friend and her brother. She became tense and irritable, and Agnes couldn't tell if Johanna was happy with the arrangement or dismayed by it. Yet she didn't think all that much about it at the time, so besotted was she with Philip.

It was only now, when she recalled how often Johanna looked at Philip with adoring puppy eyes, she wondered if she had been *jealous* of her, longing to be in her place... in Philip's bed...

Was *that* why she decided to isolate herself in Northwick Priory? Out of some sort of *guilt*? She'd hinted as much, years ago, the last time Agnes saw her before she left Meonbridge for Northwick.

Yet it was clear now that, as Sister Rosa, Johanna *had* found her vocation at the priory. The few times she returned to Meonbridge, she looked like a woman much at peace with herself. She was also more outgoing and decisive than Agnes could ever recall her being when she was younger. And, not only that; she conveyed a joy that Agnes had not seen in her since she was a little girl.

John had said it was the humility and piety of Northwick that Rosa so much valued. It was those that brought her peace and joy. If all that was now changing, as John said, surely, Rosa must be distressed? Might she be regretting her decision not to stand for election? Or might she be thinking she needed to stand up *against* the changes?

Agnes tried to imagine how Rosa might be feeling, but of course she couldn't. That world of piety wasn't her world, but she could understand if Rosa was grief-stricken, or even angry.

Goodness, such turmoil in a place you'd least expect it!

.   .   .

Agnes didn't have to ask John if he wanted to confide in her. It was only a few days later he decided to tell her the *whole* story about Northwick Priory – the part she'd wondered about but hadn't known.

It was a rare warm day in a rainy summer, and she was waiting for her brother to come home before she left their ma, who, despite the sunny weather, had descended into one of her despondent moods. They, and Lizbet, who came with her often, had spent a good while this afternoon in the garden, tending to the burgeoning vegetables in the potager, but at length Ma complained about her aching leg and said she'd like to rest. When John came back, he found them all sitting on a bench in a shady corner near the house.

John's brow was slick with sweat, and his shirt was soaked through. To Agnes's eyes he was in need of a good wash, a change of clothes and a mug of ale. But, as he approached, his face bore signs of contemplation, and she wondered whether the upheaval at Northwick was still on his mind.

Nonetheless, he gave Ma a smile, and she brightened a little, as she always did when John came home. And he tickled Lizbet under the chin, and pretended to find a cherry stone behind her ear, which made her giggle and skip about. But then John touched her shoulder to calm her down. 'Lizbet,' he said, 'would you like to stay and chat with Grandma Alice a little longer, whilst your ma and me go for a stroll, just down to the orchard and back?'

Agnes caught her daughter's eye and nodded. Lizbet was habitually a helpful child, and she didn't disappoint. 'I'd like to,' she said, 'though Ma and me must go home soon, to make Pa's supper.' Agnes couldn't suppress a laugh.

Even Ma tittered. 'So is it *you* making the supper this evening, Lizbet?'

The girl blushed a little. 'I would, if Ma 'd let me.'

Agnes clicked her tongue. 'You're very good at *helping*, Lizbet, but you know you're too young yet to cook over the fire.' Not that it would be long. Her big sister Alice was now twelve, and often prepared the pottage for the family. 'Anyway, you're right, we'll go home soon. But I daresay your Uncle John needs to stretch his legs a while after a long day on his horse.'

He patted Lizbet's head. 'Promise we won't be long,' he said, and set off down the garden.

Agnes was soon walking alongside. 'I assume you wish to say something to me, brother?'

'It's hard to get you to myself, without Ma or any little ones overhearing.'

'Is it a secret then?'

He shrugged. 'You're the first person I've told. I suspect you can guess it's to do with Northwick?'

And so, it all spilled out. Astonishingly, John had fallen in love, with a woman at the priory. She was a widow who'd sought sanctuary from her husband's brutish family, and was preparing to become a nun. When he first met her, in May last year, she'd just begun working alongside Rosa, interested, apparently, in learning about the management of Northwick's estate. She was with Rosa when John arrived for one of their discussions. By then, John said, Mother Angelica rarely sat in on the conversations, leaving it to Rosa to listen to John's advice and pass on anything she thought the prioress should know.

John looked so happy as he told Agnes of the first time he saw Anabella. 'She came into the chamber with refreshments, and each of us reacted to the sight of the other at the same time. I felt my cheeks flush red, and the tray Anabella was carrying wobbled, making the cups upon it rattle.' He beamed, his eyes brightening for a moment. 'You'll scarce believe it, sister, when I say how instantly I *knew* I'd found her – the woman I wanted to be my wife.'

Agnes suppressed a scoff. 'With a single glance?'

'I know it sounds unlikely. But Anabella felt it too. Or so she told me later.'

'You saw her again?'

'Only twice. As you know, I wasn't going to see Sister Rosa quite so often, not since they hired another bailiff. But, once I'd met Anabella, I couldn't stay away.' He laughed. 'Rosa did know it was *Anabella* I was going to see, rather than her.'

'And she didn't object? How strange, not to say improper, for Rosa to *encourage* you to meet a woman who was preparing to become a nun.' She blinked. Was Rosa – Johanna – really acting the go-between?

Again? Hopefully her motives this time were more honourable than they'd been eighteen years ago. But of course, they would be. Sister Rosa was a very different woman from the unhappy girl who'd wanted to hide herself away in a priory. Not that her intervention this time, however well-intentioned, would necessarily have a happier outcome...

Agnes didn't share these unhelpful thoughts with her brother. He'd come to her for encouragement and advice, so now wasn't the time to put obstacles in the way of his happiness, but to help him find a way of winning it.

'I agree with you,' he said. 'But Rosa said she wanted to see me happy...'

Agnes raised an eyebrow. Was Rosa perhaps trying to *make amends* for the mistakes she'd made all those years ago? Or was she herself making too much of Rosa's motives? 'Anyway, tell me more about Anabella.'

He told her about the death of the woman's husband, and how his family was trying to force her to marry his younger brother. But the brother was a brute; a man she loathed. Somehow, she'd escaped the family's clutches, and Mother Angelica had granted her sanctuary at Northwick. In gratitude, Anabella had agreed to give the fortune she'd received as dower on her husband's death to the priory... 'Apparently,' said John, 'it was the loss of this fortune to the family that particularly aggrieved them.'

Her "fortune"? So, Anabella was no villein. Well, she wouldn't be... Agnes didn't know how priories worked, but understood that nuns came only from wealthy families, like the de Bohuns and, she supposed, that Godeffroy family. Mother Angelica, kind as she apparently was, wouldn't have given refuge to just *any* woman.

Another scoff bubbled on her tongue. Was it likely, then, that a woman of Anabella's station would want to marry a villein like John, albeit he was a bailiff? Would she want to live here, in Meonbridge, in this cottage? For a few moments, Agnes thought the notion was absurd. Yet, if the men in Anabella's wealthy, high-born family were all violent and brutish, a gentle villein such as John might well make a much more appealing husband, regardless of *his* lack of "fortune"...

She stifled the scoff again. She had no reason – or right – to ridicule his plan. She too wanted to see her brother happy.

However, all that aside, was it even possible for Anabella to go back on her arrangement with the old prioress? 'Yet you,' she said, 'and Rosa are actually encouraging Anabella to *renege* on that agreement?'

John's face fell, and it occurred to her that her words had sounded harsh.

'When she fled to Northwick,' he said, 'she were only thinking about escape. Obviously, she'd not imagined then a happier future might one day be possible.'

Agnes nodded, but then she gasped, as she realised that John's relationship with Anabella, with its happy outcome, was perhaps no longer attainable. 'But, John, since you're no longer visiting Northwick, are you still in contact with Anabella?'

He pursed his lips. 'Only through Sister Rosa. We exchange letters, as you know, and she passes news between me and Anabella.'

Agnes frowned. 'Yet how will it be possible for you two to be together now?'

He sighed and the corners of his mouth turned down in the deepest of grimaces. 'I dunno,' he whispered. 'Somehow, I've got to get her out of the priory, but I don't know how...' He rubbed his hand across his beard. 'And that prioress will almost certainly put obstacles in our way, even refuse to let her leave.'

'Can she do that?'

His eyes grew wide. 'Once Anabella's taken her vows, she can. I've been afraid she might be forced to do so quite soon, though Rosa thinks it'll be at least another year... If that's true, I've got time to make a plan.' He ran his fingers through his hair. 'But I've no idea of what such a plan might be.'

'Are you hoping I might come up with one?'

'Not exactly, sis, but if you could think about it too, I'd be grateful.'

The July weather was warm enough but rather wet, yet Ma – despite her melancholy, which came and went – nagged herself into spending as much time in the potager as she could manage, with the help of a couple of cottar women.

Ma still enjoyed her garden, if not quite as much as she used to. These days, she had little else to do but tend her garden and her house, and prepare meals for her son, whereas, before Lady Margaret died, she'd be up at the manor house every week, occasionally to do some sewing but more often just to talk and share a cup of wine and sweetmeats.

More than a year had passed since Dickon's betrothal to Angharad and his grandmother's murder. At first, Ma had been steadfast, wanting to be strong for Dickon, *her* grandson too, and for those of her friends and neighbours for whom her ladyship's violent death was such a dreadful shock.

But, a week or so after her ladyship was laid to rest beside her husband in the tomb inside Saint Peter's, Ma's steadfastness began to fail her. She seemed no longer able to help others with their grief, when her own was so overwhelming she could scarcely bear it.

'It's even worse,' she told Agnes then, 'than when your beloved pa died in the plague. Hard as it might be to imagine.'

Agnes had indeed found it difficult to imagine, when Ma and Pa had been so devoted to each other. Yet the losses in that first plague were so great — nearly half of everyone in Meonbridge — perhaps Ma's grief was tempered simply by being just one of so very many?

But Lady Margaret's death *was* somehow more terrible and shocking. The violence of it, the depravity, the madness. And, for Ma, it was a devastation. Her spirit diminished into melancholy, which hadn't left her since. True, some days she was bright enough and almost garrulous. But then, for days, her sadness overcame her, and although she managed to potter about, carrying out her chores, sometimes working for hours in the garden, she spoke little and her face was long and grey.

Agnes helped Ma in the garden when she could spare the time, which wasn't often, with her family and her own potager to care for. Yet how could she leave her mother to endure her continuing grief alone? So, each day, she'd serve dinner to Jack, Geoffrey, Jack's apprentice and the two journeymen, and the girls, then leave Alice to clear up whilst she walked up the road to her childhood home, just for a brief chat.

But, today, having sent Lizbet to fetch the men from the workshop, she was on the point of dishing out the food when there was a loud knock upon the door. A woman called out in an urgent voice, and Alice ran to the door and opened it. Gillot, one of the women who helped Ma in the garden, was outside, flapping her arms in agitation.

Agnes put down the pot and spoon she was holding and hurried across the room. 'Whatever is the matter, Gillot? Something amiss with Ma?'

The woman had clearly come here at a run, for she was quite out of breath. 'Yes, Missus Sawyer... She's 'ad a fall... a bad one. I sent Betta to fetch Simon Hogge... but I think ye'd best come too, for she ain't looking good...'

Agnes's heart turned over. 'What do you mean, "not looking good"?'

'Broke her leg, I reckon.' Gillot flapped her arms again, and made to leave.

'Go back to her. I'll come.' She took off her apron and gave it to Alice, whose bottom lip was trembling.

'Will Grandma be all right?'

She gave her a quick hug. 'I don't know, sweeting, but I must go to her. Tell your Pa what's happened, and you serve them their dinner.'

Alice put her mother's apron on over her kirtle. 'Can I come up after dinner?'

'Mebbe. But stay here for now and tend to your pa.'

With that, she ran out of the door, and up the road.

Simon Hogge had arrived a few moments before she did. Gillot and Betta had apparently carried Ma in from the garden and laid her upon her bed. Ma was awake but drowsy and saying nothing. Simon looked up as Agnes hovered at the door of the tiny room.

'Ah, Agnes,' he said. 'I've not yet had a chance to properly examine Alice's leg but, from the look of it, I'd say it's broken.'

Gillot and Betta were standing by, their faces creased with worry.

'What happened?' Agnes said.

'We was in the orchard and Missus atte Wode were up a ladder...' said Gillot, chewing at her bottom lip. 'I told 'er she shouldn't do it. Betta or me could've gone up instead—'

Agnes couldn't stop her frustration bursting out. 'Then why *didn't* you? That's what you're there for, to do the jobs Ma can't – or shouldn't – do anymore.' Her voice was raised, and the two women cowered under her fury.

Betta began to weep. Gillot's daughter was barely more than a girl and, for a moment, Agnes was sorry that she'd shouted. She hadn't lost her temper like that in a long while.

She forced herself to calm down. 'Oh, don't cry, Betta. I daresay Ma insisted it was she who climbed the ladder.'

Betta continued to snivel but Gillot nodded. 'She did, missus. I'm sorry now I didn't insist back. But Missus atte Wode can be very…'— she hesitated, as if searching for the right word—'…stubborn.' She grimaced, and Agnes tutted.

'What was she doing up the ladder?'

Gillot chewed her lip again. 'Thinning out the apples…' Her cheeks coloured.

'Oh, Gillot,' said Agnes, shaking her head, 'that's *exactly* the kind of task you and Betta should be doing.'

Gillot's face crumpled too, as Betta leaned her head against her arm, tears tumbling down her face. 'I know it, missus, and I'm sorry…'

'Agnes?' Simon then called out. 'Will you come?'

She whirled away from the unhappy pair and went into the little chamber. 'What do you think, Simon?'

'The leg *is* broken. There's an open wound, but I think the break is clean, so I'm hoping I can set it easily enough.'

Ma gave a little cough and tried to lift her head. Simon hurried forward and gently pushed her shoulders down onto the bed. She let her head fall back. 'Are you going to set it now?' she whispered.

'Soon. But, now you're awake, I'll have to give you some dwale, to ease the pain.'

Ma groaned. 'I remember Margaret falling in her garden…'

'Indeed,' he said. 'Two years ago.'

'She slept for days after you set her leg…'

'Two, I think,' said Simon. 'The body needs rest after such a shock.'

She groaned again. 'You'd best get started. The sooner you do, the sooner I can be on the mend.' She shuddered then, and closed her eyes.

Simon looked at Agnes. 'I'll need your help. Or someone's…'

She winced. 'To stretch the leg?'

'If you don't want to, might Jack oblige?'

'Am I strong enough?'

'Alice herself has helped me several times over the years.'

Agnes knew that, but was she as brave as Ma? Yet how could she refuse? It was scarcely a lot to ask, to help mend her own mother's leg. She agreed, and went to tell Gillot and Betta they could go. 'I'll let you know how Ma gets on.'

Gillot nodded glumly. 'I'm sor—'

Agnes held up her hand. 'I know you are, Gillot. I'm not blaming you for what's happened. Take Betta home now, and get some rest. You've had a shock as well.'

In truth, she *did* think they were to blame, even though Ma could indeed be very "stubborn", as Gillot put it. But there was little point making them more miserable than they were. Ma wouldn't want her to do that.

The women left and, returning to the little chamber, Agnes drew up a stool close to where her ma's head lay, her greying hair, freed now from its wimple, spread out across the pillow. She took her hand, as Simon came to the other side of the bed, holding a flask which she presumed was wine mixed with the poison Simon used to dull the senses of his patients whenever he had to operate upon them.

'The dwale?' she said, and he nodded.

'Can you help her drink it?'

Agnes slid one arm beneath her ma's shoulders and lifted her up high enough to let Simon put the flask to her lips and slowly tip the wine into her mouth. At first Ma spluttered, but gradually began to drink. She turned her eyes to Agnes, and Agnes smiled encouragement.

'Keep going, Ma,' she whispered, as the flask emptied, and her ma's head and shoulders sagged back onto the pillow.

'She's asleep,' Simon said at length. 'We must make haste, to set the leg before she wakes again.'

Agnes gasped. 'Do folk sometimes wake up whilst you're still working?'

'Once only in my own experience. And, in that case, the man was especially stout. I should've given him a lot more dwale.' His forehead puckered. 'Anyway, if you come here'—he pointed to the end of the bed—'you can pull down gently on Alice's foot, whilst I pull the other way and knead the ends of the bones together.'

She did as she was asked. She presumed he'd then fit a splint around the leg. Honey, a bundle of wooden laths and a roll of linen were laid out upon a small table at the side.

'Are you ready?' said the surgeon and she nodded. On his direction, she grimaced and pulled down, whilst he kneaded at Ma's leg, until he was satisfied the bones were straightened. At length, he stood up. 'Done.'

He cleaned the wound with wine and smoothed a little honey gently over it before wrapping a long length of linen round and round the leg. He tied it tightly, then, using the laths and more linen bandaging, constructed the splint.

'Alice will wake up before too long,' he said, 'but I expect her quickly to fall asleep again, and you should let her – encourage her – to sleep. Rest is the best remedy to recovery.'

'Will she ever walk again?' said Agnes.

'D'you remember with her ladyship? It took many weeks – months. She tried to hurry it, but set it back. It takes time and patience.' He gathered his equipment together and put them in his satchel. 'But Lady Margaret *did* walk again, nimbly and without pain, and I see no reason why Alice shouldn't do the same.'

13

Northwick Priory
July 1366

Tears pricked Sister Juliana's eyelids as the psalm's lovely words and cadences tumbled into disarray. Standing in her usual place, so all the sisters could clearly see her guiding gestures, she knew a few were paying her no heed. For their singing, far from offering up to God a beautiful hymn of praise, was a hideous discordant noise.

She was glad when the psalm came to its close, yet what followed was almost worse. The prayer the sisters recited every day was becoming increasingly unintelligible. For, whilst some were intoning the prayer at the appropriate speed and pitch, a few seemed to be chasing through it. But it wasn't just the speed. Juliana could hear syllables of words were being skipped, the customary pauses missed, and even whole sentences ignored, so some of the sisters finished the prayer long before the others. She gently wiped her eyelashes with her fingertips. It was so unseemly, and so irreverent.

And she knew full well who the culprits were.

Two of the young nuns whom Sister Beatrice referred to as the prioress's *acolytes* had been practising a tentative form of this impudence for weeks. But this evening the mockery was manifest. And it was not only those two, but also Sister Gracia who, as mistress of novices, surely should know better? Yet she was scarcely much older than the girls and seemed to have developed an empathy with them. Unsuitably so, in Juliana's view.

Compline at length stuttered to a close, and the sisters filed out of the chapel. Most went sedately and in silence. But the girls, though not Gracia, bustled out, almost pushing past their sisters.

Juliana watched them go. What did they hope to gain by their disrespect? She presumed it was to end the office quickly so they could scurry off, as they were now doing, to whatever diverting pastime awaited them. Yet even they – disrespectful and ill-mannered as they were – had not attempted to escape the chapel *before* the office ended. Did they then hope to *influence* the other sisters to fall into line with them? But that could never happen: Sisters Rosa, Beatrice and Amata, and she herself, would always stand steadfast against it.

Yet, possibly, the girls were simply bored and found their crass behaviour amusing?

As soon as they were beyond the door that led out into the cloister, she heard them explode into foolish giggles. So it *was* just for fun? But it had been going on too long.

Juliana left her station and followed the other nuns. So far, she had kept her views about this to herself, but she was certain Sister Rosa – as well as Beatrice and Amata – would be as aggrieved as she was about the desecration of the holy offices; offices that, under Mother Angelica's rule, had been a source of calm and reverence and beauty.

Sister Rosa was ahead of her, and had almost reached the transept door and the steps that led up to the dorter. Juliana sped up just a little. As she came up behind her on the narrow stairs, she murmured her name, and Rosa turned.

'Juliana! We have not spoken for some days.'

'Indeed,' she whispered, 'but I should like to. Now, or later, as best suits you...'

'Goodness,' Rosa said, 'that sounds serious.'

They reached the dorter and Rosa took Juliana's elbow and drew her to one side, out of the hearing of the other sisters in the chamber.

'Now will suit me well enough, but not here. Shall we go back down into the cloister?'

Juliana nodded, and they took the stairs again.

She recalled then that the two girls had seemed to be heading for the cloister, despite it being the time for all the sisters to retire. But they were nowhere to be seen, and she supposed they had gone to the prioress's chamber for a little more entertainment of one sort or another.

'Do you have something specific you wish to say to me?' Rosa said.

'I do. And I am certain you will not be surprised to learn that it concerns the holy offices.'

'Ah,' said Rosa. 'No, it does not surprise me.' They set off along the first wing of the cloister, walking close together. 'But I shall not pre-empt your concern, albeit I daresay I know the nature of it.'

Juliana took a breath, to calm herself, so she did not seem too overwrought. 'I am certain you will be as distraught as I am about the growing chaos of the offices. Brought about by the... the brazen... the mocking...the *insolent* behaviour of a couple of our younger sisters...' She stopped, and took another breath. Her heart was racing. Her distress was bursting forth, whether she wanted it or not.

Sister Rosa noticed. 'You are upset, dear Juliana. I do of course know why. And I share your anguish.' Turning her face to Juliana's, she nodded encouragement. 'But do go on...'

Juliana poured out her grief at the dishonouring of the offices. 'You must have noticed, Sister Rosa. For a while now, in *all* the offices, a habit has arisen amongst those very few of our sisters for the psalms and readings to be gabbled, presumably to get them over with as fast as possible. They miss out words, or even sentences... And this evening, their behaviour was especially flagrant. You must be only too well aware...'

'I am. Those girls are deliberately defiling the beauty of our devotions. And I agree, just now, it was exceptionally shameless...' She smiled. 'Do you know about the demon Titivillus?'

'Titivillus? No.'

'Then let me tell you of him,' Rosa said, 'to lighten your distress a moment. For it is said that Satan'—Juliana crossed herself—'gave to his demon Titivillus the task of listening in to choirs singing psalms and other holy songs, and collecting together any omitted syllables or words and putting them into a sack. Titivillus was to take his sacksful of omissions to his devilish master to be used as evidence against offenders on the day of judgement. When those girls come at length before Saint Peter to be counted, they might find that what was once a source of merriment was not so amusing after all.'

Juliana laughed lightly. 'So, their habit of gabbling through the holy offices is not new? Others have done it before them?'

'Evidently so, else Titivillus would not have a job!'

They walked in silence for a while, and Juliana's brief gaiety subsided. 'Anyway, I am sure you have noticed too that those girls habitually shirk the night-time offices altogether. With, I think, the prioress's acceptance, or even *encouragement*? Such disrespect of our sacred duties is surely the most intolerable of the prioress's changes.' She exhaled with a shudder. 'It does grieve me deeply...'

Sister Rosa exhaled too. 'Me also.'

'So, are they seeking to *destroy* the sanctity of the offices, or is it merely for their amusement? And what might the prioress's reason be for turning a blind eye, or worse?'

Rosa was silent for several more paces. 'I think, for the girls, it might well be amusement. They might not see it as wickedness. Yet their behaviour has undoubtedly been precipitated, or at least not censured, by the prioress herself.'

Juliana let out a deep sigh. 'But why is she so hostile to what is surely Northwick's most important purpose?'

'Because the prioress has no vocation, and never has had. She was forced to come here as a girl and has always resented it. Piety, humility, modesty – all those good Benedictine virtues, which Angelica always upheld so faithfully – mean nothing at all to Evangelina. Indeed, I think she might *despise* them. She is exulting in her new power to make her life both opulent and fun, in contrast to the humble, ascetic life she no doubt feels she has *endured* most of her life. Relishing her freedom to eschew those aspects of the religious life she has always loathed, such as attending offices, especially those that require her to leave her bed in the middle of the night.'

Juliana gasped. 'Do you *know* she feels that way?'

Rosa smiled. 'Not exactly. Evangelina has always rejected piety and prayer. Mother Angelica told me how much it grieved her.' She sighed. 'I suppose it is inevitable that, now Evangelina is in charge, she will do as she pleases.'

They were silent once more for a dozen or so steps before Juliana spoke again. 'Am I to deduce that the prioress ensured her election *so that* she could make these changes?'

'Indeed,' said Rosa.

Juliana came to a halt, and turned to Sister Rosa. 'Yet surely, Sister, you could have stopped her.' Then she felt her cheeks suddenly flush hot.

But Rosa merely sighed. 'The prioress of Northwick has always been a Godeffroy, and I knew, one way or another, Evangelina, being a Godeffroy, *would* win. Therefore, I decided not to stand.'

'Yet, do you now regret it, now you see what the prioress is doing?' The moment the words were out, she cringed. Why was she being so impertinent? Yet Rosa did not seem to resent her question.

'I suppose, in some ways, I do. For now, we have a problem. We are bound by the rule of obedience to accept whatever the prioress decrees, yet I, and I am sure you, Juliana, cannot bear to acquiesce without complaint. So, what are we to do?'

'You are right, and I do not know. I want to shout my protest from the rooftops, but I do not have the courage, either to break my vows, or to suffer the prioress's rebuke.'

'I too am struggling with the prospect of setting my vows aside. Yet I do believe we – and not only you and I, but Beatrice too, and Amata, and Sister Dulcia – cannot just stand by whilst Northwick's peace and piety are destroyed.'

'Shall we not be able to complain when the bishop's visitation comes to Northwick?'

'Of course, but, if they adhere to their three-year cycle, it will not be until'—she thought a moment—'next April or thereabouts.'

'So should we then complain directly to the prioress?' said Juliana. 'Even if she does not care about the lack of piety on her own account, might she not accept that there are those of us who do?'

'I fear that she might not. The changes she has made seem to be largely for her own benefit, with little concern at all for the welfare of her sisters.' Turning to face Juliana, she took her hands. 'Let me think upon it, and pray. Perhaps God will give me guidance on how we should proceed?'

Sister Beatrice was having difficulty keeping her temper under control. Sister Helen was at her wit's end because the servants were grumbling that they couldn't be in two places at the same time. Yet that was what was being demanded of them. The prioress, as usual, was taking her dinner in her chamber, together with a couple of her *acolytes*, whilst down here in the frater, all the other sisters were awaiting the service of their meal. The servants were running back and forth trying their best to deliver food, from the prioress's new private kitchen to her upstairs chamber, as well as from the main kitchen to the frater.

And, just now, the prioress had had the audacity to send Maria scuttling downstairs to upbraid Sister Helen for not ensuring the food delivered to the chamber was still hot.

In Beatrice's eyes, Sister Maria was a brazen strumpet. Since Evangelina's election, and her invitation to the girl to join the prioress's little coterie, she'd become impossible. Although Maria was the kitcheness and, in principle, subject to *Beatrice's* direction, she no longer bothered even to pretend to have any interest in the frater kitchen and what little attention she did give was only to the staff of the prioress's private one. As a consequence, Sister Helen was now having to spend time dealing with the frater *kitchen* staff – who weren't her responsibility – and her attention was thus spread too thinly over the frater servants, who were.

Which was why the prioress's food had waited overlong to be collected by the servant tasked with carrying it upstairs.

When Maria came to deliver the prioress's accusation, Helen lost her temper in a way Beatrice had never seen before. Helen was the sweetest, mildest, most even-tempered of women, yet being criticised for failing in a duty that wasn't hers was clearly deeply hurtful. She lunged towards Maria, an indignant finger pointing at her face.

'If *you* fulfilled *your* tasks down here instead of drifting around upstairs—' she started, her voice on a rising pitch.

But Maria slapped her pointing finger aside and, her eyes flashing, squared up to Helen. 'How dare you argue against the Reverend Mother's just cause for complaint. Whatever the prioress demands, it's your *duty* to provide!'

Helen burst into tears and ran from the frater.

Beatrice hurried forward. 'Sister Helen's right, Maria. And speaking of "duty", since the prioress's new kitchen was installed, with its *separate* staff, and *separate* food...' she frowned, 'and since you, as kitcheness, are no longer carrying out *your* duties in the frater kitchen, Helen has too much to manage. What you, and the prioress, are demanding of her is unreasonable.'

Maria pouted. 'The Reverend Mother needs me with her in her chamber. I don't have time to deal with *kitchen* staff—' Her eyes glittered with contempt.

Beatrice struggled to maintain her calm. 'But that's your appointed role, Maria. You were given that honour by Mother Angelica and the present prioress hasn't discharged you from it, as far as I'm aware. It follows that, at the dinner hour, your place is here, ensuring the kitchen – the *frater* kitchen – is functioning as it should be.'

Maria pouted again. 'The Reverend Mother needs me—' she whined, but Beatrice held up her hand.

'She doesn't *need* you specifically during dinner. Indeed, it would minimise her complaints if you were here, doing your job, ensuring dinner's served efficiently to *all* the diners in the priory.'

Maria tossed her head and spun around, with as much of a swish of her skirt as a nun's habit would permit. 'I haven't got time for this. Tell Sister Helen to send the food up to the prioress again – and *hot* this time.' And with that she scuttled off, out of the frater and presumably back upstairs to the prioress's chamber.

Beatrice took several long, slow breaths. How liberating it would be simply to release her fury in a scream. But of course, she couldn't. Nuns didn't scream, especially when they were aging cellaresses.

Instead, she went in search of Helen, and found her sitting on the low wall of the arcade that ran around the cloister, leaning her back against the upright of a pointed arch. She was no longer weeping.

'Helen?' said Beatrice, as she approached. 'Have you recovered your serenity?'

She wiped her cheeks with the back of her hand. 'I'm so sorry,

Sister Beatrice, for my unseemly – childish – behaviour. I shall come at once.'

'Unseemly, perhaps,' said Beatrice, with a smile, 'but quite understandable. The situation is intolerable, yet Maria – and I presume also the prioress – seems disinclined to take any steps to ease it.'

'Then we have to make the best of it.' Helen straightened her back, and they hurried back to the frater and the kitchen to restore order, ensure the sisters had their meal, and appease the prioress with a second serving of her food.

It had been chaos – if briefly – but well before the time the bell was rung for the meal's end, order had been restored, and Beatrice and Helen had managed to take a bite themselves.

Before the office of Nones, they had a little time to go through their accounts together, so Beatrice could pay her regular visit to Sister Dulcia for the figures to be entered into the ledger.

Understanding as she knew Dulcia would be, Beatrice wasn't looking forward to this conversation, for her expenses as cellaress had increased considerably in recent weeks. Establishing the separate kitchen and hiring the additional staff had taken money from *her* budget, and the food to be provided for the prioress and her guests was on top of what she regularly bought or sourced for Northwick's sisters. And the prioress's food was different too, more unfamiliar and expensive. The cellaress had always been responsible for supplying food for visitors but, in Angelica's day, visitors were given the same food as the nuns. Whereas, recently, Evangelina had invited a rash of illustrious guests to dine with her, and she sent down lists of special dishes well in advance for her new cook to prepare.

Beatrice was aggrieved greatly by it all. But she was also worried. For, if this excessive spending by the prioress continued, Beatrice would be obliged to cut down what she provided for the sisters. She'd already instructed the kitchen staff to reduce the portions just a little. So far, she thought the sisters hadn't noticed, but if their meals had to be made even smaller, they *would* notice, and would object. Quite rightly so.

Meals in Northwick's frater were never lavish but always more than merely adequate. The gardens and orchard supplied a good quantity of vegetables and fruits, all year round apart from the leanest months of spring. Mother Angelica had insisted that fish be provided more than once a week, and the home farm supplied a little meat. So, the sisters' diet was both varied and nutritious.

But that might soon have to change.

Food the priory couldn't produce itself, like fish and salt and spices, which had to be bought in, might have to be restricted or even omitted altogether. Beatrice patted her belly. She was well aware she ate a little more than she should. But she enjoyed her food – as did the sisters – and what a sorrow it would be if that small pleasure was denied them. Yet she could imagine it might well happen. For if funds to supply the frater grew ever leaner, she might have to consider also limiting the quantity of *home* supplies that contributed to their meals. She'd have to *sell* more than she usually did simply to make a bit of extra income, leaving the frater kitchen short.

After Nones, as the sisters filed out of the chapel, Beatrice caught up with the treasuress and touched her arm. 'Sister Dulcia,' she murmured, 'are you free to talk?'

'Why yes, of course, Beatrice. Now?' Her brow puckered. 'But your face is long. Is our conversation to be gloomy?'

'I fear so, Dulcia. Yet it's a conversation that must be had.'

They strolled together around the cloister towards the tiny chamber that Dulcia had set up as her treasury. In Angelica's day, Dulcia had worked *with* the prioress in her chamber, but Evangelina had apparently decided she didn't want to share her chamber with anyone, and both the treasuress and even the subprioress had to find themselves little spaces elsewhere in the priory, each large enough for a chair, a table and a stool, and, in Dulcia's case, a couple of coffers for the storage of her ledgers.

Beatrice took the stool, as Dulcia sat down at her desk.

'I know what you're going to tell me, Beatrice,' the treasuress said, then, leaning closer, whispered, 'The prioress's changes and demands are running away with your budget.'

'I've brought the figures,' said Beatrice, 'but I'm most unhappy with them. Moreover, I've no idea at all how I can continue to provide what the sisters have become accustomed to, whilst still meeting the prioress's demands. Something will have to change, and it assuredly won't be the prioress's needs that suffer.' She grimaced. 'Imagine me suggesting she cease having so many visitors, or cut down on her consumption of meat and wine and sweetmeats. What response do you think I'd receive? She'd accuse me of failing in my duty, as that strumpet Maria did only hours ago.'

Dulcia laughed but it was evidently neither in amusement nor in scorn but in sympathy for her plight. 'Oh, dear Beatrice, I do understand. As cellaress, you're most affected by the prioress's *adjustments*, shall we say, to Northwick's way of life. You, and Sister Rosa perhaps. She had to wage something of a battle with the prioress over the repairs needed to the dorter roof.'

'Yes, I know of that. Yet, as we all do, Rosa has also had to battle with herself over whether she's willing to break her vows of obedience in order to resist Evangelina's assault upon the priory's precious funds.'

'Goodness, strong words, Beatrice.'

Beatrice coloured slightly, yet she'd no need to be contrite in front of Dulcia. 'Indeed, but young Maria did infuriate me this morning, accusing poor Sister Helen of not doing her duty, when she's in fact worn out by the unfair demands upon her...'

'Especially when Sister Maria herself seems to be neglecting *her* duties as kitcheness...'

'You've heard of that?'

'Sister Helen divulged it to me recently – in the quietest of whispers, I can assure you.' She smiled wryly.

'Poor Helen,' Beatrice said, shaking her head. 'Yet I think she and I can come to a satisfactory arrangement if we think and pray upon the matter. But no amount of thought or prayer will put extra pennies in my coffers.'

'What are you thinking?'

Beatrice told her of her proposal to buy in less food and to restrict the amount of home produce sent to the frater kitchen. Also to sell more of what the priory's estate produced in order to earn a little extra income. 'It'll grieve me greatly if our sisters can't benefit fully from the excellent output from our farm and gardens, but I see no other solution.'

'You're not practising these limitations yet?' Dulcia flushed slightly.

'For I've fancied recently the portions of some of our dishes are a little smaller than they used to be...'

Beatrice groaned. 'Oh dear, Dulcia, I was sure *someone* would notice before too long. It doesn't surprise me that it's you.'

'But so far the reduction has been small, whereas you're saying you think the sisters will soon have to manage with a much greater restriction in their diet?' Beatrice nodded. 'Mother Angelica would be so disappointed.'

'That's what I've been thinking. Angelica always insisted upon good food, and enough of it, if no more than necessary for the health and well-being of our sisters, and our ability to work and pray.'

'And she was right. Whilst I fear our new prioress isn't much interested in our sisters' health, nor our ability to pray.' She frowned. 'Yet I'm baffled by her attitude. If we continue down the path she's laying, Northwick will, at length, tumble into ruin. We've by no means *yet* reached that parlous state, but I can see it happening in, say, less than a year.'

'So, what should we do?'

Dulcia shrugged. 'As you rightly say, our vows make it difficult for us to confront the prioress, or to criticise her actions.'

'I wonder if Sister Rosa might be willing? She's already tackled Evangelina once. She might be disposed to try again.'

***

Sister Amata was stumbling a little as she and Sister Rosa took their after-dinner stroll around the cloister. Some days Amata felt in need of someone else's support, and today she'd tucked her arm firmly into Rosa's and was leaning heavily against her. It wasn't that she felt unwell, or even that she was in pain. Her left hip did hurt a little, and made her unsteady. But it was more that her *heart* was aching at the changes wrought at Northwick since Evangelina became its prioress.

She was particularly offended by the air of "fun" that seemed to be pervading Northwick, albeit only for the prioress and her favourites, but to the detriment of those sisters who considered their priory to be a house of prayer and not of bawdry.

In truth, the depth of her outrage surprised her, for Amata *wasn't* someone who disparaged joy. Indeed, she delighted in laughter, when it was merry and innocuous. Unlike the Evangelina she'd known for more than thirty years, right up until last November: a woman who hardly ever smiled, let alone laughed, whose face was always long, whose words were often harsh or hostile, as if she found no pleasure in her life at all. How odd then that such a profoundly austere woman was now embracing *jollity*, in the company of three young nuns, two of whom, in Amata's view, were determined *only* to have fun.

In some ways Amata felt sorry for the girls. Perhaps they sought amusement so desperately in order to mask their disappointment with the lives they'd been forced to live? She herself had come to Northwick as a child. She hadn't *chosen* to become a nun, yet she was willing to accept her fate. She learned to find peace and comfort in the rhythms of the religious life. Was it just her nature? For she was biddable, and had learned to find pleasure in simple things.

But she'd always had Angelica to help her...

Yet so had Evangelina, although hadn't she refused to *let* her aunt help her adapt to priory life? She resented from the start what she considered her incarceration and seemingly allowed herself to grow more aggrieved as time went by. But now she was in charge, she could run Northwick exactly to suit herself. Loathing piety and prayer, and eager to break free from any hint of humility, it seemed inevitable she'd try to make Northwick the sort of place she believed she'd been deprived of all her life.

As for her acolytes, as Beatrice called them, they were all young women of marriageable age when they came to Northwick. She presumed they'd failed to make a marriage, or their fathers had run out of money for their dowries. It was common enough for younger aristocratic daughters: if, for whatever reason, marriage wasn't possible, becoming a nun was invariably the only other option.

Nonetheless they weren't dour like Evangelina had been. Well, Letitia was a little gloomy at times, or maybe just more serious-minded than the others. Amata thought she might make a contented nun, if only she'd permit herself, though under Evangelina's tutelage that seemed unlikely.

But Maria and Felicia were flibbertigibbets, for whom fun and laughter – and, now, dogs – filled their days, whether or not it was fitting in a house of prayer. It was they who walked the dogs – Letitia apparently wasn't interested – squealing and giggling at the creatures' antics, which in their eyes could do no wrong.

Just as Amata was thinking about the dogs, two of them rushed forward and, yapping wildly, hurled themselves against her skirts. Crying out, she tottered sideways and fell against Rosa. But Rosa was strong and steady and helped her upright. Then, supporting her with one hand, she flapped furiously with the other at the dogs.

Felicia hurried forward. 'Duchess! Duke! Do leave poor Sister Amata alone...'

The animals took no notice, continuing to paw at Amata's skirt. Then one of them closed its little teeth over the hem and, snarling, began to tug, its tail wagging in excitement. Small as the dog was, it was surprisingly strong, threatening to pull Amata over.

Rosa tutted and, letting go of Amata, lunged forward. She thrust one dog out of the way, and grasped the other by the scruff of its neck, as it tried to cling onto Amata's habit. But its jaw opened and the fabric fell away, and Rosa let the dog drop to the ground.

'Sister Felicia,' she said, glaring, 'you should keep these animals under better control. They are a menace dashing about the cloister, getting under everyone's feet.'

Felicia had the grace to look sheepish. 'I'm *so* sorry, Sister Rosa. But sweet Duchess is *so* naughty, always scampering off, wanting to get into mischief.'

'Then you should keep her on the leash,' said Rosa. 'It is not good enough to blame the dog. They are your responsibility, and *you* would have been at fault if Sister Amata had been unbalanced and fallen over.'

Felicia bent down and attached a leash to each dog's collar then, dropping a diminutive curtsey, she scurried off.

'Thank you, Rosa dear, for rescuing me,' said Amata with a grin. 'I do quite like dogs, and those little creatures are so pretty with their soft white fur and fluffy ears...'

Rosa took Amata's arm again and they continued walking. 'They might *look* charming enough, but having them scampering about the cloister disturbs the sisters' tranquillity. This is not the first time I have seen a sister almost tumbled off her feet.'

Nor was it the first time Amata had had a dog encounter.

A week ago or so, she and Sister Anne had been walking to the chapel for Vespers, when all three dogs raced up behind them and then dashed past. Felicia ran on after them, but as Maria tried to follow, Anne caught her by the sleeve. Her eyes were glaring.

'Sister Maria!' she hissed, evidently trying to keep her voice low in the vicinity of the chapel. 'It's unseemly to allow those dogs to rush about the priory unsupervised, and especially near the chapel.'

In response, Maria pouted and glared back. 'The Reverend Mother has no complaints,' she said, and declared that Anne had no sense of fun. Unsurprisingly, Anne was incensed by the girl's insolence.

'But a priory isn't a place of *fun*, Maria,' she retorted, clearly trying to rein in her anger. 'Why don't you understand that?'

After Maria stomped off after Felicia, Anne took Amata's arm again. 'Those dogs are the final provocation,' she said. 'What was the prioress thinking of, bringing *animals* into our sanctuary?'

'They *are* quite charming,' Amata said, but Anne vigorously shook her head.

'Charming! I don't think so. They leave little... *piles*'—she wrinkled her nose—'in all sorts of places, in hidden corners. Including in the dorter. And of course, those silly girls don't clean up after them, so the servants have been grumbling...'

Amata tutted with distaste. 'I'm not surprised. I know I'm not the only one to have noticed little drifts of fur beneath our beds. But how horrible to find something so much worse...'

She told Rosa about that incident, and Rosa frowned. 'I agree with Sister Anne. A priory is not a playground for small dogs.'

'Yet, Maria suggested the prioress was *happy* to have them running about the place.'

'Well, she did buy them.' Rosa tilted her head. 'Extraordinary, really.'

'Indeed. Who'd have thought a woman could alter her disposition so completely, and at her age! Everything she does now is for pleasure,' Amata went on. 'There's often laughter and squealing coming from her chamber. And so many visitors, Rosa, it's so unseemly! I know Mother Angelica did occasionally invite important visitors to her chamber, but she'd never entertain them there alone...'

'No, indeed. It was often I who chaperoned her. There was never feasting and drinking, just a modest meal – the same, more or less, as was being served in the frater. Also, little merriment, but rather whatever thoughtful conversation the visitor had come for.'

'Yet Evangelina often entertains her visitors *alone*. And again, it's the sound of banter and amusement that emerges from the chamber, not the hum of serious debate.'

'Oh, I am sure Evangelina does not engage in sober conversations with her visitors. For, she never passes on any outcomes to Sister Dulcia, or Beatrice or me, as she would have to if, for example, expenditure on building works was agreed.' Rosa frowned. 'It is evident that Evangelina has no intention at all of improving the fabric of the priory, but is exploiting Northwick and its funds simply for her own advantage.'

'So, what is to be done? Surely, Rosa, it can't go on?'

14

Northwick Priory
July 1366

Rosa felt defiance bubbling up inside her. The conversations she had had with Juliana about the defilement of the holy offices, and with Amata about Northwick's decline into a place of entertainment, had intensified her own anguish, and her enmity towards Evangelina's changes. Then Beatrice had told her about the prioress's misappropriation of funds for her own use. 'Dulcia has agreed,' she said, 'it can't go on for ever, though we are not, apparently, at *immediate* risk of ruin.'

Rosa had already stood up to Evangelina about the dorter roof, and her concerns about the bailiff. Now, she felt driven to assert herself, to ensure that *all* the sisters' criticisms reached Evangelina's ears.

Beatrice urged her on. Although she had no suggestions for how to make it happen.

But could *she* assert herself? Could she go to Evangelina and enumerate all the complaints against her? Was she bold enough to do that? Yet an alternative occurred to her: could she speak *loudly* and more *overtly* about all these matters with the other sisters, instead of merely whispering them in private? She liked the idea. She would not have to confront Evangelina directly, but could be confident that Letitia, who was forever following her about, would listen in on such conversations and report them back.

For a while, she found herself impatient to *fight back* – a notion she could scarcely believe she was associating with herself. Yet how could she, of all people, launch a rebellion against her superior? What of her sacred vows?

Perhaps speaking out would not break them? Besides, was this not more *important* than her vows? God would understand... For such disobedience would be *serving* Northwick, whereas Evangelina was *destroying* it...

Over the next few days, Rosa reiterated with other sisters the conversations she had already had with Juliana, Amata and Beatrice. But now she let her voice ring out loud and clear. The other sisters knew what she was doing – and why – and, whilst not quite as bold as she, they also aired their opinions well above a whisper. Wanting to be sure she was overheard by Evangelina's spies, Rosa repeated the conversations several times, varying her words each time to suggest the exchanges were spontaneous.

She expected the prioress soon to summon her, as she had before, to reprimand her for spreading what she might well designate as "lies". But days passed and no such summons came. Had Letitia not been following her after all? That seemed unlikely, and Rosa was sure she had noticed her lurking behind an arras in the frater, and dipping in and out of the arches of the cloister.

Two weeks passed, and still the prioress ignored her. Beatrice had come to her several times, asking if she had been hauled before Evangelina for a reprimand. But the answer was always no.

'I do not understand it,' Rosa said. 'I am sure Letitia would have overheard at least one or two of our conversations. Has she not mentioned them to the prioress?'

Beatrice shrugged. 'Or has Evangelina chosen to ignore them?

After all, she is in charge, so she might not be troubled by our complaints.'

Rosa frowned. Could that be it?

Evangelina *might* well now feel indomitable. Yet, in fact, her support in Northwick was scarcely strong. Her election had been won only with the votes of the two ancients, Mildryth and Katerina, both of whom were now barely part of the priory at all, shut away in the lodgings set aside for corrodians. The prioress's backing day-to-day came principally from her three young favourites, together with Sisters Gracia and Clarice. And also, regrettably, Mariota, who, according to Beatrice, still felt bound by obedience to Evangelina.

Indeed, *obedience* was Evangelina's weapon. The Benedictine rule required sisters to give wholehearted, *unreserved* submission to their superior, regardless of whether or not they liked or approved of her commands.

Not to submit was unthinkable. For forty years, the sisters' willingness to obey had not been much tested. Mother Angelica's demands were at least acceptable, if not *always* entirely welcomed. But how very different it was now.

Rosa sighed. What was she to do? Nothing? Get on with her work, go to chapel, and let matters take whatever course they would?

Or perhaps have *more* loud conversations? Or even go directly to Evangelina and complain...

She could not decide. Despite her earlier impatience and rebelliousness, *now* she did not know how far she was truly willing to compromise her vows...

Rosa engaged in no more conversations – loud or quiet – with the other sisters, but prayed a lot, and continued privately to question her own motives. Days passed but, at length, she realised the time *had* come, and she readied herself for confrontation.

Yet, the very morning she was planning to present herself before the prioress, Anabella sought her out. It was well after Terce, not long until dinner. Most sisters were still about their daily tasks, and Rosa was in the sacristy. It was there Anabella found her. She was quite breathless when, knocking fleetingly upon the door, she at once pushed it open and stepped inside.

'Goodness, Anabella,' said Rosa, 'whatever is the matter? You look upset.'

Anabella sank onto the stool. 'I am. Because of what I have just heard.'

'What? From whom?'

Anabella took a couple of deep breaths. 'I have just come from the novices' chamber. Sister Gracia has me read to the children, or teach them singing, or their letters. She says it is good training for me for when I take my vows and am appointed an obedientiary.'

'Take your vows? Is she suggesting you might take them soon?'

'Oh, I do not think so. More justifying *me* teaching the little novices instead of her.'

Rosa shook her head. 'Sister Gracia was not the ideal choice for mistress of novices, but when there are so few of us...'

'Indeed, but that is not what I came to say. For Letitia was there too. Why, I do not know. But, whilst I was reading with the little girls, she and Gracia were gossiping.'

'About what?'

Anabella's eyes grew wide. 'About *you*, Sister!' She wrung her hands together. 'I could not believe what I was hearing.'

'Tell me.'

Anabella flushed and stared at her fidgeting hands. 'I had to tell you,' she whispered. 'Yet, now I am here, I am not sure I can bear to...'

Rosa's neck grew a little warm and she flapped the edge of her wimple. She was not sure she wanted to hear it, yet she had to know. Despite her fears, she attempted to make light of it. 'Well, you are here now, so why not tell me?'

'It was Letitia who said it,' Anabella continued. 'She did not even try to keep her awful comments quiet. Indeed, I am sure she *intended* me to overhear...'

Ah, so had Evangelina put Letitia up to this, whatever it was? 'Go on,' said Rosa.

'At first, I thought what she was saying was just light-hearted gossip... Because she asked Gracia if she knew that, when you, Sister Rosa, first came to Northwick, you called yourself *Dolorosa*. "Do you know it means sorrow?" Letitia said, and Gracia nodded. "Anyway," Letitia went on, "apparently, Rosa said *sorrow* was a fitting name because she had to spend her life thenceforward *atoning for her sins.*" She sniggered at the word "sins", as if it was amusing.'

'What was Gracia's reply?'

'She just said "But her name's Rosa." And Letitia told her Mother Angelica persuaded you to change it.'

'That is true. I *was* called Dolorosa, and dear Angelica did encourage me to give it up. I am glad she did.' She smiled, but was apprehensive about what else Anabella might have to tell.

Her face crumpled as she continued. 'Gracia then asked Letitia, "What sin could Sister Rosa, of all people, have to atone for?", then added, "Apparently she was so ashamed by what she'd done, she could no longer bear to live a normal life."'

Nausea rose in Rosa's throat. What *did* Evangelina know? She leaned forward to take one of Anabella's restless hands. 'Is there more?' she whispered.

'Well, they speculated about what your sin might be. Letitia suggested envy, and Gracia said pride. But then, as one, they squealed and cried out "lust", and collapsed into hysterical giggles.' She shuddered. 'Oh, Sister Rosa, I was mortified to have overheard it.'

At length, Rosa thanked Anabella for having the courage to tell her what she had heard. She admitted nothing, but neither did she deny that any of it was true. Yet, when Anabella left, she collapsed back into the chair, her heart thumping with agitation. Had Evangelina *prompted* Letitia to gossip about her like this? To stop her attempting to rebel?

Rosa's defiance bubbled up again. How outrageous that Evangelina should try to *intimidate* her into submission.

Yet the defiance dwindled soon enough, and apprehension took over once again when, the next day, both Beatrice and Amata spoke to her separately, with a similar story to Anabella's.

The gossipmonger this time was not Letitia but Maria, and she had apparently shared her story not just with Evangelina's cronies, but also with Anne and Helen. Rosa cringed: was Evangelina attempting now to turn her *friends* against her?

Beatrice had overheard Maria's exchange with Sister Helen, for it happened in the frater, just before dinner. Unusually, Maria had been in the kitchen, supposedly supervising the preparation of the sisters' meal. When she came back into the frater, she drew Helen to one side, as if to share a confidence. Yet she did not whisper in her ear. Instead, she spoke more than loudly enough for Beatrice easily to hear.

Helen had been horrified by Maria's suggestion that Rosa had committed a sin. 'What sort of sin?' she cried.

Maria had shrugged. 'Pride? Envy?' Then she sniggered. 'Lust?'

Helen gasped. 'That's unthinkable, Maria. Sister Rosa is the kindest, most humble and chaste person I can imagine.'

Maria pouted. 'Maybe *now*, but was she always?'

'Helen seemed to falter at that suggestion,' said Beatrice to Rosa now, 'so, later, when we were alone, I told her she should ignore Maria's lies. That what the little strumpet said couldn't possibly be true...'

'Yet I *did* come to Northwick, Beatrice, believing firmly that I needed to atone for my sins...'

She scoffed. 'Your *sins*? I don't believe it.'

'But *I* most certainly *did* believe that I was guilty.'

Beatrice, bless her, did not ask for details. 'Yet how could *Maria* have come by such knowledge?' she said instead.

'From Evangelina, I imagine. How *she* came by it, however, I do not know. But I first learned she knew something of it last October...'

'Before the election? Was *that* why you didn't stand? Because she threatened to say all of this?'

Rosa nodded sadly. 'Now she is saying it again, albeit through the mouthpiece of her favourites. She wants to stop me criticising her.'

'She must consider you a threat.'

She agreed. At which, Beatrice said they should step up their rebellion. Although Beatrice did not know the full truth of her story, whereas Rosa worried that Evangelina might go further and reveal *everything*. If, of course, she did know "everything". Yet Rosa was certain only Angelica had known the whole story, and was even more certain she would not have divulged her secret to anyone, let alone to Evangelina.

However, she was not, after all, quite brave enough to take the risk.

'No, Beatrice, much as I should like to, I am not yet ready for rebellion after all.'

. . .

Days after Evangelina had set her favourites to discomfit Rosa, Anabella came to Rosa again, in an even greater panic than before.

'I have had a quarrel with Sister Gracia,' she said. 'She repeated what Letitia said the other day, and insisted I tell her what I thought.' Her fingers plucked at her skirt again. '"How can you believe that?" I retorted. "It makes no sense!"'

Rosa quailed a little inside but tried to keep her expression neutral. 'What was Gracia's response?'

'She took offence at me questioning her judgement. Then what she said threw me into a panic...'

'What was that?'

Her eyes widened. 'She said it was time I took my final vows. "The prioress is keen for you to commit to Northwick," she said.' Anabella's dark eyes grew even wider. 'I am afraid now she might force me...'

Rosa frowned. 'She *might* have expressed such a view to Sister Gracia, but I doubt it. It sounds to me as if Gracia was bullying you.'

'But why would she do that?'

'Well, understandably, the prioress *must* be keen for your generous gift to remain in Northwick's coffers, and once you take your final vows, it will be safe. Until then, there is always the chance you might change your mind. Gracia undoubtedly knows that and was urging you to commit in order to gain Evangelina's favour.'

'But why try to push me into a decision *now*? Do you think the prioress knows about John?'

'How could she? Even if she somehow knew you were in my chamber at the same time as John, why would she construe you were there for any reason other than as my chaperone?'

Anabella gave a feeble grin. 'I suppose you may be right.'

'Anyway, as regards you being pushed to make your vows... You have been here only a little over a year. It usually takes two or even three years before a novice makes her final vows, so you should not be *pressed* into it for a while yet.'

'Yet Gracia said, as I was not a *young* novice, I could take my final vows much sooner if I wished.'

Rosa pursed her lips: she had not thought of that. 'Yes, that may be true. Yet you must not let yourself be bullied. I assume from your agitation you *are* having doubts about committing to the religious life?'

Anabella's cheeks grew pink. 'I am afraid I am. It is many months since I last saw John, yet I think about him every day... How I do now regret being less than encouraging the last time we spoke, that last day he came to Northwick. At the time I was reluctant to renege on the arrangement I had made with Mother Angelica.'

'But Mother Angelica is no longer here, and Northwick is no longer the haven of peace and refuge you thought you had fled to.' She pressed her lips together. 'In truth, Anabella, even if you *do* feel guilty about defaulting on your gift, I think you should do what is right for *you*, not Northwick.'

How peculiar it was that she should be saying such a thing...

Anabella cast her eyes down. 'I *do* feel uncomfortable about it. Yet, despite my short acquaintance with John, I do believe most strongly I could find happiness as his wife. Greater happiness than I might find as a nun.' She looked up again with anguished eyes. 'Is that very deceitful of me?'

'Not deceitful, no. When you came here, you were in a panic to escape your husband's family. You could never have imagined that, only a short while later, you might meet a man who could be the husband you always hoped for.'

'You are very understanding.'

'I have told you of my relationship with John, that I think of him as a sort of cousin, or even brother. I care about him, and am keen for him to find happiness with a wife and family, if such were possible.' She leaned forward to touch Anabella's still restless hands. 'I am also very fond of you, and wish you too to find contentment in the life you have ahead of you. I do recognise you might well not find that in the religious life. So, committing yourself to it if you have the chance of an alternative future that might suit you better, would be unwise, or even wrong.'

'Thank you,' whispered Anabella. 'Yet, how do I tell John of my decision?'

'Be patient. John and I have been exchanging letters. I shall tell him what you have said...' She smiled. 'The prioress does not seem to have thought of censoring letters, or preventing their passage to and fro, so, for a while at least, I can continue to communicate with John.'

Anabella returned the smile, if wanly. 'Thank you so much, dear

Sister Rosa.' Then she chewed her bottom lip, as if she was thinking what else to say. At length, she murmured, 'Did you ever have the chance of an alternative future, or was this always what you wanted?'

'Not *always*. For a while, I did imagine myself with a husband and some children. Indeed, my father found me a suitor, but he was not right for me.' She would not explain what happened with Sir Giles. 'But, later, I *chose* to come to Northwick. I came to realise that becoming a bride of Christ instead of the wife of some worldly man *was* in fact what I desired. My choice has most definitely proved right for me.'

Anabella looked up, her mouth twisted with unease. 'So why did Letitia say you came to Northwick to atone for some dreadful sin?'

'I shall not explain the details,' said Rosa, wondering how much to say. 'But I *was* most unhappy before I came here. My choice to come was indeed made partly so I could atone for sins I believed I had committed as a girl. But work, prayer and Mother Angelica's compassion were my salvation, and I threw off my despair much more swiftly than I could ever have imagined. The regret and melancholy of my girlhood passed away, not because I forgot about them but because I found *purpose* in my life.'

'Yet now, all that past sadness is being raked up again.' Anabella shook her head. 'But why?'

'To ensure I keep my criticisms of the prioress's changes here at Northwick to myself.'

15

NORTHWICK PRIORY
AUGUST 1366

Felicia always accompanied the subprioress whenever she had occasion to meet Rafe Byllynges. After Sister Clarice's first meeting with the bailiff, back in April, when Felicia and Mother Evangelina went with her, Felicia had asked if she might thereafter go with Clarice every time.

'I'd love to learn how the manor farm is run,' she said, and Sister Clarice had looked astonished.

'Are you *really* interested in farming, girl?' she said. 'It does seem most unlikely.'

The prioress had smirked. 'Yet perhaps Felicia needs a new interest? After all, she doesn't have a special role at Northwick...'

Felicia nodded eagerly. 'Oh, yes, yes, Reverend Mother. Please let me.'

The subprioress shrugged, and Felicia imagined she knew well enough the real reason for her sudden interest in seeing Rafe more often. 'Very well, Reverend Mother,' said Clarice, 'I agree. In truth, I do not care for being alone with a man who is not a priest, and will be glad of Sister Felicia's company.'

Since then, Felicia had gazed upon Rafe Byllynges' face many times. He always let his eyes linger upon her a little longer than he should have, if only when the subprioress's gaze was elsewhere. Felicia permitted her eyelashes to flutter as she looked away, to signal her appreciation of his attention, yet not to appear too eager. Nonetheless, each time her heart did a little flip, and her neck grew warm beneath her wimple.

She had thought him handsome from the moment she first saw him. But, recently, mere admiration had become desire.

She and Sister Clarice were stepping through the gate in the potager wall and saw Rafe waiting for them a few yards away. At that moment, the sun burst forth from behind the clouds, its brilliant rays lighting up his face, already burnished brown from his outdoor life. Then, as he took off his hood, and bowed his head in greeting, his hair gleamed gold in the dazzling light.

Felicia had gasped. How like her own hair his was: the colour of rich butter, though his was much wilder than hers. When she was a girl, she had been so proud of her long yellow tresses. They had been the envy of her two older sisters, who both had dull brown hair. She loved to wear it loose, decorated with just a ribbon or a garland of little flowers, whilst her sisters wore theirs wound into modest plaits. When the time came for her to marry, she would of course have to hide her hair under some sort of headdress, in public anyway, but she still imagined letting it fall free for her husband to enjoy...

What a dreadful shock she had had when she learned that her father's sudden, unexpected penury meant she would never even *have* a husband to admire her hair. Worse, given no other option than to become a nun, she was grief-stricken when she was required to have her lovely hair hacked off.

She had cried piteously when the sister came to cut it, and ran off to beg Mother Angelica to spare her. The prioress expressed regret, but shook her head. 'As Christ's brides, Felicia, we willingly accept the loss of our hair as a mark of our chastity and our humility, and our commitment to the holy life.'

Yet Felicia had not stopped sobbing, even as she most *un*willingly surrendered to the sister's shears and watched her beautiful curls fall in great swathes onto the floor. She wept all that night too, soaking her pillow, her sheet and her pallet. But, the next morning, Sister Gracia, the novice mistress, had taken her aside and told her sternly the crying had to cease.

'In two days, Felicia,' she said, 'you will be taking your final vows. Thenceforward, your head will be covered by a wimple and a veil. Why would you even *want* long hair? It'd be *so* uncomfortable and hot, crushed inside a coif. Short hair is so much easier to manage.'

Be that as it might, Felicia had been heartbroken at being shorn so brutally of her crowning glory, and was determined to recover it. Ever since that upsetting day, she'd quietly allowed her hair to grow, and managed to give the slip to the sister with the shears. Her hair wasn't *really* long, but, if she took off her coif there was enough of it to fall almost to her shoulders. Enough for a man to run his fingers through and lift it to his lips to kiss...

As Felicia had gazed upon Rafe's golden hair, and the handsome face beneath it, the very thought of him kissing *her* hair, and her neck, and then her lips, made her tremble and feel a little faint. And at that moment she resolved that, somehow, she simply *had* to find a way to meet him on her own.

Arranging the tryst had demanded all of Felicia's cunning. How could she slip Rafe a message without Sister Clarice noticing? Moreover, although she knew Rafe could read, her own skills barely ran to writing a coherent message.

Nonetheless, a few days later, when the Reverend Mother was away from her chamber, leaving Felicia alone, she found a scrap of paper and a quill and quickly sketched a setting sun, a ringing bell, a rough plan of the courtyard behind the priory and an arrow over one of the buildings.

And only a day or so after that, Sister Clarice announced that the bailiff was going to take them to watch some of the wheat and barley being harvested.

The weather was warm, and some of the men working in the fields had abandoned their tunics. It was scarcely a fitting sight for the subprioress, yet Clarice seemed fascinated by their exertions and, for a long while, her gaze was fixed upon them, as their strong muscled arms swung their scythes effortlessly from side to side, felling a great sheaf of stalks with every stroke.

Whilst the subprioress was thus engrossed, Felicia locked eyes with Rafe and tilted her head. His eyebrows arched. Stealthily, she partly withdrew the scrap of paper from her wide sleeve for him to see. He nodded. Then, later, after Clarice had had her fill of scything, and declared it time to leave, Felicia stepped forward to pet Rafe's dog, Tynker, and, with her back turned towards the subprioress, tucked the note under her collar.

Back at the priory, she could not wait to tell Maria, but Maria wrinkled her nose.

'Isn't it a dreadful risk?' she said. 'And, anyway, isn't he just a cottar?'

'Oh, not at all. His papa is some wealthy villein. But you haven't seen him, Mari. He's *so* good-looking...'

'And no doubt knows it, and has swived every girl in Northwick manor.'

Felicia pouted. 'I thought you'd be happy for me, finding a little excitement amidst this dreary life.'

Maria sneered. 'It's not *that* dreary. We have the best of everything, you and me and Letty. Don't you realise that?'

'I suppose so. But I can't bear to think my *whole life* is going to be like this, never experiencing what women are *supposed* to...' She paused. 'Love...' She had blushed. 'Relations with a man...'

'Motherhood?' Maria said. 'You want that too? Here?'

Felicia's blush deepened. 'No, of course not. But it's not inevitable, is it?'

'Not *inevitable*, no. But more than possible. Can you imagine the uproar it would cause?'

In truth, she had quite consciously *set aside* that possibility. Nonetheless, she was not going to let it stop her. She *needed* this! It was unbearable to be forbidden for ever the normal association between a woman and a man. Especially when this incarceration had not been her choice...

That evening, when most of the sisters were in Compline, Felicia had slipped away. She hurried to the courtyard behind the chapel and hid just inside the empty building she had marked on her sketch for Rafe. How she prayed he had understood it, and would know where to come.

The courtyard was, in principle, a good place for them to meet, for it was well out of sight of the sisters and the servants and hardly anyone came here in the evenings.

On three sides were one storey buildings, the first side a row of tiny one-room cottages set aside for corrodians, folk who paid the priory to look after them in their old age. Northwick had no *paying* corrodians, but one of the cottages was occupied by the two ancient nuns, Katerina and Mildryth, who would be well asleep by now. The buildings along the second side were barns, some used for storing hay and grain, and winter vegetables, and others empty, like this one she had chosen. On the third side were larger cottages which she was certain were unused. Except, she abruptly realised, for one. All of a sudden, her heart turned over and her neck grew clammy despite the evening chill. For did not Father Edgar live in one of those cottages...?

Yet, surely, he had no reason to be out and about at night...?

<hr>

Rafe drew his hood forward, tight about his head, as he entered the courtyard and edged his way towards the building Felicia had marked. He kept close to the line of buildings, staying in the shadows as best he could. The light was almost gone, but, in his walk up from the village, his eyes had become accustomed to the gloom.

He hoped he'd understood Felicia's little sketch correctly and it was *tonight* she'd asked him to come. He felt surprisingly uneasy: he was used to tumbling wenches, but never a nun. It scared him the little jade might have set a trap for him. He'd already been in trouble with the nuns, caught stealing priory goods, and, though he was still doing it, he didn't want to lose his job by being found out doing something even worse. But Felicia *was* delectable, and it was obvious she was taken with him too. Of course, he didn't know what she expected from him – or how far she was prepared to go. Yet it must be worth trying to find out...

As he approached the building she'd marked with an arrow – a storeroom, he thought it was, with a door and a tiny window – he stopped and peered into the deepening gloom. Was Felicia there? Should he call out? He bit his lip, his unease bubbling up again. What a fool he'd feel if she'd tricked him.

But then he heard a whispered 'Rafe?' and saw the door was slightly open.

Edging forward, he put his hand against it and pushed gently. 'Sister Felicia?'

'Yes,' she said softly. 'I'm in here.'

He opened the door a little further and slipped inside. The room was so dark he couldn't see his own hand.

'Close the door,' she murmured. He then heard the striking of a flint and a flame sprang out of the gloom.

'You came prepared,' he said, and stared in the direction of the flame. And there she was. On the cusp of collapsing into giggles, by the look of it.

'I'm so glad you came,' she said, and hurried to him. She reached out and took his hand.

How bold she was! Not that he resisted. Yet, weirdly, his nerves seethed again. It wasn't like him to be shy. But how strange it was to be touched by a woman dressed from head to toe in black. A woman who'd presumably taken a vow of chastity, yet seemed only too impatient to break it.

In truth, seemed *desperate* to do so...

Yet he wasn't willing simply to dive in. It was unlike him to be cautious but, on this occasion, he wanted to take it slowly, to find out what she wanted from him before he got himself into a predicament he couldn't readily escape.

The storeroom wasn't completely empty. A few boxes were scattered about, strong enough to sit on. He led her to them and indicated they should sit down side by side. In the candlelight, her face was beaming, excited, eager. But he held her hand, and asked her questions about herself, and told her about his life.

She allowed the talking for a while, but he could sense her rising fervour, as she withdrew her hand from his and placed it against his cheek. 'Don't you want to kiss me?' she said.

'Of course I do,' he said, 'but I'm not so ungallant as to press you.'

She giggled. 'Oh, I'd not mind.' She leaned her face forwards, close to his, and brushed her lips against his beard. He couldn't help but clasp her head in both his hands and plant a kiss onto her mouth. She returned it enthusiastically, as if she'd been kissing men all her life.

As he grasped her wimpled head, he could feel hair beneath it. He'd thought nuns had their hair cut short. 'What's under here?' he said.

'Would you like to see?' she said, and at once unpinned the veil and tugged off the wimple, and then the coif. As she did so, her hair – it was fair like his own – fell in waves about her ears. She ran her fingers through it, and crooked her head. 'Would you like to touch it?'

How could he resist? He put his hands once more about her head, and let his fingers comb her curls. 'Lovely,' he murmured, lifting a lock of it to his lips and kissing it.

Felicia emitted a deep moan, then took one of his hands and put it against her breast. He could feel the throbbing of her heart beneath the fabric, and the warmth and softness of her breast. But he forced himself to remove his hand. 'No, Felicia. No more, not now.'

'But soon?' she said.

He wasn't at all sure he *did* want more. 'Mebbe,' he said. 'But it's dangerous. We might get caught.'

'Not here,' she said.

He shook his head. 'Even here. You might think no one comes here, but you never know.'

Yet she seemed unwilling to give him up. 'Oh, *please* do let us meet again,' she said, pleading in her voice.

At length, he nodded. 'But not here. Can you get away from the priory?'

Her eyes lit up. 'Of *course* I can! Just tell me where...'

He cringed. Her unnatural excitement bothered him.

'How shall we arrange to meet?' she asked, her eyes shining in the candlelight.

'I'll leave signs,' he said. He'd done the same with other girls...

Since that first meeting, they had met several times, in the priory storeroom or in a barn just outside the village. Rafe discovered just how far Sister Felicia was prepared to go. It still troubled him, seeing a nun naked, making love to her... Fornication was a sin, but fornication with a nun seemed somehow much, much worse.

Sometimes he thought they should stop meeting, and he should pray for pardon on his knees. Yet Felicia was so beautiful, and so very willing...

Despite his fears and his forebodings, he wasn't ready yet to give her up.

16

MEONBRIDGE
OCTOBER 1366

Agnes stood at the cross-passage door of her mother's house and looked out across the garden. Autumn was advancing, the days mild now and dry, after a damp summer. Gillot and Betta had come almost every day to tend Ma's potager and orchard. The rain had spoiled some of the crops, but the orchard fruit mostly survived, and Gillot had brought along more of her relatives to help bring in the harvest.

As for Ma, she had spent the last three months sitting on one or other of the new benches Jack had made her, sited in the potager and the orchard, where she could watch the cottars work and give them some advice. Agnes could see her now, sitting just inside the little gate that led from the herb and flower garden into the potager.

Both she and Simon had forbidden Ma to set a foot upon the soil, or venture onto the grass around the apple trees, or even heft any garden implement. And Gillot had received instructions to send Ma back to her bench if she ever tried to help.

But, in fact, Gillot's reports to Agnes – even now, three months after her fall – were that Ma seemed loath to join the women labouring on her croft. She didn't even offer them much in the way of counsel or instruction. She sat and watched them working for a while, then, leaning heavily upon her stick, eased herself up and hobbled away back into the house. Where Agnes sometimes found her, sitting in her chair – made for her years ago by Jack as a birthday gift – invariably fast asleep.

Simon had visited Ma every day for weeks. He'd been pleased with the outcome of the operation: the bones had knit well, he said, and the wound healed very nicely.

Yet she was obviously still struggling to walk.

'Does it hurt still, Alice?' Simon asked her the other day.

'Not hurt, but it does feel *different*... Strange... I can't say how exactly... And my *other* leg still aches, like it did before.' She tapped the right side of her skirt. 'I feel lopsided, and must lean hard upon my stick to be sure I don't topple over.'

'Even when the bones have mended, and the flesh wound healed, it can sometimes take a long time for the muscles to regain their strength.'

'But maybe my aged muscles won't ever mend?'

'You must remember how long it took her ladyship's leg to fully mend? Several months...'

'I think of Margaret every day...' Her eyes seemed to fill with tears.

Agnes thought her ma might be going to say more about her ladyship. Such as how long it was exactly before Margaret could walk again in her own beloved garden, and how frustrated she'd been with the debility her broken leg inflicted.

But, instead, Ma closed her moistened eyes and seemed to fall asleep.

Agnes gestured to Simon to go outside so they could talk without disturbing her.

'You know, Agnes,' he said, 'Alice is walking better than her ladyship did this long after her accident.'

'Yes, I can see that too. Her gait's uneven, with the lop-sidedness she speaks of but, despite it, she can move quite quickly if she wants to...'

Later, Agnes told John what Simon had said. 'So, Ma *can* walk well enough,' she said, 'but she doesn't seem to *want* to. She's lost confidence in herself, and I think her leg reminds her constantly of Lady Margaret. It's melancholy that's stopping her recovery, John, not a lack of healing.'

John agreed. 'But what can we do to help her?'

'Talk to her, I suppose,' said Agnes, 'though neither of us has the time to sit with her for hours. Yet I'm worried she's struggling to cope.'

'She still cooks my meals,' he said, 'but she doesn't seem to want to talk much, not like she used to, before the accident.'

'Maybe I should encourage Eleanor to visit her more often?'

'Eleanor visits Ma?'

'You *know* they've always been good friends, and Ma used to enjoy their chats. More so I think than those she has with *us*...' She rolled her eyes.

'Maybe Eleanor's stories of her sheep are more fascinating than our conversation.' He grinned, and Agnes laughed.

'I'll ask her if she can spare the time.'

Eleanor was delighted to be asked to visit Ma more often.

'I'm so sorry if I have neglected her,' she said. 'It's no hardship at all to visit, for Alice and I have always found so much to talk about.'

'Yet, recently,' said Agnes, 'Ma's grown more downcast and quiet.'

'Yes, I've noticed, especially since her accident,' said Eleanor. 'I shall do my best to bring her lively news, although our lives are scarcely exciting.'

When Eleanor next came, she brought her little daughters with her, Christina and Cecily, and Agnes had no difficulty persuading Lizbet to come too, for she loved playing with "little ones", as she called them. She brought with her a bag full of the wooden animals Jack had carved for the children over the years. A few of them were past their best, with missing legs and ears, but many were worn smooth and shiny from years of being clutched by little hands. The three girls sat together at the table, and Lizbet collected together a few of Ma's bowls and boxes to act, first, as byres and barns, whilst they played at farms, then, as Noah's Ark, albeit most of Jack's carvings were sheep and cows...

Ma sat in her usual chair close to the fire, and Agnes drew up stools for herself and Eleanor.

Ma's eyes had lit up when Eleanor arrived. 'It's been such a long while since I've seen you,' she said. Eleanor exchanged a grin with Agnes, then leaned down to take Ma's hand. 'Only two weeks, Alice. But I daresay time seems to pass more slowly when you are not as active as you used to be.'

'Oh, yes, I do remember,' Ma said, though Agnes wasn't at all sure she did. 'But it's good to see you again, and the little ones too this time...'

'I had to bring them with me, as Tilla, the cottar girl who minds them, came this morning to say her mother needs her to help gather nuts, as the weather seems set fair for a few days.'

'How much I used to enjoy foraging for hazelnuts and walnuts,' said Ma. 'And how you liked to help me, Agnes, didn't you?'

Agnes wasn't at all sure she *did* enjoy it, but she'd not spoil Ma's merry mood. 'In good years, we could pick basketsful of them,' she said. 'I'll take the girls out with me soon, but I don't expect to collect as many as we used to, Ma.'

'They lasted us months,' continued Ma, 'provided I stored them properly.'

'Which you always did.' Agnes turned to Eleanor. 'Do you ever forage in the woods?'

'Not for nuts, but I did take Tina and Ceci to look for berries a month or so ago. It was fun, but, oh, what a mess they made of their hands and faces, not to mention their aprons! They were covered in black juice! Hawisa had a terrible time trying to get the stains out.'

Ma brightened a little more, as she recalled collecting brambleberries in the little wood at the bottom of her orchard. It was on the other side of the river that ran along the bottom of the croft, and, years ago, Pa built a little bridge to cross at its narrowest point. Agnes smiled at her ma's tale. Picking *berries* had certainly been fun, for she ate them straight from the bush and, like Eleanor's girls, left impossible purple stains upon her kirtle.

'What news of your flock?' asked Agnes. 'Time soon for tupping?'

'Next month. But September and October are busy months for us, ensuring the ewes are fat enough, but not too fat, before they are put out with the rams.'

'Does Emma Ward still work with you?' Ma said.

Agnes looked up in surprise. Surely Ma *knew* Emma married Will Cole five years ago? Or had she just forgotten?

'Emma *Cole*, yes,' said Eleanor. 'Will is still our shepherd, and Emma joins us at the busy times, lambing in the spring, and this autumn the preparation of the ewes. She's always been so good with the sheep, almost as good as Will and Walter.'

'And do you work with them too?'

'Not really. I know I do say "*we*" when I speak about the flock but, ever since I had these two'—she gestured at her girls—'Wat has been unwilling for me to spend much time up on Riverdown. I'm permitted to take the girls up there, to show them the new lambs, or to walk the pastures, watching the butterflies and bees and gather wild flowers...'

'"*Permitted*"! *That* doesn't sound like the Eleanor I once knew!' Ma let out a laugh. 'The young woman who made her *own* mind up about what she would and wouldn't do.' Briefly, her eyes twinkled.

Eleanor joined in her laughter. 'Indeed, I was quite confident all those years ago. But, when we were trying to have a family, Wat had my best interests at heart, and I was happy to do as he asked. Yet, now we have our family, it's I who am resisting work.' Her eyes were bright. 'I have often been up to Riverdown these past few weeks, watching the others work, and I enjoy that. I've taken the girls with me this year, so they can understand what rearing sheep involves. Cecily does seem interested, Christina less so'—she pretended to pout—'and, when they are older, they might occasionally work alongside their Papa, as I used to. But, as for me, I find I no longer wish to wrestle with the sheep myself.'

The talk of sheep and children carried on, and Ma seemed brighter than she'd been for days. But at length her eyelids drooped, and Agnes got up to put a cushion behind her head, so she could doze in comfort for a while.

Once Ma was asleep, Eleanor stood up and, taking her elbow, drew

Agnes away to the cross passage, where they could still keep an eye upon the girls, but be beyond Ma's hearing if she woke up.

'How well do you think Alice is recovering?' said Eleanor, her eyes showing her concern.

Agnes sighed. 'Not as quickly as we'd hoped. It can take a long while for broken bones to mend, and maybe longer when you're quite old. Yet it's not her leg concerns me – nor Simon – but her mood...'

'I agree, although today she seemed brighter than when I saw her last. Yet she does seem forgetful... They were small things, I know, not remembering it was only two weeks ago I came, and the matter of Emma's name. They are of little consequence, but Alice has always been so alert and mindful of everything around her.'

'I suppose it's normal as we get older, to forget small details? But, as you said, it seems to have worsened since the accident. I think it reminded her of Margaret, and how much she misses her.'

'You think that has thrown her into a deeper melancholy?'

'Is it possible?'

'I'm sure it is. Moreover, she is no longer quite as active, or busy out of doors, as she used to be. That too must add to her despondency.'

At length, Eleanor gathered up her children to go home. 'The girls have played so happily with Lizbet,' she said. 'Why don't you visit me and bring her with you? I can't recall the last time you came to my house.' She hesitated. 'But can you leave Alice, do you think?'

'Gillot or Betta can always come for a couple of hours.'

'Perhaps we can talk again about Alice? I should so like to help her fully mend.'

Another two weeks passed before Agnes had time to pay Eleanor a visit. It'd been a while since she'd been to her fine house. Eleanor had always been close to Ma, but recently, Agnes felt a friendship was growing between them too.

It was Eleanor's servant, Hawisa, who answered her knock upon the door. Hawisa was invariably brusque to visitors, almost rude, but she loved Eleanor like a daughter, having cared for her since soon after she was first orphaned. She opened the door wide and gestured, not impolitely, to Agnes and little Lizbet to come in. They followed her through the hall, with its fine furnishings, great fireplace and chimney in the wall, and into a smaller room at the back of the house, the parlour. Eleanor rose to greet them, and Cecily and Christina jumped up from the floor and, squealing, ran to grab Lizbet's hands and drag her over to where they were playing.

Hawisa brought refreshments, then closed the door behind her as she left.

'I've been meaning to ask you,' said Eleanor, 'if you have any more news of the priory?'

Agnes had told her months ago about the election and about John no longer being able to visit Rosa.

'Nothing more,' she said. 'I know he and Rosa have exchanged a few letters, and he told me the new prioress has been making changes that Rosa doesn't like. What's more, the prioress has given her a job that means she's no longer at the heart of managing the priory.'

'Oh dear, she must be dismayed.'

'I'm sure she is, though she does seem to be accepting what has happened as God's will...'

'Perhaps that is for the best, if she can't do anything to counter this new prioress?' She offered Agnes a sweetmeat. 'Hawisa is a fine pastrycook,' she said, smiling.

Agnes bit into the little tart, crumbs falling into her lap. It tasted of almonds. She licked a few more crumbs off her lip, then grinned.

'John too must be disappointed,' continued Eleanor, 'for he seemed to enjoy his visits.'

'He did. Though in a sense it was his fault for suggesting to Rosa that Northwick needed their own bailiff again. But he did still visit, just much less often. Until, that is, he found a new nun had arrived...'

Eleanor's eyes widened. 'A new nun?'

'Well, not yet a nun. A novice. A widow, actually, fleeing from her husband's brutal family.'

'Goodness! But what has a widow novice who is not yet a nun to do with John?'

Agnes flushed slightly, realising she hadn't *intended* telling Eleanor about Anabella. After all, John had told her to keep his relationship a secret, until he'd decided what to do to save it. 'Oh dear,' she said, 'I wasn't supposed to tell you...'

Eleanor's eyes widened again. 'Why? Is it a secret?'

'Yes, but now I've started...' She took a sip of the wine Hawisa had poured into her cup. She related John's story of Anabella bringing refreshments for him and Rosa, and the immediate attraction he and Anabella seemed to feel. 'He fell for her at once, he said, and she for him. I've always thought such instant love a fantasy, but John insists it's real.' Eleanor looked delighted. 'He visited twice more after that, and Rosa gave them the chance to talk—'

'*Rosa* did? What an unusual thing for a nun to do...'

'I said the same to John, but apparently Rosa told him she wished him to be happy...' Eleanor's head tilted. 'I think Rosa's a *very* different person from the Johanna we remember.'

'You've said as much before.' Eleanor nibbled at a little tart. 'So do you know anything more about this widow?'

'Not much, but her name is Anabella Sitwell... Sitwell was her married name—'

Eleanor dropped the remains of her tart in her lap, and gasped. 'Anabella Sitwell? How extraordinary, but I'm sure I know her! If it is the same woman, I knew her a little when we were girls. Her father was a merchant, an associate of my papa in Winchester. But when he moved his family to Bishop's Waltham, he and Papa kept in touch. Our two families visited each other once or twice, so Anabella and I were thrown together, though we were not exactly friends, because of the difference in our ages, five years or so, I think. This was all before the mortality...'

'But Sitwell was her *married* name,' Agnes said again, 'not that of her family...'

'Yes, yes, I realise that.' She took a sip of wine. 'I remember Mama didn't like Anabella's mother at all. Bella was still a child when her papa died – I can't recall exactly when or how – and her mother remarried. And, only shortly afterwards, I heard that she – Anabella – had been forced to marry. It was the same year Wat and I got married, so she would have been only fourteen years old or so. Her husband's name was Sitwell...'

Agnes laughed. 'How do you know all this, Elly?'

'It does sound unlikely, doesn't it? But I've probably never mentioned that I have an aunt who lives in Bishop's Waltham, my mother's younger sister. I've only met her once – she and Mama were never close – but, ever since my darling mama died, my aunt and I have corresponded, just occasionally, and it was she who told me of Bella's family, and her marriage to a Sitwell...' She grinned. 'My aunt is something of a gossip.'

'From what I've heard,' said Agnes, 'the Sitwells are a nasty lot.'

'Indeed. That is what Aunt told me. Not murderous, but certainly bullying. She said she pitied poor Anabella, being made to marry into such a family, and so young. But apparently her mother was a Sitwell too, which is why the match was made...'

Eleanor had been perched on the edge of her chair, with the excitement of her story. She eased back now against the cushion. 'Poor Bella!'

'Or perhaps fortunate Bella, given she's now escaped their clutches?'

Eleanor sipped her wine a while and took another sweetmeat. Then she sat up sharply. 'But if John can no longer visit Northwick, neither can he visit Anabella. What is to become of their affection?'

'That's the problem. It's been this way for almost a year, and John's terrified she might soon have to take her final vows, before he's had a chance to ask her to be his wife.'

'Can he not just go there?'

'The prioress has *forbidden* him to visit.'

'How extraordinary! Do you think she knows of their relationship, and is set on keeping them apart?'

'I've wondered that, but John seems to think not. What he did say was Anabella promised a small fortune to the priory if they took her in – a sort of dowry. So, I imagine the prioress will be eager for her to commit, so the money goes into her coffers.'

'How awful that sounds, for a prioress to force a woman to become a nun just so she can have her money. Anyway, what is John going to do?'

Of course, Agnes didn't know the answer to Eleanor's question.

A little later, she told John about Eleanor knowing Anabella.

He was astonished and immediately excited. 'D'you think she might be able to help me make Anabella my wife?'

'How on earth could she do that?' said Agnes, and John's brief elation faltered.

She patted his arm in a gesture of support, but inwardly she was exasperated. Given how old John was, and what great responsibility he held as Meonbridge's bailiff, why *did* he still act the callow lad at times?

17

Northwick Priory
October 1366

Evangelina had been incensed when, back in the summer, Letitia told her how Sister Rosa was openly criticising the changes she'd been making at Northwick. *She* was prioress, not Rosa! Had the woman forgotten her vow of obedience?

Almost certainly not.

Yet she was evidently still a rival, whether or not she was actively plotting to depose her.

Having dismissed Letitia to give herself time to think, Evangelina had paced around her chamber for a while. So far, Rosa's complaints had been shared only with her cronies but, in time, mightn't she try to convince Evangelina's own favourites to take her side?

She had to stop it happening.

But, rather than merely threaten Rosa privately, as she'd done over the election, this time, she thought, it would be amusing to give Rosa a taste of her own medicine. Over the following few days, she told Letitia, Felicia and Maria what she knew of Rosa's past. Of course, it was scarcely very much, but enough for the girls to tell a story that might cause mirth, as well as unease, amongst the sisters, or some of them, at least.

And, as it turned out, the gossip the girls spread worked rather well. For Rosa promptly stopped airing her criticisms and, in fact, *none* of the sisters had voiced any grievances for months. Everyone had taken to keeping quiet and getting on with their work.

Evangelina felt quite smug about it: she'd brought the recalcitrant Sister Rosa, and her cronies, sharply to heel.

Rosa might no longer be sharing her grievances openly, yet Evangelina still wanted Letitia to *keep an eye on* her, as she put it. For she didn't trust her. Fortunately, Letitia, whilst happy to be a member of the coterie, was also more than willing to spend much of her day in the company of the other nuns, sleeping in the dorter and eating in the frater. She was glad too, not to say eager, to attend all the holy offices, even the night time ones. Which meant she could easily keep watch on Rosa.

Unlike Maria and Felicia, Letitia had a rather serious, and largely pious, nature. An odd girl, really. Yet, she *was* an excellent spy, which sat rather peculiarly alongside her piety. Perhaps she saw the spying as a game, or a challenge?

When she first asked her to keep an eye upon Sister Rosa's movements, she'd impressed upon her how important the role was.

'For, as you know, Sister Rosa's been fomenting dissent amongst the sisters.' Letitia nodded, although she also seemed a little ill at ease. 'Thus, she's broken her vow of obedience, and must therefore be considered dangerous.' Letitia looked alarmed at that but still agreed to do what Evangelina wanted.

Yet, when she recently asked Letitia to continue watching, the girl demurred. 'But, Reverend Mother,' she said, 'ever since we spread that gossip in the summer, Sister Rosa has not repeated her criticisms of you once. Surely, there is no longer any need—'

She shook her head. 'She presumably learned I'll not tolerate dissent, but we can't rely upon her acquiescence continuing... So, keep an eye on her a little longer, eh?'

Letitia pursed her lips but didn't refuse.

But she soon reported that Rosa wasn't spending much time at all in the company of her particular cronies, Beatrice and Amata, but kept largely to herself. 'When she is not in the dorter or the frater, or attending the holy offices,' Letitia said, 'she is mostly in the sacristy or the chapel, carrying out her duties.'

Evangelina nodded. Edgar had complained that he so often encountered Rosa in the sacristy when he went to write his sermons, he'd almost given up trying to work there.

'She does still occasionally speak to Sister Dulcia,' continued Letitia, 'in the treasuress's chamber.'

'But not to Beatrice or Amata?' said Evangelina. 'And she finds no reason to go out into the gardens?'

'I have not seen her, Reverend Mother.'

'And how does she seem? Her mood?'

The girl shrugged. 'I am not sure I can say. She does seem somewhat melancholy, but Sister Rosa always has been rather serious, has she not?'

Evangelina smirked. 'Indeed...'

Evangelina asked her brother to attend her in her chamber, for another of their private conversations. When her maid showed him in, Evangelina sent Maria and Felicia away.

They went with a hint of resentment, presumably thinking they were being excluded from something interesting. Over the past year or so, they'd spent more and more time in her company, and doubtless believed themselves entitled to be privy to all their prioress's plans and decisions.

But, in truth, Evangelina didn't entirely trust her young disciples – nor Sister Gracia, nor even Clarice – to remain her steadfast allies. Yet she was certain she could trust her brother. After all, she could have him dismissed from his post if he displeased her. Not that there was ever any antagonism between them: the bond they'd formed as children was still strong.

Edgar had seemed encouraging about the changes she was making to the priory. He surely recognised that she *deserved* a less austere life than the one she'd been forced to suffer since she was fifteen. He *understood*.

'What did you want to talk to me about, Eva?' he said now.

She poured him a cup of wine, then sat down in her great chair. 'I'm planning to go on a journey.' She leaned back against the cushions, and took a long sup of her wine.

Edgar frowned. 'Is it wise to leave the priory without your presence?'

'You mean the business with Sister Rosa?' He nodded. 'Oh yes, I think so.'

She'd told him back in the summer about Rosa airing her grievances against her. When she described how she'd set the three young nuns to spread gossip about Rosa, he'd seemed amused. But, at the time, she'd still been nervous about leaving the priory – much as she wanted to – in case Rosa's compliance didn't last.

But it had.

'Northwick seems to be at peace again,' she said. 'Rosa evidently realises I've the power to expose her sordid past. She hasn't vented her complaints for months, and neither have her cronies.'

'So you believe it is tranquil enough for you to go away?'

'I do.'

'Then tell me more about your travels. Where are you going and how long will you be away?'

The Benedictine rule discouraged nuns from going outside their priory, but Angelica had never forbidden the sisters from leaving Northwick for a few days. Indeed, she encouraged it, if it was to visit a sick relative or close friend, or take part in some family occasion. In the first few years of her life at Northwick, Evangelina had made several visits home, specifically to see her little brother, Edgar. But once Edgar had himself been sent away to train for the clerical life, she'd little reason to go home, for no love was lost between her and her parents. Moreover, she'd no friends or acquaintances to visit, so, in all the ensuing years she'd not put a foot outside the priory.

But, as prioress, she was free to travel as she wished, because *she* decided what she did and didn't do. She also had the power to decide what Northwick's sisters could and couldn't do. And her decision was that, if they wished to leave the priory for whatever reason, they needed her express permission. A permission she'd by no means always grant...

Of course, she realised this revealed her vengeful streak. But, over all the years she'd been here, none of the sisters had been her friend – indeed, many had shown her active dislike. Those who now supported her did so, not because they *liked* her, but simply because she was now prioress.

However, *because* she was now prioress, her position in the Godeffroy family was much higher, and she received invitations to visit family members. And it was one of these she now intended to accept. The son of a cousin she knew slightly was marrying into a wealthy Southampton family, and she'd been invited to attend. How much she was looking forward to enjoying the lavish marriage feast that would be provided.

When she told Edgar about the invitation, his brow wrinkled. 'I do not think I know that cousin.'

'I've met him only once, when we were children. You were still a baby.'

'If you are so briefly acquainted, is it not surprising he has invited you to the wedding?'

'Angelica was invited to many weddings of family members she barely knew,' she said. 'Simply *because* she was a prioress. And now it's *my* turn to be venerated for my status.' Edgar waggled his head.

'However, I've decided,' she continued, 'to combine the family visit with another, to stay in the home of Sir Toby Edenborough, who's dined with me here more than once.' Edgar raised an eyebrow, and she grinned. 'Ha! I see you disapprove, brother.'

He shrugged. 'Do you have good reason for such a visit?'

'I'd scarcely spend the night in a man's house without good reason.' She let out a derisive laugh. 'He's *married*, Edgar: his wife and family will be present, so there'll be no impropriety. But, yes, my visit does have purpose, a most *important* purpose. It's for the *benefit* of Northwick.'

'Explain?'

'Our Godeffroy family is, of course, the priory's principal patron and that won't change. But Sir Toby is one of Southampton's most successful merchants, and holds lands and manors throughout Hampshire and

Dorset. And he's eager to offer the priory further patronage, and not inconsiderable funds. How could I ignore his generosity? He's invited me to his home for the explicit purpose of discussing the details of his proposal. I'm sure, brother, you'd not say I should refuse?'

Edgar seemed to consider what she'd told him, but at length agreed her visit had an honourable purpose. 'And how long will you be away?'

'Ten days or so.'

'That is a long time to be abroad, with many days on the road. You have not said how you are travelling, and who with...'

'Letitia shall accompany me. Felicia and Maria will no doubt be offended'—she rolled her eyes—'but I can't take them all. And I'm also taking two manservants, to protect us.'

'Men you trust?' His eyebrows lifted.

'Of course. I appointed them myself a year ago.'

'Who are they? Are they *capable* of defending you from attack?'

'Oh, I should think so. One's the porter, the other man a gardener. Both trusted servants. But *also* both once soldiers for the king.'

'Soldiers? Aren't they rather rough sorts of men to be accompanying a prioress and a young nun? Surely, you should have a priest with you as well?'

Evangelina grinned. Did Edgar want to come too? 'But I was hoping, brother, you'd keep an eye on Northwick for me whilst I'm away.'

His expression then was hard to read. Was he irritated she was going away without him, or glad? 'Of course,' he said at last. 'Who will be in charge?'

'Nominally, Sister Clarice. She undertakes most of the administration anyway. And Beatrice and Dulcia can be relied upon to do their part in keeping the priory running smoothly.'

'I still think you should have a priest with you, even if it is not me,' he said, frowning.

'But where would I find one?'

'How about the priest from the village church? Or ask Cousin Nicholas – I am sure he could find one for you.'

'But I'd have to *pay* him,' she said, pressing her lips together.

'Are you then not paying your manservants?'

'Additionally, you mean? Of course not. They're paid well enough as it is. But I'll be covering their board and lodging for what is, after all, a holiday...'

Edgar's face was inscrutable again. Did he disapprove of her plans after all? But she'd not ask. At length he shrugged. 'I presume they have agreed... Anyway, Eva, ask Nicholas. I am unhappy at the prospect of you travelling without the comfort of a confessor.'

Irritated as she was by his resolve, she'd not ignore it. She smiled thinly. 'Very well, brother, I will.'

The day of Evangelina's departure dawned dull and damp. Not at all the weather she'd anticipated for her travels. In truth, she was annoyed. Why today, of all days, did it have to rain?

The horses were delivered at first light: palfreys for her and Letitia, rounceys for the manservants, plus a packhorse to carry the panniers containing the clothes Evangelina was taking with her. She'd bought a special outfit for the wedding, more of a gown than a habit, made from the finest silk.

Some days ago, the hackney man had brought the palfrey Evangelina was to ride, so she could try it out. She wasn't an accomplished horsewoman, not that she'd admit it. Before she came to Northwick, she rode often enough, as all young ladies had to, though she never much enjoyed it. For her, horse-riding was a disagreeable necessity, rather than a pleasure.

What she recalled with particular dislike was how, as a woman, she was required to sit. Her mother had been strident in her insistence that, for propriety's sake, Evangelina simply *could not* sit astride a horse, as men did, but must perch sideways upon a saddle with a footrest. And what Evangelina mostly remembered now was how uncomfortable it was, and how lacking in control she felt.

Thus, when she was making her journey plans, she decided to try out her mode of travel, to prepare herself. When the hackney man came with the pretty dark brown palfrey, and two saddles, Gerard, the porter, had shown him to the courtyard at the rear of the priory, behind the chapel, well out of sight of the sisters and the servants.

The hackney man had bowed briefly, and tipped his hood. 'M'lady. Which saddle d'you want to try out first?'

'The sideways one,' she said, grimacing.

'That's the one on now. You need my help to mount?'

'If you please.'

There was a mounting block in the courtyard, and the man had led her and the palfrey towards it. She put a foot onto the block, and the man, with an indelicate shove, eased her up onto the saddle. She settled both feet onto the footrest.

'Lead me around the courtyard,' she commanded, and the man tipped his hood again and, taking the horse's reins, walked her in a wide circle around the court's perimeter.

'What d'you think, m'lady?' he said.

She breathed out loudly through her nose. 'Let me take the reins.'

He handed them to her, and she made a circuit of the courtyard on her own. But, sitting sideways, she had to keep twisting her body around to face the direction of travel. It was ridiculous! How could she travel *miles* like this! She must have done so as a girl − and in those early years in the priory, when she journeyed home to see her brother − but, now, well, she simply wasn't willing to ride in such discomfort.

When she returned to where the man was waiting, she grunted. '*That* was dreadful! Let me try the proper saddle.'

'Are ye sure, m'lady?' he said, scratching underneath his hood. 'It surely ain't seemly for a lady like yerself.'

She grunted again. 'Nonetheless, I'm not willing to make my journey unable to see where I'm going without dislocating my back.'

She had dismounted and the man changed the saddle to enable her to sit astride: a position she'd never tried before. Of course it *was* unseemly, but there was a reason why men rode that way: they could see where they were going and had control over their horse.

Remounted, Evangelina took the reins at once and moved off across the court. She clicked the palfrey into a gentle trot, and would have tried a gallop if there'd been the space. How exhilarating this was. The horse was responding to her. What did she care if her splayed legs were regarded as improper. She was comfortable, and she was in command.

When she returned once more to the hackney man, she'd nodded. 'This one,' she said. 'This is the saddle I shall use.'

He'd shrugged. 'Very well, m'lady, whatever you say.'

Now, Evangelina was sitting astride her palfrey, a voluminous cloak swathed about her to conceal the "improper" splay of legs beneath her skirts.

Letitia hadn't demurred at the sideways saddle provided with her mount, and was sitting upon it with apparent ease and comfort. But Letitia was young, and she'd doubtless had more recent practice of riding with her body twisted forwards.

Despite the gloom, the sun was clearly rising, as the sky lightened, and a faint brightness glowed behind the clouds. It would soon be time to leave.

A few of the sisters had come outside to wave them off: Sister Clarice, and Gracia. Mariota, too, and even Dulcia, though Evangelina suspected she'd come out of duty rather than a sincere wish to bid her farewell.

Clarice's eyes weren't the only ones to start at the sight of the prioress sitting legs *astride* her horse. Felicia and Maria were pointing and whispering behind their hands. Shortly, Clarice came over and, leaning forwards, spoke quietly to her. 'Reverend Mother, surely it is indecorous for you to ride this way.'

Evangelina sniffed. 'Clarice, if you had to ride the distance I'm about to, you'd do the same.' She tossed her head in Letitia's direction. 'It's all very well for youngsters, but riding sideways is an excruciating, not to say, dangerous, way to travel. And I'm not prepared to do it.'

Not that she cared what Clarice, or any of the sisters, thought. The important point was, she'd reach her destination without twisting her back or falling off her horse.

'You can pray for the success of our expedition,' she said to Clarice. '*All* aspects of it.'

'Of course I shall, Reverend Mother,' said Clarice and stepped away.

Once Felicia and Maria had stopped sniggering behind their hands, they sidled over to Letitia. With pinched lips and hooded eyes, they looked up at her, sitting straight-backed and smug upon her horse. Evangelina couldn't hear what she was saying but Maria stood on tiptoe and, steadying herself against the palfrey's flank, said something to Letitia. Her head waggled as if she was annoyed. Felicia too looked peeved. As Evangelina had predicted, both were undoubtedly irritated they'd not been chosen to accompany her.

Letitia did indeed look self-satisfied. Yet Evangelina knew she wasn't especially enthusiastic about the trip.

'What shall I be doing, Reverend Mother,' she'd asked, 'when you are with your family, and then in consultation with the gentleman?'

'You'll accompany me at all times, Letitia,' she'd said. 'You'll share what will undoubtedly be a lavish wedding feast, and you'll listen in to my discussions with Sir Toby.'

In truth, Felicia or Maria would have made more lively and sociable companions at the wedding. But Letitia's solemnity and intelligence made her the better choice for the patronage negotiations. She'd listen closely, and digest the details, and, later, be able to corroborate what was agreed.

Evangelina looked around at the manservants she'd assigned to her protection. The rounceys were snorting and prancing, impatient, she supposed, to be on their way. The men themselves looked cheerful enough. Both had asked for extra pay but, despite her firm rebuff, hadn't refused to come. Doubtless pleased to be set free from their chores for a few days...

The old priest was sitting quietly on his mare a little distance from the rest of the party. He and his horse looked accustomed to each other, and she supposed they travelled often together around his parish. Despite his physical ease atop his horse, his face looked strained. She'd met him for the first time yesterday evening.

She recognised him, and he her, for he'd come to Northwick before, when Angelica was prioress. Cousin Nicholas had arranged for the old man to accompany her, and Edgar invited him to lodge overnight in his rooms. The two men seemed to get on well. But when Edgar brought him to meet Evangelina, for some reason the old priest recoiled, and their subsequent conversation was curt and brief. She wondered why he'd agreed to travel with her, but supposed it was the fee she'd offered for his pains.

Anyway, it was time now to depart. She was surprised to find her stomach fluttering with unease. She'd been looking forward to the "expedition", as she called it, but was now nervous about the journey. Nonetheless, they had to make a start.

Glad the earlier dampness hadn't after all turned to rain, she clapped her hands. 'Come, everybody, let us be on our way, whilst the heavens are on our side.'

She pulled on the reins then, gently squeezing the palfrey's sides with her legs, guided it forwards to the front of her company. She heard Letitia click her tongue, and she was soon at Evangelina's side. The priest fell in just behind them, and the two manservants took up the rear.

Evangelina took one last look at the small group of nuns bidding them farewell. She was irritated to note that most of Northwick's sisters, including Rosa, Beatrice and Amata, hadn't come to see her leave, and neither, disappointingly, had Edgar. But, no matter.

She raised her arm in a parting gesture and, pressing her legs against the palfrey's flanks once more, she set off at a gentle trot, out through the priory gate.

18

The sun was well risen before Edgar realised he had forgotten to bid farewell to Eva and her little entourage. They would be well on their way by now.

As he splashed cold water onto his face and hands, then quickly dressed, he found himself fretting slightly about his sister's safety. He was still unconvinced of the wisdom of her trip, partly because of the potential danger on the road but also the possibility of trouble here at the priory.

Yet Eva had been prioress for more than a year and was impatient to take advantage of her position to go travelling. The family wedding invitation was not the first she had received, but he supposed that, until now, she really *had* thought it unwise to leave Northwick, even for a few days.

He was mildly vexed that *he* had not been invited, for he too would have welcomed the chance to get away for a day or so. As for the visit to the new prospective patron, he was sceptical. Obviously, more

184

patronage would be a fine thing for Northwick, but he suspected Eva was proposing to use the money not for the priory's benefit but her own.

That was, after all, what she had been doing ever since she was elected.

She evidently believed he *approved* of all the changes she had been making. And why not, for he had never quarrelled with any of her plans. Yet he did not admire what she had done at all. He had always thought she would make a terrible prioress, and his prophecy was proving correct: the changes she had made so far were good only for her, and for her close companions.

He was not so troubled by the lack of attendance at the daily offices, for he was not especially pious himself. But the changes that entailed a drain on Northwick's funds, with no advantage to the priory as a whole, he did think these were wrong.

There was no necessity for Eva to have a separate kitchen, or eat special foods, or entertain guests so lavishly and so often. Aunt Angelica had never done any of that. And Eva had no need of new, expensive clothes or ridiculous little lapdogs scampering about the place, getting under everybody's feet. Nor did she need to antagonise the other sisters by openly flouting the rules of the order, neither sleeping in the dorter nor eating in the frater. Keeping herself apart from her sisters, save from her "disciples", was *not* how a prioress was expected to behave.

But he had not said any of this to his sister. In their conversations, he always – or nearly always – pretended to agree with her. She did not realise he was humouring her.

In truth, he did not quite know *what* to think. Perhaps his sister *did* deserve to live a gayer, more comfortable life for a while, given what she had been "forced to suffer", as she put it, the past thirty years?

Yet, surely, it was not supportable if, by doing so, she brought Northwick to its knees?

In some ways, he did not much care what happened to the priory: if it fell into ruin, he would be out of a job, but might that be a boon? He did not actively dislike his life here, but the work was tedious and lacking in scope. With just seventeen nuns, and two child novices, there was little for him to do. Of course, when he was in the mood for indolence, having so few commitments was a boon. Yet he often thought that being a *parish* priest might be more stimulating, and stop him feeling his life was wasting away.

Though there was also a part of him that *did* care about the priory: Eva's unawareness – or was it *deliberate disregard?* – of the welfare of the other nuns was unchristian, but also callous, even wicked...

However, he suspected Eva's reign would not last long: Rosa and the other sisters would soon enough rise up against her. When Eva told him about her disciples spreading gossip about Sister Rosa, he had pretended to be amused, whereas, in fact, he was surprised Rosa had apparently acquiesced so readily. Perhaps she was biding her time, plotting her rebellion...

A small part of him did hope so.

When Evangelina said she was leaving Felicia and Maria behind, Edgar's heart had quickened. With his sister away, her young assistants would presumably have little to do. He rarely had a chance to speak to either of them. When they came for confession, the exchange was brief and ordinarily one-sided. But he liked the idea of having a longer conversation with them, learning why they had come to Northwick. For both came from wealthy, high-born families, and Felicia in particular was very pretty. He was puzzled by why such women would be confined in a priory instead of getting husbands.

As he shut the door of his lodgings and made his way out of the courtyard and towards the fields, to take his customary walk, he wondered what the girls were doing now. As it was mid-morning, all the sisters should be hard at work, at whatever occupation they were assigned. Maria, he recalled, was kitcheness, so would be supervising the preparation of the sisters' dinner. But what role did Felicia have when she was not attending to the prioress? It surprised him to realise he had no idea.

Edgar took the rough track down through Northwick village, which passed the common land where the manor's tenants grazed their sheep and cattle, then continued on towards the river. He stepped carefully onto the little bridge, for its planks were rotten and water spurted up between the gaps from the river rushing close beneath, on its way to power the priory's mill downstream. Then he struck out across the water meadows, towards the woodland that stretched in a wide arc... Edgar was not a man of action, but he enjoyed his daily walk, a four miles or so round trip. He found it brought a measure of solace in a life otherwise full of disappointment. It also gave him time to think. Though thinking was not inevitably a blessing, for it could give rise to an uneasy restlessness that could be hard to shift.

His discontent was not just with his wearisome profession. More so, it was with his enforced celibacy. Edgar had no intimate experience of women. Nor should he have, in theory, but, in practice, most young men – even priests – did gain some carnal knowledge, albeit only with a whore. Yet, when he was younger, the opportunity to bed a woman, even one of low repute, never came his way. And, as he grew older, his very lack of knowledge made him nervous.

Nonetheless, he quite liked women. Most men thought them naturally weak-willed, even half-witted. Yet he had learned they could be both intelligent and strong. His aunt, Angelica, had undoubtedly been both. And several of Northwick's nuns – Rosa, Beatrice, Dulcia – were clever and resourceful, excellent managers, as well as solicitous and kind. A couple of the younger ones could make the skin beneath his collar feel hot and clammy: Sister Juliana was pretty and her mood invariably sunny, and Sister Helen, if admittedly plain-faced, was sweet-natured, and warm.

Then of course there was Felicia. She was frivolous and shallow, but he did not admire her for her mind or disposition, but for her face, and what he imagined of her figure. Her beauty was much *enhanced* by the framing of her wimple, and the sight of Felicia's pale cheeks and pretty mouth would cause his loins to stir... Worse, when by chance the folds of her habit somehow got caught up – such as when she leaned across a table – and strained against her body, he could see the outline of her breasts quite clearly... He closed his eyes at the memory of the last time he had seen it. Each time, he had wondered if she was doing it deliberately, to tease him. And, each time, he had rebuked himself for thinking of her so ungallantly.

But, despite his desire – his *lust* – for Sister Felicia, it was impossible to approach her, and even more so to suggest an inappropriate liaison, however much his body might urge him otherwise...

Yet, now Eva was away, and Felicia presumably at a bit of a loss, might he be able to spend a little time with her? Or with both her *and* Maria, so as not to scare her off? But, on what pretext could such an encounter possibly take place?

He pondered upon it for the entire length of his walk, but nothing came to mind.

Edgar was in need of a breath of air. It was the third day following Evangelina's departure and, ridiculous as it seemed, he was missing her. It was a dry evening, but hardly warm, so he wrapped his thick wool cloak about his shoulders before pulling on his boots.

As he stepped outside his lodgings and closed the door, he saw a figure slipping into the darkness of one of the storerooms off the courtyard that he knew was unused. The figure was a nun, he was certain of it, from the fullness of her garments. But who was it? And what was she doing in an empty storeroom?

He at once abandoned his plan of a stroll, and went back indoors. There was a small window next to the door from which he could keep watch. He could see the storeroom well, for the sky was clear and the moon bright enough to cast some light onto the courtyard.

His legs began to ache as he stood behind the tiny window, its shutter rolled back, his eyes fixed upon the storeroom door. He shuffled from foot to foot, to ease the ache, but didn't let his eyes drift from their target. Time passed, how much he didn't know, but it was clear enough the nun was up to mischief in that storeroom. Meeting someone illicitly? One of the younger nuns, then... Sister Gracia, perhaps, or Maria, or even Felicia... And who might she be meeting? Some man from the village, he supposed.

Waiting and watching was tedious as well as uncomfortable, yet he was keen to know the identity of the lovers, if indeed that was what they were.

At length his patience was rewarded, when he saw a man emerge from the storeroom and stride across the courtyard in the direction of the village. He was certain the man was the priory's bailiff, Rafe

Byllynges, for he had not bothered to lift his hood and his yellow hair shone in the light of the still rising moon. Moments later, the nun too appeared at the door, looked about her briefly, then, lifting the skirts of her habit, took to her heels and ran swiftly in the other direction, back towards the priory. His heart turned over when he saw the shape and slenderness of her form, for he then knew it was Felicia.

He left the window and, shuffling over to his bed, sat down upon the mattress edge. Leaning forward, with his elbows on his knees, he clasped his face with both hands and moaned. It was as if all the stuffing had been knocked out of him. That lovely girl, for all her high birth and fine upbringing, was just a whore.

Perhaps he was not interested in her after all.

Felicia had been rather vexed when she learned the Reverend Mother was leaving her behind and taking Letitia with her on her jaunt. On the other hand, she supposed it was quite amusing to have nothing much to do. There would be a meeting between Sister Clarice and Rafe... And perhaps she could arrange one or two little *extra* assignations?

What was more, the prioress's absence offered the opportunity for a little mischief making. Though, what sort of mischief, she had not thought. Nonetheless, she had felt a shiver of delight at the prospect of having just a little *fun*.

When Mother Evangelina had been gone a day, that evening, Felicia and Maria, already at a loose end, sneaked away from the other sisters to the prioress's chamber to gossip and giggle with one another. By chance, they discovered the prioress's private stash of wine and became quite merry as they downed cup after cup in a short space of time.

'Do you think Sister Clarice, or Beatrice, will come looking for us?' Maria said. 'To shoo us back into the dorter?'

Felicia let out a most inelegant snort. 'What a shock they'll have if they find us like this! But, God willing, they'll forget about us altogether...'

Despite her initial coolness about Felicia's assignations with Rafe,

Maria seemed eager enough to hear about them, and Felicia was happy to tell her.

'As you're clearly enjoying it so much,' said Maria, wrinkling her nose, 'it's fortunate you've not yet got with child.'

Felicia blushed a little. 'Rafe's very careful. He knows *exactly* how to avoid unwanted consequences...'

'A gentleman indeed.' Maria huffed. 'My brother was not so expert...'

Felicia had been shocked to hear of Maria's intimacy with her brother. She'd told her of it when they both first came to Northwick and were sharing why each had been sent here.

Maria used to spy upon her three brothers when they were bathing in the river, and sometimes she and her middle brother slipped away to be alone.

'But somehow Papa found out,' she said. 'And, of course, he took the attitude that I'd *seduced* my brother against his will. My brother, the rat!'—she rolled her eyes—'happily agreed with Papa's premise. So he received no punishment, but went out into the world with his inheritance and, eventually, a wife. Whereas *I* was cast as a Jezebel, a licentious, weak-willed daughter of Eve.'

Despite her fury at the injustice of it all, Maria had laughed. 'I was deemed unfit for marriage. "No worthy man would want you," declared my dear mama. Papa agreed, and thus I was confined here in Northwick.'

She had come a year or so before Felicia herself. 'Did Mother Angelica *know* why you were sent here?' Felicia had asked.

'Not that I was bedded by my brother... My father simply claimed I was wayward and needed the calm routine of convent life. I'm certain the prioress doubted the truth of it, but she agreed to take me. Northwick needed some younger nuns...'

Poor Maria! Poor *her*! To be so cruelly forsaken by their own papas....

Felicia sighed, as she came back to the present. She no longer had any interest in her family, only in what diversion she might find, both now, and in the years to come. 'It is true,' she said. 'I am enjoying my encounters with Rafe. And yet...' She tilted her head.

'Yet what?'

She licked her bottom lip. 'I should *quite* like to try another man...'

Maria gasped. '*Sister* Felicia!' she cried, then collapsed into a fit of giggles. 'How *outrageous*! You really *are* a daughter of Eve!'

Felicia felt her cheeks flush a little, but it was true. It was not so much that she was bored with Rafe, but rather that she liked the idea of discovering how it might be with another...

'Who do you have in mind?' said Maria, her eyes wide.

'Oh, I've no idea. We hardly have much choice here, do we?'

'I'm sure Northwick village is *full* of willing men...'

'True, but I should like a different *sort* of man... A man of noble birth, perhaps...'

'Not much chance of that!' Maria poured more wine into both their cups, then drank hers down in one. 'Though, on the other hand...' She appeared to be musing.

'What are you thinking?' said Felicia.

At length her eyes lit up. 'Well, we do know *one* man who is at least of gentle birth, if not exactly noble. And he might well be eager to make your more *intimate* acquaintance...'

Excitement bubbled in Felicia's chest. 'Who? Who?' she cried.

Maria grinned. 'Father Edgar!'

'Father *Edgar*?' cried Felicia. 'Oh, no, Mari, not him.'

'Whyever not? He's quite good-looking, with his blue eyes and thick black hair. And he's not especially old...'

'But he's a *priest*.'

'All the more reason for his likely interest,' said Maria. 'After all, he may have little, or even no, experience of women. How amusing to discover how such an untried, *innocent* man might perform...'

Felicia found herself blushing again. She could not deny Edgar's face was handsome, and his figure appeared as trim as that of any younger man. She had always considered him attractive enough, but not as a man with whom she might be intimate... A *priest*, after all... 'But how could I possibly approach him?'

***

Edgar had still not summoned up the courage to approach Felicia. Despite her liaison with the bailiff, the thought of her still made his innards roil. Moreover, he could not drive the image of her from his head.

In truth, he was both disappointed and relieved by the situation. She might be his last opportunity to know a woman's body, yet what he wanted from her was a heinous sin, made even more so because he was her priest, her spiritual guide, her trusted advisor... So, he resigned himself, with a heart that was sometimes heavy and sometimes light, to acceptance that his brief reverie of holding Felicia in his arms would never come to pass.

Not long after Edgar's reluctant surrender to perpetual chastity, there was a light knock upon the sacristy door. For once the room was not occupied by Sister Rosa.

'Come in,' he called, not thinking whom he might be bidding enter. The door opened, and a wimpled head peeked around its edge.

Edgar leapt up from his chair, his heart thudding.

'May I come in, Father?' Sister Felicia said. He nodded dumbly, and she slipped inside.

He sank back into his chair and gestured to her to take the stool. She sat, her hands folded in her lap, her eyes cast down. His stomach churned, and he yearned to put out a hand to touch her. But he restrained himself.

'You wish to speak to me, Sister Felicia?'

She nodded but did not lift her eyes.

His heart was thumping now so powerfully, he thought it must be visible through his shirt. He glanced down briefly. 'Well, Sister,' he said, 'what is it?'

She lifted up her head and her lovely eyes – moist, perhaps with weeping? – seemed to be boring into his.

'I have a problem,' she said, 'for which I really *do* need your advice.'

He leaned forward. 'I am here to help.'

She tilted her head, then her tongue tip grazed her lip. 'I... I...,' she started. She looked away, then whispered, 'I keep having such *unsettling* thoughts... I wondered if... there was some remedy for banishing them? Some penance I could undertake, some prayers I could recite...' She turned back to face him, her lips slightly apart.

Edgar straightened his back and, clasping his hands together, dug his fingernails into the flesh. Oh, good God, *she* had unsettling thoughts!

All the penances he had contemplated to sublimate his own desires flooded into his head: praying for hours prostrate upon the floor, or upright but with arms outstretched; rising hourly at night to pray – indeed, *denying* sleep entirely; forgoing pleasure of every kind, including food; wearing a hairshirt or tying a cilice around his waist or thigh... All these things he had considered for himself. Should he recommend them to Felicia too?

He thought about it for a while, but, at length, he shook his head. 'I know of many penances you could attempt, Felicia. But, in principle, if you deny your body lawful pleasures, such as nourishment and sleep, it will draw back from seeking forbidden ones...' He sat back. 'Could you consider some such denials for yourself?'

'Perhaps...' She bit her lip. 'But, Father, do you not want to *know* the thoughts that are so plaguing me?'

It was chilly inside the sacristy, yet his armpits were hot and damp, and he tugged at the collar of his cassock, as the heat rose up his neck, soon to flood his cheeks. He couldn't think straight with her here in front of him. Couldn't fathom how to answer her. *Did* he want to know? If they were connected with Rafe Byllynges, could he bear to hear them?

'Only if you feel compelled to tell me,' he said. 'This'—he indicated the sacristy—'is not, after all, the confessional.'

Shifting slightly on the stool, she leaned towards him across the corner of his desk. The cloth of her habit, trapped by the desk edge, strained against her body, revealing the curve of her breasts. He could see their gentle rise and fall as her breathing seemed to quicken.

Her bottom lip then quivered slightly, and her eyes grew wide with what looked very much like fear. Was she *afraid* to tell him...? Dreading his response?

He havered, not knowing what to do or say, until, with a sudden rush of comprehension, he knew: Felicia's wide eyes and quivering lip were not a sign of fear at all. They were an *invitation*. This tale of unsettling thoughts was a ruse: she had come to taunt him, perhaps aware of his innocence with women.

For she herself was *not* an innocent: Sister Felicia was a whore...

He unclasped his hands, the flesh of his palms and thumb pads now red and sore with the stigmata of his fingernails. He folded his arms across his chest. What he *should* do was give the slut a string of penances, and send her packing...

He stared at her, her head inclined, her slender body still aslant his desk.

She was *offering* herself to him, he was certain of it. How could he pass up what might be his only chance? Despite his duty to his position, despite the imperative for control, his insides churned again, confusing his resolve.

'And yet...' he began, not knowing quite what he was about to say, until the words rushed out of him, more or less unbidden. 'In my experience, acting out one's desires can often help to mitigate them...' He gasped. What was he saying? That was the *opposite* of what he should advise...

'Oh, do you think so?' she said, her eyes wide again. 'But how?'

Once more, she ran her tongue lightly over her bottom lip and Edgar felt nausea rise up from his belly. He was about to suggest an act so wicked he might well burn in hell for it. He might condemn her too. Yet wasn't she already lost?

'It is unsafe here,' he said, his head reeling.

'For acting out?' She tilted her head again. 'I know of a place more private...'

The storeroom? How humiliating to go where another man – a lowly bailiff – had already swived her...

'As do I,' he said, thinking of a disused barn he knew, tumbledown but hidden beneath the boundary trees of a fallow field. He told her where it was.

'I do not know it,' she said, then giggled. 'Yet, why would I?'

Edgar smiled, charmed by her despite himself. 'I think we should go incognito,' he said. 'Do you still have your secular clothes?'

They agreed to meet that evening, during Compline, an assignation time he knew she was familiar with. He left his lodgings for an evening stroll, dressed as a simple countryman. For a worrying few moments, he wondered if Felicia would actually come, or if her promise to do so had also been a ruse.

She was breathless when she arrived at the agreed meeting place, the little bridge that crossed the river, which she had said she knew. Her eyes were bright. 'I managed to escape the dorter with a small bundle of my clothes,' she said, 'and changed in one of the empty storerooms off the courtyard.'

He knew well enough the one she meant.

'But, as I left,' she carried on, 'Sister Amata suddenly appeared in the courtyard, heading for the ancients' cottage.' She giggled. 'I thought she might see me! But I suspect her eyesight is not too good, and I was able to slip away when she was knocking on the cottage door.'

She then did a twirl. 'Do I look like a village girl?'

Her gown was plain enough, in a greenish fabric not of the finest quality. Her hair was uncovered, gathered by a ribbon into a sort of twist. He wondered why there was so much of it, but didn't mention it. Instead, he nodded. 'You'll do. But let us get away from here.'

19

MEONBRIDGE

OCTOBER 1366

As soon as Rosa knew Evangelina was to be away from Northwick for a week or so, she decided she too would go on a journey: to Meonbridge. She wanted to see John, to speak to him about Anabella, but also to talk to his mother, Alice. Alice had had such a close friendship with Mama, Rosa imagined she must have been devastated by Mama's death.

Rosa thought of her mother often – much more so now than she had when she was alive. She regretted being such a "difficult" daughter, as Mama had called her, in the year or so before she came to Northwick.

She wanted too to spend some time with her childhood friend, Agnes, although she was not exactly sure what she wanted to talk to her about.

Despite her irresolution about how – or even if – she should challenge Evangelina about the harm she was bringing to Northwick, she was unable to let the idea go that she had a *duty* to do so. Some of

Evangelina's changes were sacrilegious, and Rosa was sure most – if perhaps, not all – of the other sisters would support her if she did confront the prioress.

Yet she continued to find it almost impossible to reconcile rebellion with obedience.

She could discuss her concerns with Beatrice, although Beatrice tended towards enthusiasm for rebellion, whilst Rosa remained unsure she wanted to be persuaded...

However, if she could discuss the rights and wrongs of rebellion with Beatrice, she could not raise her other worry: Evangelina's threat to expose the reason she came to Northwick.

Yet, she did also wonder how much she cared, and also which was more important, her own reputation or Northwick's future. Who could help her decide?

Sharing her doubts with God had done little to ease the load, which was disappointing, not to say distressing. But, once she had decided to go to Meonbridge, it came to her that there was someone there who might be able to help her decide: Agnes. Once her closest friend, indeed the most intimate friend she had ever had, Agnes was the one person who knew, and understood, her past, however painful it might be to recollect it.

Rosa had told Beatrice of her plans to go to Meonbridge. 'I do not intend asking permission for leave from Sister Clarice,' she added.

Beatrice tapped her nose. 'How long will you be gone?'

'A few days. No more than four.'

'Are you travelling alone?' She looked concerned.

'I have arranged for Jack Bowmaster from the village to accompany me. You know him, I am sure.'

'A respectable fellow. You had dealings with him when you were acting subprioress, I think?'

'Indeed. Meonbridge is not so very far, but I could scarcely travel unaccompanied. In the past, the ride has taken me three, or at most four, hours so, if we leave early in the morning, Jack will be home again by the middle of the afternoon. I trust him to ensure I keep on the right road, and to protect me from rogues.' Beatrice looked briefly horrified, as if she never travelled abroad herself and knew nothing of the dangers of the road. Nonetheless, she spoke no more of rogues.

'Will you be visiting Master atte Wode?' she said instead.

'I shall. Also his mother, who was close to my mama from when they were young. I have had little opportunity to talk to her since Mama died, such a long time ago.'

She thought to mention Agnes too, but at length did not, for no good reason other than her own anxiety about what might pass between them...

Rosa had not been to Meonbridge since her mother's funeral – nearly two years ago. At the time, she had been recovering from a fever, the fever that had prevented her from attending the celebration of Dickon's betrothal to Angharad Fitzpeyne... The fever that had kept her from her mother's side the day she died. She had been disappointed enough to miss the betrothal, but not to have been with her mama at the moment when she passed into the next life had distressed her beyond measure.

When John brought her the news of her mother's death, her grief had been overwhelming. Not only at her loss and the manner of it, but also because of her regrets about the past. Despite Amata's pleas that she was not yet recovered, she refused to miss the funeral. How glad she was she made the journey. For she was able to comfort Dickon in his own devastation – the boy was still only fifteen – and was glad to see how deeply the tenants, too, mourned their lady's passing.

She had not returned to Meonbridge since. With her mother no longer there, and Dickon visiting only rarely, she had no one to return for. Yet there *were* folk she wanted to – needed to – talk to: Agnes, John and Alice. Indeed, she did wonder why she had not come to see them before now. It was well over a year ago that Evangelina was elected prioress and John was banished from Northwick. In all that time, she could have – should have – visited. Although Evangelina did discourage the sisters from leaving Northwick: indeed, she more or less forbade it.

Yet Rosa had much to say to John, and Alice, *and* Agnes. She also felt she needed the comfort of "home". Which was extraordinary, when she had felt no such need in all the previous fifteen years. *Northwick* had been her home, and her sanctuary, but it no longer seemed like either...

When she arrived, she wandered through the manor house, reminding herself of times past – when she was a child, when her mother had been such a strong presence in her life. How strange it was now to be the only de Bohun here... To move from room to room and find them empty, and to go out into the gardens and walk in and out of the potagers and the herbary and the arbour, and find no longer any trace of her mama.

But she was relieved to see the gardens were in good order, indeed it was clear they had been flourishing. It was autumn, so much of the colour in the flower gardens had faded, although some of the roses still clung on. But the potagers were still burgeoning, with leeks and parsnips, cabbages and kale, all set out neatly in long rows and evidently well-tended. Was this Dickon's doing, to ensure his grandmother's precious gardens were taken care of?

She recalled how, following the pestilence, her father had refused to permit any of the tenants to help Mama in her gardens. Everything had grown wild from months of neglect, yet much more work was needed in the fields, and there were not enough men – or even women – left to do it all. So, the manor's gardens simply had to be abandoned. The vegetation grew even wilder, and Mama battled on alone trying to bring the roses and the honeysuckle under control, and to recover what she could of the potagers.

After she died, the manor's gardeners would of course maintain the potagers and orchards, but the flower gardens might have been allowed to wither. Yet she imagined Dickon knew how important to his grandmother the colourful swathes of flowers had been, and especially the walkways and arbours with their magnificent show of honeysuckle and climbing roses. He must have decided he could not allow her memory to be tarnished by neglecting them. Meonbridge's young lord was clearly thoughtful and compassionate as well as wise.

Rosa decided to talk to Alice first, then John. She would leave the likely difficult conversation with Agnes for another day. So, after dinner the first day, John brought his mother to the manor house, then left her with Rosa in the hall.

'I've work to do,' he said, 'but I'll be back later to fetch Ma home.'

Rosa took Alice's hand and drew her forward. 'Would you like to sit upstairs in the solar, or stroll around the garden?'

'Oh, the garden, I think,' said Alice. 'For a little while... I haven't seen it for so long ...'

Rosa led her back to the great door, which led out onto the bailey. They took the steps down carefully. Alice was still limping slightly, presumably from the fall she had last summer. Rosa remembered how long it had taken Mama's leg to heal, and she had been younger than Alice was now. Nonetheless, as they strolled across the bailey towards the entrance to the manor's gardens, Alice's energy seemed to revive.

'I can guess what you want to talk to me about,' said Alice, the light in her eyes just as Rosa always remembered it.

Rosa smiled. 'So much time has passed since Mama died, and we have not had the opportunity to talk about her, to reminisce. I thought we would both have happy memories to share.'

Alice returned her smile, if wanly. 'Not a day goes by when I don't think of Margaret. I do miss her so...'

'I thought as much. I know you spent many hours together, especially in recent years...'

'We did. We never ran out of things to talk about. Though what they were I couldn't tell you now...' She grinned.

'Mama considered you her closest friend—'

'Despite the difference in our stations...'

'That was of no consequence to Mama. She greatly valued your company and your wisdom.'

'And I hers...'

Just beyond the physic garden, they reached the orchard which had, at its centre, a circular tunnel arbour thickly planted with vines and white roses. They came shortly to the hidden archway, half way round the circle, that led into the fragrant, flowery interior of a little enclosed herbary, with a lawn and fountain in the centre. Rosa drew Alice over to the little turf seat nestling beneath an arching trellis overwhelmed with honeysuckle, and they sat down.

Rosa's cheeks warmed slightly as, looking down at her lap, she decided to make a confession. 'How guilty I still feel,' she said, 'that, when I left Meonbridge seventeen years ago, Mama and I were not on the best of terms.' She looked up. 'I presume you know about that?'

'Margaret did tell me of it, and how very sad it made her.' Alice touched Rosa's hand. 'But I know too your bond grew stronger as you found contentment in your life at Northwick.'

Tears pricked Rosa's eyes; how thankful she was that Mama had been able to share her thoughts with Alice.

'Young girls can be difficult,' continued Alice. 'Before Agnes disappeared – you remember?' —Rosa nodded, her heart turning over— 'I didn't understand her, nor what was happening. It was so distressing...'

Rosa swallowed hard. Was Alice about to raise the reason Agnes ran away? She had not planned for their conversation to go that way...

But Alice was carrying on. 'For a whole year, I thought I'd lost her forever. But then, when she returned, with Jack and baby Dickon, I forgave her everything, so glad to have her home...' She smiled. 'That is what mothers do. Margaret was very troubled when you went to Northwick, apparently under some sort of cloud, but she was so proud of the woman you became, she understood and forgave you your decision.'

Rosa coughed to clear the slight catch in her throat. 'Thank you for telling me, dear Alice,' she whispered then fell silent.

But Alice soon filled the void. She eased herself to her feet and took a turn about the herbary, stepping over to the fountain, although the water was no longer bubbling. 'I must keep moving,' she said, looking back at Rosa. 'My leg still pains me, but walking helps.'

Rosa made a move to stand, but Alice shook her head. 'No, no, I can manage.' She took two more turns, then returned to the turf seat. 'I remember when Margaret broke her leg. It took a long time to heal, but she found gentle walking every day helped.' She grinned. 'I'm trying to do the same.'

Despite her physical frailty, Alice seemed glad of the chance to talk, and to ask questions. Perhaps John and Agnes did not give her much opportunity for conversation?

She came to sit back down again. 'I've another story about your mother I think you might not know,' she said.

'Am I really so ignorant of my mother?' Rosa grinned.

Alice shook her head. 'Some things mothers keep from their children, to save them shock or grief. And I suspect Margaret might never have told you how badly she was afflicted by the mortality?'

'The mortality!' Rosa gasped. 'Surely Mama was not struck down?'

'She was, when you were still away with the de Courtenays. She didn't want anyone to know – though I did, and Sir Richard. But I'd like to tell you of it now.'

Rosa listened wide-eyed, as Alice told her how her mama had alone nursed Philip's foolish wife, Isabella, after she left the manor house to see the healer, and came back afflicted with the terrible disease. Mama was unable to save Isabella, but then found she herself was sick. She refused to allow anyone to come near her, nursing herself alone. Until, at length, the buboes burst and she recovered.

'How strong your mother was, to be brave enough first to tend alone to Isabella, and then to nurse herself,' said Alice.

'She might have died.' Rosa's heart ached with a mix of horror, relief and pride. Tears pricked her eyes as she recalled how "difficult" she had been when she returned home from Courtenay Castle, not knowing how close she had come to losing her mother.

'She might, but she didn't. I know she prayed constantly for salvation, and in the end, God spared her, because he saw her willingness to sacrifice herself for others' sake.'

Rosa grasped Alice's hands and squeezed them. 'Thank you so much for telling me that story, Alice. Of course, I knew Mama was strong, but not how selfless and courageous she was.'

'I believe you are much like her,' said Alice, tilting her head.

Rosa flushed. Once, she *had* felt strong, if not exactly courageous; all those months ago, before Angelica died. But, since then, her confidence had been severely shaken. She said so, and Alice looked surprised. So she told her about the election – although not the reason why she did not stand – and how distressed the new prioress's changes were making her.

Alice said nothing for a while. 'Sometimes, I suppose,' she said at length, 'it's difficult to find the strength to overcome such dreadful setbacks.' She got up again, and this time held out her hand for Rosa to accompany her on her stroll around the herbary. Alice tucked her arm into Rosa's and squeezed lightly. 'But your mother did find the strength, many, many times, and I'm certain you will too.'

In her exchange of letters with John in the months following Evangelina's election, Rosa had mentioned that Anabella would not make her final vows for at least two years. Yet recently she realised her confidence had been misplaced and, when John entered the solar chamber, instead of being able to welcome him warmly, she felt discomfited.

'I am so sorry, John,' she said, after their initial exchange of greetings, 'but I am afraid I have misled you. For I now think it possible that, when Evangelina returns to Northwick, she might start pressing Anabella to commit, in order to confirm her dowry. Time might be shorter than we thought.'

His face was aghast. 'Why didn't you bring Bella with you?' he said. 'You could've got her out of there, whilst the prioress was away.' His voice was full of alarm.

She sighed. 'John, Bella is most unwilling to leave the priory. She is terrified that, once she is outside its walls, her husband's family might seize her, and force her to marry his brother.'

'But how would they know?'

'She is convinced they have a spy inside the priory.'

'A spy! One of the nuns, you mean?' His eyes widened.

Rosa pursed her lips. She would not try to overcome his incredulity by telling him that even nuns can pry upon their sisters. Like Letitia.

'Not necessarily a sister,' she said, 'but perhaps a servant? Anyway, Bella believes the "spy" might somehow discover she was planning to leave the priory, and alert the Sitwells.'

John snorted. 'That sounds unlikely...'

'Indeed. I too am not convinced. I asked her what evidence she had of such a spy, and she admitted she had none, just an intuition.' Yet, if it *were* true, how shocking it would be to arrange Bella's escape only to have her captured...

'Besides, if Bella had come with me,' she continued, 'the novice mistress would have known. I am certain she would have made a fuss.

It seemed preferable for me to come alone, so you and I at least could talk, and make a plan...'

'A plan?'

'To "get her out of there",' said Rosa, grinning. 'A plan secret enough to ensure that any spy does not discover it.'

John chewed his lip a moment. 'But does Bella *want* to leave?'

'When I told her I was coming here, she was very sad not be coming too. She asked me to give you her warmest felicitations.'

'"Felicitations"!' he cried. 'No more than that?'

'Oh, John,' said Rosa, smiling, 'even if she had wanted to say more, she would scarcely have said it to me. Such words are only spoken directly between beloveds. But, yes, I am certain Bella *does* want to be with you.' She tilted her head. 'Assuming you still want *her*?'

He threw his hands up. 'Of course I do!'

'She does feel guilty about letting Northwick down – reneging on her agreement with Angelica, as she puts it – but she does also realise she has no vocation for the religious life.'

John began to pace a little. 'But now *I'm* afraid she might be forced into making her vows against her will.' He rubbed the back of his neck and sighed.

'Which is why we need to devise a plan before that happens,' said Rosa. 'We must discuss it *now*. Bella will accept whatever we – you – decide, provided she believes she is in no danger of falling into the Sitwells' hands. She has to be confident that, when she leaves Northwick, it is to safety, to a marriage ceremony that will make her your wife.'

'So, are you thinking I storm the priory and carry her off?'

She laughed briefly. 'Indeed...'

John spun around. 'What do you mean, "indeed"? You're not really expecting me to do that, are you?'

'Well, perhaps not "storm the priory", no, but I think you might have to come for her, and somehow insist she leaves with you...'

'But the prioress won't allow it...'

'Unless she is *unable* to refuse...'

'What are you saying? Sounds like you're plotting something...'

She *was* "plotting", albeit she did not yet know the exact nature and detail of the plot. All she did know was that Anabella had to leave the priory and become John's wife. Soon. One way or another.

'Think upon it, John,' she said, 'and we shall talk again.'

When Rosa and Agnes were girls, they often escaped their mothers' company and fled into the garden. Their favourite place was invariably the orchard, provided none of the gardeners were working there. At certain times of year there was fruit to be scrumped. In spring and early summer, it was cherries, in late summer there would be plums. But, at this time of year, the pear and apple trees would be laden, their branches sagging to the ground, making it easy to reach up and pick them. Rosa smiled to herself as she recalled how often she and Agnes made themselves ill from overeating, greed making it impossible to resist picking just one more...

It was the orchard where she now wanted to meet Agnes, not to steal apples but to talk. Her conversation with Alice had raised her spirits hugely: she already felt stronger and more willing to stand up to Evangelina. But she still had to decide if she was truly willing to betray her vows and risk her own reputation for the sake of the priory. She had to air her thoughts with someone who might understand, and that person, she had decided, was Agnes.

Soon after dawn, Rosa sent a boy to Agnes's house with a message for her to come to the orchard after dinner. But, at dinner, she picked at her food, nervous about their conversation. After all, why should Agnes even *want* to help her when she had so cruelly betrayed their friendship?

But when Agnes arrived, she was hurrying and smiling broadly. Rosa took her outstretched hands and squeezed them. 'Thank you for coming, Agnes. It is so good to see you.' How pretty she looked. Scarcely any different from when she was a girl, albeit fine lines did crinkle beside her eyes and around her mouth, and her lovely hair was hidden beneath her matronly wimple. Rosa knew Agnes had suffered with melancholy for years but now, in her eyes, she could see the sunny, spirited Agnes of old.

'It's been too long,' said Agnes. 'John's always told us your news, and how happy you were at Northwick... And how *un*happy you are now...' She faltered. '*Are* you unhappy? Is the new prioress ruining your contentment?'

'Not only mine. Her favourites are content enough, but those who are outside her circle are as dismayed as I am by the changes she has made.'

'John said as much. I'm so sorry. It must be distressing.'

Rosa was surprised and relieved at Agnes's immediate sympathy for her plight. She had been right after all that she *would* understand...

'Indeed. Yet... Agnes...' She hesitated. 'I have something I wish to tell you, something I cannot discuss with anyone else, not even my closest companions in the priory...'

'Shall we sit down?' Agnes gestured towards the edge of the orchard.

They walked towards an ancient tree trunk, fallen over years ago and sawn by one of the gardeners to form a makeshift seat. They had used it often when they were girls as their private gossiping place, and Rosa was delighted to find it was still there. She let out a wistful sigh as she looked across towards the broad patch of dense woodland that started just beyond the orchard and, at length, led up to Riverdown. 'How we used to love coming here,' she said.

'We did.' Agnes slid her hand towards Rosa's and touched it lightly. 'What is it you want to talk about?'

Rosa let her fingers respond to Agnes's touch. 'The problem at Northwick is not only the changes the prioress is making.' She looked away, aware that, now she had come to this point, she was almost afraid. 'There is more...' She paused again, and Agnes pressed her hand lightly in encouragement.

'Because I have criticised her for what she has been doing, the prioress – Evangelina – is threatening me... Threatening to expose why I entered Northwick all those years ago... In truth, I do not understand how she could *know*, but cannot decide whether or not to risk her threat...'

Agnes's brow was furrowed. 'So why *did* you go to Northwick? I thought you simply decided you wanted to be a nun?'

'Not exactly. I have never told anyone the true reason, other than

Mother Angelica, but I feel the time has come for me to do so. Are you willing to listen? It does involve you...'

Agnes nodded slowly. 'Ah, I see. Very well, if it might help...'

'Thank you, dear Agnes. We might be here some time.'

She shrugged. 'I've all afternoon.'

So Rosa embarked upon her long confession. 'Although I have found peace at Northwick, through prayer and work, I have never fully overcome the guilt and shame that drove me there.'

'What guilt?' said Agnes, her eyes wide. 'What shame?'

'Shame at harbouring what I knew was an unnatural affection for my brother, which made me jealous of *your* relationship with him. *Guilt* at betraying you, my closest friend, by helping him seduce you.'

'I always thought you were unhappy...'

'I realise now how very confused I was: my unseemly passion for Philip, my irrational desperation to please him, my pitiable jealousy of you, my inexcusable lack of consideration for your feelings or your future − *you*, my closest friend! All conspired to make me deeply unhappy.'

Agnes took her hand and squeezed it. 'Johanna...' she whispered.

'Then there was the appalling way I treated poor Sir Giles. I knew he was a good man and a fine potential husband. How I regret the hurt I must have caused him. Albeit I am certain he has found great happiness with Lady Gwynedd, and his family.' She exhaled. 'At the time, I was horrified by Giles's physical appearance, yet I think I might have been persuaded to overcome my shock if it had not been for Philip's murder.' She looked up at Agnes. 'Instead, I decided to renounce the world of men and become a nun.'

'Of course, I wasn't in Meonbridge when Philip died,' said Agnes. 'But I do understand how devastating it must have been for you, yet not why it led you to such a decision.'

Rosa fingered the crucifix that hung on a cord about her neck. As a girl, she had believed that Philip's death was somehow a punishment from God − both for him, and for herself, because they were both sinners.

But, when she said it, Agnes frowned. 'Then I was a sinner too.'

'Perhaps. Yet, I still believed what happened to you was *my* fault. Although life turned out well for you, how easily it might not have!

You might have died in childbirth or fallen into dishonour...' She touched the cross again. 'I have spent fifteen years trying to atone for what I did. Yet, despite my constant piety, God has not helped me to forgive myself. Although,' she lowered her voice, 'it is not my own forgiveness that I need, Agnes, but yours.'

Agnes shook her head. 'You don't need my forgiveness. What I did with Philip, I did freely – eagerly. It was wrong – sinful! – but I was responsible for my actions. I knew it was dangerous, and chose to ignore the danger. My plight, and flight, were my responsibility, not yours.' She stood up. 'Let's walk a while,' she said and held out her hand.

Rosa took it and stood up too. Agnes led her back towards the apple trees. She stopped at one whose heavy-laden branches were nestling in the grass, clusters of red-tinted apples clinging to each one's entire length. She plucked a fruit and held it out to Rosa. 'I ate of the forbidden fruit quite willingly,' she said, smiling. She picked another apple and bit into it. 'I'm so grateful that my life has, as you say, turned out well, when it might have been so different. I couldn't be more fortunate to have Jack, and my lovely children...'

Rosa bit into her apple too. She was not sure she could wholeheartedly accept Agnes's dismissal of her guilt, but she was glad of it, nonetheless. The weight that had burdened her for so long did now seem a little lighter.

They ate their apples, then, arm in arm, made a long circuit of the orchard, saying little. Then Agnes asked Rosa if she ever regretted becoming a nun. She didn't respond immediately, finding herself surprised by the question, as if she'd never thought of it.

At length she answered. 'Yes, I do believe it *was* the right decision. For if I had not entered Northwick, I would never have found the peace of mind or joy in life that I discovered under Angelica's rule.'

'But might you not also have found contentment as a wife and mother?'

She laughed lightly. What a question to ask a nun! 'I might. After all, there is no reason why, if I had allowed myself, I could not have made a marriage as successful as, say, yours, or your parents' or indeed my own parents'. It is possible. But I made my decision and obviously I cannot unmake it. So, I must be content with my life in Northwick.'

She pursed her lips. 'Yet, to *be* content, I must somehow change it back to the way it was.'

Thus, the conversation reverted to her determination to confront Evangelina for her violation of Northwick, *and* her fear of being "exposed" for doing so.

'But how much does that really matter?' said Agnes. 'It's clear the priory is more important to you than anything else. If you suffer personal disgrace in the pursuit of setting Northwick right again, can't you live with that? Isn't the priory's sanctity more important than your own?'

Which was, of course, what she had been thinking. 'Although, as I have said, I cannot imagine what Evangelina can truly know about my past. Angelica would not have told her, and I am certain no one else knows the full story.'

'So, the risk of you falling into disrepute is small?' said Agnes. 'And, therefore, worth taking?' Rosa nodded. 'What would you have to do?'

'We, the sisters, can denounce Evangelina at the bishop's visitation. That is when the bishop comes himself or sends his representatives to examine us. She will almost certainly deny everything, but we could pursue it until the truth is out.'

'So, there is a *proper* means for sisters to rebel?'

'I had not thought of it like that, but yes, there is.'

'Then that is what you must do, at whatever time you feel is right.'

The next day, shortly after Prime, Agnes came once more to the manor house, and asked to speak to Rosa. Much buoyed by their conversation yesterday, Rosa was pleased to see her again, and wondered what more she had to say.

They sat together on one of the stone seats built into the long walls of the great hall. 'After I returned home yesterday,' said Agnes, 'two thoughts occurred to me. The first might help you further assuage your guilt about the past. The second might resolve one of your present problems. And both involve Eleanor Nash...'

'Eleanor?' Rosa was intrigued. 'What on earth can she have to do with any of this?'

When she explained, Rosa agreed that Eleanor should come to speak to her. If she was willing, they would return in the afternoon.

Rosa had never known Eleanor well. There were only two years between them but, despite Eleanor being the daughter of one of the wealthiest freemen on the manor, their paths had rarely crossed.

Eleanor and Agnes joined Rosa in the solar room, where they could talk without the chance of being overheard. After the usual exchange of pleasantries, Agnes explained that Eleanor had two pieces of information that she was sure Rosa did not already know.

'The first,' said Agnes, 'concerns Philip's death.' Rosa gasped. What might *Eleanor* know of that? 'For I suspect, Rosa,' Agnes continued, 'you don't know exactly *why* Philip died.'

'Robert Tyler...' she said, and Agnes nodded.

'Yes, he was responsible, but I warrant you don't know *why* he wanted Philip dead. For, until Lady Margaret was attacked two years ago, *none* of us in Meonbridge knew the real reason, apart from her ladyship herself and Eleanor.'

Rosa's mouth fell open, and she closed it quickly. 'But I understood that Robert lost his senses, and murdered Philip out of resentment and rage. I daresay that, at the time, I did not try to comprehend the why and wherefore of it, for, as you know, I believed my brother's death to be somehow God-sent.' She glanced at Eleanor, who appeared not to question what she said, but took a sip of the wine Rosa had poured them earlier. 'So, is there some other explanation?'

Eleanor put down her cup and nodded. 'Shortly before Lady Margaret died, at the hand of Margery Tyler,' she said, 'she bid me explain to the assembled company the connection between her own imminent death and Philip's. The connection *was* the Tylers.'

'But I think I'm right,' Agnes said, turning to Rosa, 'that *you've* never learned the truth. When you came for her ladyship's funeral, you weren't told then?'

'I do not recollect being told anything new.'

'Then, let me tell you now,' said Eleanor, 'what I told the company that day, at her ladyship's request.'

Rosa was both bewildered and shocked by the story Eleanor told.

What she herself had understood – Robert Tyler's part in Philip's murder, and that played by Gilbert Fletcher and his other henchman –

had quickly become what most folk thought in Meonbridge. But, as she now learned, Mama and Eleanor knew about Robert's *other* crime, forcing his own daughter, Matilda, to abort her baby. A baby that was also Philip's....'

Rosa gasped. Philip had lain with Matilda? So, did he always plan to dishonour Agnes too? She felt sick at the thought of it, but took a few deep breaths, and asked Eleanor what happened.

'A short while after his marriage to Isabella,' said Eleanor, 'when she was already with child and spurning his advances, his eyes had strayed towards Matilda. Her father then became so unhinged with wrath and indignation at Philip's defilement of his daughter that he not only ordered the abortion but also Philip's murder...' She hesitated. 'But what I have to tell you next, Rosa, is even more shocking.'

How right she was. Rosa's horror heightened as she heard that Matilda's older sister, Margery, had deduced – quite mistakenly, of course – that it was *Mama* who had demanded the abortion of Matilda's baby, and *that* was the reason for Margery's attack.

Rosa let out a cry. 'But Mama would never do such a thing!'

Eleanor shook her head. 'No, no, of course she wouldn't. Margery claimed her ladyship did it to protect Philip's and the de Bohun family's reputation, but *no one* in Meonbridge believed that to be true. Margery was terribly deluded, just as her father had been years before.'

Of course that had to be true. 'When John told me of Mama's death,' said Rosa, 'he said Margery must have lost her wits, and I agreed with him. For I did not believe she could possibly think what had happened to her family truly warranted such a very *evil* deed. Of course, I still presumed that it was *Robert* who had brought ruin down upon them, when he lost his senses, and murdered Philip.' She shook her head. 'But John did not tell me anything of this other horror... the matter of the abortion. Did he not know of it then?'

Agnes pursed her lips. 'He did know, yes, for he was there when Eleanor related it to the company.' She laid her hand upon Rosa's. 'But I suspect he didn't want to tell you about it, or about Margery's slur against her ladyship, thinking your grief at your mother's death would be more than enough for you to bear.'

Rosa grasped Agnes's hand and squeezed it. 'Yes, I think you must be right, Agnes. It is certainly in John's nature to take care not to cause me more anguish than I was suffering already.'

They all three sat quietly for a while, sipping wine. Then Rosa turned to Eleanor.

'How was it that you knew about all this?' she asked.

Eleanor sighed. 'I had once been Matilda's closest friend, and she told me the whole story at the time and begged me to take it to her ladyship. She *denounced* her father for forcing the abortion, and accused both him and her own husband, Gilbert, of Philip's murder. Her testimony about the murder ensured that Robert and Gilbert did not get away with their crimes, but no one other than Lady Margaret and I – and Matilda of course – was ever privy to the rest.'

'Why?'

She shrugged. 'In truth, I do not really know. Perhaps it was more a case of oversight than intent? For so much was happening in those difficult months after the mortality had passed on. There was a great deal more for people – the de Bohuns and all of Meonbridge's folk – to worry about than the motives of a man who'd lost his wits and then his life.'

'Yet I'm sorry it's taken so long for *you* to learn the truth,' said Agnes. 'It's undoubtedly been distressing.'

Rosa sighed.

Then Agnes tilted her head. 'But what this does mean, Rosa – and is one reason why I wanted Eleanor to tell you the truth – is that Philip's death *wasn't* God-sent punishment at all, but simply the result of one *man's* hunger for revenge.'

Agnes locked eyes with Rosa, and Rosa nodded.

Yes, she was right of course. Bless Agnes, for trying to help her overcome her guilt. Could she do so? She was still not sure. Yet, in truth, was it not clear? Robert had Philip murdered in revenge for his violation of *Matilda*.

It was *nothing* to do with her, or with Agnes.

How difficult it all was to comprehend. But she would think more about it later. For now, Rosa turned to Eleanor. 'So, what was the other thought you had?'

'It is to do with Anabella Sitwell.'

20

Northwick Priory
October 1366

Evangelina had expected to return to Northwick riding the crest of a triumphant wave. Aside from spending some time with her family, the most important reason for her trip had been to settle the promised endowment from Sir Toby Edenborough. An endowment he'd led her to believe would be substantial. She'd imagined having the funds to spend on more silk gowns as well as wimples, on more extensive entertaining, and on providing more tapestries and carpets for her chamber. Albeit she'd thought she might implement one or two small improvements to the sisters' lives as well, to show she did also have their interests at heart. Not that she'd decided precisely what the "improvements" might be, other than that they'd not cost very much...

But now it seemed *none* of that could happen.

For, despite his earlier enthusiasm for beneficing the priory, Sir Toby Edenborough had changed his mind.

At the dinner table, he hummed and hawed. 'My dear Lady Prioress,' he said, perspiration beading on his forehead, 'I regret to tell you that my...um, circumstances... have, um, altered.' He took a large swig of his wine. 'Business troubles... quite unforeseen... And the upshot, I regret to say, is that, at this moment, I do not have the funds...'

Sir Toby's wife was a picture of embarrassment throughout the conversation, her eyes fixed upon the fine white cloth covering the table, her hands kneading at her napkin, her elegant shoulders hunched. Was she ashamed of her husband's failure to deal with his "business troubles"? Or were they also leaving *her* short of funds to run her household? But then Evangelina wondered if Sir Toby was *inventing* his business troubles... Somehow, she did suspect it. It seemed so unlikely a man of his evident wealth should suddenly find himself without reserves... Yet she could scarcely demand to know the real reason for his change of mind.

So she swallowed her suspicions and, with as much grace as she could muster, expressed her disappointment and hoped he might reconsider as soon as he was able.

'Of course, of course, my dear Lady Evangelina.' He beamed. 'As soon as I have overcome what is, I am sure, only a temporary setback, I shall most assuredly reassess my pledge to Northwick...' He gestured to his servant to pour them all more wine, swallowed his in a single gulp, then demanded more. Evangelina took several sips of hers, but took no more of the food congealing on her trencher.

It had been a most unsatisfactory conclusion to an otherwise delightful trip.

How good it was to have escaped the confines of the priory, and to stay and dine in the grandeur of Sir Toby's mansion. She'd been given the most sumptuous of their guest chambers, and the food served was of the very best quality, rich and plentiful.

The wedding too had been a magnificent occasion. She cared little about the intrigues and manoeuvrings of the marriage market, but greatly enjoyed the splendour of the celebration. For the young wife of her cousin's son came from a very wealthy family, who spared no expense to display their power and influence to their wider kin, friends and neighbours. Moreover, as a prioress, she'd been given an honoured place on the top table, and was asked to give her blessing to the couple.

How much she relished the deference she was shown, and how well she thought she rose to the occasion.

All that had been most satisfactory. She'd had high hopes of a successful outcome to her discussions with Sir Toby, and was flustered, not to say distraught, when they came to nothing.

For how could she return to Northwick without the prize she'd promised?

It was fortunate Letitia hadn't after all witnessed Sir Toby's *volte-face*. When she enquired later how the negotiations had progressed, Evangelina had already decided not to admit the truth.

'A charming man, Sir Toby,' she said.

'He is. Has he offered the endowment you expected?'

They were already on their way back to the priory, riding upon their palfreys, well-wrapped up against an autumn day that was chilly but at least dry. Alternating between walk and trot, the horses were ambling sedately, making it easier for Evangelina to respond. 'Indeed, he has. He was as good as his word.'

At the chapter meeting the next day, she announced the outcome of her visit. A fine endowment, she called it. A splendid benefactor, she said of Sir Toby.

Nearly all the sisters applauded eagerly, and she couldn't help but notice that Rosa and Beatrice looked wrong-footed. Had they *hoped* she might return empty-handed? Of course they had...

Yet how would she deal with it when the money wasn't forthcoming after all? And for how long could she hide the truth?

Evangelina stood up from her grand chair and beamed, content for now to bask in the glory of her apparent success, albeit she knew it might be short-lived. She didn't yet have a plan to explain that white was black, but she'd surely think of something before too long...

That evening, she sent her favourites off to sleep in the dorter, wanting to be alone in her chamber. She was already less confident that a viable plan might come to her. She fretted too that her deception might be discovered soon, if Rosa or Beatrice, or more likely Dulcia, enquired when Sir Toby's funds would arrive...

She'd have to prevaricate a while. Then, if no plan did present itself, she'd disclose Sir Toby's so-called difficulties, and blame him wholly for misleading her.

Evangelina didn't feel quite herself. Not ill exactly, but somewhat less than her best. She was keeping to her chamber, and ate alone, insisting the girls took their meals in the frater with the other sisters.

Letitia didn't seem to mind at all. She was unusually cheerful after the trip. She'd also enjoyed being out of the priory and in elegant surroundings, and was delighted to answer the other sisters' eager enquiries about what she'd seen and done.

But Maria and Felicia had no interest in her stories. Out of jealousy, Evangelina supposed. Yet it wasn't only that. She wondered what they'd got up to in her absence, for now they seemed to be whispering together a good deal, just the two of them, like giddy maidens sharing secrets. Indeed, their behaviour was not at all fitting for the professed nuns they were, albeit she *was* mildly intrigued by the nature of their confidences.

But she'd not ask either one for details.

All three girls were spending less time in her company than they used to, and the gaiety they'd shared the past twelve months had faded. It was her own doing, of course, but she was downcast by the thought that the power and influence she'd been enjoying was slipping away already, and had little desire for merriment.

Yesterday, responding to an anxious Sister Clarice, Evangelina claimed to be suffering from fatigue. 'Riding such a distance is surprisingly debilitating,' she'd said, 'particularly when you've not done so for many years.'

'I cannot recall the last time I sat upon a horse,' said Clarice. 'It was courageous of you, Reverend Mother, to attempt the journey.' She smiled. 'But most worthwhile.'

Evangelina forced an answering, if feeble, smile. 'Indeed.' She feigned a yawn and leaned back into the cushions on her chair. 'Nonetheless, I'd welcome another day of rest, so please remain in charge a little longer, Clarice. Tell the sisters I'll be fully myself tomorrow.'

In truth, she had to be. She'd ostensibly won a splendid prize, and should be savouring her success, not skulking away alone.

So, after three days of seclusion, Evangelina gave herself a mental shake and put on her best gown and silk wimple.

However, when she summoned the obedientiaries one by one to her chamber, to report any concerns that might have arisen in her absence, her low spirits soon returned, when she discovered Clarice hadn't been exercising quite as much control over the other sisters as she'd expected. Particularly in respect of Sister Rosa.

It was Sister Gracia who mentioned that Rosa had left the priory not long after Evangelina herself. 'Though I did not learn of it until the next day,' she said. 'I went in search of Anabella, needing her to come and help me with the novices. I found her in the sacristy, and was surprised to find her alone.'

'No Rosa, you mean?'

'Indeed. I asked her where Sister Rosa was, and she dissembled, claiming not to know.' Gracia smirked. 'Given Rosa and Beatrice are such cronies, I asked Sister Beatrice if *she* knew where she was.'

'Did she?'

'She dissembled too, but not for long. She said Rosa was in Meonbridge, her home.'

Evangelina bristled. 'Did she say why?'

'I did not press her. I presumed it was to see her family...'

'But Rosa *has* no family. Her father's been dead for years, and her mother died a year or two ago. And I believe she has no siblings...'

Yet Rosa did know *other* people in Meonbridge, such as John atte Wode, the bailiff who used to come to Northwick to advise her and Mother Angelica on husbandry. At the time, Rosa appeared to be quite close to the man, or as close as any religious nun and secular man could be...

Or had there been *more* to their relationship? Had they been lovers...?

Evangelina suppressed a splutter of incredulity at such a notion. Yet she *had* very briefly toyed with the idea a while ago... After all, Rosa had been alone with the man quite often...

As the possibility blossomed in her head, Evangelina looked up sharply. 'Thank you, Gracia,' she said curtly. 'I'll speak to Sister Rosa about her little expedition...' She flicked her hand in a gesture of dismissal.

Gracia looked disappointed but curtsied before slipping from the chamber.

Evangelina took several turns about the room. *Was* it possible? *Had* Master atte Wode given Rosa more than mere advice on the management of fields and livestock?

She laughed out loud. No, it was too improbable, for Rosa of all people to engage in anything so sordid. And yet, if it were true, Rosa would have been deprived of her lover's devotions for twelve whole months... It would scarcely be a surprise if she'd taken the opportunity to run to him, to resume where they'd left off...

Evangelina snorted, relishing the implausible scenario she'd conjured up.

Back at the table where Hilde had recently placed a flagon of wine, she poured herself a cup and sank down into her chair. Her elation at the unlikely possibility of Rosa's indiscretion dissipated, as she thought more about the implications of her trip to Meonbridge.

For she'd left Northwick without permission, not bothering even to ask Clarice if she might go, but simply taking advantage of Evangelina's absence to slip away. It was disobedience... Worse, it was *defiance*.

She thumped the arm of her chair. Damn Rosa! She *was* a threat after all. If she was willing to depart the priory without leave, might she also be ready to reiterate her complaints, or even try to lure more of the sisters over to her point of view?

Evangelina took a gulp of wine. The hand holding the cup was shaking. It was unlike her to be nervous, but she was. For she was vulnerable. The promise of Sir Toby's money was a sign of her power and influence. But, now she'd failed to obtain the endowment she had promised, might she be in danger of losing the loyalty even of those sisters who currently took her part?

She drained her cup in another two great gulps, but, in her haste, a few drops spilled onto the whiteness of her wimple. With an anguished cry, she jumped up and, not bothering to unpin the veil, wrenched the entire wimple up and over her head. She plunged it into the bowl of water she used to rinse her face and hands, swishing it around to wash away the stain. She'd never been given to tears, but a few now brimmed, as the water reddened but the stain on the precious silk merely faded. She rubbed at the pinkness, and at length it faded a little more. It mightn't notice when it was dry... Yet, it was spoiled, and all because of her agitation.

Miserably, she returned to her chair, and slumped back against the cushions. What had she been thinking of before the incident with the wine? Rosa, of course... The thorn in her flesh...

Who, despite, only a few months ago, being intimidated by the gossip-mongering about her, had now, apparently, recovered her resolve.

She'd no idea what, if anything, Rosa might be planning, but was certain she'd become a threat again. A threat she surely had to counter. She had to reassert her authority, and *enforce* Rosa's obedience.

But how?

In truth, she doubted *any* inappropriate relationship existed between Rosa and John atte Wode. Yet, true or not, could she simply use the notion as a pretext for condemning her? Somehow, she had to undermine Rosa's self-assurance. If the story *was* true, surely Rosa would do anything to keep it secret. But, even if it wasn't, wouldn't she be desperate to avoid her reputation being sullied?

When Rosa responded to her summons, Evangelina didn't bother with pleasantries but launched straight in with an accusation.

'What made you think you could leave the priory without permission?' she said, her voice rising.

But Rosa didn't flinch; her back stayed straight, and she maintained a steady gaze. 'You were not here to give permission.'

Evangelina whirled around. 'But Clarice was here, in my place...'

Rosa shrugged. 'I needed to go to Meonbridge. My reasons for doing so were private, not a matter for discussion. I was away for just three days, and I am certain I was scarcely missed.'

'Not so!' cried Evangelina. 'Sister Gracia noticed you were absent.'

'What was that to her? Gracia and I have almost nothing to do with one another ordinarily...'

Evangelina grunted. This could develop into a pointless tit for tat, whereas what she had to do was knock Rosa's confidence. She changed her tone. 'Did you speak to Master atte Wode when you were in Meonbridge?' she asked, tipping her head as if in innocent enquiry.

'Of course. I know nearly everyone in Meonbridge, and I took the opportunity to speak to many of them...'

'But you made a *special* point of seeing him?'

'No more so than anyone else.' She lifted her chin and stared directly at Evangelina.

Irritated by Rosa's composure, Evangelina whirled away with a swish of her skirts. Then, sidling back, she came up behind her. She leaned in close to Rosa's ear. 'I'm not sure I believe you,' she murmured, her tone deliberately intimidating. 'Why would you travel all that way, merely to chat to a few tenants?'

She side-stepped and came round to face Rosa, tilting her head again. 'No, I suspect there's rather *more* to your relationship with the Meonbridge bailiff...' Rosa's eyes flew open wide, and Evangelina smirked. 'Perhaps your relationship with him is... unnatural?'

Rosa cried out. '"Unnatural"? How dare you suggest such a thing!' Her hands, which had been clasped demurely at her waist, were now flung wide, and she briefly lunged towards Evangelina as if she meant to strike her. But she threw no punch and quickly retreated, shaking with what Evangelina assumed was fury.

Yet was it fury at being accused unjustly, or because a misdemeanour had been exposed?

She didn't know, and didn't care. All she wanted was for Rosa to submit.

She came up close to Rosa once again. 'I always thought there was something *unsavoury* going on between you,' she continued, with a sneer. 'That was why I dismissed him. I can't tolerate debauchery in my priory.' She turned away, as the flagrant falsehood made even her face flush.

Why *had* she dismissed John atte Wode? She could scarcely recall the reason. Was it to do with Rosa? She thought for several moments. She'd wanted to sequester Rosa in the priory, to isolate her from outside influences... Yes, *that* was why she banished him...

She turned back, expecting to see Rosa still angry at the slur against her. But she was composed again, her hands once more clasped at her waist.

'You are *wrong*,' said Rosa, quietly but firmly. 'There is nothing illicit between John and me, and most certainly nothing "unnatural", as you so vilely put it. He and I have always been more like cousins, because of the closeness of our families. If you choose to identify that familiarity as "unnatural", so be it.' Her eyes were glaring. 'I cannot stop you wagging your offensive tongue.'

Evangelina spun around, astonished. 'Offensive tongue!' she cried. 'Is that how an obedientiary speaks of her prioress?'

'I would not expect to speak thus of any prioress worthy of her station...' She paused. 'Mother *Angelica's* tongue was always gracious and respectful, even when delivering a reprimand...'

Evangelina threw her hands up. 'Mother Angelica, Mother Angelica...' Then, without looking back, she flicked a hand in a gesture of dismissal. 'You can go...'

Rosa moved towards the door.

'I'm still watching you,' said Evangelina.

'I do not doubt it,' Rosa said, and quietly left the chamber.

Evangelina had rather forgotten about Anabella Sitwell, until Sister Gracia came again to see her.

'I had intended mentioning it the other day,' said Gracia, her tone peevish.

'What?' said Evangelina, snapping. She found the woman tiresome. She'd never much liked Gracia, and let her continue as novice mistress to keep her out of her way. As prioress, she'd little interest in any children sent to Northwick, and preferred them kept out of her sight and hearing. Their irritating mistress too. Gracia was overly fond of gossip, which could be useful, but in Gracia's case, it seemed she brought information to Evangelina simply in order to *ingratiate* herself with her. Evangelina suppressed a snort: the woman was well-named.

Gracia flinched a little at Evangelina's sharpness. 'I thought I might remind you, Reverend Mother,' she said, 'that Anabella still hasn't made her vows. In principle, there is no urgency, but, as she's a grown woman, I wonder whether she should be encouraged to commit?'

Evangelina frowned. 'Do you have a particular reason for suggesting it now?'

Gracia shuffled her feet a moment then looked up. 'Anabella is very much a favourite of Sister Rosa, and, as a novice, her vows are not truly binding. The sooner she makes her final vows, the sooner she is bound in obedience to *you*, Reverend Mother.' She lowered her eyes, and kneaded her hands together.

'Wise thinking, Gracia,' said Evangelina, and realised she had forgotten about Anabella's fortune too. Her committal to Northwick would confirm the funds of Anabella's that Dulcia already held, which would help with the impending shortfall in the priory's finances. But she'd not mention *that* to Gracia, or indeed to anybody else. 'We'll make a joint effort to encourage her. She's been here more than a year, so it's not too soon, as you say... for a woman of her age.'

She stepped forward and took Gracia's restless hands in hers. 'Thank you for bringing it to my attention. I'm glad you've the best interests of our little community at heart.'

Gracia looked up again and nodded, though her mouth wore more of a smirk than a gracious smile.

When Gracia had left the chamber, Evangelina poured herself another small cup of wine. She felt mildly light-headed. Making Anabella take her vows would bring two most worthwhile benefits. It would commit her fortune to the priory's coffers but, also, Gracia was right that it would also ensure her obedience and might indeed help distance her from Rosa's influence.

That was certainly an objective worth pursuing, and soon.

21

The conversations Rosa had had with Alice, with Agnes and with Eleanor had greatly heartened her. She had returned to Northwick from Meonbridge full of energy, and with greater courage to confront Evangelina – indeed to overthrow her.

She had sought out Beatrice as soon as she got back.

'Goodness, Rosa,' said Beatrice, her eyes alight, 'you look *much* happier than you did a few days ago. Am I to deduce your visit to Meonbridge was a success?'

'It was. I was persuaded to be brave and do what is right for Northwick.'

'Which means stopping Evangelina, or even ousting her?'

'Both. We can denounce her at the visitation.'

'Yet that's some months away, if they adhere to the usual plan.'

'Thus, we have time to assemble our evidence, and coach those sisters who share our views.'

Beatrice beamed.

'But there is another matter...' continued Rosa, biting her lip. 'You do not know, I think, that Anabella formed an affection for Master atte Wode when he came to advise us on the estate? It is, naturally, a secret. Only I know, and Juliana, for she and Anabella are friends.'

'I didn't know,' said Beatrice, 'though I do recall seeing them together once or twice in the frater, in your company. Yet that was months and months ago, before the prioress dismissed him.'

'Indeed. Their association was brief, but they quickly developed what John refers to as an "affinity". Both are in despair that they have been forced apart.'

'So, isn't the match hopeless?'

Rosa shook her head. 'Despite their short acquaintance and long separation, the bond between the two of them remains strong. John is eager for Anabella to be his wife, and she has confessed to me that she has no vocation for the religious life and wants only to be with him.'

'How do you know this, Rosa?'

'I have been liaising between them by letter.' She blushed at the seeming impropriety. It was of course an unusual thing for her to do, to aid and abet a secular love affair... She was also well aware that the last time she "liaised" between two lovers, the result was a disaster, or nearly so... Yet this situation was quite different. 'Perhaps it is wrong of me to do so—'

But Beatrice raised her hand. 'I disagree. There's no value in Anabella becoming a bride of Christ if she has no vocation.'

'Exactly. In Angelica's day, her change of mind would have been met with understanding and compassion. But now...'

Beatrice frowned. 'I imagine the prioress will soon be pressing her to make her vows, in order to secure her dowry?'

'She has already started, and Anabella is terrified she will be forced to do what she no longer wishes.'

'So, she should leave Northwick soon, to ensure Evangelina doesn't have her way.'

'Precisely.'

'And do you have a plan to *liberate* her from the priory?'

Rosa outlined the plan she had agreed with John, and with Eleanor too, when she was in Meonbridge.

Rosa had been astonished to discover that Eleanor was acquainted

with Anabella and relieved that she was keen to help her and John find
the happiness she too thought they deserved. 'Though, of course,'
Eleanor had said, 'Walter will not countenance me being put in any
danger, so whatever plan we devise must ensure I am kept safe, as well
as Anabella. I am truly eager to help, but I cannot ignore my
husband's wishes, indeed his *demands*.' Her eyes had danced with
gentle mischief.

John too would not consider a plan that put Eleanor at risk, but, at
length they constructed one they all thought would both work and not
endanger anyone.

'Most importantly,' Rosa said to Beatrice, 'it must be done soon, to
ensure Evangelina does not have the opportunity to force Anabella's
hand.'

It was only two days after her conversation with Beatrice that Rosa
had her bruising encounter with Evangelina. She was stunned by her
accusation. For Evangelina unwittingly used the very words she had
used of herself years ago in respect of her feelings for *Philip* and,
because of that, Rosa was, for a few moments, quite overcome. But she
soon recovered, realising how ridiculous the accusation about John had
been. Evangelina was grasping wildly at implausible slurs simply to try
to silence her.

Rosa realised too that, since Evangelina had returned from her,
apparently successful, trip, she seemed unusually downcast. When she
next saw Beatrice, she asked her if she had any explanation. But
Beatrice simply shrugged.

Yet, only a few days later, Dulcia provided a possible reason for the
prioress's mood when she asked Rosa and Beatrice to join her in her
chamber. Her face was pale and drawn.

'I need to speak to those I trust,' she said, looking from one to the
other.

'Whatever's the matter, Dulcia?' said Beatrice, covering Dulcia's
hand with hers.

She bit her lip. 'I'm afraid Northwick's finances are reaching a
precarious state. I've been warning of dwindling funds for months...
But now our coffers are truly running low...'

'But won't Sir Toby Edenborough's endowment replenish them?' said Beatrice.

Dulcia frowned. 'There's no evidence the endowment is forthcoming.'

Rosa gasped. 'You mean he has reneged on his promise?'

'Not necessarily. It's the Reverend Mother who has promised it. But I've received no confirmation from Sir Toby of his pledge...'

'Are you thinking he has made no such pledge?'

Dulcia bit her lip again. 'I don't know, but I do wonder if that's the case. And, if he hasn't, Northwick will run out of money quite soon.'

'Goodness,' Rosa said, 'I had not realised the situation was so dire. So, is Evangelina dissembling over the matter of the endowment, or does she truly believe it is on its way?'

'Again, I don't know, and I'm anxious about asking her outright.'

They parted with no plan of what to do. She did not say it, but it occurred to Rosa that now was scarcely the time for Anabella to leave Northwick, thereby depriving the priory of her dowry. If Sir Toby's promised endowment was not coming after all, Northwick might soon be destitute.

There was an hour before dinner, and she hurried back to the sacristy to think.

How could she do something she knew would hasten the priory's decline, when all she wanted was to save it? It seemed a reckless, indeed wicked, thing to do. Yet, it was *Evangelina* who had brought Northwick close to ruin through her profligacy. It was *she* who was wicked, and must be stopped from doing any more damage.

Rosa sat up straight and flexed her shoulders. Surely the time for rebellion was now?

Yet, was "liberating" Anabella rebellion? Yes! It would be her first serious act of mutiny. Despite her worry about the priory's finances, surely it was still wrong to force Anabella to become a nun when she had no vocation?

She stood up and smoothed down her skirts. Anabella was ringing the bell for Sext and therefore dinner, and it was time to join the sisters in the frater.

As she ate, Rosa thought more about how to deal with Evangelina. Of course, she knew how nuns dealt with recalcitrant sisters or incompetent prioresses: the bishop's visitation. Yet the next visitation was not due until next April, which was surely too long to wait. Should she – or, more properly, Dulcia, as treasuress – write to the bishop to ask if Northwick's visitation could be brought forward, as the sisters had serious concerns to raise?

She scooped up the last morsels of her meagre meal, and emptied her cup of tasteless ale. Yes, that was what they should do.

It was only days later that Anabella's "liberation", as Beatrice had it, was to be carried out. Anabella herself was nervous. Rosa had gone through the plan with her several times but, although she was excited at the prospect of being freed from her commitment, she was still frightened something might go wrong.

'Suppose the spy learns of the plan?' she said to Rosa, her eyes wide with evident concern.

'But how could she, even if she exists? No one in Northwick knows what is to happen except you and I. Beatrice and Juliana are now privy to the fact that you are to leave Northwick, but I have deliberately avoided telling them the details of how it is to be accomplished.'

Anabella nodded. 'I must be brave.'

They were sitting in the sacristy, the door slightly ajar, so they could hear anyone approaching. Suddenly Anabella got up and, throwing open the door, whirled away, out into the chapel, busying herself with checking the status of the candles.

Rosa followed her. 'Yes, you must,' she whispered. 'But I think the biggest risk – albeit it is not great – is not that the *Sitwells* will learn of your departure and try to capture you, but that one of the prioress's favourites, especially Letitia, might discover it. However, Eleanor, John and I devised the plan most carefully.'

'I can scarcely believe Eleanor Titherige is coming to my rescue.' Anabella plucked one of the altar candles from its holder and held it out to Rosa, her head tipped in enquiry.

'Yes,' said Rosa, taking the used candle from her, 'we can use the remains of it in the sacristy. I shall fetch a new one.' She took the precious stump to the little chamber and, unlocking the cupboard that held her store of candles, withdrew a new one and returned to the chapel. Anabella took it and inserted it into the empty candlestick.

'She and I were never *friends*,' she continued, 'because of the difference in our ages. But she was kind to me, when our parents visited each other and she was obliged to play with me. We were our families' only daughters.' She smiled. 'How generous of her now to want to help me.'

Rosa had already explained Eleanor's long ago affection for John, and his for her. 'Eleanor wishes to help both of you,' she had said. 'She has found happiness herself and wants you to have the same.'

'But it is so long since John and I spoke to each other...'

'Surely, you are not changing your mind?'

'No, no!' she cried. 'That wonderful letter you brought me, from John, convinced me this was what I wanted.'

Rosa recalled the moment. Of course, she had not read the letter but, as Anabella quietly perused the words, she could see there were many of them and the writing looked well-formed. John must have been practising... Anabella's breast heaved with emotion as she folded the paper and tucked it inside the little purse she wore tied to her girdle.

'I am glad to hear it,' Rosa said. 'It is happening tomorrow, so prepare yourself.'

The following afternoon, when Rosa and Anabella were once more in the sacristy, as they usually were in the hour or two after dinner, Juliana knocked lightly on the little door and put her head around it. She was smiling.

'A visitor for you, Anabella,' she said, her eyes bright with suppressed excitement.

Anabella gasped, and Rosa took her hand and squeezed it. 'Thank you, Juliana, please escort her to the second guest chamber. We shall go there now.' Juliana nodded and hurried away.

'Right,' said Rosa. 'The time has come.' She took Anabella's hand again. 'Courage!'

Anabella smiled nervously, then straightened her back. 'Courage!' she repeated.

The guest chamber was one of two designated by Angelica as rooms where sisters' relatives or friends might stay overnight, and where they could meet in private during their visits. Mama had stayed several times in this room, finding it comfortable enough, if narrow.

When Eleanor entered the chamber with her servant, Hawisa, Rosa smiled warmly at her. She gestured her to sit on the only chair. But Eleanor ignored it and came forward, her hands outstretched towards Anabella. 'Goodness, Anabella, how very long it has been.'

Anabella took her proffered hands. 'I cannot thank you enough, dear Eleanor, for coming to my rescue.'

'It seems extraordinary,' said Eleanor, her eyes bright, 'that you should be thinking of this as "rescue". Though of course I know nothing of life inside a priory...'

Rosa narrowed her eyes. 'If it were not for our present prioress,' she said quietly, 'Anabella would not have to *flee* at all, but simply affirm the religious life was not her vocation after all. We learned only yesterday that Evangelina is on the point of *demanding* Bella make her vows, so you have come not a moment too soon.'

Eleanor nodded, then turned back to Anabella. 'Are you clear about the plan?'

Anabella giggled briefly. 'Sister Rosa has explained it many, many times.'

'We shall stay together here a while,' said Rosa.

'Is there any danger of the prioress wishing to meet me?' said Eleanor.

'Surprisingly,' said Rosa, 'very little, for Evangelina shows no interest in the sisters' visitors. Anyway, she has not been informed of your arrival. In normal circumstances, she would have been. But, this time, Juliana understood there was no need. Both the prioress and all the other sisters are about their usual afternoon business, and are unlikely to discover you are here.'

The timing of Eleanor's visit – mid-afternoon – had been chosen to ensure that, when she left the priory with Anabella, Anabella was unlikely to be missed for many hours. For, in the mornings, she worked alongside Sister Gracia in the novice chamber, teaching the little novices their letters and to sing. But, every afternoon, she helped Rosa in the sacristy and chapel. As a general rule, Anabella did not mix much with the other sisters, and indeed her only friends were Rosa and Juliana. So, no one *except* Rosa and Juliana would likely notice if Anabella was missing from the offices or supper or even the dorter. The plan was not infallible, but Rosa was confident enough that it would work.

'I presume the men did all remain outside?' she said to Eleanor.

'Oh, yes,' she said. 'They understand what is expected of them, and when.'

It had been agreed that Eleanor and Anabella would leave shortly before the bell was rung for Nones, a bell Rosa would have to ring herself. This signalled to the sisters throughout the priory that the current period of work had ended, and they should go to the chapel for the next office. Of course, these days, only a few of the sisters did go to the chapel but the others would stop their work and gather together in the frater or the cloister. It was vital that, before that happened, Eleanor and Anabella were on their way to Meonbridge.

Rosa grasped Anabella's hand and squeezed it. 'God speed.'

Anabella's bottom lip was trembling. 'Thank you, Sister Rosa, for all that you have done for me. I shall keep you in my prayers.'

'And I you. But, go. And, please, send word of your safe arrival.'

She nodded, but her eyes were glassy. 'You are going to face such denunciation when my disappearance is discovered...'

'I expect it, and am prepared to deal with it.' She gave Anabella a little push. '*Go.*' She smiled at Eleanor. 'Thank you.'

Anabella led Eleanor and Hawisa back towards the gatehouse, taking a route agreed to best avoid running into any other sisters or servants. Rosa let out a great sigh as she was left alone. She must give them time to provide Anabella with her disguise and ride away from the priory, but it would soon be time for her to ring the Nones bell, and so she made her way to the chapel.

She prayed that the plan they had devised went smoothly. By arrangement, one of the men-at-arms would now be deep in conversation with the porter, sitting in the little lodge behind the priory's great gate and sharing with him a flask of good strong ale. Anabella, Eleanor and Hawisa would slip into the gatehouse, where the squire, Piers Arundale, was waiting. He would strip off his de Bohun livery for Anabella to put on, leaving him clad in a peasant tunic. He was then to hurry from the gatehouse and go into the village, from where he would, at length, find his way back home to Meonbridge by one means or another. The three women would leave the gatehouse at the same time, their horses brought forward for them to mount and ride away. If anyone in the priory happened to see the party both come and go, they would have noted the same number of riders leaving as had arrived.

As anticipated, no one remarked upon the fact that Anabella was not at supper in the frater, nor in the chapel in the evening, nor that she was missing from the dorter. Rosa had exchanged a glance with Juliana at supper, and, as they entered the chapel together, Beatrice raised an eyebrow in her direction, and she nodded.

In the dorter, because the beds were divided by, albeit flimsy, screens, it was easy enough for the sisters to assume Anabella's bed was occupied, though most of them commonly paid her little attention. Nonetheless, Juliana took it upon herself to slip into Anabella's narrow cell and make a mound of clothing to simulate a body in the bed – in case any of the sisters did, by chance, decide to look. She mentioned it to Rosa later.

Thus, Anabella's absence from the priory was indeed not noticed until the following morning, when Sister Gracia expected to find her in the novice chamber immediately after Prime.

Rosa was in the sacristy as usual when there was a loud rapping upon the door, and Gracia threw it open and barged into the little room.

'Where is Anabella?' she demanded, without greeting or preamble, her eyes flashing with accusation.

Rosa had been expecting this. 'Why do you imagine I might know, Sister Gracia?' she said, keeping her fingers crossed inside her sleeves.

'You are her friend. She works with you.'

'Not in the mornings, as you well know...' She pretended to think. 'But I admit I did not see her at breakfast. Is she ill?'

How much she did hate all this falsehood, but told herself it was for the best of motives. Although that scarcely made it any the less a sin… But she would atone for it all later with a string of testing penances.

Gracia went off in a temper to look for Anabella in the dorter but soon returned, more vexed than ever. 'She is not in the dorter, nor the frater, nor the chapel. So, where *is* she?'

Rosa was finding it difficult to maintain a credible air of ignorance but managed it sufficient to send Gracia away, suggesting she had best inform the prioress that Anabella seemed to be missing.

Some while later, she was summoned to Evangelina's chamber. The prioress had apparently sent out a search party which, after an hour of searching, had reported that Anabella was nowhere to be found, either in the priory or the village.

'Well?' demanded Evangelina, staring hard at Rosa, her eyebrows knit together in a furious frown.

Rosa braced herself. This was, after all, what she was going to have to do from now on: stand up to Evangelina. The disobedience inherent in her steeliness was painful but essential. She had to bear it, to accept that her unfitting behaviour was directed towards a greater good.

'I do not know where Anabella is,' she said. 'But I imagine she has left Northwick to escape you forcing her to commit to final vows she no longer wants to make.'

Evangelina looked rattled. 'You encouraged her in that view…'

'Not at all. I listened to her, as she came to realise the religious life was not after all for her—'

'Ha! That's applied to many of us here in Northwick, but we've learned to accept our fate, and accept it with good grace.'

Rosa wanted to laugh out loud, but dampened the outburst with her hand. The idea that *Evangelina*, of all people, had accepted her "fate" with "good grace" *was* laughable. She had done anything but accept it. But Rosa bit her tongue: she would not voice her opinion. She held up her hands. 'Anabella had a choice, and she made the one that she thought best. I know, however, how much she regretted reneging on the agreement she had made with Mother Angelica…'

'Regret's all very well,' said Evangelina, bitterly. She paced the floor a while. 'If her remorse was at all heartfelt, she'd know her decision to leave was wrong – iniquitous!' Her eyes glittered.

"Iniquitous" seemed unwarranted. Rosa pressed her lips together.

Was Evangelina going to try to track Anabella down and bring her back to Northwick? If so, she had to stall her, long enough to ensure Bella was John's wife before the prioress discovered her.

Evangelina stopped pacing and stood before her. 'So, I ask again, where is she? How did she leave without my knowledge, apparently without *anyone's* knowledge. Except, I imagine, *yours?*'

Rosa did not answer. After all, if she said nothing, Evangelina might be enraged but be no closer to finding Anabella.

But Hilde, Evangelina's maid, sidled up to her mistress and coughed. Hilde was scarcely more than a girl, appointed by Evangelina soon after she became prioress to be her personal servant. She was a village girl, but she seemed brighter, more vigilant, than most of the other servants in the priory. But now she was chewing at her bottom lip and her eyes were averted – with fear, perhaps? Yet her chin seemed set and, when Evangelina turned to her, her mouth stilled and, looking up, she gave what Rosa could only interpret as a sly grin.

'Well?' said Evangelina, irritation in her voice.

'Yesterday, yer ladyship,' said Hilde, 'North'ick had some visitors. Folk who'd never come here before.'

Evangelina rounded upon Rosa. 'Who were these visitors? And why wasn't I informed?'

Rosa applied an expression of astonishment to her face. 'I have no idea,' she said.

'The *ladies*,' Hilde continued, her eyes alight, 'came with an entourage of armed men.'

'Ladies? Armed men!' cried Evangelina.

'Four o' them,' said Hilde. So, did the maid *see* them herself?

'And you claim to know nothing of this?' said the prioress to Rosa.

She shook her head. 'I was attending to my commitments all afternoon.' Which was true, in a way.

Later that morning, it emerged that it was Letitia who had seen the party arrive and depart. It was *her* sighting that Hilde had recounted.

Evangelina insisted upon Rosa's presence in her chamber once again when she questioned Letitia about what she knew. Why, Rosa could not imagine. She was bemused. Letitia *was* of course a spy – the spy the prioress had directed to watch *her*, to find out if she was fomenting dissent amongst her sisters. But now, she wondered, had Letitia also been spying upon Anabella? Yet, if so, why? Evangelina had never hinted she knew anything of the real reason Anabella wanted to run away from Northwick. Indeed, her recent accusation of Rosa's own "unnatural relationship" with John suggested she knew *nothing* about him and Anabella.

'Why were you outside the priory?' Evangelina asked Letitia. 'On *two* occasions?'

Letitia flushed. 'I wasn't outside. I was in the upper chamber of the gatehouse, Reverend Mother... Reading...'

The second-floor chamber of the gatehouse housed a small collection of religious volumes. Valuable books, stored there because the building had strong doors and heavy locks. Letitia was, in fact, one of only three sisters who held a key: the others were Evangelina and Sister Dulcia. Quite why Evangelina had permitted Letitia to have access to the little library had always mystified Rosa. Although the girl was one of the most literate of the sisters and, as the prioress seemed to have assigned her no task other than spying, perhaps she had more time than most to read?

'So what exactly did you see?'

'Six riders, two women, four men in livery,' Letitia said. 'I did not see who met them or escorted them into the priory, but the men stayed outside the gate, so I assume only the women entered.'

'And you also saw them leave?'

'Not long after they had arrived, I heard the commotion of horses being brought up, and again looked out of the little window. And I saw them all mount up and ride away. The Nones bell rang soon after.'

Evangelina looked frustrated. 'That was all?'

Letitia shrugged. 'Before they left, I thought I heard voices and some scuffling down below, but whose voices they were and what they were doing I could not say.'

'So, we don't know if it was *Anabella* this visitor was meeting?' said Evangelina.

'True, Reverend Mother,' Letitia said. 'Though it is surely too much of a coincidence that she disappeared from Northwick the very day some visitors came and went...' She tipped her head.

Rosa's heart felt suddenly a little lighter. A coincidence, indeed. But *no more than* that, if neither Letitia nor anyone else knew it was she and Anabella who had received the visitors. She breathed out in relief. At what point, she wondered, might she herself admit the truth? It might take days for John and Anabella to be married.

She must not give Evangelina an incentive for pursuit too soon...

Evangelina frowned. 'So Anabella *must* have gone with them, somehow or another. For she's not here!' She rounded once more on Rosa. 'So, I ask again, who were the visitors?'

But Rosa merely shrugged, and Evangelina, her face taut with frustration, turned back to Letitia. 'Yet why didn't you report these visitors to me as soon as they arrived? Why keep silent until this morning?'

Letitia flushed, and looked at the floor. 'I am so sorry, Reverend Mother. You are right, I should have. But I presumed the visitors were for you, as usual...' She trailed off. But it was scarcely unreasonable for her to assume the callers were for Evangelina, and it was presumably only after they had left that poor Letitia must have realised they were not. By then it was too late, and she was doubtless too afraid to tell her.

During the exchange between the prioress and Letitia, Hilde was standing back, her face wrought with what did look very much like fear. Yet, why should Anabella's disappearance from the priory concern the maid? Rosa thought again of Anabella's claim that somebody was spying on her: how unlikely that had seemed. Yet, might it be possible that *Hilde* was that spy—

'Rosa!' The prioress's voice cut in to her musing, sharp and urgent. 'Are you listening?'

Startled, she looked up. 'I am sorry? Ah, no, I apologise, my mind was elsewhere...'

'Well, perhaps you'd bring it back to the here and now,' said Evangelina, and clicked her tongue.

'Yes, of course,' said Rosa, and pushed the matter of Hilde from her thoughts.

. . .

One morning, a few days after Anabella's departure, when most of the sisters were in the frater eating a meagre breakfast of dry bread and weak ale, the sounds of a commotion outside the priory reached their ears. Sister Clarice rose from the table and hurried from the frater. Rosa got up too and followed her.

They reached the gatehouse a few moments later, and Clarice ran to the porter's lodge, with Rosa close behind her. The porter, Gerard, was not there, but they could hear him outside the gate, apparently in loud conversation with someone. Clarice exchanged a look of alarm with Rosa.

'I suppose we must discover who has come, and what they want?' she said.

'We must,' said Rosa. 'It sounds as if there might be several men, judging from the uneasy clip-clopping of their horses' hooves.'

Sister Clarice was shaking. 'What can they want?' she said, her voice tight with panic.

'There is only one way to find the answer.' Rosa left the lodge and walked out to the gate, this time with Clarice following her.

Gerard was an old man, albeit he used to be a soldier, and a fierce one, by all accounts, and took no nonsense from most of those who requested entry to the priory. But, now, he was flanked by a band of men, three dismounted, the rest still astride their horses, and one of them was shouting at him, and gesticulating with his hands.

Rosa knew at once who they must be: the Sitwells. She knew too what − or who − they had come for, but could not imagine what had prompted them to come. Except that perhaps she did, if Anabella's theory about a spy was right after all? Yet, if that spy was *Hilde*, how could such a girl have any connection with the Sitwells? It all seemed most implausible.

Not truly feeling brave, but knowing *she* had made this happen, Rosa folded her arms across her chest, tucking her hands into her sleeves, and stepped forward. Clarice did the same, coming up behind her.

'Can we help you?' said Rosa loudly, addressing the tall man accosting poor Gerard.

The man turned, and glared at her. He was handsome, but his eyes were hard, and his mouth was set in a sneer. 'And you are?' he snarled.

Clarice gasped. Rosa too was shocked. She had rarely been spoken to in such an insolent tone.

Gerard was also clearly affronted. 'Oi, don't you talk to the sisters like that!' he cried out, shaking his fist.

But the man – Master Sitwell, she presumed – flung one arm backwards, striking Gerard hard against his ear, and the old man stumbled although he did not fall.

'Oi!' he shouted again, regaining his balance and starting forwards once more.

But Rosa raised her voice. 'No, no, Gerard, leave this to us.' She stepped closer to the Sitwell man, and held his gaze, although her heart was beating wildly. 'I ask again, sir,' she said, more quietly, 'how can we help you here at Northwick?'

'You can tell me where my brother's widow is,' he said. His voice was not uncultured, but he had the manner of a ruffian. 'We've heard the bitch is missing.'

Clarice moved closer to Rosa and whispered into her wimple. 'I think we should allow the Reverend Mother to deal with this,' she said. 'Inside.'

Rosa murmured agreement, then spoke again to the man, trying to keep her voice composed. 'This is not something to be discussed out here. Come, sir, come inside and you can address your enquiry to our prioress.'

To her surprise and relief, he calmed down and agreed. He even bowed. His name, he said, was Humphrey Sitwell, and he was the younger brother of Anabella's deceased husband. So, this was the man Anabella had said was planning to take her husband's place. Rosa gestured to him to follow her.

However, when *all* the men, both those on foot and mounted, moved forward to pass through the priory gate, Rosa spun around, holding up her hands. 'No, no, we cannot permit so many men to enter. Just you, sir,' she said to Humphrey, 'and one other. The others must remain out here.'

He seemed to baulk a moment, but she smiled. 'You surely do not imagine, sir, you are in any *danger* in a priory full of nuns?'

He breathed out heavily, then gestured to one of the other men to follow, and to the rest to wait outside the gate. Rosa led the way through the gate, towards a winding staircase inside the gatehouse. 'We have a chamber upstairs here, where we may speak with male visitors. No men are permitted within the priory's precincts.'

That was not strictly true, for Evangelina often invited men to join her in her private rooms, and even Angelica had held meetings in the prioress's chamber, as long as she was chaperoned. But the rule would serve today. The gatehouse had two upper chambers, the one on the second floor where the library was stored, and Letitia sat and read, and kept an eye on the comings and goings down below. The other, on the first floor, had been used as an office by Sir Thomas Chatterton, the erstwhile priory steward, until his dismissal by Evangelina, after which no replacement steward was ever sought.

Sister Clarice's face showed huge relief at Rosa's decision. 'Shall I go and ask the Reverend Mother to attend us here?' she murmured.

'If you would, Sister,' Rosa said. 'I shall await your return with our visitors and Gerard.' She raised an eyebrow at Clarice, trying to convey the need for urgency.

Indeed, it was not long before she did return with Evangelina. It was now Rosa's turn to be relieved, for she had worried the prioress might refuse to come, given she did not know the answer to Master Sitwell's question.

However, Evangelina did not look pleased to have been summoned. She swept into the chamber with an imperious rustle of her skirts and took the only chair, which stood behind the large table Sir Thomas once used as his desk. She dismissed Gerard, then gestured to everyone else to take the stools. But Humphrey Sitwell stayed on his feet, pacing slightly.

'Please do stand *still*, sir,' said Evangelina, sharply. 'You're giving me a megrim.'

He stopped and curtly bowed his head, but stood before her, clasping and unclasping his fists.

'Master Humphrey Sitwell, I understand?' said the prioress. 'Please explain why you are here.'

Rosa could see him glaring at Evangelina, just as he had glared at her outside. He was evidently attempting to intimidate her, but she thought Evangelina, for all her weaknesses, would not be frightened easily. Anyway, Eleanor had told her the Sitwells were apparently braggarts, who liked to brandish weapons but rarely used them.

'They have a reputation for being bullies, but not murderers,' Eleanor had said. Which gave Rosa cause to think the nuns need not be overly intimidated by Humphrey's steely eyes, although that was not to say it was wise to underestimate him.

When he did not immediately give answer, Evangelina's eyes narrowed. 'Well, sir, speak!'

He lurched forward, slammed his hands down upon the table, and – true to his braggart reputation – began to shout.

He wanted to know where Anabella had gone. Of course, Evangelina did not know, and Rosa was saying nothing. Then he asked about her dower.

'What dower?' said Evangelina.

'The property, valuables and coin she was donating to the priory.' He grunted.

'Ah, that. It's all still in our coffers. Anabella had no opportunity, or perhaps desire, to take it.'

'Then you can hand it over,' Humphrey snarled. 'It was my brother's property and now it belongs to me.'

But Evangelina shook her head. 'I've no reason to think Anabella will not return to Northwick, in which case our arrangement for her to donate her property as a dowry will stand...' She gave him a triumphant smile. 'So, Master Sitwell, I shall keep it locked up here – for the time being, at least.'

Not unexpectedly, Humphrey was furious at her response. He drew his sword and flourished it at her. His companion leapt forward to his side, brandishing his own weapon.

Clarice screamed, and Rosa closed her eyes. Had Eleanor after all been wrong?

But Evangelina sprang to her feet, banged the table with a fist and roared her displeasure. 'How *dare* you raise a sword in a house of God! You dare to threaten a *prioress*? A bride of Christ, a servant of the Lord? Oh, no, no, Master Sitwell, you will *not*! For God is witness to your cowardice and your iniquity and will assuredly *strike you down*!' She thrust both hands heavenwards, as if drawing God's wrath down upon him, and Humphrey Sitwell blenched, lowered his sword and backed away. Then, gesturing to his companion, he retreated to the door.

But, at the door, he wheeled around. 'This isn't finished, *madam*,' he said, with a growl. 'I shall find the bitch, one way or another, and then I shall be back.'

Rosa was impressed by the way Evangelina had stood up to the Sitwell man so boldly but, when she told Beatrice all about it afterwards, they agreed the prioress was not "keeping" Anabella's money in expectation of her return, but in order to have it for herself.

'Do you think the prioress will make any effort to find Anabella?' asked Beatrice.

Rosa doubted it. Troubled as she was by her own duplicity in all that had occurred, she was determined to keep Anabella's whereabouts a secret as long as possible, and steadfastly denied she knew the identity of her visitors. Gerard, the porter, was unable to say either, albeit he was supposed to identify all comers to the priory. He said he had been distracted, which of course he had. Letitia had seen the party come and go but, although she could describe them in some detail, she insisted, with complete justification, she had not seen any of them before.

Thus, no one claimed any knowledge of the people Anabella had, apparently, escaped with, and Evangelina, it seemed, soon lost interest in making any effort to discover who they were, or where they had taken Anabella.

22

NORTHWICK PRIORY
NOVEMBER 1366

It'd been sheer chance Hilde had spoken to Letitia the afternoon Anabella Sitwell disappeared from Northwick. They ran into each other in the frater, when she came downstairs to fetch some refreshments for Mother Evangelina. Moments before, Hilde thought she'd heard some sort of commotion at or near the gatehouse, and she asked Letitia if she'd heard anything, knowing she spent her afternoons in the gatehouse library, reading.

Letitia nodded. 'I saw two women with an escort come and go.'

'Why didn't you tell the prioress?' said Hilde.

'Because I assumed they had come to see her. Visitors are always for the Reverend Mother these days.'

'But she's had no visitors this afternoon. And she'll be angry to find out you saw them come and didn't tell her.'

As far as Hilde knew, Letitia kept her distance from the prioress for the rest of the day. So, the next morning, when Anabella was discovered to have left the priory, Hilde took it upon herself to tell

241

Mother Evangelina what Letitia had said, and Letitia was brought before her to be questioned.

How red Letitia's face was when she tried to explain why she'd not reported the visitors' arrival! Mother Evangelina was furious with her.

But Hilde's own heart had been banging like a drum all through the conversation. For she too hadn't reported the coming of the visitors or, more seriously, Anabella's going, and she was desperate to get a message to the man who paid her for that very information.

Hilde was supposed to keep watch on Anabella, and let her dead husband's family know if she left the priory for any reason. It troubled her that what the Sitwells wanted was to seize Anabella and force her to marry her husband's younger brother, Humphrey. But he paid her well, and she needed the money to help her widowed ma.

She couldn't get away until the evening, when she left the priory to go and see her mother in Northwick village, as she did every day. Only then could she arrange for the message to be sent to Master Sitwell to tell him what had happened. But how terrified she was about what he might do next. For, because she'd *failed* to tell him of Anabella's disappearance – albeit it were so sudden and unexpected – he'd be furious with *her*, and maybe not only furious but violent...

Yet how was it her fault? There'd been no warning. The visitors had come and gone long before Anabella were even discovered to be missing. But that wouldn't stop a man like Humphrey Sitwell deciding poor little Hilde was to blame.

Hilde hadn't seen anything of it, but she'd heard that, a few days later, Humphrey Sitwell came to the priory and demanded to know where Anabella was. Of course, Mother Evangelina didn't know and, apparently, he got very angry and threatened her, before she sent him packing. Hilde was relieved to know her message had got through. Except, later that evening, she found out Humphrey had also visited her ma and told her Hilde was no longer of any use to him, when she'd failed so miserably in the one task he paid her to do.

The next day, hoping to redeem herself by helping the Sitwells find Anabella, Hilde started to make enquiries amongst the sisters and the other priory servants, to try to discover who the visitors were, and where they might have taken her. She claimed to be asking on Mother Evangelina's behalf, even though the prioress of course had no idea she was doing it.

Hilde knew Letitia was an informer too. The prioress got her to spy upon Sister Rosa, and had done so for some time, to make sure she wasn't doing anything she shouldn't be. Mother Evangelina was, Hilde thought, a bit afraid of Sister Rosa. Despite her being so stern and haughty, the prioress seemed worried Rosa might try to bring her down. She knew naught about the details but Hilde thought Sister Rosa had been a rival for prioress, though she did wonder why *she* didn't get elected. For Rosa was a much nicer person than Evangelina, and would surely have made a better prioress. So, why didn't the sisters pick her?

Anyway, she decided to ask Letitia what she knew. 'You ever notice ought going on 'tween Sister Rosa and Anabella?' she said, when she and Letitia were alone for a few moments in the frater.

'What do you mean, "going on"?' said Letitia.

'Oh, I dunno. Summat suspicious?' She didn't actually know *what* she meant. 'Sister Rosa seemed to be Anabella's only friend.'

'Anabella was quite friendly with Juliana too. But anyway, no, I cannot think of anything I would describe as "suspicious".' She thought a while... 'Though, a *long* while ago, before Mother Evangelina became prioress, before the election, I did once see Anabella, then Master atte Wode, leaving Sister Rosa's chamber...'

'Who's Master atte Wode?'

'He has not come here for a long time. He was a bailiff, from the manor where Sister Rosa grew up. For months, when Northwick had no bailiff of its own, Master atte Wode came to advise Mother Angelica and Sister Rosa on running the estate. He stopped coming when Rafe Byllynges was appointed, months and months ago.'

'So, tell me more about them leaving Rosa's chamber.'

'I am not sure there is much to tell. I suppose I *could* say their behaviour was a bit unusual, for both did seem flushed and agitated.'

'As if they'd had a *tryst*?' Hilde felt a little breathless.

She shrugged. 'Or some disagreement. But I thought no more about it, for as far as I was aware they barely knew each other. Master atte Wode often visited Sister Rosa, and Anabella *was* her assistant – and, I suppose, her chaperone – so maybe it was not suspicious at all.'

Excitement bubbled in Hilde's chest. 'But suppose there *were* summat more between them, this bailiff and Anabella...' she persisted.

'That is a fanciful notion, Hilde. I only saw them *once*...'

'Yes, you only *saw* them once, but they might've met lots of times.' Her head was full of the possibilities. Then something else occurred to her. 'That place Sister Rosa comes from, it's called Meonbridge. It's where she slipped off to when Mother Evangelina was away.'

'How do you know that?'

'I overheard her telling the prioress. The Reverend Mother were ever so angry with her for leaving the priory without her permission.' She grinned. 'So I reckon that's where this bailiff comes from too. And if there *is* summat 'tween him and Anabella, maybe it were *him* who came to take her away?'

'Goodness, Hilde, you are conjuring an entire, and most unlikely, story with no evidence at all. Anyway, I am certain Master atte Wode was *not* amongst the men who came, though I suppose he could have been disguised as one of the men-at-arms...'

But that was enough for Hilde. "Unlikely story" or not, it was believable enough, and it did all make some sort of sense. Anyway, it was good enough to be passed on.

That evening, when she went see her ma, she first paid a visit to the man who'd take a message about Meonbridge and its bailiff to Master Humphrey Sitwell.

23

Agnes could scarce believe John was finally getting married.

The wedding was intended to be quiet but not clandestine. Sire Raphael agreed to waive the reading of the banns, but advised John to marry Anabella in public, to ensure their union was witnessed.

When John told Agnes what the priest had said, she'd agreed. 'You and Anabella must be sure that, if the Sitwells, God forbid it, do ever come to find her, you can prove she's your wife, not only in God's sight, but in that of your friends and neighbours.'

John nodded. 'I'd thought we'd have to wed in secret, to be sure the Sitwells didn't find out, but I see now it's not a good idea.' He grinned. 'I'll be glad too to have folk there, to witness my union and my joy.' His mouth pursed slightly. 'Though I'm sorry Rosa can't be with us, given it's all down to her Anabella's even here.'

Agnes gave his arm a squeeze. 'She'll be thinking of you, and will pray for you both.'

Despite the gloomy time of year, their wedding day dawned fine and clear, albeit the air was chilly.

Agnes had told Anabella that Jack would like to escort her to Saint Peter's, and she'd happily agreed. At the appointed hour, all wrapped up well against the cold, but with the bright winter sunshine warm upon their backs, Anabella took Jack's arm and, with Agnes and her ma behind them, they walked the short distance through the village from the atte Wode croft down to the church.

Yesterday, word that John was to be married had been sent around the village, albeit the name of his future wife wasn't divulged. And now Agnes could see up ahead a good crowd of women, men and children was gathered on the green, in front of Saint Peter's porch. The onlookers cheered heartily as the four of them walked by, happy, she supposed, their bailiff had at last found himself a wife. But she heard a few women murmuring their curiosity about his bride's identity and whether or not she was comely, for Anabella's face was veiled.

John was waiting in the porch, with their brother Matthew at his side. John beamed as Anabella came closer, and he held out his hands towards her. Jack freed her arm from his and put her hand into John's. 'Your bride, brother,' he said, and amiably cuffed his shoulder.

John beamed and whispered something into Anabella's ear, then led her into the porch, where Sire Raphael was waiting. The crowd all shuffled forward and stood in a wide arc, so they could hear and see the taking of the vows. When Anabella removed her veil, a murmur hummed through the onlookers – of appreciation, Agnes was sure, for Anabella did look very lovely.

The short ceremony began. Sire Raphael asked John to declare his dower and he placed a gold ring onto Anabella's finger as a token of his wealth.

Agnes smiled at her brother's declaration. He wasn't, of course, *wealthy*, but how far he'd come from the relative poverty of their father. For, as bailiff, John had acquired land and coin, so, albeit he *was* still a villein, he was now one of the more prosperous in Meonbridge.

Jack too had provided well for his family, not through the acquisition of land or property, but by the energy and skill he put into his business, mostly building or repairing houses and barns. Indeed, one of the fine new houses Jack was constructing was for John and

Anabella. John had promised her a new house – in fact, *Ma* had insisted upon it.

'You can't be living with your old ma once you're wed,' she'd said. 'Anyway, this place is far too small and humble for a man of your standing.' The light of pride in her son's advancement shone in her eyes. Agnes thought it likely Ma might go and live with John and Anabella eventually, when she became too frail to live alone. But, for now, she was content to stay in the home where she'd brought up her family. Content, too, to have the newly-weds live with her until their house was ready.

Agnes had wondered whether Anabella would mind living in such a lowly cottage, when she clearly came from a much more prosperous background than either the atte Wodes or the Sawyers. But when she asked John about it, he'd shaken his head.

'Bella truly doesn't mind at all. She's said how glad she'll be simply to be my wife, and safe from the unwanted attentions of those wretched Sitwells. And I reckon she and Ma will get on well. Bella may be almost gentry'—he'd grinned—'but she's got no airs and graces, and cares little for the trappings of that life.' How very joyful John had looked. And how pleased, and relieved, *she* was that he'd found happiness at last.

After the exchange of vows, Sire Raphael declared them man and wife, and invited them, and everyone else, to go into the church, to celebrate Mass and for him to bless the couple.

Despite the discomfort of her leg, Ma had dismissed any notion that she wasn't capable of providing the marriage feast. She got help with the cooking from her neighbours, but Dickon had sent word that she could use the manor kitchens if she wished to. He insisted too that the feasting and the dancing should be held in the manor house's grand hall, so as many villagers as possible could join the celebration.

Once Anabella was safely John's lawful wife, all sense of subterfuge and secrecy evaporated, and the occasion was as happy and agreeable as any wedding Agnes could recall in Meonbridge. The village's musicians – Adam Wragge, Will Cole, Nick Cook and Alan Fuller – were all older now, yet still lusty and energetic in their playing. Their customary routine of songs and dances brought merriment and laughter, and, when Agnes glanced across at Anabella, she saw her face was shining with what was unquestionably joy.

Agnes thought back to the day Anabella had arrived in Meonbridge. She had been waiting with John at Eleanor's house for the return of Eleanor with Hawisa, Anabella, the three men-at-arms and Anabella, disguised as a squire in Piers Arundale's livery.

John was clearly nervous, rocking from foot to foot. He'd not seen Anabella for a year. How anxious he must have been to see her! When they heard horses' hooves approaching, he ran out onto the road. She followed him out to watch them arrive. It was almost dark, so they could see little, but the sound of riders was unmistakeable. Yet, as the riders came to a halt outside the house, John hurried back indoors, and Agnes went with him.

Shortly, three figures ran towards the door – Eleanor, Anabella and Hawisa – and John held it open wide to let them in.

Agnes went forward, smiling, as they came into the light and warmth. She held out her hands in greeting. 'We're so glad to see you back, Eleanor, and welcome, Anabella, to Meonbridge.'

They took off their hoods and cloaks, and Hawisa carried them away.

'Come over to the fire,' said Agnes. 'You're both red with cold.'

'Thank goodness the weather is dry,' said Eleanor, 'but it was still a chilly ride.' She looked around, presumably seeking Walter, for when he emerged from the shadows at the far end of their hall, she ran to him. 'You see, Wat, I'm back! Safe and sound. And with Anabella.' She took his hand. 'Do come and meet her.'

Walter's face was a mixture of relief and, maybe, a little irritation that he'd been obliged to submit to his wife's decision to rescue her erstwhile friend. But he allowed a smile as he went forward with Eleanor, and welcomed Anabella into their home.

'The squire's garb suits you well, Mistress Sitwell,' he said, and Anabella gazed down at herself.

'Oh, my goodness,' she said, 'I'd forgotten I was wearing it.' She laughed lightly. 'I must say it is very comfortable, especially for riding. Perhaps I should always dress like this?'

Eleanor and Walter joined in her merriment but suddenly John was at her side.

'I do hope not,' he said, and came to stand in front of her. He beamed, and lowered his voice a little, though Agnes could still hear him. 'You do, of course, look lovely in whatever clothes you wear, but I would prefer you in a gown...'

Anabella raised her eyes to his, but her lips parted slightly. 'Suppose *I* prefer to wear men's breeches?'

Out of John's sight, Agnes and Eleanor both suppressed a giggle. But John seemed not to realise Anabella was jesting, and his mouth dropped open briefly in apparent disbelief.

Then his eyes sparked a little. 'I will not—' he began, his tone clearly vexed at the prospect of a breech-wearing wife, but Anabella at once laid her hand upon his arm and gave him a warm smile.

'Oh, John, don't look so serious. I didn't mean it! In fact, tired as I am'—she turned to Eleanor—'if someone could bring my valise, I shall change into a gown right now.'

John's face reddened, suggesting he felt a little foolish that he'd misconstrued his future wife already. And when he looked around and saw Agnes shaking her head at him, he came over. 'Did she *plan* to make me look an idiot?' he said, quietly in Agnes's ear.

'I doubt it, brother,' she said. 'You managed that all by yourself.' She grinned. 'Anabella is clearly a spirited woman... Much like another whom, many years ago, you once held in your heart...' She gestured with her eyes towards Eleanor, then let the memory sink in. 'Don't forget that women of their kind can't be bullied. You learned that lesson the hard way, John. Don't fall into the same trap again.'

He thumped his fist against his leg. 'What a fool I am!' He rolled his eyes. 'I'll try harder to heed your wisdom, sister.'

'Yet it's clear,' she went on, 'Anabella wouldn't have spoken that way to you if she didn't feel at ease in your shared affection.'

He grinned feebly. 'So, you think I haven't *completely* ruined it?'

Agnes laughed lightly. 'Almost, but not quite.' She leaned into his ear. 'Anabella was courageous to leave the priory and make the journey here to Meonbridge. Brave simply to do it, but also to take the chance that your affection was still strong, after such a long separation.'

'You're right, and I can't tell you how pleased I am to see her.'

'Tell *her* that, then,' said Agnes, gesturing now towards the stairs. Anabella was descending, dressed in a blue gown that suited her very well. 'She must be exhausted by her exploit, yet has done this'—she pointed to the dress—'to please you…'

But he wasn't really listening, for his eyes were fixed upon Anabella. 'How beautiful she is,' he murmured. 'I've never seen her in anything other than a nun's dark and shapeless tunic.'

Agnes touched his arm. 'One last thing, John. Don't *presume* she's here to wed you. She is, of course, but I recommend you woo her all over again, to prove your affection and desire.'

'I will, Agnes, I promise. No more idiocy.' He went forward to take Anabella's hand.

Shortly afterwards, Agnes had left Anabella and John with Eleanor, and hurried home to her family. On the way, she called in to tell her ma that Eleanor was returned safely with John's future wife, and John himself would be home soon.

Ma was obviously delighted. 'I'm so looking forward to meeting her. Can I go tomorrow?'

'You can,' said Agnes. 'But, remember, Ma, Anabella's presence here in Meonbridge is a secret, to ensure her dead husband's roguish relatives don't find out where she is and come looking for her. She'll live with Eleanor and Walter till she and John are married, which will hopefully be soon. John's already told Sire Raphael of his intentions. But no one apart from our family and the Nashes can know Anabella's here.'

Not that Rosa had thought it likely the Sitwells could find out. Nonetheless, from what Rosa had said of them, Agnes fervently hoped they never would. But, once John and Anabella were married, even if they did come, it'd be too late. Those God had joined together no man could put asunder.

John had been absolutely right that Anabella was truly happy to be in Meonbridge, and to be sharing Alice's small house. Agnes supposed she was relieved to be safe from her former in-laws, and thankful to have escaped the priory. Even Rosa wasn't as happy there as she once was, but at least she'd *chosen* to become a nun, whereas for Anabella it had been a desperate measure that later proved to be a mistake.

Agnes realised it was partly what she and Eleanor had said to Rosa that persuaded her to organise Anabella's escape from Northwick, and Anabella herself confirmed it.

'It was only because of Rosa's courage I was able to escape,' she said, then sighed. 'It seems so wrong to have to speak of a priory as if it were a prison from which I had to flee.'

'Yet it was,' said Agnes. 'But only because of the present prioress.'

'Evangelina is so strange. Of course, I scarcely know her, but she is very different from Mother Angelica, who was so kind and compassionate, and took me in when I was so frightened of my husband's family. I *did* think then I might be happy as a nun. Northwick was such a peaceful place, and I felt safe there and loved. Even when I first met John, I still imagined I would continue on that path. Yet, I suppose it wasn't all that long before I realised my feelings for him were growing stronger, into the sort of affection I never experienced with my first husband, the sort of affection a woman dreams of but rarely finds.' Anabella lowered her eyes to her lap, but Agnes could still see that she was smiling.

She took her hand. 'I found it too in Jack. Do you know my story? Has Rosa told you?' Anabella nodded. 'I couldn't be more fortunate to have him, when my life might so easily have plunged into disaster. That he loved me as he did, and took on my son as his own...' She squeezed her hand. 'There *are* good men, Bella, and you and I are so lucky to have found two of them.'

'I am so sorry,' said Anabella, 'that Rosa could not come to our wedding, but I imagine Evangelina will now have clamped down on sisters leaving the priory. Especially Rosa. I am certain Evangelina sees her as a threat.' She shook her head. 'Kind, gentle, pious Rosa, a threat! It is so unlikely... But Rosa has become so brave, so determined to oust Evangelina and return Northwick to the place of piety and peace it was under Mother Angelica. Rosa has forced herself to abandon her vows and I know it grieves her bitterly...'

Agnes nodded. 'Being disobedient, fighting back... It's not in Rosa's nature to be so hostile, yet she knows now she has to be, for the greater good of Northwick.'

'How I do hope she succeeds. Northwick was a wonderful place under Mother Angelica, and, even if I no longer wish to be one of its sisters, I do long to hear it has returned to what it once was.'

Despite Ma's occasional frailty, she still managed to work every day in her potager and herb garden, sometimes with the help of the cottar women, Gillot and Betta. Even in November's chill, as long as it was dry, Ma would spend a while outdoors, cutting down dead plants, and mulching the ground around them, pruning fruit, and checking her stores of roots and onions for rot. There was always something to do, Ma said, and, to Agnes's surprise, it seemed Anabella loved helping her to do it.

As they sat now in the house before the fire with a warming cup of ale, Anabella explained how enthusiastic she was about the garden and how eager to learn all she could from Ma before she and John moved to their new house, when she would become responsible for their croft.

'My previous husband,' she said, 'had a grand house in the middle of Bishop's Waltham, but it was one of the few with little land. He could have bought one with larger grounds but, even if he had, he would not have expected me to labour in them. For he deemed working out of doors to be for peasants—' Her cheeks suddenly bloomed red, maybe at the careless, but surely unintended, insult to Ma and her, then she stumbled on. 'And... and... unfitting labour for his wife.' She looked away and spread her fingers out upon her lap. 'I didn't mind, as I was accustomed to the idea that the role of a Sitwell wife was to keep her husband's *house* in readiness for the entertainment of his wealthy cronies. For that was what my mother did.' She sighed. 'But now I am here in Meonbridge, I am excited by the prospect of growing vegetables and herbs and fruit, as well as flowers. And learning how to make salves and potions.'

She took a breath, and looked up again, her eyes bright.

'Are you sure, Bella?' said Agnes, smiling. 'It's a lot of work. Do you really want your hands to look like mine?' She held them out.

She remembered, years ago, how miserable she'd been at the state of her hands, albeit that was caused by carpentry rather than gardening. They looked like they belonged to an *old* woman, not one of only twenty. Yet now, at thirty-five, when her hands were dark and wrinkled, because of her labours on her croft, she no longer minded. She was content in her life and in her labours.

But Anabella shrugged. 'Oh, I do not care about my hands. I am so happy to be here, and a member of this family and this community. I could not be more fortunate to have found you all.'

Although Rosa had thought it unlikely the Sitwells would ever learn Anabella had come to Meonbridge, Agnes still worried that they might. She worried particularly that, as John and Anabella were living in Ma's house, the rogues might attack the atte Wode croft and terrify her.

It would be a while yet before the house John had promised Anabella was ready to be lived in, though Jack had put three men to building it. Agnes imagined at least another couple of months would pass before Ma would be on her own. Yet she worried about that too, whether Ma would be able to manage all alone, albeit Ma herself was adamant she could and would, saying yet again it was about time John had a house and a family of his own.

'I'm looking forward to a few more grandchildren,' she added, and gave her shoulders a little shrug of anticipated joy.

It was in the middle of the morning when Agnes arrived at her childhood home for her daily visit. As she turned into the atte Wode croft, she heard what sounded like men shouting, not too far away, the other side of the green, near the church. But, only a short while later, the shouting stopped, and she pushed open the door of the cottage and stepped inside.

'Did you hear that commotion?' she said, and Ma nodded.

'Mebbe some lads quarrelling?' said Ma. 'Yet why might they be idling about the village this time of the morning?'

Well, it was December, and there wasn't much to do out in the fields. But she said nothing.

Moments later, there came an urgent knock upon the door, and, opening it, Agnes was surprised to find the blacksmith, Roger Stronge, standing outside, in clear agitation and demanding entry.

'Goodness, Roger, what's going on?' she said. 'Has something happened?'

'It has, and I've come to warn you, well, to warn young Mistress atte Wode'—he glanced across at Anabella, sitting at the table preparing vegetables—'she should at once seek sanctuary in the church.'

Anabella sprang to her feet, so suddenly an onion rolled off the table and across the floor. 'Why?' Her voice was tight.

'Those former relatives of yours, Mistress, they've come looking for you.'

Ma cried out, 'No!'

'Where are they now, Roger?' asked Agnes.

'I sent them on a wild goose chase, to give me time to come here, and also to alert the constable... I sent my 'prentice to tell him to be ready when the men return.'

'Should you not find John too?' said Anabella.

'I would,' said Roger, 'but I don't know where to look for him.'

But Ma knew, as John had told her this morning.

Roger nodded. 'I'll send my lad to fetch him shortly.'

'How do you know they were looking for me?' asked Anabella, a little breathless, no doubt with anxiety, as she scurried about collecting boots, and a warm cloak and hood to take with her to the church.

Briefly and speaking fast, Roger told them how a roguish-looking horseman, accompanied by an entourage of others, accosted him at the smithy, demanding to know where the bailiff lived.

He grinned. 'I were an unfortunate choice of informant for, of course, I *knew* about my step-sister bringing you back to Meonbridge, Mistress Anabella. And that you'd married John, the very man whose whereabouts this rogue wanted to know. Anyway, I said the bailiff wouldn't be home, but out on his rounds. And I sent them off on a false trail a good distance from the village. You got time to hurry to the church, Mistress Anabella, and I suggest you go too, Alice.' He turned to Agnes. 'You too?'

'No, I'll stay here till John returns, then I can explain what's happening.'

Roger sped off, and Ma and Bella hurried from the house and down to Saint Peter's. Agnes prayed the Sitwells weren't already back in

Meonbridge, but all seemed quiet, and she was relieved when, not long afterwards, John fell into the house, his face wracked with concern for his wife.

'She's in the church with Ma,' said Agnes. 'They'll be safe there. Sire Raphael will protect them.'

'Where are the Sitwells now?' he said.

'Probably on their way back here,' said Agnes, 'and I imagine they might be in a fury at being sent on a fruitless search. I daresay they'll go back to the smithy...'

John was already at the door. 'I'll go there then...' he said, and throwing the door open, raced away from the house. Agnes sighed at her brother's impetuosity but followed him, nonetheless.

She was yards from the smithy when she heard the sound of pounding hooves, of riders galloping back into the village, no doubt churning the already muddy roads into a mire. When the men reined in their horses, it was, as she'd expected, outside the smithy. One rider leapt from his mount, clearly in a rage, and shouted, 'Blacksmith, come out here!'

Agnes stayed back, not wanting to get involved but, noticing John was concealing himself behind a nearby barn, she ran to join him.

'Poor Roger,' she whispered, and John grunted.

'Luckily, Roger is well-named, as that rogue might soon discover.'

She then saw Roger's young apprentice slip from the back of the smithy and run off. She whispered to John. 'I think Roger's lad's gone to fetch the constable.'

The blacksmith had now emerged from the room behind the forge, and the Sitwell man strode forward, sword drawn.

'You wanting me for summat?' said Roger, a smirk across his face.

For answer, the Sitwell man hefted his sword, but Roger picked up a hammer and stood foursquare before him, his shoulders broad and his powerful arms rippling. 'You thinking of threatening me?' he said. 'Not a good idea.' He raised his hammer and took the branding iron from the fire – it was red-hot, so Roger must have put it there on purpose.

The man backed away a step or two, but didn't lower his sword. 'You set me off on a wild goose chase, you scoundrel!' he growled. 'Now tell me, where's the bailiff?'

'Why d'you think I'd know?' said Roger. 'I'm not the bailiff's keeper. He could be anywhere within five miles of here—'

John touched Agnes's arm to stay her, and lunged forward, till he stood beside the blacksmith.

'And who are you to be looking for me?' he said, scowling.

The Sitwell man returned the scowl. 'Humphrey Sitwell, as I daresay you already know. And you are?'

'John atte Wode, bailiff, in service to the lord of Meonbridge, Dickon de Bohun.' John stood tall, straightening his back and puffing out his chest. But he wielded no weapon.

Master Sitwell sneered. 'You kidnapped my sister-in-law, Anabella Sitwell. Stole her away from Northwick Priory. So where is she?'

John shook his head vigorously. 'Your *former* sister-in-law,' he said firmly, 'no longer has any association with your family. I didn't kidnap her, nor steal her away. She left Northwick of her own accord, and now she's my lawful wife, as all the people now approaching will be able to affirm.' He pointed in the direction of the green.

Crossing the green was a crowd of villagers, all brandishing weapons of some kind and roaring their displeasure. How had they known to come? Yet word always did spread fast in Meonbridge. As they came closer, Agnes saw in their hands were pitchforks, scythes and sickles, garden implements and even kitchen knives.

The Sitwells' horses skittered as the noise and clamour came up close behind them. They jerked at their reins and whinnied, and one or two began to buck and rear, threatening to throw their riders. The crowd closed in still further, encircling the horses and their riders, separating Master Sitwell from his cronies.

The man's demeanour changed, from belligerence to fear. He lowered his sword and stepped back a pace or two.

'You're not welcome in Meonbridge, Master Sitwell,' continued John. 'There's nothing for you here. Your former sister-in-law is now an atte Wode, affirmed by our priest and by God, and witnessed by everybody here.' He swept his arm in an arc across the crowd standing before him, and everyone roared 'Aye!'. He stepped forward, and in a tone approaching menace, said, 'I suggest you leave and don't return.'

Master Sitwell looked as if he might still resist, still argue that Anabella should go with him. But, then the constable arrived, along with his henchmen, shouting for order and pushing their way through the villagers and the horsemen. Geoffrey Dyer took up a position between John and Master Sitwell.

''Tis true what I just heard Master atte Wode say,' he said. 'You've no cause to be in Meonbridge. You and your men should be on your way.' He threw his arm up in a gesture of dismissal. 'Now.'

At that, the constable's men all lifted up their cudgels and thumped them against their open hands.

'The lord of Meonbridge don't brook strangers threatening any o' those who live on his estates. I'd advise strongly *against* testing his resolve...' Geoffrey lifted both of his black bushy eyebrows in a way Agnes had always thought looked menacing, and Humphrey Sitwell's bluster seemed to deflate.

He sheathed his sword, and turned back towards his men. The crowd parted to let him reach his horse, and he remounted. The horse pranced a little, maybe still nervous of the press of men around it.

He glared at John and the constable. 'Very well, I can see my cause is lost.' But then he sneered. 'I wish you well of my *former* sister-in-law, Master Bailiff,' he said, 'but I warn you, the woman is a bitch. She led my brother a merry dance before she ran off with the dower he had so generously afforded her, and *pretended* to need protection from her family—'

But John held up his hand and roared. 'Enough of your slurs! Just go and don't come back.'

The crowd cheered as the horsemen rode way, and Agnes prayed that was the last Meonbridge would see of the Sitwells.

24

Dulcia was making her final preparations for the bishop's visitation. The bishop had replied very courteously to the letter she sent him last autumn asking if the visitation could be brought forward. He regretted it wasn't possible to set a much earlier date for the inspection, but he did offer February instead of April. She responded with alacrity and gratitude, and ever since, she, Beatrice, Rosa and Amata had been gathering the evidence they needed to make their claims against Evangelina.

How wretched Dulcia felt to be doing this. It went counter to everything she expected to be as a nun, requiring her to commit the sins of pride and wrath, and to deny her vow of obedience. But Rosa and Beatrice were right – Evangelina couldn't be permitted to continue as prioress. She had essentially brought Northwick to ruin financially, not to mention turning it from a house of prayer and peace into something closer to a brothel. She shuddered. How she hoped dear Mother Angelica wasn't witnessing what her niece had perpetrated against the priory she'd ruled so wisely and for so long. Indeed, how much she wished Angelica hadn't been called to God, to abandon them to Evangelina's wilful plundering.

Of course, Evangelina should never have been elected. Yet none of the sisters could have imagined she would act the way she had. Dulcia – and she knew many of the other sisters felt the same – had always found Evangelina dour, acerbic and aloof, and suspected she would make at the very least a poor prioress. But not a dangerous one!

Dulcia supposed Evangelina had bribed some of those sisters who voted for her. But she had no proof and would never ask the sisters she suspected to admit to it. There was also the mystery of Rosa choosing not to stand. At the time, neither Beatrice nor Amata, nor Dulcia herself, had understood why Rosa had made such a decision, and they still didn't.

The pile of documents the four sisters had assembled was stored in Dulcia's chamber, locked inside one of the coffers where she kept her accounts and ledgers. Between them, they had written out their charges against Evangelina, and gathered evidence to support their complaints, mostly references to the accounts, to demonstrate both Evangelina's profligacy with the priory's funds, and her failure to spend money where it was needed. Rosa had also taken it upon herself to write transcripts of private interviews she'd carried out with sisters who were willing, even eager, to voice their grief at the changes the prioress had wrought in Northwick.

A week before the bishop's commissioners were due to arrive, the four women met together in Dulcia's chamber, to check they had everything clear in their minds.

As they sat down, Dulcia noticed Amata was looking worried. She leaned forward. 'Are you quite well, Amata dear?' she said.

Amata pulled on her bottom lip. 'It's only... We've managed so far to keep our deliberations secret, wouldn't it be dreadful if Evangelina discovered us before the appointed day, and prevented us from making our views known?'

Dulcia shared an apprehensive shrug with Beatrice and Rosa.

When they wished to speak of their concerns to one another, they used to do so quietly in the cloister or the frater, or a little more loudly outside in the garden. But, since October, and their joint decision to take steps to oust Evangelina, they'd been meeting here in the treasury, to ensure they weren't overheard. To make it less obvious they were gathering, they usually met only two by two. But, now they were close to their goal of addressing the commissioners, they were taking the risk of all coming together. For Dulcia, the very fact of meeting *felt* like rebellion, but she'd resigned herself to it for the greater good of Northwick.

Rosa touched Amata's hand. 'Even if Evangelina does find out, she cannot stop us speaking out to the bishop's commissioners. It is our right and our duty to do so. That is why they come, to learn from *everyone* in the priory how it is faring, not only from the prioress.'

'Indeed,' said Dulcia. 'Anyway, many of our complaints involve the priory's finances, and I'm always required to go through the accounts with them in detail. Evangelina – *unlike* Mother Angelica – has shown little interest in actually understanding the accounts, and doesn't realise how clearly they reveal her misdemeanours.'

'I am certain she also does not know about the interviews I have carried out,' said Rosa. 'I hope the sisters will repeat their stories directly to the commissioners but, if they do not, I have the transcripts to show them. Of course, Evangelina might well deny everything. Indeed, I am sure she *will*, but our evidence is strong.'

Beatrice nodded. 'Evangelina will undoubtedly refuse to acknowledge our complaints. Or she'll accept one or two of them, for appearances' sake, and deny the rest.' She arched an eyebrow. 'But I'm confident our evidence will prove she's not telling the truth.'

They all murmured agreement.

'Shall we go through the list just once more?' said Rosa.

'I'm sure we've covered everything,' said Beatrice, 'but we could reiterate who's talking about what.'

'Oh, I thought all of us were mentioning everything,' said Amata, her forehead creasing.

Out of Amata's line of sight, Beatrice rolled her eyes, and Dulcia and Rosa smiled discreetly. 'Yes, Amata, we can, but we've already agreed which of us will speak most about a particular complaint.'

'Oh, yes, of course...' Amata still seemed a little baffled. 'Please remind me of *my* particular complaint...'

'Might you feel happier, Amata,' said Beatrice, 'if you didn't have to remember something specific but just mention those worries that come to you on the day?'

'And can you remind me what *those* are?'

Beatrice rolled her eyes again at the others.

Rosa reached out once more to touch Amata's hand. 'Can you remember, Amata dear, what has upset you especially about the changes Prioress Evangelina has made?'

Amata turned her hand around and clasped Rosa's. She appeared to consider the question, her lips pushing out and sucking in as she reflected. At length she nodded. 'Northwick no longer being a house of prayer but a place of entertainment. And those dogs! Wretched little creatures, getting under all our feet!' She tutted.

'Indeed,' said Rosa. 'So, just try to remember those, Amata, and leave the other matters to us.'

Amata wagged her head, and Beatrice's face bore an expression of sadness and regret.

'Right,' said Beatrice, sniffing slightly. 'Shall we each remind the others of our "particular complaints"? Dulcia?'

Dulcia inclined her head. 'I shall speak to the overall decline in the priory's funds and the expenses made by the prioress for items used only by her, such as her extravagant clothing, luxurious furnishings for her chamber, employing her own cook, demanding exotic food, entertaining so many people... And the dogs! I have *plenty* of evidence to back up my complaints.' The others grinned, but she placed her hands flat upon the table. 'To be fair, she has implemented a couple of low-cost improvements to make the *sisters'* lives better, with the new wimples – if not gowns – and the warmer blankets... Even so, it is much too little, and much too late...'

Rosa agreed. 'The prioress needs to do much more to increase our funds, especially as the endowment from Sir Toby Edenborough still seems unforthcoming.'

'Actually,' said Beatrice, 'I've news regarding Sir Toby I've not yet shared with you... I think Evangelina might still be clinging to the hope of his endowment, albeit at some time in the future...' She glanced at Dulcia, who nodded. 'Whereas, in truth, her hope is ... well, hope*less*.'

Rosa and Dulcia exchanged looks of surprise. 'For Sir Toby,' continued Beatrice, 'has no intention at all of providing an endowment to Northwick. I found out the other day he's a good friend of Sir Thomas Chatterton, our former steward, who'd acquainted him with exactly the sort of woman our prioress is, and advised him against investing his money in her priory. Sir Toby learned that Evangelina wasn't a judicious custodian of the priory's funds, and changed his mind about sinking his fortune into such an unworthy institution.'

Dulcia flushed. 'Oh, how dreadful to hear such a judgement placed upon our priory, when Mother Angelica was always so wise and prudent...'

'But it is not a judgement upon the priory or upon you, Dulcia,' said Rosa, leaning forward to take her hand. 'It applies to Evangelina alone.'

Dulcia gave her a wan smile, then set her mouth in a stern line. She was trembling with distress. 'Then she must *go!*' she cried out, and Amata looked up in alarm.

'I agree,' said Rosa, 'as I am sure do Beatrice and Amata. And, with hope, the visitation will be the medium through which it happens.' She sat back. 'Let me recite my own particular complaints...'

She said she would speak especially about Evangelina's unwillingness to spend money on necessary items, such as repairing the dorter roof, but also wanted to address the failure of the prioress to attend the holy offices, and her encouragement of other sisters also not to attend. 'I shall also mention,' she said, 'that Evangelina rarely holds chapter meetings but makes most decisions on her own, thus giving us no opportunity for raising issues or calling out misdemeanours.' The others murmured their agreement.

'Juliana,' she continued, 'also wishes to address the matter of the holy offices, the irreverence of some of the younger sisters in chapel.'

'Very good,' said Beatrice. 'Now, my turn. I shall of course explain the constraints put upon my budgets because of the prioress's extravagances. And thus, the decline in the overall quality and quantity of food provided for the sisters. Helen and I do our best, but it's impossible to provide our customary nourishing, if modest, diet with the meagre funds available.'

The other sisters agreed. 'I believe one or two of the sisters are even going to bed hungry,' said Dulcia. 'That was *never* the case under Mother Angelica's rule.'

<hr>

Beatrice was excited, if also apprehensive, when, exactly one week later, the bishop's commissioners arrived, accompanied by a couple of clerks. They'd stay for several days, sleeping in Northwick's guest chambers and dining with Evangelina.

The first day, the chief commissioner addressed the sisters in the chapter house, explaining the process of private interviews with each one of them. Most of the sisters knew the process well enough, as they'd taken part in visitations before. It was only the three youngest nuns – Letitia, Felicia and Maria – who'd come to Northwick since the last one.

Master Foxe was standing with the two bishop's men. Beatrice stared at him. He was a representative himself, appointed to be the bishop's eyes and ears for Northwick. He'd made the arrangements for the visitation, liaising with the bishop's office to select the commissioners who would come, if it wasn't to be the bishop himself. Yet, she wondered at the nature of his "liaison", for she didn't trust the man.

'Master Foxe here,' continued the chief commissioner, 'whom I am sure all of you know, will shortly leave my colleague and me to do our work, for it is essential that those who speak to you about your priory, and listen to any concerns that you might have, should be completely impartial. Only then can we be sure to come to fair-minded conclusions about any changes that might have to be made.' He gave a tight smile, and many of the sisters returned it.

But Beatrice didn't smile; for some reason she couldn't put her finger on, she was apprehensive about what was about to happen.

The verbal examinations of the sisters would start after dinner. The commissioners and Master Foxe retired to the prioress's chamber to dine with her, whilst the two clerks ate in the kitchen, as men weren't allowed to sit alongside the sisters in the frater.

All the interviews took place in the chapter house. Evangelina was the first to be questioned, and the other sisters were agog to know what she was saying, though there was little chance they ever would find out.

After Evangelina, the sisters were examined in descending order of seniority, starting with Clarice, as subprioress, then Dulcia, who was in discussion with the commissioners for hours, as she tried to explain the sorry state of the accounts. The other principal obedientiaries – Rosa, Amata, Juliana, Gracia, and Beatrice herself, each took their turn over the course of the next day, followed by the remaining nuns. Even the ancient ladies, Mildryth and Katerina, were given the chance to air their views, whether or not they were coherent and worthwhile.

The commissioners encouraged the sisters to speak their minds, and the clerks wrote rapidly in their ledgers, describing, in as much detail as they could, the story each nun told, both the positive aspects and the negative. As Beatrice understood it, each evening, by candlelight, the clerks copied out their sketchy notes in a more fair and legible hand, ascribing each interview to the sister who'd given it. The commissioners would use these records – called the *detecta* – to assess what was working well or otherwise in the priory, what had to be changed, and what injunctions they'd impose to ensure the changes were carried out.

The sisters weren't supposed to chat about their interviews, and, although a few did whisper together in the cloister or the dorter, most maintained their vows of obedience and kept silent. Beatrice found it hard to keep her counsel, and had to busy herself with her tasks to avoid finding herself taking part in illicit conversations. Yet the anticipation was quite intense: everyone was by turns excited and anxious about what the commissioners might conclude, and found the waiting hard to bear.

The day after all the individual conversations had been concluded and written up, the commissioners read through all the *detecta* and identified those matters – the *comperta* – that demanded further enquiry. The *comperta* were then listed and any sisters who'd been accused of one or more misdemeanours were summoned to the chapter house once again to be asked to admit to or refute the accusations.

The sisters who'd not been so accused had no idea what was taking place inside the chapter house. But those who gathered in the frater in two agitated, whispering groups, sat where they could observe the chapter house door, and at least see who came and went.

Beatrice sat with Amata and Juliana, and were joined by Anne and Helen.

'Mariota couldn't make up her mind whether to come with me or sit with the others,' murmured Anne, gesturing with her head towards the group of the prioress's favourites.

Beatrice let out a modest snort. 'She doesn't look happy over there, I must admit. Still...'

At that moment, a nun approached the chapter house door, knocked and entered. It was Sister Rosa.

'Why has Sister Rosa been summoned!' cried out Juliana.

'Ah,' said Beatrice, 'I might have guessed...'

'Guessed what?' said Anne.

'That the prioress would lodge complaints of her own, specifically against dear Rosa.'

'But what could they possibly be?' said Juliana, her face distraught.

'Oh, I think that's easy enough to deduce. She'll have accused Rosa of breaking her vow of obedience, and, perhaps, incitement to mutiny.'

The others gasped, but Beatrice shook her head. 'I should have realised she'd do that. Evangelina's determined to hang onto power...'

'Even when she doesn't deserve to,' muttered Amata, in a statement not a question.

'Or, rather, because she *knows* she doesn't deserve to.'

Not much later, Rosa came out of the chapter house and walked quickly towards the frater, and her group of friends.

'Is all well?' asked Beatrice.

'Not exactly,' she said. 'Though it is scarcely unexpected.'

Beatrice harrumphed. 'I *hadn't* expected it, fool that I am! Am I to assume the prioress has accused you?'

'She has. Disobedience and fomenting rebellion.' She smiled. 'She is trying to keep me quiet.'

'But you won't keep quiet?'

'Well, I decided to admit to the disobedience, and accept a string of penances. After all, I *have* broken my vow, and I always did intend to undertake some penances when all this is over – assuming it ever is.' She let out a short laugh. 'But I am happy enough to do them now... However, I am not willing to agree to the accusation of rebellion, for I have not *"fomented"* anyone.' She looked from one to the other. 'Is that true? *Have* I goaded any of you into dissent?'

They all shook their heads. 'We did not need your goading, Sister Rosa,' said Juliana. 'We can all see for ourselves that what the prioress has been doing is wrong, and believe we have to try to stop her.' Her eyes were sparking, and the others eagerly agreed.

'I am glad you think that,' said Rosa. 'Thank you, Juliana; and all of you. However, the commissioners require me to find three compurgators to declare my innocence of the rebellion charge. Are any of you willing to stand for me?'

All immediately said yes, and Rosa blushed.

'I think you should ask Dulcia,' said Beatrice. 'Out of friendship. She mightn't wish to be seen to take sides, so to speak, but I feel you should give her the opportunity.'

'I shall go and ask her,' said Rosa and hurried away, but it was not long before she returned, smiling. 'Dulcia has agreed. She did muse on whether she herself might be accused, but I thought the notion was absurd. It is *me* Evangelina is trying to silence.'

A short while later, with Dulcia, Beatrice and Juliana at her side, Rosa returned to the chapter house, to be cleared of the prioress's accusation. When they emerged again and went to join Helen, Anne and Amata waiting in the frater, Rosa was smiling broadly.

'I presume Evangelina will be next,' she said and indeed, before too long, the prioress, dressed in her most modest gown and wimple, approached the chapter house door and went in.

The prioress was alone in the chapter house with the commissioners a good long while, until at length she emerged, stony-faced, and marched along the cloister towards the frater and the group of her supporters. She beckoned them to follow her back into the cloister and they walked, at speed, right to the other side, presumably so Beatrice and the others – the members of the "Rosa faction", Beatrice thought, with a smile – were out of hearing.

Sister Gracia's heart was thudding as Mother Evangelina practically *ran* around the cloister, whilst she and the others hurried to keep up. What had happened in the chapter house to cause the prioress such agitation?

At the opposite side of the cloister, the prioress halted and gestured to them all to come close. 'I've been accused,' she said, her voice low and bitter, 'of a number of misdemeanours. I've admitted to one or two, but can't allow the others. Thus, I'm required to bring compurgators to the chapter house to swear my innocence. I require three, and they're to present themselves within two hours.' She tilted her head. 'Which of you will stand for me?'

Gracia raised her hand at once. 'I will, Reverend Mother!' she cried, thrilled to be the first.

But, if the prioress had expected all of them to cry out 'Me!', she was disappointed. Gracia was horrified to see the others hang their heads, and fiddle with their crucifixes. The prioress's expression hardened, but none of them would meet her gaze.

Gracia tutted. 'Come on, sisters, surely we must help Mother Evangelina to overcome the conspiracy against her.' She looked around, willing the others to lift their eyes. If Evangelina could not gain absolution for those wrongdoings, whatever they were, the commissioners might dismiss her. '*Sisters?*' Gracia said again, her tone more pressing.

At length, Letitia nodded. And, a moment or so later, so did Mariota, although her face suggested she was not happy to be doing so.

'Thank you,' said Mother Evangelina to the three of them, although her expression scarcely softened. 'Shall we retire to my chamber for a while, so I can acquaint you with the accusations and my own response to them?'

As she followed the prioress, Gracia noted how the remaining sisters, those who were also supposed to be the prioress's allies, slunk away. They might do well, she thought, to muse a while upon what Mother Evangelina would surely consider their betrayal.

Beatrice and the "Rosa faction" had collapsed into merry chatter at the sight of the prioress so clearly rattled by the interrogation to which the commissioners had presumably subjected her.

'I suppose she too came to ask for compurgators?' asked Anne.

'I should think so,' Beatrice said. 'How *vexed* she looked.'

'Will she then be absolved?' said Juliana. 'She does not deserve to be.'

Rosa was no longer smiling. 'As Beatrice has already said, she will probably admit to one or two of the more trivial charges, but deny the rest. Yet our evidence is so strong, I had been confident the commissioners would see through her and find her guilty of *all* our complaints.'

'Surely, they must,' said Helen, in an agitated whisper, but Rosa shook her head.

'If she has been asked to provide compurgators that means the commissioners are willing to let them assert her innocence.' She frowned. 'It is not what I had hoped would happen.'

Moments later, the prioress slipped back into the chapter house, together with Sisters Gracia, Letitia and Mariota.

'Goodness,' said Anne, 'did you see Mariota's face? I wonder why she's agreed to vouch for the prioress when she's become so uncertain of her allegiances?'

Beatrice grunted. 'Maybe she's decided she's better off in Evangelina's camp, though I can't think why.'

When the four nuns reappeared a short while later, all had smiles upon their faces. The prioress in particular looked almost gleeful. She glanced towards the frater and, tilting her head, she smirked, then she and the others hurried away, presumably upstairs to her chamber.

'They have absolved her,' said Juliana, her voice catching, then cried out. 'Was all that evidence *really* not enough?'

Beatrice grunted again. 'I find that hard to believe, Juliana.'

Sister Rosa had gone quiet. Her back was stiff, and her nostrils flared.

Beatrice noticed her silence. 'Rosa? You look very vexed.'

'I am, although I am trying hard not to allow the sin of wrath to overwhelm me.' She gave a feeble grin. 'Oh, Beatrice, it is so unreasonable. As Juliana said, our evidence was strong. *Undeniable*! Yet the commissioners have allowed her to get away with some of the offences. Why?'

'Perhaps the commissioners – indeed, the bishop – would prefer not to find a prioress guilty of misdemeanours? Might they simply hope the injunctions they demand will be sufficient to reform her?'

'But we *know* Evangelina will not change. She will likely ignore the injunctions and carry on as before.'

Beatrice twisted her mouth. 'I daresay you're right. All that work to put the evidence together! We might have saved ourselves the effort...'

But Rosa thumped her fist lightly upon the table, in a gesture as aggressive as any of them had seen her muster. 'No, Beatrice, we were right to do it, and this is not the end. Whatever the outcome and the injunctions the commissioners impose, we shall not give up. It might take a while, but we *must* find a way to oust Evangelina.' She stood up. 'Does Dulcia know of all this?'

'I imagine not,' said Beatrice. 'She's been in her chamber all afternoon.'

'Very well, I shall go and speak to her. Do you wish to come?'

Beatrice nodded and together they hurried from the frater towards the treasury.

The following day, all the sisters convened once more inside the chapter house. It was clear that all were anxious as they took their usual places, awaiting the arrival of the officials, and couldn't help but chat nervously together.

Beatrice tried to remain composed, but Amata, sitting at her side, was wringing her hands together in her lap, and letting out loud sighs.

'All that work for nothing,' Amata muttered, echoing Beatrice's own words of yesterday.

Beatrice laid her hand over Amata's, to still them. 'Not necessarily. We don't know the commissioners' final verdict.'

Yesterday evening, all the sisters had learned that both the prioress and Sister Rosa must answer to a number of accusations laid against them. And that each admitted to some complaints and refuted others. But the details of their penances and absolutions weren't shared. Neither did they expect to learn of them now, but rather to hear a summary of the commissioners' findings, and whether any injunctions were to be imposed upon the priory as a whole.

The commissioners and the clerks arrived, and hush fell upon the gathering.

After a brief introduction from the chief commissioner, the clerks took turns to read out loud the *detecta* – the matters revealed to the commissioners – and the *comperta* – the matters discovered by the commissioners – in full. The sisters listened to the interminable presentations in silence, though when the commissioner asked if everything was clearly understood, they all said 'Aye!'. Beatrice might have liked to ask a question or two, but no opportunity arose.

'Very well,' the chief commissioner said. 'So now we proceed to the injunctions to be placed upon Northwick Priory in order to address the most serious of the failings we have discovered.' He cast his gaze sternly around the occupants of the chamber, and even Beatrice shrank into her seat a little.

A clerk then recited another list, shorter than Beatrice had expected. And how surprised she was to hear injunctions that addressed wrongdoings of which the prioress had, in principle, been absolved. Wrongdoings that were probably, in Rosa's eyes, the most grievous of Evangelina's failings, her undoing of the priory's finances aside.

Three rulings in particular struck Beatrice as significant. One demanded that the prioress had no favourites, which was a requirement of the Benedictine rule. Another ruled that she entertained outsiders much less often. A third commanded her to attend chapel daily and ensure all Northwick's sisters did the same. All these rulings addressed Rosa's principal complaint that Evangelina had changed the priory from a house of piety to one of entertainment. A complaint the prioress had apparently refused to accept, but of which she was absolved by means of her compurgators.

Beatrice was baffled. Had the commissioners, then, *recognised* the complaint, but chosen not to hold the prioress directly responsible for it? How odd.

'The list will be sent in writing to the prioress soon,' said the clerk, as he sat down, and Beatrice suppressed a snort. Sending them to Evangelina was no good: she'd just ignore them.

But, at last, it was all over. The chief commissioner declared the visitation concluded, and he and his colleague and the clerks all rode away.

Unable to concentrate on their usual daily tasks, Northwick's sisters once again split into their factions to discuss the visitation's outcomes, and the rulings imposed upon them.

The "Rosa faction" gathered once more in the frater. Beatrice thought the prioress's clique must be in her chamber.

'Well?' she said, looking from one sister to another. 'What do we think?'

Rosa shook her head. 'Nothing will change. The prioress has survived our complaints – although quite *how* I do not understand, when our prodigious evidence surely made her guilt so clear.'

Everyone nodded, but Beatrice also frowned. 'What's more, she's most *un*likely to comply with the injunctions, or, at any event, with those injunctions that don't suit her.'

'Will we truly have to wait another three whole years,' said Juliana, her face gloomy, 'before we have the opportunity to air our grievances again?'

They all exhaled wearily. Such a prospect was intolerable.

MARCH 1367

A few weeks after the visitation, Dulcia was troubled, for the most serious, and intractable, problem in the priory – the decline in funds – showed no sign at all of being resolved. The commissioners had, predictably, told both her and Evangelina that savings must be made, but what more could be done?

'I told them,' Dulcia said to Beatrice and Rosa, 'we were *already* cutting back as far as we were able to.'

'I said the same,' said Beatrice. 'I'd already applied a number of restrictions to the sisters' diet, but the food still has to be adequate, and nourishing. Indeed, the commissioners enjoined us to ensure it was. Yet it's not *our* mismanagement, Dulcia,' she continued, her voice rising, 'that's caused this dreadful shortfall, but the prioress's.'

'I agree. Although she *is* now cutting down a little on her own expenditure... She's promised to comply with the injunction to entertain outsiders less often, to eat mostly alone, and not to demand such lavish food for herself, and so far, she is doing so. She's even refraining from purchasing extravagant new clothes or furnishings. Might she be hoping to convince the sisters that she understands their grievances against her and wishes to make amends?'

Rosa shook her head. 'I do try always to be tolerant and forgiving, but I truly doubt that she has changed at all.'

'I agree,' said Beatrice. 'She'll carry on like this for a while, weeks, maybe even a few months, but then she'll revert to normal. You mark my words.'

Dulcia nodded. 'Yet I'm certain she wants to continue as prioress. So, she might be willing to continue to forego her luxuries if it ensures she keeps her position?'

Rosa did not disagree, yet she suspected Beatrice was right that Evangelina's new-found restraint was temporary. 'Anyway, what she has to do,' she said, 'is raise more funds, find new sponsors.'

'Though, under Angelica's rule,' said Dulcia, 'we managed well enough on the funds provided by our principal patron and the income we ourselves made from our farm. It *was* entirely Evangelina's extravagance that threw our perfectly workable economy into such disarray.'

'Do you think she acknowledges that?' said Rosa.

'She certainly *recognises* it,' said Dulcia, 'and has talked of finding new benefactors. But, knowing what happened with Sir Toby, I'm doubtful any others will come forward. Moreover, even if Evangelina cuts back *totally* on her excessive expenditure, it will still take us quite a while to refill the gaping hole she's gouged out of our coffers.'

Yet it was not just the finances that still troubled them all.

As they'd suspected, the other grievances they'd raised against the prioress were barely being addressed. Evangelina *still* had her favourites, albeit she did eat with them less often, so her chamber rang with gaiety and laughter less frequently than it once had.

She had, too, made a very modest compliance with the ruling that *daily* chapter meetings were required, by holding them once a week. Yet, most seriously, she still mostly failed to attend the holy offices in the chapel, and those sisters who'd followed her example – or, at any rate, attended only in the day time and not at night – continued to do the same.

'It is still not good enough,' said Rosa. 'Despite imposing the injunctions, the commissioners did not deal properly with our most serious complaints against Evangelina. She is complying only half-heartedly with the rulings, so nothing has changed. Nor will it. Northwick will continue to decline, in both piety and prosperity.'

She clasped her hands together and placed them decisively upon the table. 'Therefore, sisters, our task is far from over. We must continue to fight against her. She will no doubt imagine she can ignore the injunctions she does not like for another three years, but we cannot allow it. Northwick will be destroyed long before then, and that is something surely none of us is willing to contemplate.'

The others unequivocally agreed.

'Then I am willing,' continued Rosa, 'to be disobedient and, indeed'—she laughed briefly—'to *foment* rebellion, if that is what is required. And, finally, I think it is. Are you with me, sisters?'

25

Northwick Priory
March 1367

Evangelina was once more spending a lot of her time alone. The initial satisfaction – and indeed, relief – of surviving the visitation, with no more than a few penances and some rulings she might or might not follow, had dissipated.

Some weeks before the visitation, Letitia had told her Rosa, Beatrice and Dulcia were meeting regularly – sometimes too with Amata, and even Juliana. She'd assumed they were concocting a raft of grievances to try to overthrow her, and had asked Nicholas Foxe to help her refute their claims.

It was Cousin Nicholas who made the arrangements for the visitation, liaising with the bishop's office over the dates and who would actually come. In the past, the bishop himself had carried out the inspection, but the old bishop, Bishop Edyngton, had died last October, and although the new one, William Longe, had been elected, he wasn't yet in post. As a result, the bishop's office was, apparently, in a state of some disarray, and Nicholas had had no difficulty persuading the office that two of the bishop's commissioners – and he named two men in particular – would be the perfect choice for Northwick's visitation, as there was little untoward that required examination.

When Nicholas told her what he'd said and done, Evangelina grinned. 'You might have thought the bishop's officers would smell a rat, you saying that.'

He'd tapped his nose. 'My word is trusted. Moreover, with the office so pressed, having many visitations to arrange – not just priories, but monasteries, and churches, all manner of institutions for which the bishop is responsible – I thought they'd welcome my suggestion of an unobtrusive visit, without the bishop's presence...' He leaned forward. 'You will find those two commissioners most *co-operative...*'

'Thank you, Nicholas,' she said. 'I'm most grateful.'

She explained to him her conviction that some of the sisters were intending to raise several grievances against her.

He wagged his head. 'I recommend you accede to one or two of them. Accept a penance or two, and agree to comply with any relevant injunctions they impose. That way, the commissioners are likely to absolve you of the other complaints—'

'Only "likely to"?' she said, her head tilted.

'Oh, more than likely – certainly!'

Thus, Evangelina had survived Rosa's conspiracy to undermine her.

Yet she was a little disappointed that her own attempt to challenge Rosa had had similar results.

It'd been easy enough to come up with her own grievances against Rosa: her frequent disobedience and her undoubted scheming with the other sisters. "Fomenting rebellion" she thought she'd call it, and rather liked the phrase.

Rosa had accepted the charge of disobedience. Yet how vexing that she denied rebellion. For the commissioners then had to permit her to find compurgators to vouch for her innocence, which she doubtless had no trouble doing...

Evangelina grunted as she recalled how, in the same situation, *her* so-called supporters had failed to stand up for her. She did, at length, find three who would, but was resentful that the others had kept silent when she asked them for their help. Yet she had to quell any bitterness she might bear towards them, for, if she was going to continue as prioress, she needed all the supporters she could muster, even if they had once been disloyal.

Hilde slid into her chamber, bearing a tray of dishes.

'Your dinner, Lady Evangelina,' she said, putting the tray down upon the table and curtseying.

'Thank you, Hilde,' she said and waved her away.

She had little appetite. Standing up, she went to the side table where Hilde had earlier left a flagon of wine, and poured herself a cup. She took it back to her chair, and sat down heavily, causing the wine to splash a little and leave droplets on the dark fabric of her gown. She flicked at them idly with her fingers, and drank.

She'd thought often in the past few weeks of what happened at the visitation, and what it meant for her future as prioress. But she'd not yet devised a strategy for guaranteeing her position. It was why she was spending so much time alone: she needed time and solitude to *think*.

Since the visitation and the rulings, she *had* made some concessions. As a sop to Dulcia, and the commissioners, she'd cut back on her personal expenditure – she'd bought nothing new for weeks – and agreed to be less extravagant with her own food, and to dine more on her own than with her favourites. She was playing her part...

Yet Dulcia said it would take *months* or more to recover the deficit, even if she cut back entirely.

What she *had* to do was find another benefactor...

She'd told the commissioners she was still hopeful of Sir Toby Edenborough's endowment. Yet she knew this was a lie. Sir Toby had clearly decided against backing Northwick at all. She thought the justification he'd given her unlikely, but he'd not change his mind.

She had to find a new sponsor, but she'd lost the enthusiasm to look...

But what of Anabella's dowry? The property deeds, the jewellery, the gold... Evangelina had made no effort to hunt her down and bring her back to Northwick, despite having claimed to the commissioners she was hopeful of her return. That wasn't going to happen, she was sure. Yet she was still refusing to let Dulcia return Anabella's dowry to her. But why? There wasn't any point in keeping it, for Dulcia wouldn't permit even a groat of it to be spent.

She finished her cup, and peered over at the food. It was doubtless cold by now, but she had to eat. Standing, she went to sit at the table. She picked at the meat, and ate a few spoonsful of the sauce. It was tasty enough but plainer fare than she'd become accustomed to. Soon she pushed the dish away, and poured another cup of wine instead.

Evangelina stepped over to the window that looked out across the fields and woods towards the distant hills. The hills were barely visible, as heavy cloud had now descended, making the early afternoon as gloomy as if it were dusk. How quiet it was, both out there and here in her chamber. Excessively quiet. She'd chosen the solitude, of course, but she did miss the merriment of sharing meals with one or other of her young "disciples", as she'd once called them.

But that merriment had been one of Rosa's principal objections: "turning Northwick into a house of entertainment instead of piety", as she put it.

Evangelina looked back into her chamber. It had become quite dark. Why hadn't Hilde come to light some candles? She put down her cup and, taking up a spill, lit it from the fire and put the flame to the wick of the nearest candle, then did two more. The flames at once brightened the chamber, bringing it a little cheer. Picking up her cup once more, she paced around the room, recalling the moment when the commissioners had asked her about that particular complaint.

She had, of course, refuted it, but they countered that the evidence suggested it was true. She'd floundered a moment, denying the existence of her "disciples", for favourites were against the Benedictine code. And she could scarcely admit to her *yearning* for a more luxurious, easeful life. At length, she said, as prioress, she was required to entertain potential benefactors and supporters of the priory, and surely shouldn't have to give that up.

'Then do it more discreetly,' said one of the commissioners. 'Entertain them less often, and less generously. No more than once a month should surely be sufficient...'

She'd agreed and said no more, glad they seemed to have passed over the charge of favouritism. But consequent to the complaint about entertaining was the accusation that she had failed to attend the holy offices and encouraged other sisters to do the same. Which was true, and clearly difficult to justify. Yet she wasn't willing to *admit* to it. The commissioners presented evidence from several sisters, and moist heat gathered underneath the neck of her wimple as she found herself unable to respond other than to deny the charge outright.

At length, the commissioners arraigned her for all of her denials: the declining finances, the entertainment, the lack of piety. And, like Rosa, she had to find three sisters to uphold her avowal of innocence. Only Gracia had played her part convincingly, yet the commissioners accepted all three pleas. Albeit they did also impose the rulings, most of which she intended to ignore. After all, no one outside the priory would be checking up on her and the next visitation was three long years away...

Despite her reluctance to part with Anabella's dowry, Evangelina at length sought out the treasuress to discuss what to do about it.

'We can't simply keep it,' Dulcia said again. 'That would be most dishonourable, even theft.'

'Yet she's evidently run away, and hasn't bothered to ask for it...'

'Nonetheless, if Anabella is no longer living as a nun in Northwick, we have no entitlement to the property, however well-intentioned she was when she first offered it.' Dulcia pursed her lips. 'Do you then believe she *has* run away, and not been kidnapped?'

Evangelina shrugged. 'It's clear her husband's family – the Sitwells – *didn't* kidnap her. I understand Anabella had been afraid of that, and it was the reason she fled for sanctuary to Northwick.' Dulcia nodded. 'But, when Humphrey Sitwell stormed into the priory and accosted me, he evidently *didn't* know the whereabouts of his brother's widow.'

'You were brave to confront him as you did,' said Dulcia, and Evangelina smiled thinly.

She thought she'd shown *great* courage, but admitted to herself, if not to anyone else, that she'd been terrified and really not known what to do. It was fortunate the man backed down following her tirade.

'But he threatened to return,' she said, 'to collect the fortune he considers his, and if he did, how would we answer him? If it's no longer held in Northwick's coffers, we can justifiably send Master Sitwell packing if and when he comes again.'

'I agree. Yet where do we send it when we don't know where Anabella is?'

Evangelina did wonder now why she hadn't made a better effort to discover where Widow Sitwell had disappeared to. If she wasn't abducted, did she make her own arrangements to leave, or did someone else in Northwick help her? Such as Sister Rosa?

Immediately after Anabella's departure, Evangelina had asked everyone in the priory what they knew, questioning the sisters, the priory servants and Gerard, the porter. Gerard claimed never to have seen before any of the people who came that day, and was red-faced when he confessed he hadn't made his usual enquiries of the visitors.

'But I were deliberately distracted,' he said gruffly, evidently annoyed with himself.

None of the other servants had anything to offer. Though, when she questioned Hilde, Evangelina sensed she might be hiding something. It was Hilde who informed her about the visitors, repeating, it turned out, what Letitia told her she had witnessed. But neither she nor Letitia appeared to know any more than that some people came to the priory and left again. They'd no notion of whom the women visited, albeit it was obviously Anabella Sitwell. And they'd no idea where the party might have taken her...

Of course she'd questioned Rosa too, but she refused to give any answers. Which undoubtedly suggested guilt, but, frustrated as she was by Rosa's silence, Evangelina didn't know how to *force* her to confess the truth.

Soon after that any enthusiasm she'd had for pursuing Mistress Sitwell seemed to fade. She simply forgot about her. But now, they did need to know where the woman was.

'Have you any idea how we might find out?' she said to Dulcia.

The treasuress shook her head. 'I wonder if any of the other sisters know?'

'I asked everyone shortly after she disappeared.'

'I remember.' Dulcia flushed slightly. 'But, *then*, they might have been unwilling to say. Whereas now...?'

'Who are you thinking of?' said Evangelina.

'I couldn't say...'

Evangelina frowned. "Couldn't" or "wouldn't"? Without doubt, it was Rosa. But she'd not press Dulcia to reveal what she clearly didn't wish to. For she needed *Dulcia's* continuing support most particularly. But she'd question Rosa again sometime to try to discover what she knew...

The loss of Anabella's fortune would make a considerable dent in Northwick's coffers, and Evangelina had no ideas for how to replenish them other than to find another sponsor. However, she was bleakly unconvinced that any more wealthy men eager to invest in Northwick even existed.

On the gloomiest of March days, such as this one, when dark clouds blanketed the sky from early morning to sundown, Evangelina's chamber – despite its fine furniture and rich decorations – took on an air of melancholy, indeed, almost despair. There were moments when she wondered if she even *wanted* to be Northwick's prioress any more...

Yet what was the alternative? To have Rosa as prioress in her place, with her austerity and her piety and her strict adherence to the rules? She herself would have to sleep in the dorter alongside all the other nuns, to share their bland and boring diet in the frater, and be obliged to run along to the chapel eight times a day...

Moments later Evangelina had pulled herself together. No, she wouldn't let that happen. Even if she did feel a little bleak right now, she wasn't yet ready to give up everything she'd gained.

Wielding power over her sisters had been exhilarating; being able to do – indeed to *have* – whatever she wanted, and to live the genteel life she'd been so long deprived of, had been a thrill. But, without full and constantly replenished priory coffers, continuing to live such a life would be impossible.

Yet the priory's teetering finances were not her sole concern. In order to keep her position as prioress, she'd also *have* to confront Sister Rosa and bring her finally to heel.

. . .

Rosa hadn't been cowed by Evangelina's charge of an "unnatural" relationship between herself and Master atte Wode. It was an accusation Evangelina now wished she hadn't made, for it was patently absurd. And, far from being intimidated, Rosa had been angry and defiant, rebutting it entirely.

Besides, she knew from Letitia's continued watching that Rosa was, once more, meeting often with her cronies. Which proved she *was* still scheming to overthrow her.

Evangelina thumped the table with her fist: she had to stop her. For months, she'd been threatening to lay bare the whole truth about the saintly Rosa's past. Even though she knew almost nothing about what had driven Rosa to enter Northwick.

She did know that, when Rosa first came, she was disconsolate and troubled. A few times, Evangelina had listened in on the girl's desperate prayers, as she begged God for forgiveness for her sins. She always wondered what sins the young novice could have committed, when she appeared so virtuous and compliant, yet in all the ensuing years she never had found out.

In the past year or so, she'd threatened Rosa twice: before the election, and last summer with the gossip. Both times, the threat was to expose her so-called sins. And, both times, Rosa yielded. The mention of her "sins" had clearly frightened her.

But the acquiescence hadn't lasted.

Evangelina pushed herself to her feet and took a turn about her chamber. She had to make the other sisters see that Rosa was not the saint they thought she was. For too long she'd been prevaricating, only admonishing Rosa in private, which was scarcely a threat at all.

What she *had* to do was discredit Rosa openly, to expose her to the other sisters' revulsion. She imagined the scene in the chapter house, with her denouncing Rosa, revealing her sins. The gasps and cries of shock. Rosa's slumped shoulders and scarlet, chastened face. Perhaps her fleeing from the chamber in abject shame...

That would do it. Surely, Rosa wouldn't be able to tolerate such very *public* humiliation?

· · ·

Since the visitation, Evangelina had been calling chapter meetings every Friday. Her failure to hold *daily* chapter meetings, as the Benedictine rule demanded, was a charge she decided to confess to and agree to correct. She thought, in time, she might once more dispense with them altogether, for, mostly, nothing much was said or discussed. A few minor cavils were raised and resolved, and the gathering was invariably over not long after it had begun.

But next Friday's meeting would be different...

Stirred by her decision to denounce Rosa to the other sisters and bring her down at last, Evangelina instructed Hilde to ask Letitia, Maria and Felicia to join her for dinner in her chamber. She was feeling the need for a little merriment again. As the bell rang for Sext, there came a knock upon her door, and Letitia and Maria stepped inside.

Evangelina held out her hands as she went forward to greet them. 'It's been too long,' she said. 'But, as I'm sure you know, we're all having to cut down on our expenditure a little, and I agreed with Sister Dulcia to play my part. Yet I've missed your company.'

Letitia smiled, if rather wanly, but Maria, although she nodded, was curiously glum-faced.

'But where's Felicia?' said Evangelina. 'Isn't she joining us?'

Maria shook her head. 'You've been hidden away so long, Reverend Mother, you've not realised she's not been herself for weeks...' she said in a whisper tinged, Evangelina thought, with rancour.

'I've not been "hidden away", Maria. But I *have* had several important matters to attend to, since the bishop's commissioners were here.' Maria shrugged. 'So, what's wrong with Felicia? Is she ill?'

The girl's cheeks reddened. She was plainly reluctant to say more.

'Well? Why won't you tell me?'

Letitia stepped forward. 'Mother Evangelina, I suspect Maria is loath to *betray* her friend.' Maria threw her a scowl. 'But it is surely time you knew about Felicia...'

Evangelina spun around. 'Knew what about her?'

The girl hesitated a moment. 'That she is with child?' Her eyes were alight, as if the news was good.

Evangelina gasped. 'With child?' She sought her chair, and fell back into it. Her heart was hammering with alarm. 'How can she *possibly* be with child?' Her voice rose to an undignified squawk.

Maria looked at the floor, her cheeks scarlet, but Letitia shrugged. 'I do not know *how*, Mother Evangelina...' She blushed. 'But I do know she was sick for weeks, in the mornings... And now, well, now, the swelling in her belly is quite evident, even underneath her most capacious skirts—'

Evangelina gasped again, and sprang once more to her feet. 'Swelling? How much? How many months?'

Letitia didn't answer, but Maria, without lifting her head, murmured 'Five.'

'*Five months*!' Evangelina cried. Quickly counting back, she came to October. 'It happened when I was away?'

Maria gave a single nod.

'Go and fetch the trollop here!' Evangelina was aware she was close to shrieking, and her forehead was now pounding. How could this be happening? As if there wasn't already more than enough to drag her down...

Maria sidled off, but Letitia hovered.

'So, you don't know who?' said Evangelina.

'No, Reverend Mother, truly. But I did become aware a while ago that Felicia was pregnant, with the sickness and all. She hid herself away as best she could, hoping, I suppose, it might all go away... But of course, it has not and now...'

'Yes, yes...' She locked eyes with Letitia. 'But why didn't you tell me sooner?'

'I did not think it was my place...'

Evangelina grunted. 'Your *place* is to keep me informed.'

Shortly, Hilde came with the food, and there was enough for four. Evangelina exhaled loudly. 'You can take that away. My assistants aren't joining me for dinner after all.'

Hilde looked across at Letitia, her eyes questioning. Letitia gave her head a little shake, and Hilde sniffed. 'After I've gone to all this tr—' She promptly stopped, and chewed at her lip. Her cheeks were red. 'Sh-shall I leave some for you, Lady Evangelina?' she stammered.

Evangelina huffed. 'Don't bother. I've lost my appetite. Take it all away. Give it to the sisters in the frater...'

Hilde muttered peevishly as she picked up the tray again and backed out of the chamber, but Evangelina didn't bother to chastise her.

It wasn't long before she wished after all Hilde *hadn't* taken away the food. She poured herself a cup of wine, but it wasn't what she needed when her head was throbbing with a megrim.

At last Maria returned and, when she entered, it was clear she'd had to press Felicia to come.

'You can stand over there, next to Letitia,' Evangelina said to Maria, and what looked like fear flashed briefly in the girl's eyes. 'Hilde has taken our dinner down to the frater. You can eat it later, if there's any left after the sisters have had their fill.'

Both girls let out doleful sighs but, ignoring them, she faced Felicia, who, with her bowed head and sagging shoulders, was much unlike her usual self.

'Well, well,' she said, 'what trouble you do find yourself in, Felicia.' She pointed at the girl's clearly swelling belly. 'Explain.'

Felicia was shaking visibly, as if she had an ague, or the room was freezing cold. When she lifted her head, her face was ashen, her eyes dark with misery. Her fingers clutched restlessly at the fabric of her skirt. For a moment, Evangelina almost felt sorry for her. But not for long.

'Well? I said, explain!'

Felicia looked away. 'What *is* there to explain? You can see my predicament...'

'Indeed, I can. So, who's the father?'

'I cannot say.'

Evangelina exploded. 'What do you mean, "cannot"? Are you *refusing* to give me the villain's name?'

She nodded, and tears rolled down her cheeks.

Evangelina swung around to face the other girls. 'Do *you* know?'

'I have already said I do not,' Letitia said, then flushed, presumably hearing the insolence in her tone.

Evangelina disregarded it and turned to Maria. 'And you? I rather imagine you *do*.'

But once more Maria hung her head and remained completely silent.

'I could *beat* it out of you,' said Evangelina, her voice rising yet again.

Felicia cried out 'No!', Letitia let out a gasp, and Maria crossed herself and dropped to her knees.

Evangelina strode away from them all, and stared out through the window. It was gloomy again outside, the clouds dark and sweeping low over the distant hills. How well the weather accorded with the humour in this chamber...

As she stared, her thudding heartbeat reached her ears. Had she *really* threatened to thrash the information from girls who'd so recently been her merry companions? Angelica had never even threatened, never mind performed, an act of violence against any of the sisters, although Evangelina had heard that, in other priories, prioresses did commit such acts against unruly nuns. Could *she* do it too?

She left the window and paced the room, imagining taking a stick to Maria's back, or Letitia's... Their flinching bodies, their cries for mercy... Her heart began to race... For several moments, she thought she might enjoy it. The violence might assuage her fury. And it might give her what she needed, and more quickly...

She stopped her pacing. Yet, the other sisters would be appalled. They might even disavow her. No, angry as she was, violence was not the answer...

Yet she did *have* to know who'd violated Felicia. He had to be held responsible for his crime. But if the girl refused to give his name, without beating her, how could she *make* her do so?

Felicia was quaking, evidently in a panic. Terrified for all sorts of reasons: the threat of a beating, breaking her vow of chastity, bringing shame to Northwick, knowing her family might disown her, the whole business of being pregnant and giving birth... The girl clearly had no idea how to deal with her predicament.

But neither did she. A sense of panic rose in her too, and she returned to the window for a moment to try to calm herself. Perhaps, once the girls had left, she'd go to see Edgar; he might have some advice.

At length, she came back to Felicia. 'Does anyone else in the priory, other than Maria and Letitia, know of this?' Felicia shook her head. 'Good. Keep it that way. You might soon have to go away, to preserve your reputation and the priory's. In the meantime, you'll keep out of sight.'

Though how long could such a secret be maintained?

Felicia nodded miserably and dropped a brief curtsey. 'Thank you, Reverend Mother.' The girl looked almost relieved, as if revealing her plight had eased her burden.

Evangelina dismissed her, and the others, and sat down to think about exactly what to say to Edgar.

Edgar wasn't in the sacristy, so Evangelina went to his lodgings. From her chamber it was an inconvenient walk right around the priory to the courtyard behind the chapel. As she walked, she pulled her hood close about her head. It might be spring, but she was glad of her fur-lined woollen cloak, newly purchased in November.

She'd not been back here for a while, and was struck by its depressing gloom. The soaring height of the chapel overshadowed the courtyard and, on a cloudy day like this one, the corrodians' cottages must be very dark inside, as indeed must Edgar's lodgings. She'd not noticed that before.

She knocked upon his door, and heard him shuffling towards it. The door creaked open. 'Sister!' he cried. 'This is a surprise...'

'Invite me inside, brother, it's wretchedly cold out here.'

It was scarcely much warmer in the cottage.

'No fire?' she said, looking down at the hearth. Embers were glowing feebly. 'Why don't you add more wood? Surely, you must be cold?'

He wasn't wearing his cassock but was dressed like a labouring man, in woollen hose, a shirt, what looked like *two* tunics, with a surcoat on top and a hood nestling around his neck. He *was* cold.

Edgar pouted. 'Sister Dulcia has cut my ration. She said economies are being made throughout the priory.' He bent down and, picking a small log from his meagre supply, added it to the embers and poked them into life. 'Is that true?'

'We're all having to cut back...' She hesitated, wondering what to tell him. 'There must have been some mismanagement of the funds...'

'I cannot imagine Dulcia ever *mismanages* Northwick's funds,' he said. 'Surely, it is your *extravagance*, sister, that has caused the deficit?'

She spun around, on the point of reprimanding him for his impertinence. But she stopped herself. This was her brother talking, the brother to whom, months ago, she'd professed her firm intention to live a more comfortable, genteel life. He knew well enough, as much as Sister Dulcia – and she herself – where Northwick's precious funds had gone.

As the fire sputtered into life and began to emit a little warmth, she took off her cloak and sat on Edgar's only chair. She plucked at her skirt. 'Well, yes, I see now I overspent somewhat. But I was expecting more funds to come from Sir Toby...'

'Which are not after all forthcoming, I understand.' Edgar drew up a stool in front of her.

'Indeed. I do have to find a way of bringing more money into Northwick...'

'So you can resume your lavish lifestyle?' His eyes glinted in the gloom.

She glared at him. 'No, so the hole in our coffers can be refilled.'

'You've changed then, sister!' He laughed.

'Not really. But my survival as prioress obviously depends upon Northwick's preservation...'

Edgar got up and poured two cups of ale from a jug. He handed one to her and she drank it down. It was cold and weak and on the edge of sour. 'Anyway,' she said, 'Northwick's funds aren't what I came to speak to you about, but something just as critical to my survival here.'

He sat down again. 'Why are you telling me?'

'Because I don't know how to deal with it. I thought you might have some advice.'

'I'll do my best.'

She held out her cup for more ale, and swallowed it in one gulp, shuddering at the acrid taste. 'One of the young nuns is pregnant,' she said. 'Her belly's growing. Before long, everyone in the priory will know, unless I send her away soon on some pretext or other.'

Realising Edgar had bent down again, poking at the fire, she prodded his shoulder. 'Edgar, are you listening?'

'Of course I am.' His voice sounded a little strained. 'Which nun?'

'Felicia.'

The fire iron clattered onto the stone hearth. He coughed. 'It slipped out of my hand.' He selected another piece of wood and set it on the fire. 'Felicia, you say? I am not surprised...' He sat back on the stool again.

'Not *surprised?*' Evangelina tilted her head. 'Do you know her well?'

'No more nor less than all the sisters. But...' He hesitated.

'But what?'

'I am afraid Sister Felicia is a whore.' He leaned forward and fiddled with the wrappings around his ankles, then sat up again and adjusted the sit of his hood. 'I have observed her...' He looked up at her, and his eyes were wide.

'Observed her where?'

He pointed to the window. 'Out there, in the courtyard. Or, rather, emerging from one of the empty storerooms... With a man...'

'A man?' gasped Evangelina. 'What were they doing in a storeroom?'

He snorted. 'I suppose the answer to that question is now clear.'

'Ha! Indeed. But who was the man? Did you know him?'

Edgar hesitated again, but at length said, 'It was Rafe Byllynges. That yellow hair of his was shining in the moonlight.'

'The bailiff? Ha! I might have known it.' So, not the amiable young man everyone thought him, but a rogue who preyed upon young girls. 'And you're sure it was Felicia?'

'The moonlight...' he mumbled, as he put his cup to his mouth.

'Why didn't you tell me this before?' she said grimly.

'I did not wish to get her into trouble. I hoped it was just the once and she would seek forgiveness for her sin.' He shrugged. 'But perhaps I *should* have mentioned it...'

Evangelina tutted. 'If you'd done so, she might not be in this predicament. When was it you saw them?'

He seemed to consider for a while, then said, 'October?'

'When I was away?'

'I suppose so, yes...' He took another gulp of his foul ale.

'So, the bailiff...' She sat back. 'Felicia's refused to name him, so, thank you, brother, for the information.'

'A pity,' he murmured. 'Don't you think? Such a comely young woman...'

'Who's brought disgrace to herself, her family and Northwick. Should I send her away?'

'Where to?'

'I've no idea.'

'Then why not keep her here, but out of sight? You can watch her, and ensure she does no further damage to the priory.'

'But I don't want it to become common knowledge amongst the sisters.'

He scoffed. 'The way gossip spreads in Northwick, I would be astonished if it is not already talked about in the dorter and the cloister.'

'But, a pregnancy in the priory!' she cried. 'I'll be blamed, Edgar...'

'But you can't be blamed for the girl's depravity. Nor for the bailiff's. You cannot be held responsible for *everybody's* actions.'

Was he right about that? She doubted it. She was certain she *would* be held responsible. This was yet another rod for the blessed Sister Rosa to beat her with. Her head was spinning, and she craved the solitude of her chamber. But one more question. 'What do I do when the child is born?'

He wagged his head. 'Give it to a couple in the village. I daresay there are many who would welcome it.'

She agreed. And maybe he was right. Knowledge of Felicia's disgrace would soon, if not already, be rife amongst the sisters. There was nothing she could do now to gainsay it. What she *had* to do was to deal with the situation. To ensure no condemnation attached to her.

And punish the man who'd brought this ignominy upon them.

26

How disappointed Rosa had been by the outcome of the visitation. She and the other sisters had been confident their evidence was so strong that Evangelina could not possibly escape judgement for her intolerable behaviour.

Unjustifiably confident, as it turned out.

Were the commissioners as open-minded as they might have been? Or had Evangelina *ensured* they would acquit her by compurgation? It would not surprise her to discover that Evangelina had somehow meddled...

It *had* surprised her when Evangelina raised grievances against *her*, which, in hindsight, was naïve. She felt a lingering unease that the same process of compurgation had also enabled her to be acquitted of fomenting rebellion, albeit that *was* essentially what she was now doing... Her acquittal had come by means of a legal technicality, rather than because she was truly innocent... Although the penances she had been given for breaking her obedience vows were going some

290

way towards assuaging her unease, she was nonetheless still struggling to reconcile "rebellion" with her natural desire for harmony.

But, last week, she had told Beatrice and Dulcia she was ready for rebellion, and she was. She had finally made peace with her conscience. Her mutiny would, after all, be temporary. She would do whatever she had to do, regardless of the short-term consequences, and would repent thereafter, whatever that entailed, even if it meant spending the rest of her life upon her knees.

Since her declaration, and Beatrice's and Dulcia's eager – albeit, in Dulcia's case, also somewhat anxious – commitment to join her, Rosa had told both Amata and Juliana they too could join the conspiracy – for that *was* what it was – to oust Evangelina and return Northwick to what it had been under Angelica's rule.

Juliana was enthusiastic, although she too was nervous to be doing anything that went so much against her sacred vows. 'But I must be brave,' she said. 'Like you, Sister Rosa.' Her smile was timid.

Amata seemed a little hazy about the significance and gravity of the plan. Should she even be involved, given the recent gentle decline in her ability to grasp ideas and keep hold of memories? Yet Amata was now the longest serving member of the Northwick community, and it was unthinkable to exclude her from decisions that would mean so much to her.

Beatrice agreed that Amata had to play her part. 'It might be minimal, but she might equally have much to offer. It's hard to know what lurks beneath the fog that swirls in and out.' She grinned sadly. 'But if she falters in her understanding, we can help her. Don't you think?'

Rosa thanked Beatrice for saying what she had hoped she would. 'There are five of us, then,' she said. 'Five rebels.' She exhaled. 'Oh, Beatrice, how appalling that it should come to this.'

'Appalling, but necessary. I see no other way for us to rescue our beloved Northwick.'

Thus began the rebels' meetings in earnest, in Dulcia's chamber, where they could be reasonably confident they would not be overheard. For it was sited to one side of the cloister, out of the way of the nuns' regular passage between the dorter, the chapel and the frater.

Even so, Rosa wondered if Evangelina *knew* of their meetings. She mentioned it to Beatrice. 'Are you as baffled as I am that Evangelina is making no attempt to stop us? She must have known we were meeting before the visitation; else she would not have raised the rebellion complaint against me.' Beatrice agreed. 'I am sure Letitia is still spying,' continued Rosa, 'and will have reported back that we meet in the treasury. So why is the prioress not intervening?'

Beatrice could not offer an explanation.

It was in October that Evangelina had last threatened Rosa. That accusation, about John, had been ridiculous, and the prioress must have realised it, for she had not mentioned it again. Before that was the acolytes' gossip during the summer, and, earlier still, the threat Evangelina made to stop her standing in the election. On the first two occasions, Rosa had been cowed into submission. But she was no longer afraid of threats or accusations.

Indeed, when Evangelina made her preposterous claim about John, Rosa was ready to stand fast against it. For Agnes's counsel that *Northwick's* reputation was more important than her own had struck home. In that moment, Rosa had understood that saving Northwick from Evangelina was her obligation and her duty. If achieving it meant breaking her solemn vows, so be it.

If Evangelina chose to threaten her yet again, she would no longer be intimidated. Even if she chose to denounce her in public, instead of merely threatening her in private, she would still stand firm...

Yet, why wait for that to happen? Perhaps her best plan was to *pre-empt* any such revelation by telling her friends the truth?

Rosa asked not only Dulcia and Beatrice to meet her in Dulcia's chamber, but Juliana and Amata too. They all squeezed into the small space, for the treasury was mostly filled with chests and coffers. Juliana perched on the edge of Dulcia's desk, as there were insufficient stools for everyone.

Despite her new-found boldness, Rosa was still a little queasy at what she was about to say. She first asked them all to say a prayer with her, for humility and forgiveness for what she was about to reveal.

'Goodness, Rosa,' said Beatrice, 'whatever can it be?'

She bowed her head. 'I have kept this secret far too long. Now we are actively collaborating to overthrow Evangelina'—she arched her eyebrows—'I have decided I must be honest with you all, about myself, and about why Evangelina holds such enmity towards me. I am sorry if you find it shocking – or worse – but I *have* to tell you. I hope you will not think too badly of me, for my past, and for my long-held duplicity.'

'*Duplicity*!' said Dulcia, her eyes wide. '*You*, Rosa?'

'Indeed. Let me explain.'

The others remained silent and attentive as she told them exactly why she had chosen to come to Northwick as a girl. How she believed she had committed the most heinous sin in her unnatural affection for her brother, and in her careless disregard of her closest friend.

'When I came, I expected to spend my whole life in Northwick atoning for my sins. But, with Mother Angelica's love and help, I found peace much sooner than I imagined.'

She told them then about Agnes and their conversation in October, and how it changed her attitude towards Evangelina, and to herself.

When she had finished, Beatrice leaned forward and took her hand. 'None of us are without sin,' she said, 'and you *were* very young.'

'Seventeen.'

'Young women often harbour wild imaginings or inappropriate passions,' Beatrice continued. 'But it seems to me, from what you've told us, your long-held guilt wasn't fully justified. Your friend – Agnes – told you that you *didn't*, as you'd thought, bear all the blame for what happened. She bore it too. And you now know too your brother's death wasn't, after all, a punishment from God, but simply a man-made act of vengeance.'

Rosa took a deep breath, glad of Beatrice's understanding.

'All these years,' continued Beatrice, 'you've borne your shame and guilt, I won't say *pointlessly*, but certainly undeservedly. How thankful I am you went to Meonbridge and spoke to Agnes. She's evidently a lady of great wisdom!'

Rosa laughed lightly. 'You might not have thought that of her when she and I were young, but now, yes, Agnes is indeed both wise and compassionate.'

'Moreover,' added Beatrice, 'I imagine *all* Northwick's sisters – including most of those who are currently in Evangelina's camp – know you for who you are *now*. Cheerful, kind, pious. The woman'—she grinned—'they *will* choose to be their prioress, when the opportunity arises.'

'Hear, hear,' said Amata, and Dulcia and Juliana warmly agreed.

It was only the next day that Juliana knocked lightly upon the sacristy door, and peeked in.

'Sister Rosa?' she said. 'May I tell you something?' Her eyes were wide and bright.

Rosa gestured to her to sit down. 'What is it?'

'It is shocking,' said Juliana, 'but also a little exciting, if only because I believe it might help our cause against the prioress.'

Rosa put down her quill. 'You have my attention.'

Unlikely as it was that anyone was prying outside the sacristy, Juliana lowered her voice to a whisper. 'Sister Felicia is with child.'

Astonished, Rosa leaned forward. 'With child?' She too kept her voice low.

Juliana nodded. 'I have just learned she has been sick for weeks, you know, mostly in the mornings. And, now, I understand her belly is expanding, though I have not seen her myself.'

'Now I think of it, I too have not seen much of Felicia for a while.'

'She kept herself out of sight whilst she was nauseous. At the time, Maria made frequent excuses for her absence, but none of us thought much about it because they and Letitia have spent so much time with the prioress rather than in our general company.'

'Yet, I believe Evangelina has mostly dined alone ever since the visitation...' Rosa paused. 'No, much longer than that, ever since she came back from her expedition... I think it is since *then* that Evangelina has been alone in her chamber much more often than she used to.'

'Yes, you are right. Anyway, Felicia is still keeping to herself, I suppose because her predicament is becoming more obvious...'

'I wonder if Evangelina knows?'

'I do not know, but it is from Letitia I have learned all of this...'

'Letitia?'

She bit her lip. 'She has been so loyal to the Reverend Mother, yet I think her loyalty is flagging. Though she has not said as much. But she appears almost *gleeful* at the news of Felicia's predicament, which does seem most unkind, when Felicia must be so frightened...'

'Indeed, she must. As must also Evangelina. For having a pregnant nun in your priory reflects very badly on a prioress. It indicates she has no control or authority over her convent. Do you know how many months into her pregnancy Felicia is?'

'Five or six, I think.'

Rosa considered a moment. 'Which means the "event" happened when Evangelina was away. In hindsight, then, perhaps it *was* a bad idea for her to leave the priory?'

'Yet Sister Clarice was left in charge,' said Juliana.

'But evidently Felicia, and whomever she had her liaison with, escaped Clarice's attention.'

'I wonder who it was? The man, I mean?'

'Does Letitia not know?'

'She has not said so.'

When the conspirators met again a few days later, Beatrice had more to say about Felicia's condition.

'It seems to me,' she said, 'that every sister in Northwick now knows about Felicia, albeit few have actually seen her. She appears to be keeping herself out of sight, though she might as well not bother, with her secret already out.'

'Perhaps Evangelina has insisted upon it?' said Rosa.

'Daresay she has,' said Beatrice, 'but there's no purpose in it.'

They all agreed Evangelina was probably as terrified as Felicia about how the pregnancy and, most particularly, the birth of the child, would affect their futures, both at Northwick and as nuns.

Juliana was thoughtful. 'I wonder if Felicia might wish to leave the priory – indeed, the religious life – so she can set up home with her beau, whoever he is, and their baby?'

Rosa shook her head. 'I am afraid that cannot happen. If Felicia leaves the priory, she will be an apostate, having renounced her vows, and therefore be under threat of excommunication.' Juliana gasped. 'If she weds the father of her child, their union will be unrecognised or even condemned by the Church. Hardly a prescription for a happy married life.'

'That seems so cruel,' cried Juliana, her eyes wide with shock.

'It is. But Felicia is a professed nun and *cannot* reverse her vows. It is more likely that, when the child is born, it will be given away, and Felicia will have to undertake a string of penances for her immorality, which might be enforced solitude, fasting, or even exclusions from our communal life. But she would have to remain a nun, either here in Northwick or in another house.'

'What of the man?' asked Dulcia.

'If he is ever discovered,' said Rosa, 'I imagine he would be charged for getting Felicia with child. He might be able to absolve himself with compurgators, but if not, he too would be severely punished.'

'Yet will he ever *be* discovered?' said Juliana. 'I understand Felicia has refused to name him.'

Amata, who these days rarely voiced her opinions, let out a sudden burst of giggles. 'Or perhaps she doesn't even know who he is?' Everyone else gasped. But her eyes were bright with glee.

Beatrice tutted. 'Amata, that's very mischievous! Whatever do you mean?'

Amata tittered. 'She's such a frivolous young madam, too fond of herself, and not at all suited to the religious life. Even less suited than our prioress!' The others joined in the jest.

'You're not wrong there,' said Beatrice. 'But am I to deduce that you've been spying on her?'

'Oh, no, *I* haven't been spying,' said Amata. 'But I *have* been to visit Katerina and Mildryth.' Her brow wrinkled. 'I found out Sister Mariota hasn't visited them for months... All through the winter! Apparently, she just sends a servant occasionally to make sure they've sufficient food and fuel. But not to visit them herself, when *she's* the infirmaress, well, it's shocking...'

'How remiss of Mariota,' Beatrice said. 'It's not as if the infirmary itself is busy.' The others murmured agreement. 'However, did you learn something of interest from your visit to the ancients?'

Amata giggled once more. 'They're not quite as "ancient" as you might imagine. I feared they might quickly fade away, shut away like that from the sisters and the priory. But they seem content enough. And, when they can, they keep an eye on any comings and goings in the courtyard.'

'Albeit with a somewhat cloudy eye,' said Beatrice, grinning. 'Though I can't think much goes on out there for them to watch.'

'No, indeed,' Amata said. 'Recently there's been very little. But, some months ago – Katerina couldn't recall *exactly* when – she did see something that looked suspicious, on *several* occasions.' Her eyes were merry once again.

'Well, don't keep us in suspense,' cried Beatrice.

Amata leaned back and laughed heartily, then dabbed at her eyes with the edge of her wimple. 'I shouldn't laugh, for it's really not a matter for merriment. Yet it did give Katerina a little cheer when she told me what she saw...'

Beatrice tutted. 'So, are you going to tell *us*?'

Amata leaned forward. 'Sister Felicia, and a man... Late in the evening... Coming out of one of the empty storerooms.'

'How did Katerina know it was Felicia, if it was dark?' said Juliana.

'There was moonlight! Even with her rheumy eyes, Katerina said she was quite certain it was Felicia.'

'And did she also know the man?'

Amata's cheeks were flushed as, with a flourish of her hands, she declared, 'It was the bailiff! Master Byllynges.'

Everyone gasped again.

'Does Katerina *know* the bailiff?' asked Rosa, frowning.

Amata wagged her head. 'I asked her what he looked like, and the man she described, with his height and his yellow hair, was surely Master Byllynges.'

'There might be other men in Northwick with such hair and stature,' said Rosa.

'Yet Katerina did seem sure.' Amata splayed her wrinkled hands upon her lap. 'And she saw Felicia again on more than one occasion, with the bailiff and, apparently, with some other man...'

'Then why did she not report it?'

'I asked her that, and she said she remembered what it felt like to be young...'

'But if she didn't want to betray Felicia,' said Beatrice, 'why tell you now?'

'The serving girl told her about Felicia's condition, and Katerina thought she'd better after all tell someone what she'd seen...'

Dulcia sighed. 'It seems, then, Rafe Byllynges might be the culprit, or one of them at least. What a pity if it *is* him... Such a personable young man...'

'Mmm,' said Beatrice. 'Or *was*.'

'Was?'

'Indeed. Master Byllynges recently left Northwick for what I'd assumed was a few days, to visit a relative or some such. But what Amata's just told us makes me wonder if maybe he's gone for good, abandoning not only Northwick but the young nun he has abused and brought to shame.'

How astonished they all were at both Amata's news and Beatrice's. In truth, Rosa did feel somewhat sorry for poor Felicia. She might be a frivolous girl, even an immoral one. She might have brought her predicament upon herself. But how cruel of Rafe Byllynges to abandon her. Yet, if he were caught, he would certainly face punishment and lose his job at Northwick, so perhaps he had decided the better plan *was* to disappear and let matters take their course without him.

Although, of course, he might not *be* the culprit, if Katerina really did see Felicia with different men...

Despite the shock of it, Rosa was almost heartened by prospect of the baby, not because she wished Felicia to suffer, but because it was another grievance to levy against Evangelina. A very serious one, as Juliana had implied.

'We can't keep quiet about this,' said Beatrice. 'We were already thinking we had to find a way of raising our complaints again. Now this has happened, it's even more imperative we don't wait for the next visitation before we act. Our other grievances are serious enough, but this...' She rolled her eyes.

They all considered the situation for a moment, trying to think how best to arraign Evangelina quickly.

At length, Rosa had an idea. 'It has just occurred to me that Winchester has a new bishop – or soon will have. I wonder if we might approach him directly with our grievances? In his new position, might he not be especially eager to ensure all the priories he is responsible for are well managed?'

Dulcia shook her head. 'But he'll be terribly busy, Rosa, especially at the beginning of his reign. He won't have the time—'

But Amata almost squealed. 'Oh, but he might *make* time for us! Why didn't I think of it before?'

'Think of what?' said Beatrice.

Amata's cheeks were flushed with excitement. 'You do recall, Bea, don't you, that my family is from Wickham?' Beatrice nodded. 'But do you know the new bishop, William Longe, also comes from there?' None of them did. 'Not only that, but I'm sure you'll be surprised to hear that he and I have familial ties.' She beamed.

Rosa gasped. 'Do you think you might be able to obtain a personal audience with him?'

Beatrice looked incredulous, but Amata nodded eagerly.

'Oh, I'm sure I can. It might not be soon, as he's not yet properly in post. But I could ask my cousin, Francis, who has influence in Winchester, to write directly to the bishop...' She beamed again. 'Shall I do that?'

JUNE 1367

It was weeks before Amata received a reply from Bishop William. Her cousin, a man of some importance amongst the city elders, had the ear of many with influence and power, in business, government and the Church. Despite the bishop not yet being officially in post – his formal appointment was expected in July – he was nonetheless working in his office, and, Francis reported, was apparently more than willing to discuss any serious issues within his new diocese.

'William's well known in Winchester,' said Amata. 'He was at school there and, early on, was favoured by the constable of the Castle, who employed him as his secretary. In the years since then, of course, William's risen far and fast. He's been working with the *king* for years...'

Amata was clearly very proud that a man with, albeit loose, ties to her own family had ascended to such a venerable position. 'He's a good man, too,' she said. 'Very capable and wise, but also compassionate. Anyway, Cousin Francis says he's agreed to give us an audience.' Her face was beaming yet again.

Rosa gasped. 'You mean he *will* meet us face-to-face?'

'Francis suggested I go, being family, and one or two of you come with me.'

The sisters debated briefly who should go, and it was soon agreed it should be Rosa.

'Should you not come too, Dulcia?' she said, but Dulcia demurred.

'No, no. Much as I should like to meet the bishop, I know you'll put across our case clearly and succinctly. The bishop won't have much time to talk, so I doubt he'll be interested in poring over accounts. No, you go with Amata, Rosa, and tell him everything he needs to know.'

'But how will we get leave to go to Winchester?' Amata said, her excitement suddenly deflating. 'Evangelina will surely try to stop us going.'

Rosa nodded. 'We must conjure up some pretext for the two of us to go away. Some duplicity will be required, I am afraid. A visit to your family perhaps, Amata? I shall be accompanying you as your chaperone.'

'But Winchester is a lot further beyond Wickham,' said Amata.

'Indeed. But Evangelina does not have to know we are travelling further. We can say we plan to reside in Wickham for several days.'

Amata's forehead creased, and her so recently bright eyes were clouding once again. 'Yet what reason do I have for visiting my home?'

Beatrice cleared her throat. 'You used to visit Wickham often, Amata, when Angelica was prioress. To see one or other of your many relatives. It's only the past year you've not done so. That older brother of yours might be ailing, and need to see you?'

'But he isn't ailing, Bea,' said Amata. 'Or not as far as I know.'

'Yes, yes, but that doesn't matter.' Beatrice rolled her eyes. 'It's merely the *reason* you give to Evangelina for your journey.'

'Yes, yes, I understand,' Amata murmured slowly.

Surprisingly, Evangelina did not question Amata's reason for requesting leave. She seemed greatly distracted – by Felicia's pregnancy, perhaps? She did not even protest at Rosa's insistence on accompanying Amata on her journey.

Horses were procured and Rosa again asked Jack Bowmaster to escort them as far as Wickham. They stayed at Amata's brother's house for one night, letting him in on the subterfuge, to the old man's considerable delight. Then one of his most trusted servants escorted them on to Winchester.

Rosa almost enjoyed the journey, with the warm summer weather, and dry roads making the going relatively easy. She thought Amata enjoyed it less, but she was much older and even less adept at horse-riding than she was herself.

Nonetheless, they arrived in Winchester in good time and Amata's cousin had arranged to meet them, and provided accommodation for a few nights in his fine mansion.

'So, what is this all about, Cousin Amata?' said Francis, when he was alone with her and Rosa in the spacious chamber he used as his office. 'Are you truthfully trying to oust your prioress?'

'Sadly, yes. She's quite unsuited to being a nun, let alone *in charge* of the priory.'

'So why is she prioress?' he asked.

Amata looked slightly confounded by the question.

'May I tell you?' Rosa said.

He smiled. 'By all means.'

'After our beloved Mother Angelica died, I am sorry to say that Evangelina, believing the position to be hers by right, used guile to ensure she was elected. We do not know exactly what she did, but we do know she should not have won.'

He smiled again. 'Amata has told me it was you, Sister Rosa, who should have been elected. And that, if and when there is another election, you will be voted in.'

She flushed. 'That may be true but that is not why I, or Amata, or any of our sisters, are seeking to unseat Mother Evangelina. It is because she is harming – *has* harmed – Northwick, and we cannot allow it to continue.'

'I understand your finances are now in peril, after years of sound economy under Mother Angelica. And that the priory has become a place of bawdry?' A blend of shock and mirth was in his eyes.

'Perhaps not exactly "bawdry",' said Rosa, albeit, with the most recent news, it was not far off the mark. 'But certainly, a place that is not as peaceful and pious as it once was. For most of the sisters it is that, rather than the lack of money, that is the most painful outcome of Evangelina's rule.'

'Yet the priory cannot survive if you have no money.' He placed his hands together in a steeple, and tapped his fingers.

'That is true, of course, but it is the lack of piety that grieves us most deeply.'

Francis looked up and smiled. 'My acquaintance with William Longe leads me to believe that he will be most distressed to hear your story, and will wish to bring swift succour to your plight.'

The bishop was most amiable as he welcomed them into his office. He acknowledged Amata as a distant cousin, even though he could not have known her well, given she was more than twenty years his senior.

He gestured to them both to sit in cushioned chairs.

'Francis has outlined to me the plight in which you and your sisters find yourselves,' he said. 'It sounds a rather shocking tale. Would you like to tell me more?'

Amata seemed a little overawed, but accepted a small cup of wine. 'I think it best if Rosa tells you,' she said, 'for she has it all much clearer in her mind.'

'Of course.' He sat back down in his grand chair. 'Do go ahead, Sister Rosa. You have my complete attention.'

Although she had brought with her a few jottings on her battered wooden tablet, to remind her of what she had to say, Rosa had been practising her explanation to the bishop, to ensure she made her points as clearly and succinctly as Dulcia said she would.

She told him everything: about her suspicions that Evangelina had somehow meddled with the election; her profligacy with priory funds, providing for herself a life of luxury and amusement quite inappropriate to a Benedictine nun; her refusal to attend the holy offices and encouragement of other sisters to do the same; her negligence in respect of holding daily chapter meetings; and finally, her failure to prevent the pregnancy of one of the younger sisters.

Bishop William listened in steady silence, not interrupting or asking questions.

When she had finished, Rosa felt exhausted. She bowed her head. 'I apologise for bringing such a litany of failure before you, Your Grace.'

'It is scarcely your fault, my dear,' he said. 'But what I do not understand is why all these failings were not addressed during your visitation. You have been examined quite recently, have you not?'

Rosa looked up. 'Three months ago. Several sisters brought our many grievances before the commissioners, and the prioress admitted to one or two of them. But, most – the most serious – she refuted. The commissioners ordered her to bring compurgators, which she did, and they had to absolve her.'

'Had to?' he said, frowning. 'To my mind, such grievances as those should warrant further investigation.'

Rosa let out a long breath. 'We thought so too, and were most disappointed with the outcome. Which is why, since the visitation, we have been trying to come up with a plan for having our concerns looked at again.'

'And here you are.' The bishop smiled broadly at them both, then sighed. 'I am glad you came. Not because I *want* to discover mismanagement amongst my many monasteries and priories, but because I am anxious that such failure is corrected, if necessary, by installing a new head.'

All of a sudden, Rosa felt a little nauseous. This was going well. The bishop was unquestionably as compassionate as Amata had said he was. She thought it likely he *would* help them to oust Evangelina and return Northwick to what it once had been.

Yet she could not ignore the terrible gnawing in her heart. She *had* to mention to the bishop the grievances Evangelina had levied against *her*. Moreover, she had to confess to breaking her vows and plotting with her sisters to bring the prioress down. If she was not willing to admit to her own shortcomings, she was not being honest with him, or with herself.

She swallowed. 'Your Grace,' she said quietly, 'I have a little more to say. I have to tell you about my own part in what has happened in Northwick these past many months.'

This time she did tell him everything: first, about Evangelina's threats to reveal the unhappy past that drove her to enter Northwick. Then, about her unbearable decision to break her obedience vows; and, finally, her falsehood at denying to the prioress's face that she was conspiring to overthrow her.

She lowered her head, and grasped her crucifix. 'These sins I do acknowledge,' she whispered, 'in the fervent hope that I will, in time, gain pardon from them by constant prayer and penance.' She sighed deeply. 'It took months before I could even contemplate committing such sins. How earnestly I prayed for guidance! Yet, at length, I found that I was willing, even eager, to do so, even at the risk of forfeiting God's grace, if I could save Northwick from its dreadful fate.'

The bishop stood up from his chair, came around his desk and, laying his hand upon Rosa's head, murmured a short prayer. 'None of us is without sin, Sister Rosa. I am sure yours will be forgiven in due course.' He sat down again. 'But tell me, who is Northwick's priest? And also, who is the bishop's representative at Northwick? Do you know him?'

Amata nodded at that. 'A man visits us from time to time, helps arrange the visitations and indeed elections – though, before this last one, there'd not been an election for forty years. His name is Nicholas Foxe. He's been coming for... Oh, I don't know, four years or so?'

The bishop frowned. 'Nicholas Foxe...' he repeated, and then again. 'I am sure I know that name.' He stood up and walked about his chamber, his lips pursed in contemplation. At length he cried 'Aha!' and came back to his chair.

'I have dredged the rogue up from the depths of my memory.' He grimaced. 'And rogue indeed he is. A man given to corrupt dealings of many divers sorts.'

Amata let out a cry, but Rosa took a deep breath. So, she had been right not to trust Master Foxe, even though she had had no notion why. 'You have met him, Your Grace?'

'Not met, no, but I know of his reputation. A reputation that is not only his but is attached to many members of his family. The Godeffroys—'

Rosa did then cry out. 'Master Foxe is a *Godeffroy*? Do you know, Your Grace, that Northwick's principal benefactor is the Godeffroy family? That our prioresses have, for decades, always been Godeffroys?'

His eyes widened. 'Prioress Evangelina is a Godeffroy?'

Rosa inclined her head. 'As was Mother Angelica.'

He started in surprise at that, then smiled. 'Ah, yes, Angelica. I do remember her. Why or how, I am not quite sure...' He thought again for a while, but at length shook his head. 'No, I cannot think when or why I would have met her. But I do recall her as the most delightful, charitable and devout of women, ideally suited to the position of prioress.'

'Indeed, she was,' said Rosa. 'Amata and I deeply mourn her passing, as do most of Northwick's sisters, albeit she was very old.'

'Yet how surprising to learn *she* also was a Godeffroy,' he said, clearly bemused. 'I had not realised that. She could not have been more *unlike* the rest of her unscrupulous family... Although perhaps it is unfair of me to besmirch them all...'

'Indeed,' said Rosa. 'But if Master Foxe is one of the *unscrupulous* Godeffroys—'

The bishop slapped his hand against the arm of his chair. 'I do not want him as my representative! God only knows how he was appointed, and what mischief he might have got up to in the cause of furthering the Godeffroys' interests. For that is what they do, that clan...' His eyes were fierce with indignation. 'No, no, Master Foxe must *go*, and I shall ensure it.'

Rosa did now wonder whether Master Foxe had had some sort of hand in Evangelina's election, and indeed the visitation. She wanted to seek the bishop's view, but he was already asking another question.

'And what of your priest? Perhaps I know him too?'

'We know him as Father Edgar,' Rosa said. 'He seems pleasant enough, although we only see him at Mass and for confession...'

'What age of man is he?'

'Oh, my age or thereabouts, I should imagine.'

The bishop frowned. 'And how long has he been at Northwick?

'Ten years or more, as I recall.'

'That is unusually young for a priory's priest-in-charge,' the bishop said. 'I wonder how *he* was appointed?'

'I do not recall, Your Grace,' said Rosa, and turned to Amata. But her eyes had glazed again, as if she was finding the conversation overwhelming. 'Father Anselm was a dear man, whom all the sisters loved. But he died from great old age, and Father Edgar came in his stead.'

'And do all the sisters love *him*?' The bishop arched an eyebrow.

'I cannot speak for the others,' Rosa said. 'As I say, he seems pleasant enough, but... Somehow, Your Grace, I have never trusted him, although I cannot say exactly why...'

'Perhaps because he too is a Godeffroy?' The bishop's eyes were bright. 'It seems to me, beloved Sisters, I must investigate the goings-on at Northwick, not only your prioress and the grievances you have brought against her, but also the appointments of your priest and my so-called representative.'

He rose from his chair and came around his desk again, holding out a hand to Amata to help her stand. As Amata struggled a little to her feet, Rosa sprang to hers, feeling much more hopeful than she had when they arrived.

'Thank you so much, Your Grace,' she said, 'for giving us your valuable time.'

He graciously bowed his head and reached out a hand to each of them. Rosa grasped one and Amata took the other. 'Be assured,' he said, 'that I shall act.' Then he gave their hands a shake. 'Peace be with you both, and all your sisters.'

27

NORTHWICK PRIORY
JULY 1367

Evangelina found herself face-to-face with Sister Rosa the day after Rosa returned with Amata from their trip to Wickham, allegedly to visit one of Amata's ancient brothers. Evangelina hadn't asked for Rosa to come, but was *told* that she required an audience.

When Letitia came to tell her Rosa was on her way, Evangelina thought to refuse her entry. But Rosa simply stepped into the chamber and closed the door behind her, having gestured to Letitia to go.

'You can't just walk in here, demanding to see me,' cried Evangelina, her voice rising. 'You must wait to be invit—'

Rosa raised her hand. 'Normally I would agree, Evangelina. But your position here is no longer secure, and your authority to say who can and cannot enter this, once venerated, chamber, will, I am certain, soon be denied you.'

Evangelina spun around, her heart thumping with alarm. 'What do you mean?'

'That is what I have come to tell you. You might wish to sit down.'

Evangelina thought she probably *didn't* want to sit, if Rosa was to remain standing. She straightened her back. 'Say what you have to.'

But, as Rosa related where she and Amata had actually been these past few days, Evangelina did, at length, sink into her chair.

'We mentioned to the new bishop,' said Rosa, 'all the grievances we had raised at the visitation. In his opinion, many of them should have been investigated, not simply discharged through compurgation. We told him about the baby too...'

Evangelina opened her mouth to speak, but couldn't think what to say... She could protest that the commissioners were acting *for* the bishop, yet, if the new bishop was now disputing their findings and decisions...

Anyway, Rosa held up her hand again. 'Allow me to continue.'

She then told her what the bishop had said about the Godeffroy family: that he believed Nicholas Foxe to be a rogue, and was alarmed to learn that Edgar had been installed as priest-in-charge at so young an age. 'He also told us what Amata and I had not known,' she said, 'that Master Foxe is a Godeffroy, and he suspected that Father Edgar is one too. A fact and a possibility the bishop clearly considered a matter for concern—'

'Yet your precious Angelica was a Godeffroy,' she cried. 'Was *that* a matter for concern?'

'Of course not, for the bishop remembered Angelica for the noble lady that she was. However,' she continued, 'he is going to investigate both Edgar's and Nicholas's appointments, alongside re-examining our grievances against you. It may not happen soon, but you can expect the bishop to take action. It may mean, Evangelina, you are deposed.'

Evangelina leapt to her feet. 'Or it may not! If, after all, he discovers your complaints against me were unjustified, and Edgar's and Nicholas's appointments were properly obtained...'

'Do you really believe any of that is true?' Rosa's expression was incredulous, even scornful, and, obviously, she was right.

Yet Evangelina was damned if she was going to give up without a fight. It'd be months before the bishop declared the outcome of any of his investigations, so she had time to think of a way out of this mess. In the meantime, she was ready to retaliate.

She spun around and glared at Rosa. 'Of course I do! What I also "believe" is that you, and Sister Amata, are treacherous liars.' She realised she was shouting, but didn't care. 'You *lied* about the nature of your journey. You *invented* the wicked falsehood of Amata's brother being near to death. You knew all along you weren't going to Wickham but to Winchester...' She batted the air with her hands.

But Rosa shrugged. 'Well, evidently, if we had told you of our real plans, you would have stopped us going. We could not allow that. We *had* to put our case directly to the bishop.' She frowned. 'I do not *enjoy* telling such untruths, Evangelina. It grieves me bitterly that I should have to. But, by your heinous actions against Northwick, you have given me no choice.'

'No choice, ha! Of course you have a choice. The choice to uphold your vows—'

'But what of your vows, Evangelina? Do you embrace *any* of the Benedictine rules? Or are you content to disregard them all—'

'Damn you, Rosa, damn you!' Evangelina cried, unable to rein in her growing panic. 'Get out of here.' She flailed her arms in a frantic gesture. 'Get out!'

Rosa inclined her head. 'Gladly,' she said, insufferably calm, then slipped out of the room.

Evangelina sank back into her chair. Her heart was thumping so fiercely she thought it might burst asunder. Her head too was throbbing.

Yet was it any surprise? It was all over. Nicholas's machinations in the election and the visitation would be discovered and he'd be dismissed.

Edgar too, who'd been appointed through Nicholas's manoeuvrings, and would never have been given the post at the age of twenty-five if he *hadn't* been a Godeffroy, would be discharged too, sent to another post, perhaps the other side of the country.

She swallowed. How she'd miss him, her only genuine ally. And yet, if Rosa's grievances were upheld, she too would be deposed, as Rosa said. She might be forced to go to another priory, and everyone would know she'd been sent there in disgrace.

If that was her future, she'd not simply submit without at least trying to bring Rosa down.

For the matter of Rosa's past still remained. Evangelina gripped the arms of her chair. She *had* to expose her. She conjured in her mind revealing to the sisters Rosa's wicked past, declaring how she was enticing others to conspire and scheme to overthrow her, their prioress, flagrantly flouting her vow of obedience. They'd realise then that Rosa was a sinner and a liar, and not after all worthy of their deference and admiration.

It was only one week later that a man Evangelina didn't know requested an audience with her. Although, of course, she soon did know who he was: the new bishop's man, come to displace Cousin Nicholas.

Letitia showed him into the chamber, and she gestured to the girl to stay. Nonetheless, she went forward with hand outstretched to greet the man, a personable looking fellow, with warm eyes and a well-trimmed beard. He bowed his head, and took her hand lightly in his.

'Madam Prioress,' he said. 'I am here at Bishop Longe's request, with a warrant for Master Foxe's dismissal. I regret his services to Northwick are no longer required. I shall be undertaking them in his stead.'

'Master Foxe isn't here,' she said. 'He only comes to Northwick when he has duties to perform.'

'Yet I must speak to him, to inform him of the situation.'

She pursed her lips. 'I'm afraid I cannot help you.'

'Though I suppose you can tell me where he lives?'

After the new bishop's man had left, Evangelina lay down on the great bed, resting her throbbing head against the pillows piled up behind her. She pulled the curtains forward to block out some of the summer sunshine streaming through the window.

How confident, not to say presumptuous, Rosa had been when she came to tell her about the bishop's intention to investigate her grievances. She was *expecting* him to find in her favour, and for

Evangelina to be deposed. And, clearly, her expectations were beginning to be fulfilled.

The bishop had already acted against Nicholas. He'd now be without a job, for she'd told the new man where her cousin lived. Not that she cared what happened to him.

But she might still be able to save herself.

It would surely take a while for the bishop to deliver his verdict on his investigations, and, before that happened, she was determined to reveal to all of Northwick's sisters Rosa's sinful past and deceitful present. Surely, when they heard what she had to say, they'd realise Rosa wasn't the saint they thought she was?

When the sisters filed into the chapter house for the Friday meeting, Evangelina was already sitting in her grand chair. A few of the sisters were still murmuring to each other as they sat down, and, at length, Evangelina called for silence. She straightened her back and lifted her head high.

'Well, sisters, does any of you have anything to raise today? If so, speak now.'

She scanned the chamber, an eyebrow lifted in enquiry. But none of the sisters raised her hand or stood up to speak.

'None?' she said. 'Excellent. The priory must be functioning well.' She smiled thinly. 'And yet...' She paused. 'And yet, despite that, there *is* something amiss at Northwick. For one amongst you has long been hiding herself beneath a cloak of untruth and deceit. And she has been doing so for *years*...' She paused again, then cast her gaze around the chamber.

'How extraordinary is that?' she said at last, then lifted her chin sharply. 'And how *contemptible*!'

The silence in the chapter house was palpable. Evangelina knew it would be. After all, none of the sisters knew who she was talking about, although surely Gracia and the three "disciples" would grasp soon enough who it was she meant.

'In truth, I've known about this deceiver for a long while, but hoped her sense of what is right and honourable would persuade her to confess to her duplicity. But she hasn't, and I've seen no sign that she intends to do so. Therefore, I believe it's my duty as your prioress to tell you what I've learned, so *you* are no longer deceived by this snake living in your midst...'

There was a murmur of unease. She let her gaze skim the chamber once again. Most of the sisters' faces were wide-eyed or open-mouthed, though both Gracia and Letitia did, as she'd expected, show understanding, even if Felicia's and Maria's faces were blank.

At length, she alighted upon Sister Rosa, who was sitting, as she always did, with Beatrice and Amata. Rosa was looking directly back at her.

Defiant. *Rebellious*.

Did Rosa not *believe* she would denounce her? She'd soon find out...

Evangelina looked away again. 'I can see from your faces,' she continued, 'you can scarcely believe what I'm saying. But I regret it's true. The sister I'm referring to *appears* to be the most pious, the most virtuous of us all, a woman without sin. Yet she's been hiding from you all the very reason why she came to Northwick, many years ago. But I can tell you she came because of the dreadful *sins* she had committed...' She hesitated a moment, briefly concerned one of the sisters might ask her to elaborate upon Rosa's "dreadful sins". But no one said a word, so she continued. 'She came because she needed to spend the rest of her life *atoning* for those terrible iniquities—'

'Why are you prevaricating?' a voice called out. 'Why not simply *proclaim* the sinner's name?'

The voice was resolute. It was Rosa's.

Evangelina looked back at her and met her eyes. Eyes that showed no fear or irresolution. She faltered, lost her thread... And, unwittingly, gave Rosa the opportunity to dismiss her denunciation before she'd even made it.

Rosa stood up. 'What the prioress will not tell you,' she said, coming forward so she could address the sisters face-to-face, 'is that Sister Amata and I recently had an audience with the new Bishop of Winchester. We told him of the many grievances we raised at the visitation, grievances the prioress denied and for which she was absolved. Yet the bishop was aghast to hear that his commissioners apparently treated such serious complaints so lightly, and insisted they needed further investigation.'

Evangelina slumped back down into her chair, as Rosa babbled on about the details of the complaints and the shock the bishop had expressed. Then Rosa stopped and bowed her head. The sisters, who'd listened in silence as she was speaking, now fell to murmuring amongst themselves. Evangelina would have liked to know if their murmurs were with Rosa or with *her*.

Rosa looked up again. 'It is of course me the prioress referred to earlier as the "snake", the sinful, deceitful sister in your midst. Evangelina was undoubtedly going to tell you why I came to Northwick when I was seventeen. Well, I shall tell you myself. It is an unhappy tale, of which I am not proud. Yet it is a tale I have already told Sister Dulcia and Sister Beatrice, and indeed the bishop. But I shall now tell *you* because, although I *have* been deceitful in recent months, in my efforts to right the wrongs the prioress has committed against Northwick, I am determined to be fully open and honest with you all. No more secrets.'

Evangelina felt her authority slipping away as Rosa related exactly why she had chosen to become a nun, explaining details *she* most certainly hadn't known. The sisters let out gasps of shock and what she presumed were sighs of sympathy.

But when, at length, Rosa concluded, the cries were of support.

Beatrice then stood up and came to stand at Rosa's side. 'I trust,' she said, 'you will applaud Sister Rosa for her honesty in speaking to us so bravely, and thank her for her bold efforts to rescue our beloved Northwick from the evident decline it's suffered in the past year and a half. It's clear His Grace, the bishop, agrees entirely with Rosa – and indeed with Sister Dulcia and me, and I imagine with many of you – that returning Northwick to the house of peace and piety it once was, is of paramount importance. And *that* is what Sister Rosa has been struggling to achieve.'

Nuns didn't, as a rule, raise their voices or clap their hands in approbation, but as Beatrice and Rosa returned to their seats, Northwick's sisters did both. If not all of them. Evangelina noticed both Gracia and Maria were silent and unmoving, their faces impassive. Felicia was sitting with them, yet seemed quite unaware of what had just happened, for she was rocking gently back and forth, her hands rhythmically circling her swollen belly.

As for Letitia, she seemed to have turned to Rosa's side, for she was sharing a smile with Beatrice and Juliana. And Mariota was arm in arm with Anne, her eyes soft with what was possibly relief.

Sister Clarice, on the other hand, sat alone, speaking to no one, her fingers kneading at the fabric of her habit. Briefly, Evangelina thought of going to her, but she didn't want to ask if she was changing her allegiance. She'd know the answer soon enough…

There was nothing for it but to slip away. She rose from her chair and, as discreetly as she could, crept out of the chapter house. She was *still* prioress, with a private chamber to retreat to. She'd continue to enjoy it whilst she could, even if the comfort and luxury of it had already palled.

Only days later, very early in the morning, the sound of frantic screams and sobbing came from one of the chambers along the passage from the prioress's, one of several that, otherwise, were unused.

Evangelina hadn't wanted Felicia to be delivered of her bastard child anywhere in the priory, but she'd made no arrangements for her to go elsewhere, and, in the event, matters took their course, and Felicia was howling before Evangelina had a chance even to remove her to the infirmary. The girl had occupied the chamber for the past few weeks. Maria slept with her, and in the daytime, ran back and forth to fetch and carry whatever Felicia needed.

It was still dark beyond the shutters when Evangelina had awoken abruptly, startled by a sharp rapping upon her door, and the unbidden entry of a dishevelled-looking Maria. 'It's started, Reverend Mother,' she'd said without preamble, finding her way to the side of Evangelina's bed by the light of the stubby candle she was carrying. 'Felicia's making quite a fuss. Who should I fetch to attend to her?'

Evangelina had struggled to sit up. 'The infirmaress, of course. Sister Mariota.' A piercing wail rent the air. 'Good Heavens, is that Felicia?'

Maria nodded. 'Will Mariota know what to do?'

'No, of course not, but she knows a midwife in the village who's already agreed to come.' She swung her legs around and stood up. 'Go on, girl, go and find Mariota and tell her what's happening.

Though I'd be surprised if she doesn't already know, with that appalling din.'

Maria hurried away, and Evangelina groaned. How unsavoury this all was. It was bad enough Felicia getting with child at all, but the actual procedure of its advent into the world was something she'd rather not give thought to. Nonetheless, she supposed she should at least go and see the wretched girl and make sure she was receiving whatever attention was appropriate.

However, when she arrived at Felicia's chamber, she found Sister Amata and Sister Beatrice already there, both trying to soothe the girl and moderate her penetrating cries.

'Where's Mariota?' demanded Evangelina.

'She's gone into the village,' Beatrice said, 'to fetch the midwife.'

'Good,' said Evangelina, but then took Beatrice aside. 'But why's Amata here? Isn't she too old for this sort of thing?'

'Not really, but she is old enough to have witnessed at least one or two births at Northwick. Not nuns, but village girls...' She tipped her head slightly. 'Don't you remember them seeking sanctuary here in their distress? Years ago...'

Evangelina shrugged. If she'd ever been aware of them, she'd forgotten. 'I'll leave you to it,' she said, turning towards the chamber door. 'I daresay Mariota will return with the woman before too long... But do try to keep the noise down...'

Beatrice grimaced. 'I don't imagine I'll have any control over what Felicia does or doesn't do over the next few hours.'

Evangelina shrugged and left the room. If she returned to her bed and put her pillow over her head, maybe she could block out the worst of it.

It was late in the afternoon when Beatrice came to tell Evangelina that Felicia's baby had been born.

'A boy,' she said.

After sleeping a while longer, Evangelina had eventually left her bed and dressed, and was sitting in her chair, doing nothing more than contemplating her future. Once the child was born, she'd have to make arrangements for it, and decide what to do about Felicia. Edgar had suggested the child could be given to a couple in the village... She'd get Mariota to arrange it. But what of Felicia? And what of herself? Though of course, it might all be taken out of her hands, especially if the bishop's investigations found against her...

'A boy?' she said. 'Any indication of its father?'

Beatrice pursed her lips. 'It's not noticeably the bailiff's. No shock of yellow hair.' She hesitated. 'In fact, the baby's head is covered in rather a lot of *black* hair.'

'Black?' she said, then stood up. 'But babies don't always have their parents' colouring, so Byllynges might still be the father.'

Beatrice shrugged. 'I suppose so.'

'Anyway, perhaps you should return now to Felicia,' said Evangelina. 'I'll come to see her later...'

Evangelina wasn't sure she wanted to see Felicia or the child. She found maladies of any sort repugnant, and had no interest in babies.

However, according to Maria, several of the sisters had already visited Felicia's chamber.

'And how did they find him?' Evangelina said.

Maria grimaced. 'Well, of course, he's a baby, and babies are meant to be endearing, aren't they? The sisters are finding him quite adorable.' She havered. 'And yet...'

'What?'

'They are surprised the boy doesn't seem to look at all like Rafe Byllynges, when they'd understood *he* was the father... Which was why he'd disappeared, to escape justice...'

'So, who does he resemble?'

She hesitated a few moments before answering. 'Oh, I don't know. Babies don't really look like anyone, do they? Not when they're so small...'

Evangelina shrugged. Not that she had wide experience of babies.

'I think Sister Beatrice,' continued Maria, 'might try again to persuade Felicia to divulge the father's name...'

Evangelina winced at the memory of threatening to beat the information out of Felicia, and the others. She'd not tried again to discover the villain's name. She nodded. 'I suppose we should try to discover it, so we can bring the man to justice.'

Despite her vacillation, at length, Evangelina found she had sufficient curiosity to persuade her to walk along the passage to Felicia's chamber.

Felicia was still lying on the narrow bed, her uncovered hair – remarkably long, Evangelina noted – unkempt and strewn across the pillow. Her face was so drained of colour it was chalky white.

'Is she all right?' she said to Beatrice. 'She looks very pale.'

'The midwife says she's well enough. The delivery was long and difficult, and the girl's uncomfortable and tired.'

Amata was sitting by the bed, stroking Felicia's hand, and murmuring to her, although the girl was shaking her head defiantly.

'What's Amata saying to her?' asked Evangelina.

'She's trying to encourage her to suckle the baby.' Evangelina recoiled at the thought of it, but Beatrice frowned. 'But she's refusing even to try.'

'So, will the child die?'

'Of course not. The midwife's gone to fetch a wet nurse.'

'How's *he* faring, then?' Evangelina moved towards the makeshift crib in which the babe was lying.

'See for yourself,' said Beatrice. 'Do you wish to hold him?'

She shuddered. 'I think not. Seeing will be sufficient.'

She sidled over to what was evidently a laundry basket and looked down. The sleeping baby was tightly wrapped from neck to toe in what looked like a piece of blanket from the dorter, but his head was uncovered, revealing the thick cap of hair that Beatrice had described.

At the sight of it, Evangelina's heart turned over. She found herself reaching out her fingers, to stroke the soft skin of the baby's cheek, then touch that dark silky hair.

She bent down, to mask a sudden indrawn breath. How very much this child resembled the only baby she'd ever known, the baby she'd once so much adored... Her heart began to race as an unlikely possibility struck her.

Was this child her *nephew*? Yet how could that be? Surely, Edgar was wholly ignorant of women... *Wasn't* he?

Gulping down her bewilderment, and hoping her eyes wouldn't

betray her, she straightened up again. 'Charming,' she said to Beatrice, aware her voice was tight. She coughed to clear her throat. 'I told Mariota she'll have to find a home for him.'

'She's already done so. The wet nurse the midwife's bringing. She recently lost a child. But this little one will stay here for a day or two before she takes him away. Just to be sure he's healthy.'

Evangelina nodded: the sooner the child went from here the better...

And yet... She couldn't stop herself looking down once more at his sweet face, observing how his eyelashes fluttered against his rosy cheeks. She felt her heart constrict. For, if this *was* her nephew, he was a Godeffroy...

Back in her chamber, Evangelina's head churned with possibilities.

Just because the child had black hair and rosy cheeks didn't prove that *Edgar* was its father... She couldn't imagine *how* he might be. Yet what did she really know about him? After all, he was twenty-five when he first came to Northwick, a grown man. Who knew what carnal knowledge he may have gained before he was ordained?

She couldn't shift the notion that it might be him. She then recalled Maria saying Beatrice was going to try to persuade Felicia to name the father. Suppose the name she gave was Edgar's? The last thing she wanted was for his identity to be revealed.

For, it would be yet another depravity with which she'd be held responsible, now everyone in Northwick, thanks to Rosa, knew Edgar was a Godeffroy, albeit they *didn't* know he was her brother.

Yet Edgar himself would also suffer. Edgar, the only person she'd ever cared for. She'd already thought he'd be sent away from here, when the bishop found out how he'd been appointed. But this was much worse. He'd likely be defrocked. Even excommunicated? How could she bear for that to happen to her little brother?

No, better to let Felicia keep it a secret. If no one knew, Edgar might at least be able to continue as a priest...

. . .

Early the next morning, Beatrice came to Evangelina's chamber in some agitation.

'Felicia's on her way,' she said. 'She's demanding to talk to you… Insisting now on telling you the name of the child's father…'

Almost at once, Felicia burst into the chamber uninvited, her eyes burning bright, and lurched over to Evangelina. She was dressed only in her linen shift – shockingly still stained from her efforts to birth her son – and her hair was still uncovered, and as wild and unkempt as it had been yesterday. Beatrice hurried forward to try to calm her, but Felicia violently threw her off and lunged closer to Evangelina.

'I hear you want to know the father of that… that… bastard child?' she cried without preamble. Her mouth stretched into a mocking grin. 'Believe me, you'll regret you asked. For you won't like what I've got to say…'

Evangelina's head and heart were now thumping in a clamour of pain and terror. How could she stop the wretched hussy speaking out?

But the girl gave her no opportunity. 'You've seen it?' she barked. 'Noted its dark hair?' Recoiling from the vitriol in her voice, Evangelina gave a single nod.

Felicia sneered. 'You know already, don't you?'

Evangelina made no response, and Felicia prattled on. 'But what you *don't* know,' she spat out, 'is *how* he got his spawn on me…'

Evangelina raised a hand, but Felicia batted it away. Her eyes were glittering now.

'He raped me, *Mother* Prioress, the man of God, our trusted confessor, our priest, your *Godeffroy* cousin…' Then she screamed, 'He *raped* me! Do you understand? He took advantage of your absence to hunt me down, to violate me, and leave his bastard spawn lodged inside my belly.' At that, she flailed her arms and howled. 'I was a virgin, a bride of Christ… And now I am defiled…' She looked from Beatrice to Evangelina, her eyes huge. 'What will become of me?'

Evangelina blenched. So, it was true… She sank into her chair.

Frowning, Beatrice stepped forward. 'But I thought the *bailiff* was responsible,' she said to Felicia, ignoring her frenzied turmoil. 'Rafe Byllynges.'

The girl spun around, her cheeks bright spots of pink. 'I can't imagine why you think that—'

'Because you've been seen with him several times, in a manner suggesting an illicit liaison—'

'Who said that?' she hissed.

'That's of no consequence,' said Beatrice, calmly. 'Is it true?'

The girl seemed to falter, but at length she cried out, 'No!' She flailed her arms again. 'How could the child be Rafe's? Look at its hair...'

'Babies don't always look like their parents,' said Beatrice. 'After all, the child doesn't have *your* fair hair...' Felicia pouted, but Beatrice continued. 'And Master Byllynges *has* disappeared.'

But Felicia shook her head vehemently. 'No, no, no!' she cried. 'I've already told you, it was Edgar...' She sank to the floor, weeping, and clawing at her wild hair. 'He must be arrested, charged with his wicked crime...'

Evangelina was aghast. What she'd dreaded was come to pass: *Edgar* was responsible... She was so shocked, she couldn't think how to respond.

But Beatrice was still calm. She bent over the sobbing Felicia and, grasping her arms, raised her to her feet. Then, shuffling her over to a stool, she pushed her down onto it. 'Your claim is very serious, Felicia. Why didn't you say it months ago?' Felicia didn't answer.

Beatrice turned to Evangelina. 'I don't know much about the law, but I believe rape should be reported soon after its occurrence, like raising the hue and cry.'

Evangelina raised her eyes. 'What are you saying?'

'That, if this came to court, even if Father Edgar was accused, he might be absolved because the proper procedures hadn't been followed. It might be hard to prove his guilt without evidence of the assault...'

'Surely, there's the evidence of the child?' said Evangelina, wearily. 'A child who looks like him...' she whispered.

'True. Though the child itself does present another problem, this time to Edgar's benefit...'

Evangelina looked up. 'What?'

'It's scarcely my area of expertise,' said Beatrice, smirking slightly, 'yet I recall, in relation to those two village girls I mentioned, the child's very existence was assumed to indicate the woman gained *pleasure* from the liaison and had, therefore, consented...'

'Are you saying Edgar *didn't* force her?'

'I couldn't claim such knowledge, but, in principle, it's possible...'

Evangelina exhaled. So, might Edgar get away with this? Assuming Felicia was even telling the truth. 'What might happen to him?'

'Oh, I don't know. The bishop might take a different view. For I suspect it'll be the bishop who'll decide.'

Evangelina's brief optimism faded. She nodded listlessly.

Felicia coughed. 'And what'll happen to *me*, do you think, Sister Beatrice?' she whispered, her voice tremulous.

'I don't know that either. I suppose you'll be given a string of penances, and one of them might be your removal from Northwick.'

'So you don't think I'll be dismissed from being a nun?' Her eyes were bright.

'No,' said Beatrice. 'I do know *that* isn't possible. Or, if you were, you'd apostatise – renounce your vows – which means you could be excommunicated.'

Felicia gasped. 'So, I *can't* stop being a nun?'

'Do you want to?'

'I'd thought perhaps I might...'

'Yet where would you go?' said Beatrice. 'What would you do? Your family—'

She wailed. 'Would disown me...'

Despite herself, Evangelina's heart clenched. Had Edgar *really* raped her? Left her in this parlous state? It seemed so much unlike him, to be so callous.

'I imagine the most likely outcome is you'll stay at Northwick,' said Beatrice.

'I'd rather be sent away,' said Felicia. 'Where the nuns don't know me, or the shame I've brought upon myself...'

'Upon *yourself?*' said Beatrice. 'I thought it was Father Edgar who'd done that?'

She blushed. 'He and I together,' she whispered.

. . .

Beatrice took Felicia away, back to her chamber, and Evangelina hurried to Edgar's lodgings. Would he still be there, or might the news of Felicia's claim have already reached his ears, causing him, like Rafe Byllynges, to flee?

She was almost surprised when he responded to her knock. But, as he stepped back to let her in, his eyes did not meet hers, and his whole body seemed agitated. *Did* he already know?

She refused a seat but told him at once what Felicia had said.

The room was gloomy, despite the brightness of the summer day outside, yet she could see a redness rising to his cheeks, and his fingers clawed at his collar.

He shook his head. 'I told you, sister, it was Rafe Byllynges she'd been with. I saw them together more than once.' Despite the seeming confidence of his words, his voice was tense.

'Yet the child's colouring contradicts the notion that its father could be Byllynges. His hair is black, Edgar...' She hesitated. 'And, in truth, the baby looks exactly like you did. I remember you so well...'

He looked up at her, his eyes bright with what she supposed was fear, then slumped onto a stool. He grasped his shaking head between his hands, and let out a long sigh.

Evangelina sat down on the chair, and waited for him to respond. At length, he raised his eyes again. They were damp.

'I daresay you will not believe me,' he murmured, 'but I did not rape Felicia. The little whore seduced me—'

Evangelina guffawed. 'Seduced you? She's a nun. What would she know of seduction?'

He grimaced. 'A great deal. It is true, you know, about her liaisons with Rafe Byllynges. I saw them several times. And perhaps she also went with other men?'

'Yet how?'

'She evidently found ways of slipping out of the priory without any of her sisters noticing... I imagine she became quite practised at it.' He sighed again. 'Sadly, my own liaison with Felicia was singular – just the once...' He faltered. 'How unfortunate that it was *my* seed—'

She held up her hand. 'I don't need the sordid details. But, yes, unfortunate *you* planted the child in her, when the bailiff and any others apparently failed to do so.' She massaged her pounding forehead. 'But what were you *thinking*, Edgar, to do anything so wanton and dangerous?'

He pressed his lips together. 'Felicia is very lovely. When she offered herself to me, I was unable to resist.'

Evangelina closed her eyes. Hadn't Felicia hinted earlier – after her long tirade of accusation – that she *did* share the blame? Implying her cry of rape was false? Nonetheless, she was furious with her brother for acting with such lack of prudence. She snapped her eyes open and glared at him. 'Then you're a fool, Edgar, to be taken in by her. I can scarce believe you had no forethought for the consequences.'

'Indeed, wisdom and caution abandoned me when I followed her out into the fields.' He ran his fingers through his hair. 'Later, when I learned Felicia was with child, I knew it was at least possible it was mine.' His eyes went soft. 'And, for a while, I imagined she and I might be able to be together with our child—'

Evangelina let out a cry of derision. 'Then you are an *absolute* fool!' He looked up, his eyes now like those of a beaten dog. 'Even if she wanted to, which is highly doubtful, you must know it would be impossible? Both of you dismissed from the religious life, excommunicated? How would you live?'

He held up his hands in a gesture of supplication. 'Yes, yes, Eva, I do realise all of that. My fantasy was only temporary...' He bit his lip. 'So, what do you think will happen to me, and to Felicia?'

Of course, she didn't know the answer, and suddenly no longer had the energy to discuss it any further. How aggrieved she was that Edgar had not only failed to consider the consequences of his actions for himself, but had given no thought at all to how they might redound upon her.

She didn't know how to respond or what to do. Surely, everything was lost. Even without the results of the bishop's investigations, this was the end for her at Northwick. She'd be dismissed as prioress and, probably, sent to another priory, where she'd have to live out her days in whatever austere regime the prioress there demanded.

As she walked back across the courtyard, to return to the comfortable chamber that was still hers, she thought again about the child lying in the laundry basket in the room along the passage. She was now as certain as she could be he was a Godeffroy. Her nephew.

Her kin. If matters went ahead as planned, he'd soon be lost to her entirely, given to some cottars, to be brought up as a tenant of the priory, instead of a scion of its ruling family.

She tripped up on the step as she crossed the threshold back into the priory, and had to grasp at the stone jamb to prevent herself from falling over. She leaned against it, her heart beating a little faster at the misstep, but also at the sadness whelming up inside her. How could she bear to let the child go?

Recovering her balance, she grasped her skirts and ran through the cloister and upstairs to her chamber. Slamming the door behind her, she turned the key, then fell back into her chair, trembling, her fingers clawing at her gown.

It was of no consequence what she could or couldn't bear, for the decision about the child wasn't hers to make.

28

Rosa cautioned her sister conspirators against exultation or self-satisfaction.

'Our cause has succeeded,' she said, 'and I am glad of it. Yet it was a battle I did not wish to fight. A battle I wish profoundly Evangelina had not forced us into.'

'She's paid heavily for doing so,' said Dulcia.

Rosa had been present when the new bishop's man, Master Aylesbury, came to tell Evangelina she was no longer prioress and there would soon be another election.

'The bishop's investigations into the grievances against you are not quite concluded,' he said, 'but there is more than enough evidence to prove you have brought Northwick into both financial and moral degradation and cannot be permitted to continue as its prioress.'

She was to be sent away, he said, to a priory the other side of England. When Evangelina asked where exactly, Master Aylesbury shook his head.

325

'I am not at liberty to tell you,' he said. 'But hundreds of miles from here. Far enough to keep Northwick safe from further harm.' He smirked, but Rosa frowned at him.

'Master Aylesbury,' she said quietly, 'that was unnecessary.'

He held up his hands, and bowed his head. 'I apologise. A thoughtless and unamusing jest.'

'I'm *glad* of the distance,' said Evangelina, either not noticing or not caring about the "jest". 'Better to go far away, where no one knows me.'

Rosa detected rancour in Evangelina's voice, despite her apparent acceptance of her fate. With good reason, for the former prioress shot her a doleful glare.

'I can resume the miserable *obscurity* that's marked out my life.' She reeled over to the chair and eased herself down into it. Resting her head against the backrest, she closed her eyes, and kneaded at her forehead with her fingers.

Just for a moment, Rosa felt compassion for this woman who had been her bitter adversary for the best part of two years. Yet it had been by no means inevitable that Evangelina's reign as prioress *would* end in her demise. For most of those two years, Rosa had feared deeply for Northwick's future, watching with increasing despair as Evangelina stripped it of both its financial assets and its spiritual strength. Until she had been able to convince herself to break her holy vows and act against Evangelina, Northwick's ruin was a grave and very real probability.

How glad she could be now that she *had* acted, and that Dulcia, Beatrice and the others had supported her.

Evangelina lowered her hand from her brow and opened her eyes. 'When?' she said, addressing Master Aylesbury.

'You leaving here?' he asked, and she nodded. 'Within the month. Negotiations are being finalised with the receiving priory.'

She nodded again, her whole bearing languid, seemingly defeated. 'And what of my brother?'

Rosa was startled. Brother? Not just a Godeffroy then, but Evangelina's *brother* and, she supposed, Angelica's nephew. But neither Evangelina nor Master Aylesbury noticed her surprise, and she made no comment.

Master Aylesbury had taken Edgar away from Northwick two weeks ago, soon after Felicia had made her shocking claim, which Rosa reported to the bishop's office. Evidently, Edgar put up no resistance to arrest, and Rosa learned shortly afterwards from Evangelina that he had admitted his culpability to her when she told him of Felicia's accusation.

The bishop's man now pursed his lips. 'He has made a full confession of his fault in the matter of Sister Felicia, and the bishop has imposed appropriate penances.'

'But the blame was not entirely his,' said Evangelina, straightening her back a little.

'Indeed. When Edgar was brought before Bishop William for questioning, he claimed Sister Felicia had beguiled him. At first that seemed unlikely, until Felicia confessed her part. So, his plea was thus acknowledged, although he did accept it scarcely gave him an excuse to abuse his position and break his vow of chastity.'

Evangelina let out a deep sigh – of relief, Rosa assumed.

'He seemed genuinely ashamed,' continued Master Aylesbury, 'and declared himself willing to undertake whatever penances the bishop sought to impose, in the hope that, in the future, he could once more resume his priestly role, albeit in some other, more suitable, environment.'

'Other than a house full of nuns,' said Rosa.

'Quite,' he said. 'Bishop William, a most wise and compassionate man, was willing to exercise a little leniency towards Edgar, in consideration of his previous good character.'

'So, he's not to be dismissed from the priesthood?' said Evangelina.

'He is not. Provided he does undergo his penances diligently, and undertakes the pilgrimage the bishop has demanded.'

'Pilgrimage?' queried Evangelina. 'Where to?'

'Not yet decided. But one that will give him plenty of time to reflect upon his misdemeanours and pray for guidance in his future life.'

Edgar would not return to Northwick. His penances were to be carried out in Winchester, so neither Felicia nor the rest of Northwick's sisters would have the opportunity to witness his punishment. When some of the sisters learned that he was Evangelina's brother, they declared themselves especially disappointed to be missing it. But Rosa warned them to rein in what was surely unwarranted gloating, and pray for Edgar's eventual contrition.

Although the new election had not yet been arranged, so Rosa was not yet prioress, it seemed generally accepted in the priory that she would be, and most of the sisters were already deferring to her as if she was. Only Gracia and Maria remained aloof, seemingly aggrieved by Evangelina's demise, and Clarice was still cautious in Rosa's presence, perhaps as yet uncertain how to remedy her earlier betrayal.

The "conspirators" continued to meet, no longer to plot rebellion but to plan Northwick's recovery. Rosa still valued Dulcia's and Beatrice's advice most especially, although, if and when she did become prioress, she would hold daily chapter meetings, as the rule required, so *all* of Northwick's sisters could be consulted.

For now, she enjoyed the conversation of her little coterie, and was glad Northwick had been a house of prayer and piety, but never one of silence.

When the sisters heard of Master Aylesbury's visit, bearing news of their former priest, they were keen to hear what he had said.

'What penances will he have to undergo?' asked Juliana, her eyes wide.

Rosa tilted her head playfully. 'Why on earth do you wish to know, Juliana?'

The young nun blushed crimson, and hid her face with her hands, as if she had committed some breach of delicacy.

Beatrice laughed. 'Sister Rosa's teasing you, Juliana. There's no reason you shouldn't know, though you might be shocked at what you hear.'

Rosa repeated what Master Aylesbury had told her and Evangelina of the penances the bishop had demanded of Edgar. 'Bear in mind,' she said, 'the penances are intended not only to punish the offender but also to set an example to all those who witness his humiliation. Edgar will receive four floggings—'

Juliana gasped. 'He is to be *flogged?*'

'He is,' said Rosa. 'Let me explain. On four Sundays, he will have to parade around the cathedral, bare-headed and bare-foot, but still wearing his cassock, and carrying a large candle as an offering to the church. As he walks, he will be beaten with a stick by a priest or dean.'

'How shameful,' murmured Dulcia.

'Indeed,' said Rosa, 'but that is the purpose of it. That is his public punishment, but privately, he is also required to fast on bread and water twice a week, and to go on a pilgrimage to some cathedral or shrine some distance away from here.'

Once he had undertaken everything required of him to the bishop's satisfaction, he would return to priestly duties. 'I think he must be grateful he is neither to be dismissed from the priesthood nor excommunicated,' Rosa said, and the others agreed his punishment seemed less severe than he might have feared.

'And what of Felicia?' asked Juliana. 'Did Master Aylesbury have news of her?'

'She is to stay here in Northwick. You will remember Amata telling us that Bishop William is compassionate, and so he has proved to be. He has decided to take a benevolent approach towards Felicia. Although she will undergo many testing penances, again there is no question of dismissing or excommunicating her.'

In fact, Felicia herself was not greatly pleased to be remaining at Northwick, feeling – much like Evangelina – she might be happier going to live with sisters who did not know her. But the decision was not hers to make. Rosa vowed that, assuming she was elected prioress, she would treat her with consideration, and insist the other sisters did the same.

Felicia had not been taken to Winchester for questioning. Instead, Bishop William had sent one of his commissioners to Northwick to share the task with Master Aylesbury, and bid Rosa and Dulcia be present at the interview.

Despite Felicia's earlier insistence that Edgar had violated her, she had now changed her mind. She admitted to being at fault, that Edgar was not her only lover, and that he did not rape her.

'I not only agreed to our liaison but sought it out,' she murmured, her head bowed, 'as I did my liaisons with Rafe Byllynges.' She had hesitated a moment. 'I don't know if the child was fathered by Edgar or by Rafe, but I suppose its appearance does suggest it was the priest?'

She blushed deeply as she added, quietly, 'Rafe was practised at avoiding unwanted consequences, whereas poor Edgar had no idea...'

'And has the bishop declared what *her* penances are to be?' asked Juliana now. 'Is she too to be humiliated and beaten in a procession around the church?' Her eyes were wide with horror.

Rosa shook her head. 'Her humiliation will lie in what she will no longer be permitted, such as leaving the priory, or speaking with any lay people, or being allowed to send or receive letters. In addition, she will be kept in solitary confinement three days a week, which I think will go very hard with her, for she is so fond of company. There will also be a period of fasting, bread and vegetables one day a week, only bread and water on another.' She pressed her lips together. 'The bishop demanded too that she does not attend our daily chapter meetings, but lies face downward at the entrance of the chapel until our discussions are complete.'

Rosa cringed as she told them of this particular mortification. She had asked Master Aylesbury if the bishop might be willing to waive it, but he had shaken his head.

'It is a small enough degradation,' he said, 'and will not last for ever.'

As Rosa described the litany of punishments Felicia had to undergo, Juliana's eyes had, if it were possible, grown even wider. Rosa leaned forward and touched her hand. 'Do not look so alarmed, dear Juliana. For the penances are not permanent. If Felicia carries them out diligently and humbly, and prays steadfastly for the remission of her sins, the bishop expects to be able to lift some of them, if not all, within six months or so.'

'They will be hard for Felicia, I think, those six months,' said Dulcia, and Rosa agreed.

'Therefore, we must all help her, be generous-hearted, yet firm in our insistence that she does not falter in her penances. The sooner, then, she can be freed from them, and return to a more normal life. Though, of course, a normal life in *our* terms, not Evangelina's.'

It was very early morning, and the day seemed set fair, when all the sisters gathered outside Northwick's gatehouse, to await the escort that would accompany Evangelina on her long journey to the priory to which she had been exiled. The animals were being prepared in the courtyard, with panniers of supplies being loaded onto packhorses, and the riding horses saddled.

The palfrey Evangelina was to ride was being fitted with a sideways saddle, which Rosa knew Evangelina would detest. She recalled the fuss Evangelina had made last year, when she was embarking upon her short expedition to visit her family and stay with Sir Toby Edenborough. For Evangelina had insisted upon riding upon a standard, forward facing, saddle, despite the impropriety of sitting astride the horse.

When Master Aylesbury was making the arrangements for Evangelina's journey, and asked Rosa if she thought Evangelina could ride or would need a carriage, she suggested that a horse would be fine, but also mentioned the matter of the saddle.

Master Aylesbury grinned, rather wickedly, she thought. 'Perhaps, then,' he said, 'I shall order up the sideways saddle for her.'

'Is that not unkind?'

He agreed, but thought making Evangelina's journey uncomfortable might lend useful weight to the penalty. Rosa demurred but he did not change his mind.

At length the horses were brought round, and the escort assembled. Master Aylesbury himself was going, together with two armed retainers, a priest and a stern-looking nun from Winchester. But there was no sign of Evangelina. Time passed, and Master Aylesbury looked up often at the sky, as the sun rose and the air warmed, and he was clearly impatient to be on their way.

He came over to Rosa and asked if someone could be sent to hurry Evangelina along. 'We need to leave,' he said, 'else we shall not reach our lodgings before nightfall.'

Striding over to the group of waiting sisters, Rosa asked Clarice to go and tell Evangelina she had to come now. 'If she is trying to put off the moment of departure,' she said, 'tell her that moment has already passed, and Master Aylesbury is demanding her immediate presence.' Then she leaned closer to Clarice's ear, and spoke quietly. 'If she does not come quickly, I believe he might take her bodily and sling her across the saddle like some baggage.'

Clarice looked aghast and hurried away.

Shortly, Clarice reappeared outside the gatehouse, with Evangelina close behind her. She was carrying a modest bag, in which, Rosa supposed, she had stowed her personal belongings. Yet it was scarcely large enough for more than a couple of gowns. Had any of the silken garments found their way in there, or was Evangelina now sufficiently humbled to have left them all behind?

The stern-faced nun came forward and took the bag from her. Evangelina resisted its confiscation, but the nun shook her head, giving the bag to one of the retainers who attached it to a pannier. Master Aylesbury gestured to Evangelina to mount the palfrey, leading it and her over to a mounting block. Rosa saw her scowl when she saw the saddle, but she did not resist. She stepped onto the high block, then Master Aylesbury, grasping her other leg somewhat roughly, helped to propel her up into the seat, where she settled, grim-faced, her feet resting on the platform.

Soon, everyone was mounted and Master Aylesbury bowed to Rosa. 'We shall depart,' he said, 'and *I*—he emphasised the "I"—'shall see you again in a few weeks.' He had told Rosa he expected the journey to take two weeks or so, imagining neither Evangelina nor the stern-faced nun could ride more than twenty miles a day, if that.

Rosa once more felt compassion for Evangelina. The journey would be hard, and by the time she reached the priory, wherever it was, she would no doubt be dispirited and exhausted. Yet Rosa could not be other than pleased that Evangelina was gone from Northwick, enabling her and her sisters to try to return their beloved priory to the place it once had been. Nonetheless, she would pray for her, and urge all the sisters to do the same.

A few days after Evangelina had left, Dulcia came to Rosa to ask what she should do about Anabella's dowry.

'Evangelina intended to try and find out where she'd gone,' she said, 'but evidently never did so.'

'Evangelina did realise I knew where Anabella was,' said Rosa. 'Initially, after Anabella left, I refused to tell her anything. But I would have told her, if she had asked me later, once I had learned that Anabella was safely married. But of course, she did not ask.'

Dulcia clapped her hands. 'So, is Anabella wed to Master atte Wode?'

Rosa wondered now why she had not, long ago, told Dulcia and Beatrice that all was well with Anabella. She had told Juliana as soon as John sent word that he and Anabella were man and wife, but they had agreed to keep the good news to themselves, in case the Sitwells got wind of it.

'I am sorry I did not tell you months ago, Dulcia. I should have. But now I can tell you all about them, and you can arrange for her property to be returned.'

However, she held fast on telling Dulcia about the Sitwells. It was only recently that Rosa herself had learned that they had invaded Meonbridge. John did not write to her about it until July, when her mind was so occupied by upheaval and rebellion that she had not told anyone else about it.

Now, she was not sure she wanted to discuss the Sitwells with anyone in Northwick. Hopefully, their association with the priory was at an end. What she did want, however, was to discover how the Sitwells found out where Anabella was. Anabella had always suspected someone was spying on her, a servant perhaps, who had some link with the Sitwells. At the time, Rosa had thought the notion quite implausible, but she now recalled how, last October, after Anabella had escaped the priory, she had noticed how troubled Evangelina's servant, Hilde, had seemed. She had wondered then if it was possible that *Hilde* was the spy.

How such a girl could have any connection with the Sitwells, she could not imagine, but, somehow, they *had* discovered where Anabella had gone. She would not do it now, but, if she was elected prioress, she would question Hilde about whether she was responsible for the Sitwells' assault on Meonbridge. After all, if the girl was prepared to take secrets about the priory to dangerous outsiders, she could scarcely be allowed to remain one of its servants.

. . .

Northwick's sisters had to wait for Master Aylesbury to return from delivering Evangelina to her new priory before an election could be held to appoint their next prioress. One or two suggested Rosa should simply assume the role, but Rosa shook her head at them.

'We must wait for Master Aylesbury,' she said. 'I am sure he will make the arrangements quickly once he has come back.'

She rejected also the notion that there was no need for two candidates to stand, as it was obvious that "everyone" would choose her. 'No, no,' she said, 'we shall do it properly. Perhaps there is another sister whom some might prefer, so we must allow a fair election to proceed.'

She asked Juliana to ask the other obedientiaries who amongst them would stand against her, thinking of Beatrice or Dulcia or even Clarice. Dulcia was unwilling, as she was eager to remain as treasuress, and Clarice's former disloyalty to Rosa made her too embarrassed to put herself forward.

But Beatrice did agree. 'On the strict understanding,' she said to the other sisters, 'you don't vote for me.' Everyone laughed, and Rosa joined in. Bless Beatrice for her support.

It was September when Master Aylesbury returned to Northwick. He was beaming as he entered the prioress's chamber, which Rosa, Dulcia and Beatrice were using once again to meet outsiders, as Angelica had used to do, as long as she was chaperoned.

He bowed to them all.

'You look well,' said Rosa. 'Did you enjoy your travels?'

He frowned. 'Not the outward journey. Your former prioress was most irksome, complaining the entire time about the horses she was riding, the saddle she'd been forced to sit upon, the lodgings and the food... How delighted and relieved I was when we finally reached our destination, and I could hand her over.'

'Did the prioress receive Evangelina with any warmth or grace?' asked Rosa.

His eyes crinkled. 'Not warmth, I'd say, but grace? Yes, perhaps. Out of Evangelina's hearing, the prioress did say she considered her arrival as a gift from God, some sort of challenge, I think she meant, to which, through prayer and love, she hoped to rise.' He pursed his lips. 'I chose not to enquire more deeply...'

'Of course, she doesn't know Evangelina,' said Beatrice. 'She might revise her view in time...'

Master Aylesbury laughed. 'Indeed. I would certainly not consider Sister Evangelina a "gift" but, clearly, I am not as charitable as that venerable prioress.' He rubbed his hands together. 'Anyway, Sisters, Evangelina is no longer our concern.'

Rosa was glad of that, but nonetheless did hope the prioress might draw out the best in Evangelina, and that Evangelina herself would, in time, find some contentment in her new life.

'So, to the election,' Master Aylesbury was saying, rubbing his meaty hands together once again. 'Soon, I think?'

'The sisters are eagerly awaiting it. I have told them two candidates must stand, else it would not be an election but a coronation. Sister Beatrice will stand against me...' She smiled at Beatrice.

'I doubt Sister Beatrice is *against* you in any way—' said Master Aylesbury, and Beatrice tittered.

'Quite right!' she said.

'But I understand your wish to do things "properly",' he continued. 'So, I shall summon up some officials from the bishop's office, and make the usual announcements, and then we can proceed. Shall we say the Friday after Michaelmas?'

'I am sure that will be suitable,' said Rosa, and Beatrice agreed. 'I shall inform the sisters at our chapter meeting tomorrow. They will be delighted.'

In truth, not *everyone* was delighted.

Most were indeed excited by the prospect of the election, and many told Rosa they were going to vote for her. Not, they said, that they did not like Beatrice, but they had always thought of Rosa as Mother Angelica's successor, and was certain Rosa would have been Angelica's choice.

But two sisters did remain unwilling to throw off their seeming resentment at what had happened to Evangelina. Gracia and Maria did not appear to want to vote for either Rosa or Beatrice. They were distant and resentful, spending time together and away from the other sisters.

'I am not sure,' Rosa said to Beatrice, 'quite why they are so resentful.'

'Neither of them is carrying out her duties properly either,' said Beatrice. 'Gracia seems to be ignoring the novices, and the little girls have been spending much of their time with Juliana. As for Maria'—Beatrice rolled her eyes—'she spends no time at all in the kitchens, leaving all the work to Helen. I've tried to talk to her about it, but she refuses to listen.'

Rosa pressed her lips together. 'Of course it cannot continue. I do want to mend bridges and, once I am elected'—she blushed at her assumption, but Beatrice waggled her head—'I shall try to bring them both round. Clarice and Letitia have already done so...'

'And Mariota is relieved her loyalties are no longer divided. I daresay the *dis*obedientiaries'—she grinned—'will come round eventually. Let's hope the election is the turning point.'

The election was a joyous day. Rosa tried to bring a degree of seriousness to the occasion, but the sisters seemed to be treating it more like a party, with the matter of the election, and the dropping of black and white balls into the urn, something akin to a game. The bishop's officials were bemused by the sisters' high spirits but did not attempt to rein in their enthusiasm.

Beatrice contributed to the atmosphere by cheerfully repeating her wish that no one vote for her. Nonetheless, when the urn was upended, there were three white balls, the chosen colour for a vote for Beatrice. She frowned at the sight of them. 'What did I say?' she said, casting her laughing eyes around the chapter house. The sisters giggled but none confessed.

Rosa suspected Gracia and Maria had chosen white. They might have refused to vote at all. She was glad they had. It did not matter if they still felt unable to give her their support. She would try to recover their support in due course. But whose was the third white ball? Katerina and Mildryth seemed to be enjoying the occasion, sitting in the chapter house surrounded by the sisters they had both known for so many years. But Mildryth's eyes did look baffled as well as happy, so perhaps it had been her... No matter...

According to tradition, Rosa took herself off to the dorter, ostensibly to signal her resistance to being chosen. But when Dulcia and Juliana came to ask her if she was ready, she decided not to prolong the waiting.

They went down the narrow stairs from the dorter to the entrance to the transept, then she permitted the two sisters to take her arms and pretend to drag her into the chapel. As she recalled was the case two years ago, the nave was full of people, not only Northwick's nuns, but the priory's servants too, as well as the bishop's officials. Rosa walked forward towards the altar, as cries of joy erupted on both sides. She knelt and the canon from Winchester pronounced her the prioress of Northwick.

A few days after the election, Master Aylesbury came unexpectedly to Northwick and asked to speak with Rosa, Beatrice and Dulcia. They gathered in the prioress's chamber.

Rosa planned to have the great bed removed to the small adjoining room that she once used as her office when she was putative subprioress. Now, as prioress, she intended to continue sleeping in the dorter with the other sisters, as was the Benedictine way, and without the bed, the large chamber would be much more suitable for visitors, especially when they were men.

'Sisters,' said Master Aylesbury, taking the seat at the table that Beatrice offered him, 'I need to speak to you about the Godeffroys...' They all let out a small cry of surprise. 'Indeed,' he went on. 'I have received a visit from Nicholas Foxe, acting on their behalf.'

'What did that rogue want?' said Beatrice.

Master Aylesbury cleared his throat. 'I have not yet told you this, but Bishop William has expressed the view that the Godeffroys should no longer hold sway over Northwick. The priory needs to find another benefactor—'

Dulcia gasped. 'But how, Master Aylesbury? And how are we to manage if the Godeffroys withdraw their funding?'

He coughed. 'They already have, Sister Dulcia. Master Foxe, or whoever sent him to see me, was much angered by the bishop's command. Nicholas had been instructed to offer more, in order to retain their control over the priory—'

'More?' spluttered Dulcia, but he held up his hand.

'Of course, I declined the offer, and made it clear that Northwick wanted nothing more to do with the Godeffroy family or their money.'

Dulcia looked aghast, but he shook his head. 'Do not be alarmed, Sister Dulcia. For I have news of a much more satisfactory answer to your funding needs.' He paused for a moment, then gave them one of his beaming grins. 'Sir Thomas Chatterton, your former steward, has already agreed to provide funds in the short term, although he confessed, if sadly, he was not sufficiently wealthy to endow Northwick fully.' He turned to Rosa. 'Which he said he would have gladly done now you are prioress. But he strongly recommended approaching Sir Toby Edenborough again, who he was certain would now be more than happy to renew his proposal for a generous endowment. Moreover, he also knew another couple of gentlemen who might be interested.'

Dulcia relaxed back into her chair, her cheeks soft with relief.

Beatrice clapped her hands together. 'Good for Sir Thomas,' she cried. 'And let's hope he's right about Sir Toby. *That* gentleman will make a most agreeable benefactor.'

Rosa felt suddenly light-headed. 'Thank you, thank you, Master Aylesbury,' she said. 'We could not be more glad to hear such splendid news. Sir Thomas was a fine steward until Evangelina drove him away. I do hope he will consider resuming that role for Northwick in due course. As for Sir Toby, how disappointed we were when he withdrew his offer when, as Beatrice says, we had thought he was exactly the kind of benefactor we needed.'

'No obligations or demands,' said Master Aylesbury, grinning. 'Anyway, I shall keep in touch with him.' He turned to Dulcia. 'You can at last look upon the hole in your coffers with confidence that you will, before too long, be able to refill it.'

Dulcia let out a deep sigh, and Rosa took her hand and squeezed it. 'This does not mean that all our problems are at an end. But at least we can now see a way forward, to return Northwick to what it used to be.'

Master Aylesbury stood up. 'Well, Sisters, I shall leave you to your deliberations.'

'Will you not stay for dinner?' said Beatrice, but he shook his head.

'Thank you kindly, but I have other matters to attend to this morning. Another time.'

Rosa rose to her feet too, and held out her hand to him. 'Master Aylesbury,' she said, 'do you think we now know each other well enough for us to call you by your given name?' He took her hand, shook it warmly and beamed.

'By all means, Mother Prioress. My name is Richard.'

'Oh!' said Rosa. 'That was my father's name, and that of my nephew, although the family call him Dickon. In future, may all the sisters use Richard to address you?'

'I shall be honoured to be considered theirs, and Northwick's, friend.' He bowed to Rosa and Dulcia, and Beatrice escorted him to the door.

29

Rosa relaxed into her chair and surveyed the scene before her. How cheerful the frater looked, bedecked with holly and mistletoe and ivy. And how bright the lofty chamber was, with the extra candles she had allowed winking on every side.

She recalled Christmases at Meonbridge when she was a girl, and how much effort her mother put into decking the great hall: with huge swags of pine and ivy, and so many candles it was bright as day. As a child she had found the spectacle a thrill, and even when she was older and leaning towards adolescent melancholy, the sight and smell of Christmas in the manor hall always raised her spirits.

Of course, Northwick could not afford de Bohun extravagance, but she had encouraged the sisters to gather in festive greenery and make swags and garlands sufficient to festoon the frater. And how right she had been to do so. Perhaps it *was* a frippery, but it brought everyone great cheer, an excellent antidote to the worry and despondency of these past two years.

She let her gaze run over the assembled company: fifteen nuns and the two little novices, and a small group of those priory servants who did not work in the kitchen. Angelica had always invited the servants to join in the festivities, but Evangelina had insisted they ate in the kitchen on Christmas day the same as any other. Why, Rosa did not understand, as Evangelina herself had not shared Christmas dinner in the frater.

But Rosa saw no reason not to reinstate Angelica's stance, and how very cheering it was to see everyone all talking and laughing together.

She wished Sir Thomas were here, to witness the result of his very generous donation, provided specifically for the sisters to have a good Christmas dinner. And what a splendid effort Beatrice and Helen had made, providing the best food possible for everyone.

The chamber was alive with excited chatter as the sisters took their usual places at the frater tables, but invited the servants who were dining to sit alongside them. Then, on Beatrice's signal, the kitchen servers had marched into the frater carrying dishes before them, and, coming to stand before Rosa, laid the platters down along the length of the high table. Everybody clapped their hands and Beatrice beamed.

Rosa had laughed. It was not so different from the Christmas feast at Meonbridge, albeit the procession there had been longer and the range of dishes huge. Of course, there was much less here but, just like then, the wonderful smells that arose from the dishes set before her, a blend of sharp and sweet and spicy, were very tempting.

Cook had excelled himself, for there were little pies, and various roasted birds, and a rich and spicy meat brewet, as well as pears cooked in wine and custard tarts, and a variety of little sweetmeats. Rosa smiled as she recalled how, at home, a whole roasted pig, its mouth stuffed with apples, was always borne in on a great platter. Such a thing was beyond Northwick's means, even with Sir Thomas's donation, and was anyway far too rich and extravagant for a priory's fare. But the fare they did have was plentiful and delicious, and accompanied by wine: a true celebration, not only of Christmas and Christ's birth, but Northwick's resurgence and rebirth.

Nibbling on a custard tart and sipping at her wine, Rosa cast her eyes again over the merry throng in front of her. Was it all perhaps a little *too* merry? Yet it was only for one day.

Northwick's sisters had always enjoyed Christmas day. Celebration was never denied. The cellaress tried to ensure the food was a little special, although, last year, as funds declined, Beatrice was unable to provide much more than the usual plain fare. But, even then, the sisters made the best of what they had, sang songs and told each other stories. It was scarcely boisterous.

Yet, up in Evangelina's chamber, the past two Christmases were almost riotous, if only for those few members of the prioress's coterie. For days, they dined on rich food, played raucous games and, apparently, invented little plays, and even danced. They also all drank rather too much wine, and the sounds coming from the chamber were more akin to the rowdy jesting one might expect to hear coming from an ale-house or a stew.

Today was not at all like that.

She looked either side of her, at Beatrice and Dulcia. Both were at ease, their faces flushed with wine and good humour. Far from being troubled by the merriment, they were relishing it.

As was, by the look of happiness on her face, Sister Clarice, whom she had allowed to remain as subprioress, despite her lapse of loyalty.

'Oh, Reverend Mother,' she had said, wringing her hands together in her lap, when Rosa told her of her decision. Her eyes filled with tears. 'I am so sorry—'

But Rosa had held up her hand. 'No need for regrets, Clarice. Let us leave them in the past.'

It was in her interests, and Northwick's, that she bore no grudges to any of those who had taken Evangelina's part against her. Their community was small. She had seen how unhappy the place could be when it was riven by animosity and rancour. She was determined it would not happen again.

Yet she sensed those sisters who had once been strong allies of Evangelina – Clarice, Letitia, even Gracia and Maria – were in fact relieved that life in Northwick was returning to something like normal. But she still needed to reassure them. So, she had given new jobs to

Maria and Letitia – as chambress and sacrist – in the hope they would understand the trust she was placing in them.

As for Gracia, she had decided to give her the role of almoness, as Amata wanted to retire anyway, and spend more time with the "ancients". But Gracia had been rather shocked at what she considered a demotion.

Rosa had shaken her head. 'It is most certainly not demotion, Gracia. You were not really suited to being mistress of the novices, especially when the only novices in your charge were little girls.' She had raised an eyebrow. 'Do you not agree?' Gracia had nodded stiffly.

'The job of almoness,' she went on, 'is vital. Almsgiving is one of our principal purposes. For years, Amata carried out the role with great industry and compassion, until the past year or so, when our funds ran so low...' Gracia's face stayed stiff, but she did nod understanding. 'We must all give thought to those less fortunate than ourselves, and, as almoness, you act for us in ensuring they receive our help.'

Gracia had nodded again. If she was not happy, it was not her place to show it, and she knew that. She was the one sister Rosa thought would take time to acknowledge that her support of Evangelina had been a bad idea. But she would not attempt to hurry her.

Beatrice leaned in to her now, breaking into her recollection. 'It's going very well, don't you think?' she said.

'Excellent, Beatrice, truly,' Rosa said. 'Thank you so much.' She smiled and touched Beatrice's arm.

'It's Sir Thomas who deserves the thanks,' she said. 'Without his donation, I couldn't have provided such a splendid feast.'

'I have already thanked him, as I am sure you have too. What a boon he has been to Northwick these past few months.'

Beatrice agreed, then gestured towards Felicia, sitting with Maria and Letitia, her face alight as she shared some laughter with her friends. 'You were right to let her come,' she said.

'Oh, how could I not,' said Rosa. 'It would have been heartless to make her miss the festivities. She knows she has to return to her solitude and her penances tomorrow. But, at least for today, she can be the young woman she is and have a little fun.'

'I've noted,' said Beatrice, 'none of the sisters are treating her with anything other than kindness.'

'Indeed. How glad I am they are. Felicia has months of penances still to fulfil, but I am hopeful that, in due course, she will return to us a full member of our community.' She paused. 'Do you know anything of the baby?'

Beatrice shrugged. 'Not much, but I understand the boy's thriving with his new family. But he'll never know his mother was a nun. Or his father a priest...' She raised an eyebrow.

Rosa nodded. 'I wonder where Edgar is now. I understand from Richard Aylesbury that he has disappeared. Apparently, he undertook two penances then asked the bishop if he might defer the others. He left Winchester to go on a pilgrimage to the shrine of Our Lady of Walsingham, but has not returned.'

'Like Rafe Byllynges,' said Beatrice, with a wry grin. 'Which, in his case, is probably just as well. Sir Thomas, by the way, is still seeking a replacement. A *married* man, he suggested'—she grinned—'who might present less of a distraction to the younger nuns.'

Rosa could not help but smile: that would undoubtedly be for the best.

She supposed Edgar would now be dismissed from the priesthood, perhaps even excommunicated. She bowed her head. He was a foolish man, but not a wicked one. She would pray for him, and hoped he found his own kind of salvation.

Rosa was determined that Northwick would return to a place of piety and peace, but not one of melancholy and gloom. Whatever Evangelina had thought – indeed whatever the younger nuns now thought – Northwick had been a house of light and joy under Angelica's rule. Because, although Angelica was strict in her avowal that a priory's principal function was prayer and work, her avowal came with love and compassion.

Rosa had disapproved of the frivolity and merry-making that had been a constant feature of Evangelina's days mostly because it was had at the *expense* of the prayer and work. Northwick became a place of noise.

In principle, a priory was supposed to be a place of silence, with sisters allowed to speak only at prescribed times of the day. But, under Angelica's rule, *quiet* rather than silence had been customary. Silence was often demanded in the frater, whilst a sister read the daily reading. And in the chapel, no speech was permitted other than what was needed to praise God. But in the cloister and the dorter, talk was allowed as long as it was restrained. At work, where sisters worked with others, if conversation was required it was permitted, as long as it did not degenerate into idle chatter.

Rosa was aware that it was not really for her to pick and choose the rules she wished to follow. Yet, Angelica's example showed that relaxing the rule of silence into one of quiet made for a generally happy atmosphere. And she thought Bishop William would not criticise her for striving to make Northwick Priory a contented place.

MEONBRIDGE

DECEMBER 1367

Rosa would have liked to spend Christmas in Meonbridge but would not leave her sisters to enjoy the festivities without her. Instead, she planned to travel on Saint Stephen's day, to spend a few days with her family, leaving Clarice nominally in charge, with Dulcia and Beatrice ready to help, were help required.

December was never a good time for travel, and Sir Thomas insisted on hiring a carriage to take her in greater comfort than a horseback ride. Dulcia had stowed Anabella's fortune in a casket, and it was travelling with her, so Sir Thomas also provided an armed escort for her journey.

She was grateful for the carriage, albeit it made her nauseous with the constant lurching from rut to rut. She was damp too from having often to alight and stand out in the drizzle whilst the escort laboured to free the wheels stuck in the mud. The journey had been difficult and slow, and how guilty she had felt about the men assigned to attend her – soaking wet, their boots and hose mud-coated, and undoubtedly chilled to the bone – when they might have stayed home with their families to continue their festive celebrations. When they arrived in

Meonbridge, she would insist they were given food and warmth and rest before they attempted to return home.

Dickon's face was beaming as he came forward to greet her. He held out his hands, and drew her over to the blazing hearth. He took her sodden cloak and helped her to remove her muddy boots, then poured a goblet of warm spiced wine and bid her sit and drink.

He sat down beside her. 'So, Northwick is safe once more,' he said. 'The wicked prioress has gone, and you are in her place.' His tone was light-hearted.

She smiled, but shook her head. Even if he was jesting, she could not bear to speak of anyone in such terms. 'She was not wicked, Dickon, just a terrible prioress. One who might have brought the priory to utter ruin.'

'But you saved it.'

'My sisters too. We had to unseat her to stop the damage she was doing.'

'And now you are the rightful prioress.'

She shook her head again. 'I do not see it as entitlement, but a privilege. I simply want to return Northwick to what it was under Angelica's reign.'

He nodded.

Rosa had not seen Dickon for three years, since her mother's funeral. Then, he had seemed still a boy, needing comfort for the loss of his beloved grandmother, but now he was most definitely a man. Tall, powerful, handsome: the image of his father. Except that Dickon was a much more amiable and admirable man than Philip.

Like Evangelina and Northwick, she thought Philip would not have made a good lord of Meonbridge, perhaps for more or less the same reason. Much as she had adored him as a girl, she was certain he would have managed Meonbridge and the other de Bohun estates *entirely* for his own benefit. He would have given no consideration or care to the people who lived and worked on them. Of course, that was the usual way of things: most lords *did* consider their property as simply the bringer of their own wealth, the men and women who created it worth no more than the ploughshares or the cattle – in some cases even less so.

But Dickon did not think like that. For he was already following the example set by his grandmother, rather than his father or grandfather. Mama was, she now knew, much wiser than either of her menfolk, as well as compassionate, not only towards her family but also her tenants, whom she regarded as her neighbours.

She recalled how scornful she had been as a girl of her mother's attitude towards Meonbridge's tenants, believing her father's – and Philip's – aloof and punitive approach to them more appropriate. How wrong she was! For it was *Mama* who found the solution to the riots that threatened Meonbridge after the devastation of the pestilence, and Mama who ensured that Meonbridge manor and all the de Bohun estates were, for the most part, places of contentment as well as industry. She was confident that, under Dickon's lordship, Mama's efforts would not be undone.

Rosa was looking forward to seeing Anabella again. It was more than a year since her escape from Northwick, and she had not had the chance to visit her and John in their new house. She felt excited when John invited her and Dickon to join the family for a feast.

Anabella's eyes were bright with happiness as she held out her hands to Rosa. Rosa hurried forward, and they embraced, something they had never done before, and Anabella was like a giddy girl in her excitement to show Rosa her new home.

John too was beaming, happier than she had ever seen him. Happy to have a wife he adored and who adored him, and, perhaps, to have a house that matched his station. But, when he turned, bent down and rose again with a bundle in his arms, she could see that the greatest joy was almost certainly reserved for his child.

He stepped forward, plucking at the blanket around the baby's face. 'How proud we are,' he said, his voice catching slightly, 'to introduce you to our son.' He smiled, as Anabella came to stand by him.

Rosa peered down at the baby, sleeping peacefully, apparently undisturbed by his father lifting him from his cosy crib. 'When was he born?' she asked.

'Two months ago,' said Anabella. 'Would you like to hold him?'

Rosa faltered. She had never cradled a baby in her arms. She thought of Felicia's baby: she had seen him several times before he was taken away by the midwife's daughter, but never picked him up. Some of the other sisters had been keen to cuddle him, but she had not wanted to. The child had been the result of an illicit union, which had ended in grief for both his parents. Yet why should that make a difference? *He* was not responsible for his parents' failings...

But *this* baby was the product of love. Why should she not wish to hold him in her arms, when this, surely, was what she had hoped for when she helped Anabella give up the sisterhood and become John's wife?

She reached forward, and John put his son gently into her arms, cradling his head in the crook of her elbow. She was startled by the weight of him, despite his tiny size, and was delighted by the dark lashes that grazed his cheeks. Looking up at Anabella, and then at John, she smiled broadly.

'How enchanting he is, your little boy,' she whispered, and rocked him gently.

'Tell me a little more about Anabella,' Dickon said to Rosa, grinning. It was the day after their visit to the atte Wodes'. 'I'd like to hear about her escape from Northwick — planned and executed by you, I understand?' He laughed. 'Which seems a very *in*appropriate action for a nun.'

She returned the laugh, yet she still shuddered at everything she had had to do to recover Northwick. She still had months of penances to fulfil before she would feel absolved.

'Indeed, it was most inappropriate. Not only plotting Anabella's escape, but also Evangelina's overthrow. It is something I wish never to have to do again, for it went against everything I hold sacred.'

She told him all about the plot to "liberate" Anabella, as Beatrice had it. 'I did not know if the plan would work,' she said, 'but Eleanor, and your retainers, and, in particular, Piers Arundale, played their parts well.'

Dickon laughed. 'Ah, yes, Piers. Did you know it took him two weeks to return to Meonbridge?'

She gasped. 'Two weeks? No, no one told me that.'

'It just so happened no carts were plying their trade between Northwick and Meonbridge that week, as he'd hoped, so, in the end, he gave up waiting and decided to walk. But he took a wrong turning, and found himself down by the sea at Portchester, before eventually finding his way home.' He guffawed. 'The other fellows here still tease him about it.'

Later, Rosa asked her nephew about his life at Steyning Castle, training with the Earl Raoul de Fougère, who had been the liege lord of both her father and her brother. 'What about that squire who gave you trouble a few years ago?' she said.

'Edwin de Courtenay? He's been lying low since all the uproar. He gets on with the training and doesn't cause any trouble. He's not entirely without friends, but he does still spend a lot of time on his own. But he certainly no longer threatens me.' He grinned.

'So how long is it before you complete your knightly training?'

'Three years yet,' he said. 'But I'm in no hurry to leave Steyning. I enjoy my life there. In truth, if it wasn't for my position here, I'd probably stay, in service to Earl Raoul.' He gave her a wry smile. 'But of course I have the de Bohun estates to manage.'

'They seem well enough managed without you here,' she said, then wondered if that was quite tactful.

He grinned. 'True enough. But, in truth, Aunt, part of me *wants* to take up my lordship and make Meonbridge my home. I love it here.' He grinned again. 'And I know Angharad will be happy to live here, and follow in grandmother's footsteps as the wise and gentle chatelaine.'

'So, do you expect to go away?'

He nodded. 'King Edward's battles against the French are still not done, and if the earl decides to raise a force to support him, of course I'll go. The earl's near seventy, and might not fight himself, but he has a strong force of knights and men-at-arms to call upon, and I mean to be amongst them when I'm ready.'

EPILOGUE

JANUARY 1368

Edgar looked about his new lodging. It was meagre, worse even than his paltry cottage in Northwick Priory. A straw pallet on the floor. A stool. A basin and a jug. No hearth, no table, no chest for his clothes. As well he had brought so little with him. It might be a dismal life here, but it would be one without commitment or limitations.

He had never hated his role at Northwick, but he resented being forced into the priesthood and being denied the life of a normal man.

Here he was just Edgar – whether educated man or labourer, he did not yet know.

He lay back on the pallet, staring at the ceiling, the rafters black and hung with cobwebs. Had he made the right decision?

When he was still in Winchester, by chance he met his cousin, Nicholas Foxe. Nicholas had been dismissed from Northwick even before himself, but the Godeffroys sent him to speak to his replacement, Richard Aylesbury.

'They hoped,' he said, 'I could overturn the bishop's directive that

Godeffroys were no longer Northwick's benefactors. I wasn't surprised to find Master Aylesbury playing the bishop's lackey, refusing our request outright.' He had shrugged. 'But I scarcely care. The nuns now left in charge of Northwick are viragos and termagants, and I'm glad no longer to have to deal with such perfidious women.'

He laughed, and Edgar joined in. Yet he knew Rosa, Beatrice and Dulcia were not "viragos" at all and certainly not perfidious, but simply strong-minded and good-hearted women who wanted their beloved priory back. He imagined they must be *highly* delighted no longer to be involved with the likes of Nicholas Foxe.

Edgar sighed. Nicholas would no doubt procure himself another job, but he himself had neither job nor source of income.

The bishop was still waiting for him to fulfil his penances before deciding whether to dismiss him from the priesthood or find him some lowly clerical position. But he would wait in vain. Edgar kept delaying, claiming agues here and megrims there, and the bishop was tolerant in accepting his excuses.

Nicholas suggested he might work for a month or so for a Godeffroy uncle, and the bishop did not object, provided Edgar pledged to return to Winchester to do his penances. For several weeks no demands came from the bishop, but then, in October, a message arrived to say his patience was wearing thin. Edgar hoped his uncle might offer him a full-time position, but no such offer came.

So, he returned to Winchester and at length accepted the mortification of the penance for two Sundays in a row. How humiliating it was being beaten bare-foot three times around the cathedral, in full view of a jeering crowd of onlookers. After the second Sunday, he could not face a third and fourth, and asked the bishop if he might defer them, and undertake the pilgrimage instead. He was surprised when the bishop agreed.

Bishop William suggested the shrine of Our Lady at Walsingham as a suitable destination, and Edgar did not demur, knowing he wanted only to get away from Winchester and the bishop's influence. It was scarcely the right time of year for travel but, a week later, having packed his few belongings into a travelling bag and determined some sort of itinerary, he hired a palfrey and was on his way.

He knew he never would reach Walsingham. Perhaps he never

intended to. More seriously, he would not return to Winchester, and his penances. He would be an apostate. Dismissed from the priesthood. Even excommunicated... That frightened him, but he would not go back.

He thought about his sister, wondering how she was faring in whichever priory or abbey she had been exiled. He was sad to know he would never see her again, but in truth he never did support her in her wild mismanagement of Northwick. What he should have done was *stop* her, not pretend to agree to her vilification of Sister Rosa and making the priory her own private fiefdom.

If he had done so, everything that followed might have been avoided.

After many days of wearying travel and exhausting contemplation, he had found himself here in Cambridge. Riding through the city gate, he liked the look of it. Instead of finding an overnight lodging in an inn, he paid two months' rent on this hovel.

Soon, he would look for work. It did not matter what. It would be a different life. It might be good or it might be bad. But it would be one that he had chosen.

Evangelina had never spent so much of her day in the chapel and upon her knees, reciting psalms. The penitential psalms. She knew all seven of them by heart. Yet she didn't feel any more penitent than she had when she first came here.

How long ago was that? She counted on her fingers. September to January... Four months.

Four months of Fridays blighted by psalms and fasting on bread and water. Four months of lying on a hard, narrow bed in a dorter full of snuffling, snoring nuns. Four months of enforced awakening twice every night, to stumble to the icy chapel to recite Matins and then Lauds.

And, every day of those four months, she'd worked. Not as sacrist or cellaress, or any kind of obedientiary, but alongside the priory servants and lay sisters, toiling, as they did, in the garden or the kitchens or the laundry.

All of it, the psalms, the fasting, the menial labour, were part of the penance the bishop had imposed. But none of it made her feel more contrite. If the prioress was reporting to the bishop on her progress, she couldn't possibly have said Evangelina was ready for remission.

So, was she simply to continue doing the penances for ever? She sought out the prioress, to ask how long they would endure.

The prioress sighed. 'You must realise, Evangelina, that it is up to you. The bishop requires signs that you show remorse for your transgressions, not that you simply carry out the penances. Yet I see no such signs.' She smiled thinly. 'Unless you are keeping them well-hidden?'

Evangelina pressed her lips together. She supposed she could pretend. Why hadn't she considered that? She was *doing* the wretched penances, so why not gain benefit from her efforts? Yet, she couldn't fathom what "sign" the prioress might expect to see. It was so long since she'd felt sorrow or regret for anything, she was quite out of practice with the notion.

'No, Reverend Mother, not hidden,' she said. 'Simply absent...'

'Then I fear your penances must continue. The bishop is hoping – indeed, expecting – to be able to grant you remission of your sins, but he can scarcely do so if you are not willing to repent.' She sat down and folded her hands together upon the desk. Evangelina remained standing before her, and the prioress raised her eyes. They seemed full of what Evangelina thought might be fear, or at least anxiety.

The prioress lowered her voice. 'Evangelina, I am *deeply* concerned that, if you do not show your repentance soon, the bishop might feel obliged to... to excommunicate you, to force your hand.'

Evangelina gasped. The famously kind and compassionate Bishop William Longe? 'Would he do that?'

She shook her head sadly. 'I do believe it is a possibility. One, surely, you would not wish to risk?'

Evangelina closed her eyes a moment, sensing a mounting megrim.

Ever since she'd been here, she'd been denied her black veil, the symbol of her profession as a nun. Its denial was intended as a mark of degradation, putting her on a level with the lay sisters, the servants in the priory. Of course, she hardly cared, as she'd never wanted to *be* a nun. But the prioress, genuinely wanting her to atone, clearly hoped she'd soon regain her veil and become a full member of her sisterhood.

But did she want that herself? Did she even care about the possible excommunication?

In truth, she didn't know. She'd been letting the days slip past, with the penances, the toil and the humiliation, without even thinking about how her *life* was passing. She'd scarcely considered the matter of contrition, what it would mean if she achieved it, or if she even wanted it.

'I'll think about it, Reverend Mother,' she said at last, and backed out of the chamber.

Evangelina stood up from the tub of undergarments she was kneading. She let the water run off from her hands before easing her aching shoulders. She wiped her hands against her apron and winced. As usual, they were sore, from the hotness of the water and the ashes she'd just added to help whiten the sisters' linen.

She recalled her last conversation with her brother, before Master Aylesbury removed him from Northwick to Winchester. Both knew their time at Northwick was at an end, and they'd be punished for their actions.

Edgar was remorseful, wishing he'd not after all succumbed to a young woman's wiles. 'It was my own fault,' he'd said, 'allowing my frailty to get the better of my wit. I have brought my miseries upon myself.' He looked up at her. 'You too, sister?'

She'd shaken her head. 'I don't regret what I've done, even if I'm going to suffer for it.' She repeated what she'd told him two years ago, of feeling cheated out of the comfortable life she'd expected as a girl, and her bitter resentment of the bleak, austere existence she'd had to bear.

But, in response, he'd shrugged, and shaken his head.

Her mouth had fallen open in dismay. She always thought he'd understood, but maybe she was wrong. Perhaps, after all, he didn't think her justified in what she did. She'd have liked to ask, but didn't want to force him to disavow her.

They'd sat in silence for long moments. Then, at length, he'd taken her hands in his. 'So, sister, we are to be parted, perhaps for ever. It is possible, even likely, we shall never meet again.'

Their eyes had met, and his were as desolate as she felt.

***

A MESSAGE FROM THE AUTHOR

If you've enjoyed reading *Sister Rosa's Rebellion*, please do consider leaving a brief review on your favourite site. Reviews are of enormous help to authors, both in terms of providing feedback and in building readership. Thank you!

And, if you enjoy my writing, perhaps you'd like to join "Team Meonbridge"?

In return for your support, I will send you updates on my writing, and occasionally ask for your help or feedback. As a small "thank you" for joining the team, I will send you an unpublished short story or novella featuring some of the Meonbridge characters.

If you are interested, please visit my website at www.carolynhughesauthor.com and select **JOIN THE TEAM!** to open the sign up form.

I look forward to your company!

AUTHOR'S NOTE

I hope you've enjoyed reading this story of medieval nuns as much as I've enjoyed writing it!

However, I want to make it clear that this picture of a medieval nunnery should *not* be taken as the norm! I suspect that most of the 140 or so nunneries in medieval England were probably more like Northwick under Mother Angelica, reasonably pious and tranquil, working hard to make ends meet, although there were a few very wealthy institutions. But there is evidence – from the bishops' visitations, which were how all religious institutions were monitored and managed, including religious houses and churches – that a few *were* badly managed, had prioresses who were useless and/or self-seeking, where discipline was lax, piety at a minimum, the inmates possibly feeling like prisoners.

For background information, I am indebted to *Medieval English Nunneries, c. 1275 to 1535*, a vast tome written in the 1920s by a well-known medieval historian, Eileen Power. Her book has been criticised for overstating the case for mismanagement, and especially depravity, in medieval nunneries, but I don't feel she does especially overegg the situation. She draws on reports from the bishops' visitations, which describe the "goings-on" in some nunneries, sometimes in considerable detail. They certainly make surprising – and entertaining – reading!

And yet, I feel, it is perhaps surprising that *more* nuns did not succumb to misbehaviour, given the circumstances in which some of them had entered their cloistered life.

Anyway, I have drawn on Eileen Power's descriptions of particular cases of prioresses or abbesses who brought either financial failure or shame, or both, to their houses. Then, of course, I have used my imagination to develop a story that I hope gives a flavour of what life *might have been* like in those few houses that had the misfortune to be headed by a woman who was more interested in her own comfort and advancement than the well-being of her sisters.

If you would like to find out more about the background to *Sister Rosa's Rebellion*, do have a look at this post on my blog, which gives some insight into what I learned from my research into medieval nunneries, and how I drew on some of the more surprising, and rather shocking, aspects of the lives of a few nunneries in order to create a story that I hope is intriguing as well as engaging:

https://carolynhughesauthor.com/2024/11/25/goings-on-in-medieval-nunneries/

Note: I have referred to the nuns of Northwick as "Sister [name]", although I believe that, at the time, fully professed nuns were usually titled "Dame", and only novice nuns were called "Sister". However, I chose to use "Sister" for all the nuns, simply because I felt it was a term with which we are familiar, whereas "Dame" might seem less natural, having connotations nowadays that are unconnected to nuns.

Note: Just a reminder that you can find a Glossary of medieval terms for all the Meonbridge Chronicles on my website at https://carolynhughesauthor.com/glossary-of-terms/

ACKNOWLEDGEMENTS

I am of course indebted to the many people who continue to help me along my writing and publishing journey. I wouldn't have started, let alone completed, the journey without their help.

For *Sister Rosa's Rebellion*, I must once more thank my "beta readers", who read an early version of the manuscript, to help ensure the story flows, the characters are likeable (or not, as appropriate), the plot "works" and the book is, as a whole, an enjoyable read. David and Rhonwen, thank you so much for your time, skill and insight. I really do appreciate it!

My warmest thanks go to my lovely editor, Hilary, for yet again helping me to wrangle the story into shape and encouraging me to continue telling my Meonbridge stories.

And, finally, of course, thank you too to Cathy Helms at www.avalongraphics.org for adding such a beautiful cover to the latest book in the Meonbridge Chronicles series.

ABOUT THE AUTHOR

CAROLYN HUGHES has lived much of her life in Hampshire. With a first degree in Classics and English, she started working life as a computer programmer, then a very new profession. But it was technical authoring that later proved her vocation, word-smithing for many different clients, including banks, an international hotel group and medical instruments manufacturers.

Although she wrote creatively on and off for most of her adult life, it was not until her children flew the nest that writing historical fiction took centre stage. But why historical fiction? Serendipity!

Seeking inspiration for what to write for her Creative Writing Masters, she discovered the handwritten draft, begun in her twenties, of a novel, set in 14th century rural England... Intrigued by the period and setting, she realised that, by writing a novel set in the period, she'd be able to both learn more about the medieval past *and* interpret it, which seemed like a thrilling thing to do. A few days later, the first Meonbridge Chronicle, *Fortune's Wheel*, was under way.

Seven published books later (with more to come), Carolyn does now think of herself as an Historical Novelist. And she wouldn't have it any other way...

Sister Rosa's Rebellion is the sixth MEONBRIDGE CHRONICLE, and more stories about the folk of Meonbridge will follow.

Carolyn has a Master's in Creative Writing from Portsmouth University and a PhD from the University of Southampton.

You can connect with Carolyn through her website www.carolynhughesauthor.com and on social media:

ALSO BY CAROLYN HUGHES

Fortune's Wheel: The First Meonbridge Chronicle (2016)

How do you recover when half your neighbours are dead from history's cruellest plague?

June 1349. In Meonbridge, the Black Death has wiped out half its population, among them Alice atte Wode's husband and Eleanor Titherige's entire family. Even the manor's lord and his wife, Margaret de Bohun, did not escape the horror.

Now the plague is over, it's a struggle to return to normal life. When tensions between the de Bohuns and their tenants deepen into violence and disorder, the women must step forward to find the way out of the conflict that is tearing Meonbridge apart.

"Completely intriguing, fascinating and surprisingly emotional...more please!" The Book Magnet @thebookmagnet

---

A Woman's Lot: The Second Meonbridge Chronicle (2018)

How can mere women resist the misogyny of men?

1352. In Meonbridge, a resentful peasant rages against Eleanor Titherige's efforts to build up her flock of sheep. Susanna Miller's husband, grown melancholy and ill-tempered, succumbs to idle talk that his wife's a scold. Agnes Sawyer's yearning to be a craftsman is met with scorn. And the village priest, fearful of what he considers women's "unnatural" ambitions, is determined to keep them firmly in their place.

Not all men resist women's desire for change – indeed, they want it for themselves. Yet it takes only one or two misogynists to unleash the hounds of hostility and hatred...

"I didn't so much feel as if I were reading about mediaeval England as actually experiencing it first hand." Linda's Book Bag @Lindahill50Hill

ALSO BY CAROLYN HUGHES

Squire's Hazard: The Fifth Meonbridge Chronicle

How do you overcome the loathing, lust and bitterness threatening you and your family's honour?

It's 1363, and Dickon de Bohun would be enjoying life as a squire if it weren't for Edwin de Courtenay making his life a misery with his bullying and threats to expose the truth about Dickon's birth.

At home in Meonbridge, Dickon notices how grown-up his childhood friend, Libby, has become. Libby, seeing how different he is too, falls instantly in love. When Margery, Libby's aunt, learns of her passion, her long-held rancour against the de Bohuns is rekindled. Having hidden her hunger for revenge for years, she can restrain her hostility no longer.

Dickon must rise above Edwin's intimidation, and his lust for Libby can't end well. Beleaguered by the hazards sparked by such powerful emotions, can he nonetheless overcome them?

"An absorbing medieval tale... Intrigue, deceit, treachery and yet family love and loyalty – this book had it all." @VickiMasters9, Author of *The Castilians*

The Merchant's Dilemma: A Meonbridge Chronicles Companion

1362, Winchester. Seven months ago, accused of bringing plague from Winchester, Bea Ward was hounded out of Meonbridge by her former friends and neighbours. She struggled back to Winchester, yet, now she's here, she wonders why she's come, when the love of her life, Riccardo Marchaunt, is surely married .

But Riccardo is relieved to find Bea is alive, when he thought he'd lost her forever. He longs to marry her, but his father would forbid such an "unfitting" match. Determined to find a solution to his dilemma, he hatches a plan. Yet even the best laid plans can go awry, and love's journey never did run smooth...

"Wonderfully vivid and immersive historical fiction and I highly recommend the whole series." The Book Magnet @thebookmagnet

---

You can find out more about Carolyn's books on her website:
https://carolynhughesauthor.com/books/